BOOKS BY HORST BIENEK

Time Without Bells

Horst Bienek

Time Without Bells

Translated by Ralph R. Read

New York **Atheneum** 1988

English translation copyright © 1988 by Atheneum Publishers
Originally published in German under the title *Zeit ohne Glocken*
Copyright © 1979 Carl Hanser Verlag München, Wien

Chapter Twenty-One was translated by Steve Murray.
The ballad in Chapters Twenty-One and Thirty-Two was translated by Paul Norlen.

ATHENEUM
Macmillan Publishing Company
866 Third Avenue, New York, N.Y. 10022
Collier Macmillan Canada, Inc.

Library of Congress Cataloging-in-Publication Data
Bienek, Horst ——
  Time without bells.
  Translation of: Zeit ohne Glocken.
  I. Title.
PT2662.I39Z2413 1988   833'.914   87-17124
ISBN 0-689-11930-5

10 9 8 7 6 5 4 3 2 1
PRINTED IN THE UNITED STATES OF AMERICA

Do not tell me about the heroes and victims. Tell me about the simple people and about mighty life as it is.

—**Witold Gombrowicz**

Time Without Bells

1

"I DON'T UNDERSTAND how someone can pound nails through the hands of a living person. I *absolutnik* can't understand that." Andy was standing in the door to the kitchen, barefoot and in his nightshirt, looking at his mother, who was combing her hair. She was already dressed. She was wearing a dirty colored barber's cloth over her shoulders, which, along with the dim morning light, made her face look gray. Andy looked at his hands.

"You just had a bad dream," said Anna Ossadnik in a firm, clear voice, as if to expunge the remnants of the night from his thoughts and from the kitchen. She was not looking in the mirror, but was combing her hair with the certainty acquired from a thousand repetitions. Then she put the brush back down on the washstand and with both hands separated the hair at the back of her head into two parts. With swift, practiced movements she braided the left half, stuck the end of it into her mouth so that it wouldn't unravel, then did the same with the right half.

"Wash the sleep out of your eyes, son," she said through her teeth and the braid. "But go easy on the soap, it's our last piece for this month."

"And one foot on top of the other, so they would only need one nail to nail them both down, that must have been a pretty long nail, about five inches." Andy spoke as if to himself. In his thoughts he imagined one soldier putting one foot on top of the other and the other soldier setting the nail and pounding it with a big hammer until the nail drove through the flesh and bones and sat deep in the wood.

He put his right foot on top of his left.

"But the man on the cross must not have resisted," he decided in a calm voice.

"Are you already talking to yourself, so early in the morning?" said Anna, who had just finished the second braid. She twisted each

3

of them into a bun that she pinned skillfully in place with two hairpins. "What are you talking about anyway?"

Andy came into the kitchen, turned on the faucet, and splashed cold water onto his face with both hands.

Anna untied the barber's cloth from around her neck and took it off her shoulders carefully so that the hair and dandruff wouldn't fly around. Only now did she look in the mirror. After a fleeting glance, she was satisfied with her hairdo.

"About Jesus Christ, who they nailed to the cross." Andy spoke up loudly to drown out the sound of the water. He turned it down, bent forward for a mouthful, and began to gargle loudly.

"What makes you think of that?" Anna murmured in front of the mirror. She stretched her face this way and that to test the tightness of her skin. True, it was Good Friday. But did her son have to start in on such peculiar matters so early in the morning?

"Today, exactly one thousand nine hundred and ten years ago," Andy said, after he had spit out the water. He dried his face with a blue-striped towel into which the letters DR were woven. He had not used any soap. He didn't like the new soap, which was as light as a sponge. It made your skin stink like mold for hours afterward. Now that Paulek had stopped sending soap from France and Mamotschka had used up the supply she had hidden in the cellar, he wished he didn't have to wash at all anymore. He wet his hair so he could somehow tame it with a comb, and used his finger to mark an uneven part through his hair.

"What do you mean?" said Anna, acting as if she were doing the arithmetic. "This is 1943! No, you're right . . . Christ was thirty-three years old, that's right." She had folded the barber's cloth into a drawer in the little dressing table, from which she now took a flowered scarf that she tied around her neck. Then she looked at herself more closely in the mirror. She thought she still looked good. If you didn't know her, you would have taken her to be ten years younger right off. On Easter Sunday she would take the curling iron and make three or four waves on each side and twist the hair at her temples into two spit curls. Then for the first time she would put on her new dress made of the blue satin that Paulek had brought home from France at Christmas; it had a bell hem, pleats at the shoulders and bosom, and bat sleeves—the latest fashion. And at her age! But Paulek had insisted on it; he had even gone with her to the dressmaker's and had waited while the woman took his mother's measurements, because he didn't want Anna to pass the material on to Ulla, as she had always done before.

If it weren't for the goiter; it had begun to grow a month ago, slowly of course, but nothing could stop it. She searched for the place with her fingers and, in spite of its yielding softness, felt it as a thickening lump. It hadn't changed since yesterday, but she still couldn't get rid of the feeling that it was already clearly visible. For some time she had felt the lump whenever she turned her head quickly to the left. Luckily the goiter, if it was one, caused no pain, just occasional difficulty swallowing in the morning. In the mirror not much could be seen, and even Franzek assured her again and again that anyone who knew nothing about it wouldn't notice it at all. Maybe she asked him that so often because she wanted to hear him keep saying it. She had successfully kept the goiter secret from the children so far, but for some time she had been wearing a silk scarf for safety's sake. Now she began to fear that it might attract attention if she always wore the same scarf with the little blue flowers on a yellow background around her neck; she hoped that Paulek would soon send her new scarves from France in different colors so that she could change off.

"You're talking about the crucified Christ," she said, "but I can't get you near a church. It wouldn't hurt you to go to the Good Friday liturgy service at three o'clock with me. What do you think about that?"

"Not much," Andy said, polishing his glasses carefully. "I'd rather read a page in the Bible here at home. I won't listen to lies preached from the pulpit."

He said this as nonchalantly as possible. After all, it wasn't the first time that he'd refused to go. He really did believe in God, and that's why he had made a firm decision never to enter a church again.

"Ach ja," Anna sighed. It was not clear whether the sigh was for her son Andy, who was suddenly growing up, or for her goiter. There was reason enough to sigh about both.

The terrible thing was that if the goiter continued to grow, slowly but inexorably, she figured that in two years she would have as thick a neck as Frau Pastuschka. She drank warm salt water every morning now and prepared a tea for herself every evening of centaury, because it was supposed to contain iodine, and she took tablespoons of a frightfully stinking and even more frightfully tasting medicament regularly, which old Wieschow, the homepath from Bilchengrund, had given her. She had gone to him when the doctor just kept on prescribing white tablets for her. For a while she had believed that these tablets would help and the goiter would stop growing. She said this to the doctor, who promptly raised his fee, but two weeks later it was clear that she had fooled herself once again. Anyway, she had only gone to the doctor because Franzek had wanted her to. But with such illnesses only a homeopath could help—if anyone could—and old Wieschow in Bilchengrund was one of the most famous in the whole region. The worst thing was the fear every morning when she woke up; the first thing she did was feel her neck to find out whether the goiter had grown some more overnight. This fear persisted until she ascertained that nothing had changed. And it was the same thing every day.

In reality the goiter had not changed at all for days, and if occasionally it seemed a little larger or a little smaller, the difference was so slight that she couldn't be sure. It was her fear, her vivid imagination, and her hope that made her believe first in the growth of the goiter, then in its remission, and then even in its disappearance.

Should she have it operated on? That was the last resort, not because neck operations themselves were especially dangerous—but what was much worse, you had to count on being an imbecile afterwards, crazy, *ogupna*. Sometimes she toyed with the vain thought that it would dry up and disappear just as it had come—she had heard of such things happening. Should she let Squintok in on the secret? Good Friday was actually the best day to do it. But no, today of all days she couldn't muster the courage. She adjusted the scarf and went into the kitchen.

"I hope you'll all be at home this evening, every one of you," Anna said in a slightly hoarse voice, and cleared her throat. "Father is coming today too, he's always on the job two days in a row now, so he gets three days off. That's nice, isn't it? He'll be off for Easter!"

She bent down in front of the stove, poked around in the ashes until a few dark red embers began to glow, and tossed a crumpled sheet of newspaper on them. Then she started blowing until a little flame flickered up. "Father is taking transports of essential war matériel to the East," she said. "All top secret."

Mamotschka has put on her martyr's face today, Andy thought. But he said she'd better let Tonik know about it, so he'd stay home for a change. "Otherwise we won't see him at all during his whole leave. All he does is run after girls . . . I wonder what's in it for him," Andy murmured, not moving from where he stood.

"My Lord, how you talk," Anna said, and put a handful of shavings and thin kindling on the fire. "And on Good Friday, too! Why don't you go get dressed while I make breakfast. You can wear your shirt from yesterday. You'll get a new one on Sunday."

"Are we having your famous fasting breakfast again?" Andy yawned. His hair lay plastered against his head, parted rather crookedly. He would rather not put on a shirt at all, that would only mess up his hair.

"A piece of bread and margarine, as always, and rose-hip tea," she said. "You know that." Rose-hip tea was good for her neck, too.

There were times when we were worse off, then every day was Good Friday. But none of you remember that nowadays. You can't imagine how it was. What a hard time we had! What poverty there used to be here! What *bieda*! She could really get worked up about it.

The shavings were smoldering but not burning, so she had to blow on them again. That couldn't be good for her neck.

"Oh, come on, Squintok, give me a hand! The clouds are hanging so low the stove won't draw."

Andy blew into it and all of a sudden it worked. Little red and bluish tongues of flame flickered here and there, until all at once a flame shot up. That's the way to do it, he thought proudly.

"Would you go get dressed, Squintok," his mother said, "before the day's half gone. And get Kotik in here, too, we'll have breakfast together. And at noon we fast. Leave Tonik in peace, he has to sleep the war out of his system, it's probably still stuck in his bones."

"I'm on my way," Andy said, starting off slowly. "But don't call me Squintok!" He looked at his bare white feet, cautiously proceeding step by step on the dark linoleum. "That must *absolutnik* hurt like crazy. How can anybody stand it, nails right through your hands . . . and right through your feet," he said.

"I imagine it must be horrible," said Anna Ossadnik, setting a pot of milk on the very edge of the stove so that it would heat slowly and not boil over. In reality she could not imagine it at all.

2

VALESKA PIONTEK HAD slowed down after Halina's arrest. Everything about her was slower—her speech, her motions, her thought. Even her piano playing. She needed almost twice as much time to get dressed in the morning—and today more than ever, as she carefully fished out an old dress and a shabby coat. She didn't even want to comb her hair, but then she stood in front of the mirror for a long time anyway, hiding her hair under a black turban she wrapped herself. She saw the face of an old woman in the mirror, and it was hard for her to get used to the fact that it was her own. It was not the first time that she had made this discovery. Earlier she had tried to smooth away the crow's-feet at her temples and wrinkles under her eyes with creams and alums, to restore her former face. Today, though, the sight gratified her. A Good Friday face, she thought.

Valeska liked it when people called her a pious woman. But in reality she no longer knew whether she was truly pious. So much had become routine for her—not just her housework, not just the piano teaching, but praying too. She went to church every Sunday, even went to devotions on weekdays. But she never went to church twice on the same day except on Good Friday; then she went to confession early in the morning and to Holy Communion at three in the afternoon. In the hour of Christ's death. *Now from the sixth hour there was darkness over the whole land until the ninth hour. But about the ninth hour Jesus cried out with a loud voice, saying, "Eli, Eli, lama sabacthani," that is, My God, my God, why hast thou forsaken me? . . . And immediately one of them ran, and taking a sponge, soaked it with vinegar and put it on a reed and offered it to him to drink. But the rest said, "Wait, let us see whether Elias is coming to save him." But Jesus again cried out with a loud voice, and gave up his spirit.*

She had recited that as a child and still knew it by heart. And she would never forget it until she died. But sometimes she thought her prayers ought to be completely different and completely new, and she yearned to be as shaken before the Crucified One as she had been as a child the first time she performed the Stations of the Cross in the little church in Myslowitz.

Perhaps her prayers would be more ardent today, because she would be thinking of Halina, just as she had been thinking of Halina for days. O Lord, take her under thy protection and shield—but it didn't occur to her that Halina was traversing her own stations of the cross, far away from her, behind thick prison walls.

She brewed herself some barley coffee and ate a dry roll, which she dunked in the coffee now and then, lost in thought. Today was the most important fast day of the year. And she wasn't giving any piano lessons today either. On this day of the Lord's suffering, she wanted to be especially close to him. And she felt that she had never been as close to him as in this Holy Week. She had been to church the previous evening and had watched the Archpriest washing the feet of a few old men and women. Old Hrabinsky had been among them this time and had stuck out his good foot; he had a wooden prosthesis on the other leg, for which he had recently acquired a shoe. He had looked so happy as he walked past Valeska, smiling at her. It was hardly noticeable that he was wearing a wooden leg. She thought about how he had been hobbling along the streets for years, with that wooden stump strapped over a worn-out leather cushion, and she felt guilty watching him, because she too had laughed at him sometimes. And she felt guilty about Halina, too.

She had slept poorly that night. She woke up when it was still dark outside—no light came through the cracks in the blackout curtains. She felt no fear, but her heart was beating so loudly that she had the feeling its rhythm was being transmitted to the bed, the room, and all the walls, and thus was penetrating the entire house. Her head was full of pain, pictures, memories. She began to feel cold; she wrapped up tighter in the blanket and laid her coat over it as well, but she was still cold. Finally she hid her head under the covers, as if she could lock out the night and the world that way. She must have fallen asleep again in this position.

When she got up, it was still quiet in the house. On the way to the bathroom she met Irma. It was not like it usually was when they met in the narrow hall, when each of them would try to avoid each other or purposely look off in a different direction. This time they stood facing each other and looked at each other for a long time, silent and understanding, as if they had both had the same terrible dream, the last traces of which they thought they could see on each other's faces. Sometimes Valeska wished that she could at least share her dreams with her daughter.

"You are going to church, aren't you, Mama? Please take me with you. I want to go to confession today."

Valeska was confused. Irma had asked her for something. She hadn't simply said, as usual: "I'm going to church." She had said: "Please take me with you." And she wanted to go to confession. Valeska didn't know how to reconcile that with the expression on Irma's face, and she worried about it. Of course it would be more proper for Irma to stay home in her condition.

While she washed up, it occurred to her that the rosary from Padua, which she had been looking for for days, had probably been put into an old box in the pantry long ago. And she found the box right away; jars of gooseberry preserves were stacked on top of it. She rummaged around in Christmas tree ornaments, dried flowers, paper roses, and old film pouches, and to her surprise she found the checkered cap with the brown celluloid visor that Leo Maria had so liked to wear when he was bicycling across the countryside to photograph old village churches and new water towers.

There were times when Valeska no longer thought about Leo Maria; she didn't have time to remember their life together and his death. But then there were things that appeared without warning and brought him into her consciousness again—a lens, a still unopened package of photographic paper, or old undeveloped rolls of film (even though she had sold everything that reminded her of the atelier). At the very bottom of another drawer she discovered a bouquet of violets that he had once dried, a tin figure, a faded necktie—she was safe from nothing. She had given away his shirts and suits right after his death, she had sent them far away, to Cosel and Heidersdorf, to distant relatives whom she probably would never see again, Prohaska had accepted the best things; he had come from the Ruhr with practically nothing. Since then she had been afraid he might show up at her door in Leo Maria's suit some day. She wished she could hide all the books that he had ever read, and for a long time, whenever she put anything on the table—a cup or a plate, or a spoon or a fork—she wondered how often Leo Maria had handled it in the course of twenty years. But sometimes she thought she should preserve everything that reminded her of him, his tie pin, his fountain pen, his watch chain, his jade ashtray—that was about all; and she realized how few personal things he had possessed, aside from his clothes and old photographs, of course. She wanted to preserve them but not to be reminded of them, and so she hid his things in places where she seldom looked . . . but because of this cleverly devised plan, she was sometimes surprised by the things just at the moment she least expected them, such as now. Could Josel wear this cap? But then she hid it in the box again, and the rosary of simple brown, turned wooden beads fell into her hands. Her great-aunt Vera had once brought it home from a long journey and claimed that it had been blessed in the Church of St. Anthony in Padua. That was what made it so precious. And it was simple enough for this Good Friday too, which was to be a day devoted to penance for her.

Irma had already finished dressing. She had hung a coat loosely around her shoulders, which made her swelling abdomen stand out even more. "I'm ready," she said, as if she were to be led away.

"It's good that you dressed warmly," Valeska said, looking at her from the side. "It's not cold outside, but at this time of the year, winter is still in the church walls. Come on, take another swallow of hot malt coffee, I've already made it."

She was gratified that Irma wanted to surrender herself to her guidance. The slant of the girl's shoulders indicated to Valeska that Irma had given up her protest, even if only for today.

"Is Josel awake yet? Have you seen Uncle Willi?" Valeska asked, pushing the cup over to her daughter. And continued to talk, without waiting for an answer. "I saw the two Schimmels earlier through the window, with their knapsacks; they must be going for one of their long hikes again. It might turn into a nice day. The sky is gray but the sun is waiting up there, you can feel it, it's just waiting for the cloud cover to break, then it could get warm."

Irma drank the hot coffee in little swallows. She drank it quickly and enjoyed the warmth spreading through her body. She was silent. But not just because her mother was talking incessantly—on the contrary.

"Do you feel well? I mean, is everything okay with . . . your belly?" She looked across the table at Irma's protruding body, as if something unsettling might emanate from it that you should always keep an eye on.

"Lucie will take care of Helga until we're back," Irma said. "And I think I still have a little time to go."

It would not be much longer, she knew that, but she was hoping for a few days of rest. The child lay heavy in her body, she felt it more from day to day. She simply needed more strength now for every step, for every movement, no matter how small. Even if she was just going shopping, she soon ran out of breath. Every day she calculated at least twice when her time would come, but the result was always simply that it could happen any day now. Just don't let it be a Friday's child. That was a superstition in this region: Friday's children were supposed to be difficult children, and Good Friday's children were children of woe. Fine if it came on Easter Saturday. But best of all on Easter, then it would have to be a child of happiness.

By Easter she would probably have a letter from Skrobek, too. She was worried about him. This was already the third week that she hadn't had any news from him, and that was unusually long. He was the driver for a general, and generals never get close to the front. So he was not exactly in immediate danger, but you never knew what could happen out there. Uncle Willi had told her that the Russians were advancing so fast in the East now that they sometimes cut off whole units . . . just as the Germans had done earlier. Uncle Willi knew that from foreign broadcasts, which he was still listening to in secret even though it meant risking your life. You read again and again in the newspapers that they had arrested someone for "listening to enemy broadcasts" and "distributing enemy propaganda." She hoped so very much that a letter from Skrobek would come tomorrow. Hedwig Schuchardt had had a miscarriage when the postman brought her a letter, but it was not from her husband,

it was from a Military Section, stating that "for Führer, Folk, and
Fatherland" her husband had . . . She put the cup down so hard that
it clattered.

Whom does Irma take after, anyway? Valeska wondered. Not after
me. You could be with her for hours without her saying a word;
you could describe Ulla Ossadnik's first piano recital to her excitedly
without her commenting; you could describe a trip to her in
detail—not a question, not a peep out of her. She listened, yes.
Sometimes, often much later, in a very different context she would
mention something she remembered, from which you could tell how
closely she had been listening. Valeska could not comprehend this.
Not even after twenty-three years. People exist to talk to each other!
So that they can tell each other what is going on inside. That much
she got even out of Halina, who didn't speak much with her tongue,
but did with her eyes, her face, her hands.

She had not known for years what was going on inside Irma. And
not just since the awful news that Irma's first husband had fallen in
Poland a few days after their marriage, during the taking of Radom.
She had never been able to find out why Irma had married Heiko
in such a rush; she knew little more about him than that he came
from the West. And Irma had not wept, either, when she became a
widow. Valeska had seen no tears on her face, in any case, not even
at the requiem at the parish church of St. Peter and Paul, when they
were taking leave of the dead man to whom Irma had been married
by a judge, but had not been joined by the holy sacrament of mat-
rimony. Sometimes she had misgivings about why Irma had refused
so adamantly to be married in church.

Then when she married Skrobek, a perfectly ordinary taxi driver,
she had stepped up to the altar at St. Peter and Paul's without wasting
a word over it, to receive the marriage sacrament with him—and
since then she had started going to church every Sunday again. And
she had finally taken down the spade that she had nailed to the wall
of her room after her time in the Labor Service, as a sort of memento.
A spade on the wall! A crucifix belongs on the wall, or the enlarged,
tinted photograph of your wedding, but not a spade. All that would
have seemed very peculiar in a stranger, how much more so in her

own daughter! What would it take before Irma revealed herself to her? She didn't know.

Perhaps her brother understood his niece better, even if they didn't talk to one another very often. Once Willi had said to Valeska: "Irma's silence is her weeping." That was a statement she had thought about a lot and it had pleased her. A long, petrified weeping: that's what her silence was. And Valeska shouldn't let this silence continue to grow too much. It could push the two of them so far apart from each other again, the way they had once been before. That was why she talked so much in Irma's presence, much more than she used to: she wanted to break the silence.

Now the two women sat facing each other—silently. Then they stood up without a word and left the kitchen. No Halina would come to clear the table. When they got back from church, even more dirty plates and cups would be there, and Valeska would have to clean them up herself. "Poor Halina," she said softly.

She pushed her arm underneath Irma's, who tolerated the intimacy.

"Everything's a little later this year," Valeska said simply and matter-of-factly. "Even Easter."

In the garden the yellow of the forsythias gleamed, and the gorse glowed and flourished, spreading its scent as far as the fields and railway embankments. The tulips had grown up tall and plump with their calyxes still half closed. The blackthorn was like stars at the garden fence. The magnolia in front of her brother's garden cottage did not yet show a single blossom, only a few buds could be seen; the cold winter had frozen most of them. Maybe it should be transplanted to the south side, where it would get more sunshine. Yes, it got too little sun. But on the south side no one would be able to see it from the window. Then they would have to go outside to enjoy its blossoms.

She had always been in favor of people's displaying what they had. Especially such a splendid magnolia, the only one on this street, and one of only two or three in this entire part of town. It would never have occurred to her that it was too old to survive transplanting. Valeska could forget things that she found unpleasant or inconvenient in an astonishingly short time, and so thoroughly that later she could honestly claim that she never knew anything about them. "Look at the hawthorn," Valeska said to Irma. "In another week, if it stays this nice, this will be nothing but a sea of blossoms. Then the smell will make you drunk, yes, it will . . . the smell of hawthorn." She spoke as if she wanted to avoid something. They turned onto Schröterstrasse. If they had gone on in the other direction for about ten minutes, they would have reached police headquarters on Teuchertstrasse, and behind it, somewhat hidden, lay the prison. Constantly she had to think about Halina's being locked up behind one of the barred windows. There or somewhere else. They had not informed even her brother. With his connections to the court! But it was something political, so everyone enveloped himself in silence.

Irma knew this road as well as her mother did. There had never been a spring when she had seen a sea of white hawthorn blossoms in the front garden. She had never seen hawthorn here at all. Only dirty white narcissus, crippled, soot-covered daffodils, and plump, tall, overgrown tulips of a repulsive ugliness.

A boy was hobbling along in front of them. He had a clubfoot, and at every step his back buckled in a frightful way. She had to force herself not to stare.

"Where . . . where's the hawthorn?" she asked, fighting against a memory from the time when she was pregnant with her first child, and, afraid of giving birth to a cripple, a cretin, an idiot, she saw only cripples, cretins, and idiots everywhere. This was why she let her mother lead her over to a hedge and inhaled the smell, in the hope of chasing away the memory. It was the gorse that was so fragrant.

"Not hawthorn," she said, "hawthorn has a different smell." She was breathing heavily, and inside her coat she began to sweat.

"We've been walking pretty fast," Valeska said. "Maybe a little too fast for your condition. I can tell that it's an effort for you to be carrying two lives." She looked into her daughter's eyes, concerned. But the daughter thought her mother was being intrusive. So she walked on.

No, mothers should not look into the eyes of their grown children like that, Irma thought. They still want to be part of something that they actually lost at the moment of giving birth. And Irma wondered why it took fourteen or fifteen years or even longer before they grasped this, or never grasped it—like her own mother.

And Valeska thought: Not even my own daughter can look me in the eye anymore. Ever since the mess with Kaprzik, that idiot, she can't look me in the eye anymore. I'll pray for her today, on Good Friday, at the Sufferings of the Lord, who was flogged, spat upon, and crowned with thorns, who was nailed to the cross, given gall to drink, and stabbed in the side with a lance, I will pray for her. And I will pray for Halina. And for the poor man who brought disaster down on Halina. Yes, she intended to pray for him too. She had never seen him and could hardly imagine him.

She wrapped the rosary around her hand and around her prayer book and held them before her; both should be clearly visible here, close to the church.

From afar they could already make out red and white streamers closing off the main portal. A fire engine was parked in front of it, but the ladders had not been raised. The scene was quiet, no firemen were visible. Only a few boys were standing around at a suitable distance, gaping. There were clumsily painted cardboard signs:

PLEASE

USE THE

SIDE ENTRANCES

Valeska asked one of the boys what that meant. They guessed, not really knowing.

"The storm tore a few stones out of the tower," one of them said, pointing up at it.

Only then did Valeska and Irma notice a big hole in one of the tower windows. "But there wasn't any storm," Valeska said, puzzled.

The two women walked on. "Which priest are you going to confess to?" Valeska asked, with suppressed curiosity.

Irma looked straight ahead. "Oh, to whoever's there. I don't care," she said, irritated.

"I won't say confession to Mikas or to Jarosch. I'll go to Archpriest Pattas if he's there, I haven't said confession to him for a long time.

He'll be surprised when he hears me. And what do you think I have to confess to him!"

A smile glided over Valeska's face, and for an instant it looked as if she had forgotten what day it was. And how much had happened.

"Oh, Mamuscha . . ." was all Irma said.

3

ANDY GLANCED OUT the window of his little room. It looked dreary outside. He loved to lie in bed in the morning, not sleeping, just thinking about something or other, which he never had time to do except on Sundays or on a holiday like today. There were enough worthwhile things to think about. He liked doing this most when the sun was shining and painting wild patterns in the air and on the blanket, then he lapsed into a state where a single thought in his mind would drift effortlessly into another, and finally a beautiful, indefinable, flowing dream would result. But today the sun wasn't shining. Today he simply wanted to vanish from the house. No more arguments with Mamotschka, especially on Good Friday, about whether he would go to church or not. He had his convictions, and the older he got, the less he let himself be talked out of them.

He shut the door of his room carefully, so as not to wake anyone.

"Where are you sneaking off to so early, Squintok?" Kotik was standing in the hall in his undershirt.

"You really know how to scare someone," Andy said. He hadn't noticed Kotik coming out of the other room. He turned the key and removed it from the lock.

"What did you do to your hair?" Kotik asked. "Take a look in the mirror!" He would have liked to get a look at his brother's room. They had always slept in the same room, but a year ago Squintok had moved into the little laundry room, because he felt grown-up and wanted to be alone. The room was rather cramped and had only one narrow window, but it was his "kingdom," as he called it, and for some time now he had even been locking his kingdom shut, which only made Kotik more curious.

"What do you mean, what's wrong with my hair?" Andy asked. "I just combed it down smooth."

"That's the trouble," Kotik said. "It's much too long and straggly. Make a wave in it with water, all the *pierons* do. Or have Mamotschka put a few curls in it with the curling iron. Slicked down like that, you look like a Negro."

"What's that?" Andy asked, putting the key in his pants and taking out a pocket mirror.

"Negro? You don't know? Never seen a Negro in the dark? Well, that's the way your hair looks."

Andy looked in the mirror now. But he was not looking at his hair, he was looking into his own eyes, which were gazing back at him from the mirror. "Here, hold this," Andy said, and pressed the round pocket mirror into Kotik's hand. He took off his glasses and moved his face closer to the mirror. It was really true that his eyes were both all the way open. So you couldn't say that he squinted anymore. Tonik had been the first one to notice it; he must be the best judge, since he hadn't been at home for two years. But his teacher, Herr Hajek, had too. He decided not to let people call him Squintok from now on, although he used to like this nickname. As long as he could remember, he had squinted and all that time people had called him Squintok, everybody had, and it hadn't bothered him. But now he was not really squinting, so he couldn't go by that name anymore. He was no swindler or con man, after all.

"Stop calling me Squintok," he grumbled and put his glasses back on.

"What do you mean?" Kotik asked, amazed.

"Because I don't squint anymore, it's that simple," Andy said firmly. "And because I'm *absolutnik* sick and tired of being called Squintok." If he really meant it, he would have to get started. But he wasn't sure how seriously he did mean it. Maybe he had arrived at this decision too quickly.

"Have you got a screw loose?" Kotik said. He went up to his brother and looked him closely in the face, but not to investigate whether he was still squinting; he wondered whether anything else on his face had changed. And since he couldn't tell, he said: "Just because you're in the local Flak Service now? That kind of job won't keep you from squinting."

"First of all, I'm being trained on the sighting telescope, as a gunner, and second, let's not fight on Good Friday," Andy said, in conciliation.

"Oh, today is Good Friday. I almost forgot," Kotik said.

"Blessed Lord Jesus, you're making such a racket, you'll wake up Tonik." Anna came rushing into the hall, and if Tonik hadn't been awake before, then he would have to be now.

"Squintok doesn't want us to call him Squintok anymore," Kotik said absentmindedly. He was looking for his slippers.

"What kind of a funny idea is that? He started in on it in the kitchen already. I've been wondering ever since what he meant by it."

"Well, is that so hard to figure out?" Andy took off his glasses and shoved his face at them. "Look, I'm not squinting anymore so I'm not Squintok anymore, either! That's all there is to it."

"That's fine, son," his mother said, "we'll respect that. You're almost grown-up now."

"As if it has anything to do with growing up," interrupted Andy angrily.

"Yes, you're right, Andreas, and it makes me so happy. I've noticed for a long time how much the glasses have been helping you. And you know yourself how I insisted that you wear them. At first you didn't want to at all, you remember that? Because you were afraid your school friends would all laugh at you and call you Four Eyes, and remember how we went to the doctor and then to the optician, and you didn't like any of the glasses? And then you always had tears in your eyes for the first few days . . ."

"I can give the glasses to Kotik," Andy said. "Sometimes he complains that his eyes hurt."

"No, no, Kotik doesn't need glasses, he's got good eyes, he just shouldn't keep reading until there's no more light in the evening, that's bad for the eyes."

"Besides, I don't squint," said Kotik, insulted.

Suddenly they all noticed a strong smell. Anna was the first to say something. "Ah, blessed Lord Jesus, now the milk has boiled over!" She flung the door open and ran into the kitchen, without bothering about the noise she was making. Half of the pot had already boiled over. Why did this have to happen to her! Yet this always happened, again and again, ever since she was married. Nothing could prevent it. She had tried everything. She could stand at the stove giving all her attention to the moment when the milk would begin to rise, but then the wind would bang a window shut, or someone would ring the doorbell, or she would step into another room just for a moment.

She wiped off the stove top with a wet rag and sprinkled salt on it. The smell of burned milk could last for hours in the kitchen. They no longer gave her a milk card for any but the youngest boy, a quarter liter per day. Every other day she bought half a liter at the dairy store. His entire day's ration had just boiled over! What a disaster.

It was Squintok's fault! And she was glad to have someone to blame, because it had happened so often that she had run out of excuses herself.

Children are getting more and more stubborn, she thought. You can't even tell what they're thinking anymore. From the beginning she had been against Andreas's being called Squintok by the others, but he had adopted the name himself because the children always teased someone who squinted, so he had thought up the name as a badge of honor. That's the way it was. And now, all at once, on Good Friday, he didn't want to be Squintok anymore. Just as on Good Friday a few years ago, he had suddenly refused to listen to her reading from the book of *Miracles and Deeds of the Saints*. She read aloud from this book only once a year, on the evening of Good Friday. She had inherited this custom; her mother had read the legends aloud too, but unfortunately not just on Good Friday. It had practically always been the legend of Saint Genoveva of Brabant, because her mother would quickly forget which legend had been read last time. She was different. She put a bookmark in the book and read straight through from legend to legend. And now she had come to the martyrdom of Saints Audifax and Abachum. Yes, when children grew up, they didn't want to listen to them anymore. But she was determined to continue these readings from *Miracles and Deeds of the Saints*, year after year, until she finally finished them. Only Franzek still listened to her patiently and with the same attention as on that first Good Friday they had spent as newlyweds in their own apartment, back when she had got pregnant with Anton, who was now . . . Oh, how long ago that was!

"Will you be here this evening," she asked Kotik, who came shuffling in, in his wornout slippers, "when I read from the legend book?" She asked cautiously, almost pleading. If things kept going the way they did with the other children, then docile Kotik too would soon start to rebel.

"Squintok said he's not coming to breakfast. He wants to fast today. Think he can stand it the whole day?" Kotik was plainly perplexed. "I think he's off his rocker. A while ago he braided himself a whip out of hemp, with lots of strands and knots all over them, and demanded that I scourge his back; he wanted to find out how long you could stand it, he said. And now he wants people to stop calling him Squintok!"

Kotik shook his head and looked really worried.

4

THE TWO WOMEN entered the church through the side entrance. Valeska immediately dipped three fingers in the holy water font with a sweeping gesture, and crossed herself from left to right. Still supporting Irma with one arm and holding her close, she walked along the transept to the center of the church. Both of them had trouble adjusting to the dimness inside after the bright light outdoors. Most of the windows had been walled up from both the inside and the outside, to protect them from destruction during air raids. In the center aisle, Valeska bowed before the high altar. She just bent her right knee a little, so as not to pull Irma down with her, then they sat down in the third row. She slid toward the middle of the smooth bench and pulled Irma after her. Somehow Valeska had succeeded in holding on to her the whole time. But now Irma shook off her mother's hand abruptly. She even slid away from her a little, and tried to think about confession, not looking to the right or the left.

On the steps to the altar lay the cross, which was usually erected behind the altar. An acolyte was kneeling next to it on a purple pillow. He was sitting more than kneeling; perhaps he had had to maintain this position for too long. A woman with a child approached from the center aisle, kneeled before the cross, and touched the five stigmata on the crucifix with her lips. The acolyte wiped off the places with a cloth. Then the child followed, bending over the cross fervently and carefully kissing each wound, as his mother must have impressed upon him. The acolyte pushed him away with his left arm before the child's lips had even touched the holy feet, and polished the places twice as carefully.

Valeska silently handed Irma the open prayer book. She didn't need it herself. The praying she was going to do now she knew by heart. Irma tried not to see the book, but as her mother persisted in holding it out to her, she took it. She read the Examination of Conscience and shut the book. She had often gone to the Supine Cross on Good Friday and had touched the stigmata, or had kissed the relics of saints on pilgrimages. Now she didn't do that anymore.

Valeska looked around in the hope of catching sight of someone who would appreciate her appearance in church. But only a few people were present, and as far as she could make out, all the faces were unfamiliar. Or did they only look strange to her in this dim light?

Valeska wanted to pray her first rosary with the sorrowful mysteries for Halina. For Halina, for poor, unhappy Halina, that God might protect her, that God might stand by her, that God might free her from prison.

As far as the last point was concerned, she wished she could rely on her brother.

While her lips moved soundlessly, she slipped one bead after another through her slightly nervous fingers; sometimes, purposely or not, she would let two beads pass for a single Ave Maria. Out of the corner of her eye she observed her daughter and the few people who were going to the altar to kiss the stigmata of the Savior on the cross. Most of them were women. She recognized one of them, Frau Jaworek, all in black, whose husband had fallen at Stalingrad; he had received the Iron Cross First Class there during the siege and had been promoted to sergeant, which would substantially improve her pension. Yes, she had to have luck.

When the Archpriest stepped out of the sacristy and walked straight toward his confessional, Valeska interrupted her prayer. She nudged Irma, put her rosary in her purse, and rubbed some eau de cologne on her temples with her hands. "Pattas is in the confessional. If you want, I'll go with you . . ." she whispered to her daughter.

But Irma was not ready yet. All at once she was no longer sure whether she should go to confession. She would certainly not go to Pattas. And he would probably not be relieved by another priest for an hour. She would prefer a confessor who didn't know her. At least not as well as the Archpriest knew her. "You go first," she whispered.

But others had been quicker than Valeska, for when she reached the confessional, two people were already standing there, one on each side. She recognized one as the wife of Schachtner, the delicatessen owner, and the other as skinny Frau Smolka, who was the first to slip into the confessional booth. Valeska nodded to Frau Schachtner, but absently to show how deeply she was preoccupied with her examination of conscience. If only she had not left her rosary behind. There was still time for her to finish the rosary for poor, unhappy Halina. But it was not advisable to go get it; in the meantime someone here could get in ahead of her. She remembered where she had stopped, at the third sorrowful mystery, and continued, holding onto a finger instead of a bead: *He who was crowned with thorns for us.*

On Good Friday everybody wanted to confess to Archpriest Pattas. Jarosch, by contrast, would be quite free, no one liked to go to him. The children liked Curate Mikas best.

Valeska knew the examination of conscience almost by heart. *Heavenly Father*, she said to herself, *in deep reverence and love I pray to thee. Thou hast granted me a particularly important day today. It shall be a day of stern self-examination, remorseful confession, and of sincere* . . . that Frau Smolka, what sins could she possibly have committed? As Frau Smolka had disappeared into the confessional booth, Valeska caught herself imagining what Pastor Pattas would get to hear. I have lied, I have stolen, I have behaved unchastely, I have borne false witness against my neighbor and coveted my neighbor's wife and property . . . Earlier you could listen in sometimes, when there were no confessional booths—naturally that happened unintentionally. Once she had heard Frau Kikolski sobbing into the screen as she was confessing her relationship with Herr Buchner to the Archpriest. It had been pretty embarrassing. And except for her brother Willi, she really had not told anyone else; he was a lawyer, after all, and bound by an oath of silence . . . But for some time now they had had real booths in the confessionals at the Peter and Paul Church and in the parish church of All Saints, too, with doors that shut snugly, not a sound could escape . . . And besides, she didn't want to be distracted now in her examination of her soul for whatever sins, venial and grave (*God protect me from mortal ones*), she had to confess. *Illuminate me with the light of the Holy Spirit so that I see my soul as it is open to thy all-seeing eye.* And take Halina into thy protection, she added.

Frau Smolka came out of the confessional, with her hands folded close in front of her face. Maybe it was not supposed to be evident that she had been crying, maybe she held them there to concentrate entirely on herself and her repentance, not to be distracted by anybody or anything. Yes, that's how it should be. To Valeska, however, she was exaggerating the consciousness of her guilt a bit too plainly. What could she have done, her husband had not had leave for over a year.

She could have entered the booth now, but she wanted to wait here outside until Frau Schachtner came out the other side. True, you could not hear what was being said on the other side, but sometimes you could understand the priest in the middle when he assigned the penance to the sinners and gave them absolution, and in the case of Frau Schachtner it did not interest her in the least how much penance she was assigned.

It would be better to start with the Form of Confession now: *Let me attain thy grace through the holy sacrament of confession.* Yes, she whispered, it is my greatest sin not to have paid more attention to Halina, not to have guided her more carefully, not to have given her more strength and love, then things would not have gone so far. It's my fault, it's all my fault . . .

It took quite a while before Frau Schachtner came out of her booth. Valeska was afraid that, absorbed in her examination of conscience, she had simply failed to see her. But she finally came out with her hands folded in front of her breast like a child, and touching the tips of her index fingers with her lips. She had such an enraptured expression on her face that for a moment Valeska thought she had seen a different face, and looked after her in astonishment.

The wood sounded hollow and loud beneath her shoes as Valeska stepped into the confessional, or was it her heart that was thumping so hollowly and loudly all at once? The door fell to behind her; it was as if someone had cut off the light and the air.

The cramped cell smelled of sweat and eau de cologne. She kneeled in the dark on the footboard and brought her face up close to the screen. She couldn't see the pastor, not even his outline. But she heard his breath and smelled his tallowy skin. That reassured her. "Praised be Jesus Christ." The words squeezed from her mouth. Through the screen she heard a peculiar sound. Maybe those were syllables that died before they reached her ear. Valeska felt the heat rising within her. The sweat was collecting in her armpits. "My last confession was four weeks ago," she breathed, "I have . . ." she began.

When she stepped out of the booth, she felt a pain as if a cold iron band were tightening around her head. She straightened her turban, believing that it had slipped badly, which was not the case. She felt sweat at the back of her neck, and her neck felt stiff. She placed both her hands on her face, up to her eyes, and returned slowly to her pew. She thought about what the priest had given her as penance: the Apostle's Creed, the Litany of the Blessed Virgin, and five Paternosters with the Ave Maria. And for Halina she would pray the litany of Our Lady of Sorrows, as well. And she would repeat it for Halina every day, before going to sleep or when she woke up. Until Halina was free again.

I place myself in thy hands, Father protect and lead me through your holy angels. Extinguish all evil desires in my heart. Quell the flame of passion, give me love for thy Law . . . She recited it to herself as she had done a hundred times before, without thinking about what she was saying.

"Do *not* quell the flame of passion within me," she said. And she said it again, not louder, but more fervently. "Holy Mary Magdalene, do *not* quell the flame of passion within me." She felt that something rose within her, climbed inside her, up into her head, almost numbed her. She didn't know what it was. For a moment she didn't even know where she was. And was astonished suddenly to be sitting next to Irma again.

Irma had stretched her legs out in front of her and held her arms crossed over her high-arched body, protecting and defending it. She was breathing heavily through her mouth and looked at her mother absently.

"*Muj Bosche*, what's going on, child?"

"I think it's starting," Irma whispered. She straightened up in the pew with a jolt and grabbed on to the prayer stand; her knuckles slowly grew white. "I think I'd better go," she said. She stepped out into the center aisle of the nave with small steps. She was steady on her feet now, only a cramp in her back bothered her. She would be able to go home all by herself. "No, you just stay here, you have to do your penance, Mamuscha!" She meant it to be friendly, but it sounded like a reproach.

Valeska would not leave her alone. The two women walked along in the middle of the nave, and from a distance it looked as if they were holding each other up.

The faithful looked up from their prayer books, but when they saw that neither a miracle nor a scandal was taking place they retreated again into their prayers and spring coats.

A strange woman came up to Irma and put her arm under Irma's on the other side, but Irma didn't want to be supported at all, neither by her mother nor by a stranger, and every few steps she would try to shake them off. But her mother, as well as the stranger of whom she saw only the long hair that fell across her face, only held on tighter, just as you hold on tighter to a drunk or a lunatic who is resisting and has to be led away. Only when they had reached the street did Irma succeed in freeing herself. She was quite out of breath.

"Jesus and Mary," Valeska said, "is it already starting? You shouldn't have tried to come to church." She was really worried. She called a boy over who was standing next to the barrier: "*Hoppek*, run into the sacristy and tell them to send for an ambulance . . ."

"Are you crazy! I've still got lots of time. Stay here, *hoppek*." And to her mother: "I'm doing fine now. I had some back pains before, in the pew, maybe I wasn't sitting the right way. I can easily make it home by myself."

"You really think we can make it?" Valeska asked carefully, the way one encourages a seriously ill patient.

"Of course," Irma said decisively. "I still have a whole day left, I can feel it."

"Well, I'll stay with you," Valeska said unnecessarily. Suddenly it occurred to her that she had left her purse in the pew. "My purse!" she cried out, and rushed back into the church.

It's better if Irma has the baby at home, she thought as she walked. The Wondraczeks have always given birth at home. And basically Irma was a Wondraczek. So if it were up to her, a clinic would be out of the question. Maybe the baby won't come until tomorrow, or even Easter Sunday. A Resurrection baby, that would make her very happy. But you can't always choose; of course, the main thing is that there aren't any complications. It went smoothly the first time, and it's always easier the second time.

She saw the women praying in the pews. It seemed to her as if they had made an effort to look especially shabby and wretched on this Good Friday, the day of suffering. So as to attract even more attention on Easter Sunday in their new clothes. That's how things had always been here. Valeska had saved up enough points on her clothing ration card for a suit jacket, which she bought at Defaka and had made fashionable with a few minor alterations. She would wear it on Sunday when she went to Mass and Holy Communion with her brother. And everyone would see her walking up the nave to the front, to the altar.

Yes, there was her purse. And the prayer book lay on the floor—Irma must have dropped it. It's true, she needed a new purse. Of genuine leather, naturally—perhaps Paulek Ossadnik could bring her one from France, the next time he came home on leave. She would talk to her friend Anna about that, she could trade her something for it. Actually the suit jacket was not important to her, she just wanted to show the others that she was continuing to pay attention to her appearance after the death of her husband, even in wartime. After Leo Maria was buried, her brother had warned her not to let herself go and run around in the same clothes all the time. No one could say she was doing that now.

At the exit she dipped her fingers in the holy water again. Outside she could see Irma strolling toward the main gate, toward a large crowd that was milling around the barrier. Where had they all come from so fast?

Then Valeska saw that they were all staring up into the air, Irma too. Following their gaze, she saw that a bell was being lowered on ropes, slowly, so slowly that you could hardly see it move. "What's the meaning of this?" Valeska asked, when she reached her daughter in the crowd.

"You can see for yourself," said a man, not turning his head from the sight of the bell. "They're taking our bells away. For the war."

"And on Good Friday, too," sighed Valeska Piontek.

5

ANDY OSSADNIK WAS strolling down Eichendorff-Allee. A thin
morning fog dispersed in the light. It was very quiet. Up to now he
had passed only a few old women, their faces framed by black kerchiefs, who were obviously on their way to church. He didn't like
this morning atmosphere, no, he almost hated it, this air charged
with sleepiness, this crippling dampness, the gray that sucked away
all colors. He hated that about weekdays—amidst the flow of people,
he shared their defeats before the day even began, and even more
so on days like today, when the silence and the emptiness made him
yearn for something that was completely different.

The sky was gray and overcast, the clouds drifting ponderously
toward the east. Only occasionally did one of them tear open, re-
vealing another cloud above it, pure white and moving faster. It
wouldn't be long now before those too would break up and finally
let the sun through. Along about noon, he thought, looking up, it'll
break out.

It was a perfect day to do something with the *ferajna*, something
really memorable. Like the time when they set fire to the deserted
house by the old brickyard, or plundered the hidden warehouse in
Petersdorf. But the *ferajnas* were long gone. Their time was past,
and not only because families with children were scattered all over
the map, mostly in eastern Upper Silesia, from where they once had
come. The Globinskis had even moved to Warsaw because Angel
Face's father was a big shot there; he was prominent in the defense
industry now. Angel Face had sent him two picture postcards, one
of Marketplatz and the other of the Church of the Holy Cross; he
was fine, he had written, and he missed his old friends. Andy liked
the stamps, but he had not answered him.

His *ferajna* had also broken up because he didn't want to be its
leader anymore, since the time the boy from the Huldschinsky settlement had drowned. Wonzak had led it for a while, but it fell apart
more and more the stronger the Hitler Youth grew in their neigh-

borhood. And ever since they were no longer rivals for the leadership of the *ferajna*, they had got along much better, Wonzak and Andy —they had actually become friends, even if they didn't get together as often as before. Wonzak was a toolmaker's apprentice at the Railway Repair Works now, because he had been unable to get an auto mechanic's apprenticeship, which would have interested him much more, and Andy was a merchant apprentice at the miners' association. The miners' association is almost the same as the civil service, his father had said, they can't go broke, that's important, you never know, times can change.

Andy no longer believed it was the time for *ferajnas*. The time had come for putting boxes of sand, fire-beaters, and water barrels in the attic, for piling sandbags in front of cellar windows, for practicing air defense, for treating injuries where there were none, for splinting legs that were not broken, for searching the sky with searchlights for airplanes that had not arrived yet, for learning how to operate antiaircraft guns beneath camouflage nets, for toting shells over from the depot and then taking them back after practice.

Maybe he would meet Wonzak along the way. Where did boys of their age hang out, anyway? On the streets, at the movies, or in church; so they would have to meet on the street somewhere. He would make a detour by way of Moltkestrasse, and then across the Ring to Wilhelmstrasse, then behind the municipal theater and the Victoria baths, where a kind of meeting place had formed down by the Klodnitz. The location changed every year and no one could ever figure out why. The summer before it had been near the Lutheran clubhouse on Lohmeyerstrasse, and when the girls walked home from choir practice in the evenings, the boys whistled at them in unison, and not just because they were Lutheran. Now he could wander through the markets by the Church of the Cross, where the peddlers came from far away to sell pots and pans from Bunzlau, hand-carved whisks and cooking spoons, sauerkraut barrels and willow baskets, or to the butter market, to the herb market, to the flower market—Good Friday was a particularly lively market day in town.

Two heavy trucks came rattling down the street. The first stopped right next to Andy Ossadnik; a man in an army uniform with a white armband with the letters OD on it jumped down from the cab and asked directions to the Peter and Paul Church.

Andy was surprised that someone from the Todt Organization was asking the way to a church, of all things, and St. Peter and Paul at that, which anybody could find—you could even see the tower from here. But nowadays nothing should surprise you, his father had said. Only when the two trucks had driven on did it occur to Andy that he could have asked the man what they wanted at St. Peter and Paul. Maybe he should have ridden along and shown them the way. Anyway, it would have been more exciting to have ridden part of the way in the truck than to amble along the lonely Eichen-dorff-Allee.

A boy who looked familiar somehow was walking along in front of him. Andy quickened his pace to catch up before the next inter-section. It might be Hannes, whom he sometimes met at vocational school. Nobody else here in Gleiwitz had hair as straw-blond as Hannes's, probably not in the rest of Upper Silesia, and he had never seen so many freckles on one face before, either. Hannes Stein was his name, yes, he remembered that they had played field hockey together once, but Hannes had not been able to stick it out; you could play field hockey well only if you started when you were five years old. Andy had spoken to him once and asked him what his name was, because the freckled boy always stood around alone during recess.

"Your name is Stein, just Stein, like this stone here?" That had seemed pretty funny to him. "Strange name, sounds foreign, you can't be from around here."

"Hey, listen, you must be kidding, that's a true German name!"

"Around here, only the Jews have such true German names. Stein, Hirsch, Ochs, Lustig, Landmann."

"What's your name, then?"

"Andy Ossadnik, but everybody calls me Squintok, because I squint."

"Ossadnik sounds pretty foreign to me, I've never heard a name like that, anyway."

They had played 66 together and smoked a cigarette butt once, but that was all. Hannes Stein had been sent here to the countryside camp for children and then had not returned home with the others;

his family was supposed to have been killed in an air raid. Frau Dolezich had kept him at her place—the woman with the stationery store on Kronprinzenstrasse; now he clerked for her and was learning to be a merchant tradesman. He'd been at it more than a year.

Andy Ossadnik had caught up with the boy now. He poked him in the back. The other boy turned around—it was indeed Hannes Stein. "You're Hannes with that funny name Stein, aren't you? I'm Squintok, do you remember? Where are you headed?"

"I'm just out for a walk," Hannes said. "I always discover something new."

"Yeah?" Andy wondered how anyone could find anything new in this town, whose streets he knew almost by heart. He couldn't, at any rate. He Was interested in getting acquainted with other, more distant areas now, even if it were only Cosel, Hindenburg, or Beuthen. Of course, Kattowitz, Ratibor, or Neisse would be much better, and some day, he hoped, he would get to know cities like Breslau, Berlin, and Hamburg, too, maybe even Paris, London, and New York. He was greedy for new experiences like that. Not for remote side streets or hidden alleyways in the old part of town.

"I know everything around here," he said proudly, "and if you want to know something, just ask me."

But Hannes didn't want to know anything. For the moment it was enough that Ossadnik had put his hand on his shoulder. They walked on together, and Hannes had the feeling that he was seeing the street and even the town with different eyes now, and everything seemed more familiar to him all at once.

"Haven't you been here in town quite a while?" Andy asked.

"More than a year."

"The guys you came with have all left by now, haven't they? You're *absolutnik* the only one left?"

"Yes," Hannes said.

Now Andy was embarrassed. After all, he could hardly ask him directly if it was true that his whole family had lost their lives in an air raid. But he wished he knew for sure.

"What region do you come from?—you speak such a funny dialect."

"From Bremerhaven," was all Hannes responded, although he

actually thought the way people spoke here was funnier. He still hadn't gotten used to some of their expressions. But he didn't dare say anything about that.

"Well . . . ?" Andy hesitated. "Do you like it here in Gleiwitz?"

"Sure, of course," Hannes said firmly. "You can imagine. Otherwise I wouldn't have stayed here."

Andy could not imagine. But he was glad and proud that Hannes liked it here. He liked it here too, but he didn't know anywhere else, and he couldn't even guess how far Hannes had already traveled. Bremerhaven, that was somewhere at the other end of Germany; at any rate, it was by the sea. He had always wanted to see the sea. Maybe he would even get that far someday as a soldier. All the things his brothers Paulek and Tonik had already seen as soldiers! They were sure lucky! Paulek was even in Paris for a while. Unbelievable. Only Bruno's luck had run out; he was buried in Greece someplace. At least he got to see the Acropolis first; his last postcard came from there. Mamotschka stuck it under the glass of the kitchen buffet, and in the beginning she always cried when she got out the coffee cups. Andy himself had not gotten beyond Deutsch-Piekar or the Annaberg, and sometimes he wished that the bombs would rain down here too so that he would be shipped away to a country camp somewhere far away—to Prague, to Vienna, or maybe to Bremerhaven. But by now he was probably too old for a country camp. If the bombers came to Gleiwitz now, he would have to fire at them with the flak that was set up beneath trees and camouflage nets.

"Let's walk together," Andy said.

Yet they had already been walking together, even if they had not said much to each other.

And Hannes Stein was not exactly talkative.

"The two of us could do something or other, what do you think?" Andy Ossadnik said, without quite knowing what he and this silent boy might do together.

"Yes, we could," agreed Hannes, blushing a little, because he didn't know what the two of them should do either. "You can count on me."

He was not quite sure whether that was so, but it was a good idea in any case to get to know Ossadnik. In Bremen there was a saying that youngsters who squint, squint toward fortune.

"Are you a Lutheran?" Andy asked suddenly, and took his hand off Hannes's shoulder. He picked at his shirt, the collar of which was mended in a few places. He assumed that anyone who wasn't from Upper Silesia couldn't be a Catholic either.

"Why do you ask? What made you think of that?" Hannes was wary. Back home, he had had to give his religious affiliation in school and at the HY, and once they all had to fill out a family tree. They had questioned him all the way back to his great-grandfather. But his schoolmates or friends had never asked him whether he was Catholic, Lutheran, or even Jewish. Only since he had come to this strange town had he been asked, again and again. And not just whether he was Catholic or Protestant, but whether he believed in Jesus Christ, the only begotten son, and in the saints and martyrs, in the Virgin Mary, in the fourteen helpers in need, in the infallibility of the Pope.

"Why I'm asking? Because today is Good Friday, and because for Catholics that's *absolutnik* a day of mourning and penance. Just take a look at how people here go to church on this day, in their oldest and most raggedy clothes. They say they used to wear old potato sacks over their bare bodies. Only the Lutherans put on their Sunday best today, you can tell them at a glance."

And he took a closer look at Hannes. Well, he was dressed kind of plainly, as usual. He had probably lost everything in the air raid.

"I didn't even notice," Hannes said. "Most people are Lutheran where I come from, we were the only Catholics, because my father is from the Rhineland and married in Bremerhaven. My mother comes from the seacoast. Sometimes my father would say: 'A Catholic can't make anything of himself here.' But he did pretty well in shipbuilding; earlier they say he was constantly out of work."

Andy looked at Hannes Stein attentively from the side. He waited for him to continue talking. But Hannes was somewhat slow, in his thinking as well.

"That had advantages for me," he said after a while. "I didn't have to go to religion class."

"Are you kidding?"

The sharpness of Ossadnik's voice surprised him.

"Why should I kid you?" Hannes almost stammered.

"Can you say the Apostle's Creed by heart?"

"Sure."

"And full of grace the lord is with you?"

"What?"

"Aha, that's it." Andy was squinting a little now behind his glasses. There was something he hadn't liked about this Hannes Stein from the very beginning. He couldn't say what it was. But he had sensed it. It was his smell, yes, it was his smell. He didn't know many Lutherans. But all of them were always so clean in a certain way, so sober, so hygienic, he didn't know how to express it. There was no incense in Lutheran churches. And if someone had never been enveloped in a cloud of incense in his whole life, you could smell it. Yes, that was it.

The boy interrupted his thoughts: "You mean the Hail Mary? We call it the Hail Mary."

"Fine! Then recite it." Andy stood facing him, and looked at him threateningly.

"Hail Mary, full of grace, the Lord is with you, blessed are you . . . among women . . .'"

"Good, good, that's fine," Andy reassured him. "I believe you, *absolutnik*. Come on. Let's go."

Andy was practically transformed. Anyone who could parrot the full-of-grace-the-lord-is-with-you so glibly had to be a Catholic. Hannes had just spent too much time with Lutherans, that was the trouble. He had already taken on their smell.

Hannes Stein walked along beside Andy. His face was working up to a question. After a while he asked: "What difference does it make, Ossadnik? What if I weren't a Catholic?"

"The Lutherans," Andy said hesitatingly, "you know, they're just different, they're heathens, or Protestants, they're against the Pope. A different race, that's it."

Hannes still didn't comprehend, and stopped. "What do you mean by that?"

"Well, they're different from us," Andy said decisively. He gestured in a way that showed that for him the matter was closed and he had no wish to continue with this topic.

Hannes walked along next to Andy, silent now. In passing, he tore a leaf from a maple, pinched it to make the juice squirt out; he put the leaf to his nose and inhaled the smell of the fresh greenery. He was thinking frantically about what could have been so very different about the boys he went to school with in Bremerhaven. He couldn't figure it out.

"We have nothing in common," Andy continued. "Here in our part of the country, you know, the Lutherans have different schools, live in different neighborhoods, even have their own places of worship. I've never been in a Lutheran church, but I've heard that they have no cross and no Virgin Mary. Who do they pray to, anyway? To this . . . Luther?"

He pronounced the name contemptuously. His indignation grew. He wanted to convince Hannes.

"And their prayer books are completely different, and they don't go to Communion either. They take a host and drink wine with it, just imagine, real red wine. They're practically like Jews."

Hannes looked down on the black packed earth beneath his feet. He felt that what Ossadnik was saying could not be true, he just didn't know how to explain it to him. It wasn't that simple for Hannes. In his opinion the thoughts in his head were right, but he couldn't put the words together to express them—at least not right now. Ossadnik was always so quick with his replies.

"Here comes Wonzak, I think," Andy said, walking faster now. And another boy was hurrying across the street toward them.

Andy and the other boy said hello by sticking out their hands and slapping palms, first with the left hand and then the right. He did the same with Hannes Stein while Andy was introducing them. "Do you know each other? This is Heinrich Wons, we all call him Wonzak. An all-right guy." He said nothing about Hannes Stein.

"I thought I'd run into you somewhere," Wonzak said. "I've been looking all over the place."

Wonzak was good-looking, but it was hard to tell beneath all the pimples that covered his face like the heads of stickpins. Wonzak suffered from them so badly that he no longer even dared to speak to girls, and the ones he knew he avoided, because he thought they would be disgusted by him. He squeezed at every new pimple that he found on his face; often he jabbed them open with a needle he had sterilized in a flame, in the hope that they would go away faster, but that just made them worse; some of the pimples developed into real boils. Other boys, at least, and that helped a little, either didn't notice or didn't care. But the boil on his left cheek attracted even Andy Ossadnik's attention. "*Pjerunnje*, have you got a *szpyrka*," he said, almost admiringly.

Wonzak only grimaced, and spat. What should he say? He had been squeezing at it long enough. "That's my Good Friday mark," he said sourly. And to change the subject, he added quickly: "What are we going to do?"

"Well, I don't know," Andy said. "Hannes is new in town, he says he always can find something new to do. Maybe he'll show us how."

"Okay, make a suggestion," Wonzak encouraged him.

Hannes didn't know what to answer. "They're new things for me, anyway," he defended himself. *Szpyrka* was also something new for him, he had never heard the word before.

"We could go find palm branches in the forest, calumus or fresh birch twigs. Frau Dolezich claims that she already saw the first June bugs in the town woods."

The other two boys started laughing.

"Man," Wonzak said to Andy, "you should have left him with your brother Kotik." He was already thinking of the best and quickest way to get rid of him.

"Why don't you try to think of something?" Andy said. "Hannes is okay. He just has to get settled. Anyhow, he's Catholic."

This won points for Hannes only with Andy. It didn't interest Wonzak particularly. His association with Squintok stemmed from the *ferajna*, before Squintok had had this Catholic obsession.

"Hop a freight to Morgenroth?" he said under his breath.

Andy shook his head.

"Tschinkern? Klippe? Pitwok?"

Andy shook his head at the name of each town.

"How about Klekotka?"

Klekotka made Andy look up. But then he rejected the notion

with a wave of his hand. They could do something like that any Friday. But today it ought to be something special, something unusual. He just didn't know what.

"Oh, by the way," he said, "I don't want you to keep on calling me Squintok, that goes for everybody. Simply," he elucidated, "because I don't squint anymore."

No objection. Wonzak didn't feel like standing there and checking Squintok's eyes. For him Squintok was a name like any other; he had used it so often that he had long since forgotten the "squinting" part of it. But what was Squintok's real name, anyway?

"Sure," he said, with forced cheerfulness, "I'd just like to know what your name is now."

As long as he had known him he had been Squintok.

And that was actually what was unusual about him. True, the old *ferajna* no longer existed, and when Wonzak thought it over, if Squintok hadn't squinted, he probably never would have become the leader. Without the squint, Squintok was just like anybody else. Inferior, actually, and certainly inferior to him.

"My name is Andreas, at least that's how I was baptized. But you can call me Andy," Squintok said.

That might be all right for the new guy, but not for me, Wonzak thought. He put a hand on his belt buckle and hitched it up. As always he was wearing his HY uniform, without the neckerchief and knot, because he didn't have much else to wear. "So, what are we going to do?" he said. "We could go to the movies. They're showing *The Big Shadow* at the C.T. Lichtspielen, *I Accuse* at the Capitol, *The Golden City* at the Deli, and *Youth* at the Showplace, but that's just the title, it has nothing to do with us . . ." He had practically all the film programs of the town in his head, and usually those in Petersdorf and Hindenburg, too. There was still time before the first show in the afternoon.

As they turned onto Oberwallstrasse and headed for the Ring, more and more people were on the street. A group of nuns with rippling wimples passed them, holding giant rosaries that hung down below their knees.

"We could go to the zoo. Or to the museum," Hannes said shyly.

"What baloney," said Wonzak. "We don't have any zoo, just a

greenhouse. There's a few crocodiles there, pickled, you can take a look at them."

"Museum!" Andy said. He used the word like a reproach. He had never gone to a museum voluntarily, just once with a class from school, and he wasn't about to alter his principles.

Suddenly Andy stopped. "I've got an idea!" He jumped up and grabbed onto the thick branch of a linden, tried twice to pull himself up, and on the third attempt climbed out onto the branch and peered down to the ground.

"We'll go attack the Lutherans!" he said.

Wonzak and Hannes stopped too. "What'd you say?" Wonzak said.

"I think we should go attack the Lutherans!" Andy said decisively. "There's only three of us, but maybe we'll meet somebody on the way. We'll let those guys know that today is Good Friday."

"What Lutherans?" Hannes asked skeptically.

"The country camp in Richtersdorf, for instance. I know my way around there," Andy said. "I was there once. They don't even have crosses in their classrooms. But they're always dressed first-rate and they don't pray."

Wonzak was all for it—he was even enthusiastic. "I wish I'd thought of that!"

Hannes didn't understand. He had been at country camps a few times, the one by the school in the town woods, and the other one out there in Petersdorf. He didn't know the one in Richtersdorf. The guys in Petersdorf, he remembered anyway, were from the Dortmund area, and he sure hadn't talked about God with them.

"How about it?" Andy said impatiently. "Are you coming along or not? Nobody's forcing you to."

"I just mean, I know some of the guys there," Hannes said hesitantly.

"Exactly. So you'll go in front and cast the first stone," Andy decided.

"What am I supposed to cast?"

"Are you deaf, you *lullok*! Stones, like your name, get it?

"The *ferajnas* used to go from the foundry district to the Lutherans and engage them in real battles, and smash their kitchen windows.

You see, the Lutherans cook on Friday, they don't fast like they should. That's how you can recognize them.

"Well, let's go!"

"That's what I say," Wonzak said.

They went back the way they had come, in the direction of Richtersdorf.

"There's no real Lutheran neighborhood in town anymore. And you can't ring the doorbell first, and ask whether Lutherans or Catholics live there," Andy said, somewhat disappointedly.

"They should set their churches on fire, like the Jews' synagogues," Wonzak said.

"Don't keep saying Lutherans," Hannes protested, but he didn't sound very convincing.

6

In Kattowitz, nine o'clock had struck by the time they marched out of the yard of the Gestapo prison onto Schenkendorfstrasse. An iron-gray sky weighed heavy and low upon them. They walked three and four abreast and took up almost half the street. Only seldom did an automobile approach them, now and then a bicycle rider would pass, giving them a wide berth, and they met hardly any pedestrians. It seemed as if the traffic had been detoured on this April day, or as if people had ducked into side streets, in order to avoid them.

The column moved along slowly, about two hundred men, women, and children. Except for the children under six, they were all wearing a yellow star on the left side of the chest, as big as the palm of a hand. The kapos, who were differentiated from the others by their white armbands, circled the column yelling and flailing their sticks; they drove on the old people who were too slow for them, as if they had to prove how zealous they were to the SS escort at the head and the rear of the column.

One of the men being driven along was carrying a blanket in each hand tied up into a bundle; a stuffed briefcase, which he had secured around his shoulders with a broad leather strap, bumped rhythmically against his stomach. It was good that they had surrendered their baggage in Gleiwitz. They had been suspicious at first because they were afraid it might get lost in transit, but Herr Linz had issued them receipts, and they would get it all back in the ghetto in Riga. Some men were carrying suitcases and rucksacks in addition to blankets, and were already groaning under the load.

The man's chest pains had gotten better. He hadn't slept half the night because he had no more of his drops, and only toward morning had he dozed off, exhausted. But he couldn't have slept long. First there was only a shrill, excruciating, piercing noise, nothing but the torture of this noise; after that there was the rigid, hostile, endless white of the ceiling above him. Finally soft voices next to him,

weeping and praying: *Shma Yisrael Adonai* ... And he comprehended where he was: in the cell. His mind understood but his body
did not. It still lay unmoving on the plank bed, wedged in between
other bodies. It took a while until warmth suffused him and released
him from the stiffness, and he could prop himself up on his elbows.

Outside the window it was still dark. But the emergency light in
the cell was bright enough for him to make out the other Jews who
had spent the night with him on the hard plank bed. They were
getting up too, slow, confused, dizzy, because they too were per-
ceiving their surroundings only slowly, confusedly, and dizzily. And
now Jews were crawling out from underneath the plank beds; there
had been no room for them up above and now they were looking
for a place to sit down at least. There they fell asleep again, leaning
their backs against each other.

Later the main light of the cell was turned on, and someone yelled
a command through the peephole in the door: "Get ready for transport!"

Then they began to crowd and shove and push in front of the
two toilets, which were separated from the cell only by a ragged
oilcloth curtain. They wanted to relieve themselves before the transport started. They no longer noticed the stench. They smelled only
the chlorine that floated in waves through the cell as the toilets
flushed. He himself would never forget the penetrating smell of
chlorine since his job at the sewage treatment plant.

After a while coffee was dispensed through the opening in the
door, one ladle per person, for the children as well. Many of them
had no cup or pot with them, and they pressed the others to drink
their coffee faster, so they could line up at the end and still get some.

It grew quieter in the cell. The Jews were busy sipping at the
coffee and chewing at the bread they had brought along. When they
had been taken from their homes, they had been told they should
take along provisions for two days. But they had packed so much it
would be enough to last for three, four, or even five days. They
looked at their supplies, but when they thought about not getting
anything else to eat until they were in Riga, they consumed only
half of what they had allotted themselves. Riga was far away.

Many of them were eating home-baked matzo, which had crum-

bled in their pockets. Some ate nothing. In Passover Week thou shalt
not eat leavened bread.

The man blessed the matzo and poured some of the red wine that
Herr Kochmann had provided nobody asked where from there was
no lamb this year they glanced at the chair that remained unoccupied
Rabbi Saretzki had been taken away on the last transport this is the
bread of affliction that our forefathers ate in the land of Egypt whoever
is hungry come and eat with us whoever is needy come and celebrate
the Passover with us this year here next year in the land of Israel
this year in bondage next year free

and little Aaron asked why this night is different from all other
nights

on all other nights we can eat all kinds of herbs on this night only
bitter herbs

Mah nishtaneh ha-layla ha-zeh

And they all praised God old Salo Weissenberg said: May the day
I was born be obliterated and the night when it was said a male
child came into the world that day shall be dark and may God above
not ask about him why does God give light to the weary and life to
the sore at heart who wait for death which does not come and search
more for it than for treasures

They were silent and Aaron went to the cellar and brought the
Torah scroll from its hiding place which they had not seen now for
a year little Aaron Brauer

Then came the second call for the transport. The Jews crowded
around the toilets again, most of all the women with children. Or
they sat on the plank beds as if paralyzed, their baggage next to
them, and waited. Outside it had grown light by now. Their voices
grew quieter and then fell totally silent. The man had propped his
arms on the two blankets, his head drooped, his mind plowed through
layers where sleep and consciousness and dream mingle, now he dug
his way deeper into dream, then deeper into consciousness. He was
in the cell, and somewhere else at the same time.

*Aaron's soul had already gained admittance to the forecourt of the
Lord. The paradisiacal gardens of eternal spring and unforgettable har-
monies greeted him there. An obliging wind pushed the curtain of a cloud
from the portals of immortal light, which through its abundance of sun*

put to shame the glimmering candles of all seven-brauched menorah. The patriarchs strode toward him, and their brother and fellow warrior Moses, the progenitor of the priesthood, whose name he had borne on earth, blessed him. The seraphim and cherubim, the gatekeepers of Eternity, folded their pinions in prayer before receiving the worthy servant of the Lord and leading him before the throne of thrones. The earth watched over Aaron's husk as faithfully as Heaven did his transcended soul; and over the ivy and roses of a graveyard mound still lovingly cared for today, a Star of David shimmers night after night in blessing.

Later the man will say to his neighbor Herr Karpe, there is a time of enlightenment for us too, sometimes I think I have stumbled on it, then something not comprehensible, not visible, transforms itself as the second into a square, and my consciousness moves around within it, and I experience everything simultaneously, past and present, and if the dream is the future, then the future too, and I think it will be this way forever now. That is, I don't think it, that's just the way it is, it is the feeling that from now on nothing more will change.

Until the square shatters and the second races on, and I am in this dirty, overcrowded cell again, voices, shrieking, weeping all around me, fifty Jews in a cell which once was designed for twenty. No memory of what had happened remains, I know: something happened. Something perfect. And wait for the next enlightenment.

Herr Karpe will look at the man and say to him after a while: Why does nothing like that ever happen to me?

The iron bolt in the cell door banged open. Without needing any command, the Jews exited with their baggage. An SS man was standing behind the door, counting. He held a clipboard in his hand upon which he tallied them up.

The man squeezed through the door, the blankets in his hands, at his stomach the briefcase on which big letters in white paint spelled out:

ARTHUR SILBERGLEIT, B. 1881

Now he was one more mark on the tally.

In the hallway the Jews were received by the kapos, who led them down the stairs. Whoever was too slow or, in their eyes, dressed too well, they helped along with a shove.

In the prison yard a long column of Jews was already assembled. It almost seemed as if the column had only been waiting for them. An SS man yelled at them that since there were no trucks available today, they would have to proceed to the train station on foot. Freight cars for their further transport would be waiting for them there.

Then the iron gate opened and the column began to move. It's best not to attract attention, Silbergleit thought, and kept to the middle.

Some of the Jews who had been quartered in different cells the night before made furtive gestures of recognition back and forth. Others discovered relatives or friends whom they had not seen for some time, and now tried to get together with them during the march and exchange news.

Silbergleit didn't know any of them. Nor did he take the trouble to look for a familiar face. He walked along beside Karpe, slightly stooped because the briefcase was pulling him down, and let Karpe tell him whatever he had learned from the others.

The other Jews were from Hindenburg and Beuthen, from Oppeln, Brieg, and Breslau. Obviously Jews from all over Silesia had been assembled here in the Kattowitz prison. The Breslauers had been taken from their homes on Wednesday and had spent the first night in the prison on Kletschkauer Strasse.

Herr Weissenberg, who was carrying only a bread bag in addition to his blanket, brought the news that the Breslau Jews had been told they were being sent to Lublin, which was to be set up as a Jewish city like Łódz.

"I think it's more likely we're going to Riga," Silbergleit said.

That's what Herr Linz had told them when they left for Kattowitz. There was surely no reason to consider the words of a Party security man to be the absolute truth. But why would he have said Riga when he could just as well have said Lublin? Herr Kochmann also had talked about Riga.

"You're always saying Riga. Where did you hear that?" asked Herr Weissenberg. "We were supposed to take along provisions for two days. That would seem to indicate that we won't travel very far."

"For us this is already the second day," Herr Karpe said. "So we would have to arrive there today. And for the Breslauers it's already the third day. Some of them have nothing left to eat."

"In the railway cars there are goulash cannons," Weissenberg said. He had been a gunner in the World War and remembered how field kitchens had been hitched onto the trains.

"I suppose so," Silbergleit said. "It's a long way to Riga."

"How much farther is it to the train station? Does anybody know?" Weissenberg asked loudly.

In his childhood, Silbergleit had been in Kattowitz a few times, but that was more than forty years ago. He had been to the museum, the theater, the city hall, and the botanical gardens. At the time the prison had not interested him.

"It can't be far," said Herr Karpe, who as a salesman had been everywhere, even across the border to Kattowitz and Königshütte, even to Kraków. He thought he remembered some of the houses they were passing, also a street they were just crossing.

"At first I had the feeling they were leading us through side streets, so we wouldn't attract attention. But then today is Good Friday!"

Silbergleit remembered this as if it were very far away: "Good Friday! Then people will be in church."

An old Jew suddenly began to scream and with a wail dropped to the street next to his suitcase. This caused only a brief eddy in the column, as the kapos jerked him to his feet and drove him on with their sticks. Two younger men supported the old man between them; the suitcase was left on the street.

"Is your heart doing better?" Karpe inquired. He had lain next to Silbergleit in the night and had watched him toss sleeplessly in pain.

"Yes, thanks," Silbergleit said with a twisted smile. "This one I'll survive. And in Riga I can buy some more drops."

I know it because the jasmine was blooming and fragrant you know how much I've loved jasmine and the red and white peonies ever since my childhood it was better that you didn't come yes always jasmine on my birthday the white jasmine always bloomed

I knew that you'd come I asked Herr Kochmann to say that I had gone out of town but naturally you knew that in these times a Jew doesn't leave town and you stood out there on the other side of the street with the bouquet of jasmine in your arms waiting and looking at the house all the windows to the street were covered with wooden blinds you couldn't have known that they were nailed shut except for one in Herr Kochmann's room and he rolled the blind up just a little so the sun shone through in stripes

and said come on take a look down there your wife is waiting with the jasmine in her arms and won't go away can you stand it

7

Josel Piontek climbed onto a No. 4 streetcar on Hütten-strasse, heading east. Up front, next to the driver, hung a sign: last stop morgenroth. A name that sounded like dawn. A little some-thing to console you on this gray, gloomy, leaden morning. Ad-mittedly, it wasn't much. The streetcar was almost empty. Josel took a seat up front. From here he could look past the driver, through a large, dirty pane, at a landscape that seemed to him a repetition of something he had often seen; yet he looked at it as if hoping for the miracle of something different. Low, huddled houses; a railroad bridge stretching across a confusing expanse of tracks, signal posts, and freight cars; on the left side a birch forest and on the right the rambling, soot-colored brick wall of an industrial plant, then the wire fence of another one, and the sooty brick wall of still another. They went on for kilometers, and the eye was almost relieved at the sight of a piece of fallow land with gray, wrinkled fields and scrawny birches, trees that had developed bizarre forms in the struggle with soot and smoke from the coking plant behind them. Then small, huddled houses again, a bridge across a dirty, sluggishly flowing river. Josel took his bearings on two parallel steel ribbons, stretched across black ties, that led to infinity, where heaven and earth came together in an inescapable gray. But no matter how far the creaking streetcar traveled, no matter how often it stopped with the ratchet of the handbrake sounding like the clanking of dungeon chains, it came no closer to that infinity, which for him was called Morgenroth. Josel stared straight ahead; his head seemed as empty to him as if it had been cleaned out.

He had left early that morning, when the house was still quiet. He had heard his mother rummaging around in the kitchen. She only gets involved with some kind of work so early in the morning because she wants to make herself forget Halina's absence, he thought. Later, from the window, he had noticed his mother and Irma leaving the house; they were supporting each other, but you couldn't tell who was supporting whom. No doubt they were on their way to church; it was Good Friday, after all. He wanted to be gone before they returned. He didn't want to meet Mamuscha this morning; he knew she would attack him with her questions and keep at it and repeat the same questions over and over, until Uncle Willi showed up, or Aunt Lucie, who seemed to have settled in since Halina's arrest. This questioning seemed to calm Mamuscha somehow, but his answers certainly wouldn't. Today Josel had no desire for either questions or answers, he didn't even feel any particular desire to take this trip to Beuthen.

When he was going in the direction of Trynnek, it was still not clear to him whether he would reach his goal today, whether he would ever get there at all; it was only a dull instinct in him that drove him in a certain direction, and he didn't know whether it was the right one. But walking past the mountainous slag heaps, the clattering pit-head gear, the smoking stacks, between swampy fields and lumpy paths, between coltsfoot and yellow crowfoot, spurge and rushes, he thought about his relationship to God, to Dostoevski, to his mother, and especially to Ulla Ossadnik.

Kicking along a tin can as he walked, he considered whether he should go visit Ulla Ossadnik at the Cieplik Conservatory in Beuthen, to ask her a question and to wait for her answer. He intended to pose a single question, in the hope of one single answer. He didn't have much time left, for right after Easter he would have to leave for basic training. He kicked the can so hard that it rolled into a creek and sank.

Yes, he *would* go to Beuthen. He could have a look at how she lived, and listen to her practice; he hadn't heard her practice for a long time. He left the path across the fields and turned toward town. He tried to look as casual as possible, even walked more slowly, to prove to himself that he thought it possible, but not necessarily crucial, to visit Ulla. But he couldn't get away from his question, no matter how hard he tried.

He had something to say to Ulla that one human being has to say to another only once in a lifetime (or perhaps twice at most). But by the time he bought the ticket, he was no longer sure whether he would be able to ask her. He had been wanting to say it to her for a long time, but he hadn't succeeded in being alone with her recently, for ever since her first public appearance at Blüthner Hall, her teacher had not budged from her side. This person had been treating her like a precious porcelain doll. Or maybe Ulla even welcomed the presence of such a *czotek*. This Herr Lechter was a short, plump, but uncommonly agile person, whose face was always flooded with an unnatural, excited redness, and whose eyes almost threatened to pop out of their sockets, most of all when Ulla was around—Josel couldn't stand him. They said about Herr Lechter that he had immediately discovered Ulla Ossadnik's unusual talent at the Cieplik Conservatory, and from then on had devoted himself almost exclusively to her training. There was talk of endlessly long practice sessions; he was supposed to have sat at the piano with her for ten to twelve hours on some days, and several times a masseur had to work on her arms and hands after practice. There were even rumors of blows and torture, although nothing specific could be imagined by the word torture, simply something terrible—and all this was told not with signs of horror and shock, but rather in whispered tones of the highest praise and admiration. Josel had seen this Herr Lechter only two or three times, and it was probable that the teacher had not even noticed him. After the concert Josel had pushed his way up to Ulla and handed her flowers, and Ulla had smiled at him briefly, but otherwise she had eyes—ach, all her senses—only for her teacher. To Josel, this Herr Lechter was not just unpleasant, but also uncanny somehow. On the one hand, he sensed in this fat, sweating man something of obsession, yes, artistic fanaticism; on the other hand, he exuded a coldness and calculation that frightened Josel. Both qualities had probably been essential in creating Ulla's first great triumph of her life on that evening. That had been immediately clear to him then. But he had also sensed that Herr Lechter was in the process of remodeling Ulla, transforming her, making a very different person out of her.

So something had to happen! But what? Worst of all, he didn't know who could make something happen. Certainly not her mother—Ulla came home rarely, perhaps partly because she was ashamed of her simple parents; definitely not her father, who adored her happily and silently as before; and not her former piano teacher,

Valeska Piontek, either, who for Ulla probably was only a reminder of the degrading conditions under which she had begun. So I'm the only one left—Josel tried to bolster his courage.

He still remembered Ulla's first visit to Strachwitzstrasse. Her father in his too tight railway uniform had escorted her—no, he had practically presented her. Without being able to read music and never having taken lessons, she rattled off waltzes and fox-trots on a neighbor's piano. Mamuscha had taken a look at her, had examined her hands and stretched her fingers until the joints popped, had set the metronome and simply made the girl play according to the beat. She was astonished! She had never had such a natural talent sitting on this piano stool, and she probably would have given Ulla Ossadnik instruction for nothing. Or had all that happened later? At any rate, his mother had been the first to recognize Ulla's talent, and when she realized that there was nothing more she could teach Ulla, it was her idea to have her apply to the Cieplik Conservatory in Beuthen. She had even arranged for a scholarship. And now Ulla wanted little (and her teacher Herr Lechter nothing at all) to do with her former discoverer. Josel didn't dare reproach her for her recent absence from Gleiwitz, but he would reproach her new teacher. He began to develop a dislike of Lechter that at first turned into contempt and later even into hate. On some nights Josel caught himself quarreling with him in his mind, arguing with him, and fighting with him. And suddenly he found himself on his way to Beuthen, and then he was standing on Bahnhofstrasse, in a doorway across from the Cieplik Conservatory. Sooner or later Herr Lechter would have to come out. Then he would talk to him about all the things he had discussed with him in his mind for so many nights. Perhaps he would only walk up to him with his head lowered, bump into him, give him a shove, knock him down, or bite him on the hand, so he wouldn't be able to play the piano for a while. He wanted to do something senseless, something that would insult and humiliate the man, although he was not clear who would be more humiliated by such an act.

Once he actually had caught sight of the teacher on the other side of the street and had gone toward him; he had pulled his head down between his shoulders and was about to butt into him. But then he sidestepped at the last instant after all and only brushed against him. The teacher probably didn't even recognize him, maybe he didn't even notice him; he walked on as if a fly had merely touched him, an annoying fly. Yes, that's how he felt, like an annoying fly. What was he really, nothing more than an insect that the others would like to shoo away. He felt like the man he had read about in Dostoevski: if he couldn't be loved, then at least he wanted to be hated. So he resolved to turn around and venture an attack, but the nimble round man had already disappeared behind the front door of the conservatory.

He had seen Ulla, too, and not just once, and instead of stepping out of his hiding place, he had timorously withdrawn even deeper into the doorway. Was he scared, or even cowardly? He wished he were not even there, he wished he were no longer a person who felt and suffered, but only an object, a doorknob, a windowpane, or a doormat, just as the other man was only a sphere and Ulla only a piano key, and he wished that all people would turn into things.

And yet he had only been waiting for Ulla to catch sight of him in the doorway and, without saying a word, simply look at him and embrace him. But none of that had ever happened. Ulla had always been in a hurry, she had always disappeared without glancing to the right or left. He continued to stand in the doorway and wait, and in time the waiting, simply the waiting, had become more important than anything else. He was waiting for a change. But nothing changed. He looked up at the windows of this gray three-story building, behind which the outline of a person sometimes appeared and then vanished again, and leaning against the wall with his cap pulled down, he indulged in fantasies that let him forget reality. Then it grew dark and the windows lit up, and for a moment he thought they were lit only for him. But soon afterwards the blackout curtains, which let through only small scraps of light, destroyed the illusion. He began to wiggle his feet, which had almost fallen asleep from all the waiting. He imagined Ulla sitting at the piano and striking the keys, while the short, spherical, bald-headed dwarf with the red face stood next to her giving directions. If only he could conjure him away!

Then he sees Ulla alone at the piano, in front of an orchestra. The conductor gives the cue and her hands leap, hop, and dance across the keys, and the music reaches all the way out to him, but he hears only her, her alone, and at the end the applause bursts out and people jump from their seats and clap enthusiastically, while she bows shyly, again and again, and he, Josel, runs forward and shouts bravo, bravo . . .

He imagined it this way because he had once seen this in a movie. But when Ulla was on the stage of the concert hall in reality and the audience was applauding her, he had remained seated and had not even clapped. He had been as if paralyzed and to this very day something deep inside him had remained frozen . . . Once, at the beginning, when his cousin Andreas had still been in town, he had spotted him in another doorway, waiting like him and staring up at the windows for a long time until it got dark, and he walked away slow and tired, with his shoulders hunched, a black object on two legs that was absorbed by the darkness.

He had spoken with Ulla only when she paid a courtesy call on his mother, and that happened seldom enough. He had tried his best to be alone with her, but he had not succeeded. Perhaps it was pure coincidence, but he thought it more likely that Ulla arranged it that way on purpose. Yet he certainly wouldn't have told her about his trips to Beuthen and waiting in front of the Cieplik Conservatory.

All he had managed to do was to exchange a few words with her, and what he had wanted to say to her had remained concealed beneath a thick layer of small talk, and before they had found the time to clear away this layer and to advance to the glowing core of his desires, they had already separated again. They grew a few steps farther apart each time. Finally, Beuthen no longer seemed a neighboring town to him; rather, measured according to his soul, it was light-years away.

Sure, today he had a valid reason to go to Beuthen. Today he wouldn't wait in front of the conservatory as before, looking at the windows and dreaming; today he would march through the door, up the stairs, and ask for Ulla Ossadnik in Lechter's piano class. He would see her and talk to her. It was the war that supplied him with the reason. The war was good for something.

The war had caught up with him too. He had his draft notice in his pocket. Right after Easter he would be in the army. First to a camp at Liegnitz for basic training, and from there to the front. It was the war that made the decision, over his head and over Ulla's.

On the way past the vegetable gardens at the edge of town, he had already been planning his speech, which he constantly repeated, but the more he tried it out, the more unlikely it seemed that he would be able to give it in her presence.

I got my draft notice, Ulla, and in two weeks I might be at the front, where a shell could hit me . . . that's how he would begin. But he knew he would never start off like that. He thought about what words Prince Myshkin had used to declare his love to Aglaya, or rather to confuse her. He should have read that through again. At the time it had not only stirred him, it had aroused him precisely because the Prince had used words and phrases wholly different from those he had expected. Maybe his performance would only seem erratic and ridiculous to Ulla . . .

Josel held tight to the seat in front of him as the streetcar braked sharply and finally halted. He had to transfer now, to the Beuthen-Scharley line. It was as if he had been torn from a deep dream. There had been a time when he would have roamed half the world, asking every girl who struck his fancy whether she would love him—and now he didn't even have the courage to ask Ulla whether she at least would wait for him until after the war. Everything had turned out differently. Ulla had become famous overnight, even though the two of them had not traveled to Warsaw together beforehand, to the Church of the Holy Cross, to touch the pillar encasing the heart of Chopin. Had she forgotten, perhaps? Anyway, he would never forget.

She would soon go on tour, to the army field hospitals and many cities; she would play Schubert, Schumann, and sometimes Chopin too, accompanied by that fat so-and-so with the fish eyes. And *he* had to go to war and in a few weeks would be lying in a trench somewhere, in mud and filth, and he would take aim, bringing the sights of his carbine to bear on something approaching from the other side, a thing that previously had been a human being, a man on two legs. He would not ask Ulla, no, he simply wouldn't be able to ask her; but he would look at her silently, and read her face, her eyes, her movements. It would be reassuring for him to know that

someone was waiting for him. It would make it easier for him to
endure everything out there at the front. Perhaps it would make
dying easier for him. And it was to be no one else but Ulla. That's
what he wished for now, as he climbed in the streetcar to Beuthen-
Scharley.

It shouldn't be his mother, his sister, or Uncle Willi. It shouldn't
even be the memory of Papusch—he could drag that along with him
everywhere. He had always wanted to get away from this town, and
now it was almost time, no one would be able to stop him. He only
hoped he would be sent to the West, perhaps to France, to the
Atlantic Wall, just as old Montag had once said to him: with every
generation, a move farther to the West! And he would look around
in the big, foreign cities, and someday he would send for Ulla, if
she still wanted to go with him. Only memory held him here beneath
this gray sky and on this black earth.

Until now only a few people had been sitting on the streetcar, maybe ten or twelve, each sitting on a separate seat, as if not
wanting to come into contact with the others. At the next stop a
group of men and women, mostly elderly, swarmed aboard, shouting and calling to each other. A soldier who had been sitting in
the rear at first, now sat down up front next to Josel, because he
didn't want to be hemmed in by all the black clothes. Josel moved
over.

After they had asked each other where they were going, they began
to size each other up. It turned out they were almost the same age.
The other one, who had just spent two weeks on the Eastern Front,
had lost his right arm and was on convalescent leave now. Josel had
nothing to counter with but his draft notice, which was in his pocket.
That seemed to amuse the soldier, for he laughed so hard that his
sleeve jerked back and forth. He gave the impression of having come
to terms with the loss of his arm, or, which seemed more likely to
Josel, had not yet really comprehended the loss.

The female conductor was still taking the fares of the men and
women who had gotten on. Then they began to sing. Scattered at
first, then together in a chorus, it was not very loud, it was more a
solemn humming. Josel could have joined in, it was an old pilgrim's
song that he knew by heart:

Ave Maris Stella!
Mother Mary help!
Mater dei bella
Mother Mary help!
Oh, Mother Mary, help us.
In this, our hour of need.

The streetcar braked sharply on a curve, so the soldier slid closer to Josel. He had tried to grab hold with his one hand too late. Pain ran visibly across his face and contorted it in a grimace for a moment. Josel couldn't tell whether it was a physical pain or an emotional one because the soldier had to discover all over again that he possessed only one arm. Josel would have liked to know how long it takes to get used to the loss of an arm. He looked directly at the soldier who had slid back along the seat. He straightened his forage cap with the one hand, and gave Josel a crooked, somewhat embarrassed smile. Josel saw himself as the other man in this instant. Yes, he could in fact have been the other soldier. This notion didn't frighten him at all. Who knows what will have become of him in a year. Everything could be much worse. He squeezed his eyes shut and made himself smaller in his seat.

"What happened there?" Josel asked, tapping carefully at the empty sleeve hanging down.

"In the Pripet Marshes," the soldier said, "my arm got torn off by a shell—just sliced off like with a razor. It flew through the air, I could see it fall onto the ground, then it lay there, my own arm, my hand, a few meters away from me, can you imagine that? It was crazy. I went over to it and was going to pick it up, my arm, yet not my arm, and that's when I first felt the blood on my shoulder, felt myself getting sick. I began to stumble and fell down, right in front of my bloody arm . . ." With his left hand he made a gesture as if to wipe away the memory of it. "It got me home," he said with a grin.

That meant nothing to Josel. The whole description nauseated him. He wasn't afraid of the loss of a leg, an arm, or even an eye. He was afraid of a head wound, afraid of becoming an idiot, crazy, *ogupna*, he couldn't rid himself of this fear.

"It got me home," the soldier repeated, almost proudly. As if that were a distinction, a kind of decoration First Class.

The streetcar was rattling across a bridge now. Josel hummed along with the pilgrim's song:

> *Rosa sine spina*
> *Mother Mary, help!*
> *O tu gratia plena*
> *Mother Mary, help!*

A skinny boy with a yellow pennant in his hand stumbled forward between the seats toward the conductor.

"What kind of crowd is that?" the soldier asked.

The song had reminded Josel of something. "I think they're going on a pilgrimage to Deutsch-Piekar, it's not far from here," he said. And he asked the boy, who nodded to him and, as if in confirmation, lowered the little yellow flag, which bore the black letters IHS.

"This is Good Friday," Josel said, "so people go to Mount Calvary."

He had been there once himself, right after the war began, when Deutsch-Piekar had become German, and he remembered how they, a group of teenagers, had run from one Station of the Cross to the next to kiss the relics of the saints, which were enclosed behind a pane of glass. It was Paulek who carried a bottle of schnapps hidden under his jacket and took a swig before every relic to "disinfect" the glass. He passed the bottle around so they could do the same, and even before they reached the top of the Mount they were already slightly tipsy.

"Many of the faithful," Josel said, "climb up the holy hill on their knees, praying. That can take hours. And when they reach the top, their knees are bloody and they're completely exhausted."

The soldier slapped his palm to his forehead. "Religious insanity," he said, as if it were a conclusion that had been bothering him for a long time.

The streetcar was rumbling along so noisily that Josel had to yell to make himself heard. "You have to believe in it," he said earnestly.

"Religious insanity," the soldier repeated.

Josel had understood him the first time. If he was still looking at his neighbor a little skeptically, it was only because he couldn't associate the two words with each other.

"You must not be from around here?" Josel asked.

"Nope, I'm from Stettin, this is new to me."

Two women got on at the next stop, their kerchiefs as gray as the light outside. On their bosoms they wore buttons with the letters EAST. They remained standing in the rear on the platform and made themselves even more unobtrusive than they already were.

The group of pilgrims began a new song. A few thin voices began, but perished in the noise of the squeaking brakes. The skinny boy beat time in vain with the church pennant.

"My philosophy is very different," the soldier said to Josel: *That won't make the world go under, even though the world looks gray, it's survived full many a blunder, it will be sky blue some day.*

He couldn't help it that it consisted of lines from a hit tune. They had helped him through everything, at least up to now.

Multistoried houses to the left and right made it apparent that they had arrived in town. On the street they saw black-clothed people indistinctly in the gloomy light of the morning.

> *Over the mountains calls*
> *The church bell's dying fall*
> *Sweetly at eve*

The soldier laughed at Josel, showing his teeth, chanting: *One time over, one time under, even if your skull is smoking . . .* The streetcar slowed down with a sirenlike noise. Josel stood up. The soldier got up too.

"Do you know what you sacrificed this for?" Josel asked, tugging at the soldier's empty sleeve. "Just ask the people around here, they'll tell you."

The soldier didn't just look incredulous, he seemed to be really baffled. They stood facing each other, half wedged between the seats. Josel felt the ticking pain in his forehead again, directly above the bridge of his nose.

"Let me through, I have to get off," Josel said. And more loudly: "Go along with these people, pray the Stations of the Cross with them, pray with them at the grave of Christ, do it!"

"But why should I pray?" The soldier sat down again and wouldn't let Josel out. "Nothing else can happen to me. I'm already a cripple. Now it's the others' turn. Sometimes the world is gray, sometimes it's sky blue, that's the way it is." His face was empty. There was no expression on it at all.

Josel was able to squeeze past the soldier now. "So there'll be a world full of cripples, right?" he called to him. "Maybe that's how it will be. I told you I've already got my draft notice in my pocket, a few weeks more, I'll be at the front and then, who knows, I could get hit by a bullet, a shell could blow me to bits, and if I'm lucky, like you were, I'll only lose an arm or a leg, but maybe it'll be worse . . ." He didn't dare say out loud what he was thinking. The soldier tried to hold him back with his hand. But Josel easily shook him off.

> *I'll be that bell divine*
> *So let that voice be mine*
> *Both near and far*

he sang along with the pilgrims, even rather loudly, pushing forward to the exit, which was secured only by a chain. He unhooked the chain and stood on the step, and as the streetcar entered a curve, he jumped off, so nimbly and surely that it was clear this wasn't the first time he'd done it.

The soldier gazed after him for a while, then he sat down on the seat again and stuffed the empty sleeve into his jacket pocket. "Religious insanity," he said softly to himself, "the people here are crazy, they're all crazy." His homemade philosophy worked better: *That won't make the world go under, it'll still be needed* . . . he sang back at the pilgrims' song.

8

HALINA'S NEW TEETH were the cause of it all. Maybe Valeska should never have tried to do anything about it, but she could no longer stand seeing Halina running around with those sunken cheeks, looking old far beyond her years. And it didn't help, either, when Halina would stuff balls of wax into the pouches of her cheeks on special occasions and beam over the whole of her newly stretched face. Of course, this could only fool people who had never seen her before—for Valeska, it was all the more horrifying.

She never would have thought of it, though, if Halina hadn't been entered in Census Group III and thus, simultaneously, in the state health program; the teeth wouldn't cost her a thing. So she herself took Halina to Dr. Kozuschek, the dentist on Breslauerstrasse, who was known as much for his coarseness as for his perfectly fitting dentures. Her uppermost thought was that with new teeth, Halina might have some chance, or at least one last chance, of meeting a man who, even if he didn't exactly fall in love with her, might at least marry her. Naturally she was interested, on the one hand, in keeping Halina here in the house as long as possible—and she had already been here for almost seven years, a sizable chunk of life and even more labor, and a few secrets bound them together as well; on the other hand, she had promised Aunt Jadwiga she would take the responsibility for Halina and her happiness, and she took that seriously, she did, right down to the teeth. She wouldn't be able to hold on to Halina much longer, anyway. The Labor Office was already calling up single women for antiaircraft or armament duty, and young married women, too, if they had no children. And Valeska asked herself sometimes when her turn would come, even if she was approaching fifty. If the war lasted a while longer, they would even come for the children. Josel was not even finished with school and had already received his draft notice.

But the last thing she would have imagined was what had then happened to Halina. She couldn't get over it. She walked back and forth in the music room, plucked absentmindedly at the drapes here, picked a dry leaf from the begonia there, straightened the photograph of Gieseking on the piano, and listened nervously to the sounds in the house. She wished things were noisier, the silence made her restless. Irma had retreated to her room and had forbidden her to send for a doctor or even a midwife, because by now she believed —and probably hoped, too—that the baby would come on Sunday, as she had calculated. And she had found a note from Josel in the kitchen, saying he was on his way to Beuthen to say good-bye to Ulla Ossadnik. Maybe he would bring Ulla back with him, she even hoped so, the long holiday was here and she could play four hands with Ulla, a military march by Schubert, or the little C-major Sonata by Mozart; at any rate, she wouldn't have to keep thinking about Halina. Perhaps she could schedule a home concert for Easter Sunday. Now that Frau Reimers was here from Cologne, she had a good violin again; old Frau Dobrewollny was simply no longer up to it.

Valeska had left a window open overlooking the garden, and a light, warm wind billowed the drapes. In some places the sky had torn open and showed blue spots and islands, the gray clouds towered together and were being driven off more and more strongly to the east. If they were lucky, there might be a sunny sky that afternoon. Because of the rain these last few days, the ground was like a swollen sponge; if the sun would shine for just a couple of days in a row now, nature would explode. It was already the end of April, after all.

Valeska imagined that she still perceived Halina's smell everywhere in the house. If she weren't in the kitchen, where the dirty dishes reminded her so clearly of the girl's absence, she might believe that Halina had just gone outside for a moment and would be back with the next bang of the hall door. Now she yearned for the noises that Halina made. She couldn't by any means have described what sorts of sounds these were, but they had been so characteristic of Halina that she could immediately distinguish them from all other sounds. Yes, when she thought about it, what was particular about these sounds was perhaps their noiselessness: there was only a vibration when she walked through the hall into the kitchen, only a draft that indicated her approach, only a certain change in the light when she was standing in front of the window. Except for the sound she had got into the habit of making with her new dentures, by sucking in air through a gap in the teeth; it sounded unpleasant but Valeska couldn't get her to stop. She had snapped at Halina a few times because of this; now, she would have been glad to hear that sound.

From the hall she heard steps, heavy, slow steps. Her brother came into the music room in his dressing gown and with a hairnet on his head. He acted as if he were looking for something, maybe a newspaper, but there was no newspaper on Good Friday. Or he was looking for his book, for that thick novel, *The Saint and Her Fool*, that he had been toting around for a long time now, always with one finger between the pages as a bookmark. She had observed how the finger drifted farther back in the book from evening to evening, until he had finally clapped it shut a few days ago. She would have liked to ask him about the contents, for the title made her curious, but since the time she had discovered a book in his room with candid, if not obscene, sketches, he no longer talked with her about what he was reading.

It was practically noon and he was still running around the house in his dressing gown and with the hairnet on his head. And on Good Friday, too! On days like this, when he didn't have to go to his office, he was capable of running around like this until the afternoon, sometimes even until evening. It didn't seem to bother him at all; at least he acted as if he felt just fine. In some way it was sobering for Valeska to see her brother meandering around the house in his spotty dressing gown in broad daylight. And his hairnet, which was sprinkled with gray dandruff even though he used all sorts of hair tonics and shampoos, was almost physically repulsive to her. But she didn't dare say anything. This horrid hairnet, under which he protected the waves he designed with comb and water, irritated her greatly.

"Are you looking for me?" she asked, as a pretext for another question.

Fortunately he was busy with the sofa, tossing the cushions aside to find something underneath—for if he had looked at his sister now, he would probably have guessed her other question.

"I'm looking for . . ." Wondrak said, as if trying to remember what he really was looking for. "I don't know where I left my cigarette holder . . . yesterday. I wasn't in the music room yesterday evening . . . or was I?"

Valeska sank down on the piano stool, as if she were relieved that only something as banal as a lost cigarette holder was at stake. These days people were sometimes afraid to meet one another because they had only terrible news to tell each other. When Valeska met an acquaintance in mourning in town, she avoided her, for she didn't want to hear who it was who had fallen this time, a son or son-in-law or even husband. Anyway, the government had decreed—and the churches had not protested it, which had outraged her—that mourning could no longer be worn for an entire year, as before, but only for three months. Perhaps because they feared that the whole town would be wearing black someday.

Without rising, Valeska said: "Irma's time is here."

"Ach!" Willi called out so loudly, so surprised, that she had to assume he had just found whatever he was looking for. For he couldn't have been that flabbergasted by the fact that Irma was about to have her baby.

"We were in church this morning," she said, "that's when it started, right in church." It sounded as if she wanted to blame the church for it. "She's in her room now, and claims it was a false alarm. But I know better. Let's wait a few hours, then the pains will start in earnest."

"No complications yet?" Willi said, somewhat indistinctly because he was bent over, trying to fish the cigarette holder out from beneath the sofa.

"What?" Valeska asked.

"I mean, how did you get home? Were there any complications on the way? And how does Irma feel now?" In his effort to show more friendliness, he gained ground with this salvo of questions.

"The way it usually starts," Valeska said. "With spasms in the back. I wanted to call an ambulance for her, but you know how Irma is, she insisted on going on foot. Well, maybe it was for the best, you're supposed to get exercise right up to the last minute . . . By the way, as we were leaving, they were lowering the bells from Peter and Paul. The square in front was full of people watching."

She said this as casually as possible. It had been in the newspapers weeks ago, and they had talked about it and gotten excited and outraged too. Frau Millimonka from the Third Order, who was also a member of the Parish Council, was supposed to have gone to Archpriest Pattas and challenged him to refuse to release the bells. It was said to be a command from the Reichsmarschall, as commissioner of the Four-Year Plan, but no one had seen the order in print. The Third Order began to collect nonferrous metals on its own, so that at least the oldest bell, from 1654, could be rescued, but they accumulated only a few kilograms, because nonferrous metals had been collected from the beginning of the war and people simply didn't have any more. Valeska had even taken down her brass curtain rings and replaced them with wooden ones. But then they were told that old historic bells were not covered by the new law—and the Gleiwitz bells had been provided by the rather impoverished citizenry of the town immediately after the Thirty Years' War. But when a pastor in Cosel was arrested because he had called upon his congregation to pray publicly for the rescue of the church bells, nothing more was said about the order.

"Our beautiful bells," Willi Wondrak said helplessly. "That they're doing it on Good Friday, of all days!" At least that was cause for outrage.

"We won't have any bells on Easter. I can't imagine how we'll celebrate the Resurrection of the Lord without bells ringing . . ."

Valeska really could not imagine it, for as far back as she could remember she had gone to the High Mass on Easter Sunday; for her it was the most beautiful High Mass in the Church year. The closing chorus, *Halleluja! The strong vanquisher of Death!*, she liked better than any Christmas carol, no matter how beautiful and solemn, and she especially loved it when all the bells joined in the chorus, and their pealing mingled with the fervent singing of the faithful. After the benediction by the pastor they were accompanied on their way home by the marvelous pealing of the bells. She would never forget it. Even at the time when she was attending the little church in Myslowitz, which had only a single bell, she had been impressed by the Easter bells.

"A special company from the Reich must be doing that," Wondrak said. "I can't imagine that the Nitschke Company on Lohmeyerstrasse would dare try it on a Good Friday . . ." For a moment he considered whether he should take a look at this strange drama himself. But after a glance at his dressing gown, he decided not to.

"I'll be going to church this evening," he said, "then the whole thing will be over. It would just make me sad to have to watch them do it."

"The Lutheran churches, I heard," Valeska said, "are practically making a sacrificial event out of it. They ring the bells one last time before ceremoniously handing them over to Führer, Folk, and Fatherland. When I hear that, well, I'd rather have them come and take them on Good Friday."

Willi Wondrak felt for his hairnet, checking whether it had slipped during his search for the cigarette holder.

"Do you still remember," Valeska said, "in the new Christ the King Church out there by the town woods, when they took the bells away a year ago? The people stood there and wept—the bells had been bought only a few years before with contributions from the congregation, and it's not exactly rich people who live in that area . . ."

Valeska sighed. The bells could have made her forget her daughter, without further ado. And even Halina, poor thing. She had gone to the Christ the King Church with her then to watch. My God, she had already forgotten that.

So much was happening in these terrible times. "You start getting used to terrible things," she said offhandedly. But she would never get used to the terrible things that might happen to Halina.

"Any news?" Valeska asked brusquely.

Her brother understood immediately. After all, they had been thinking of nothing else since the day before. He answered just as brusquely: "No, none." And added, in a different tone of voice: "Can I do anything . . . anything at all for Irma?"

Yet he hoped he wouldn't have to go to Irma's room and see her in that condition. He liked his niece well enough, to the extent that nieces were tolerable at all, but women who draw everyone's attention to their swelling belly secretly revolted him. He didn't want to show it—at least not in Irma's case—but he was simply unable to make an exception. Pregnant women have a specific smell; they smell of sawdust and decaying leaves, he maintained. With Irma the smell was particularly strong. He smelled it on women who you couldn't even see were pregnant yet, and he was nauseated by it, but naturally he wouldn't have admitted it. He remembered only that he had to throw up once during Irma's first pregnancy. And no one had told him she was pregnant beforehand. He had simply smelled it. He didn't want to see Irma until she had given birth. But now he was looking for a newspaper from yesterday, one from the capital. They didn't reach Gleiwitz until a day later, anyway.

"Friday's child is full of woe," Valeska said, and sighed. She remained sitting behind her grand piano, as if she wanted to conceal herself behind the instrument. At least until Halina returned. She couldn't stop thinking about it. Even though it was perfectly clear to her—and she had discussed it extensively with her brother, weighing the situation from every angle, considering every possibility—that nothing whatsoever could be done until the holidays were over.

"The poor thing" was all she said.

She raised the keyboard cover halfway, propped it up with her left hand, and struck a key with her finger. No, she didn't want to play, not on Good Friday. And not when her daughter was possibly writhing in pain in the next room. And Halina was suffering in prison.

Not much could be happening with Irma yet. Aunt Lucie was in her room with her and would inform them if anything serious happened. Maybe it would be long and drawn out—she struck another key—maybe it would even be an Easter child. She too wished ardently for an Easter child.

"How could that ever have happened," she said after a while with her left foot resting on the pedal. "I can't get over it."

"Over what?" Willi asked, mostly out of politeness. For he knew exactly what she meant. Since yesterday they had been talking about nothing else.

"Halina," she said despondently.

"But you know very well that I left no stone unturned. I hope we'll make some progress after the holidays." He wanted to leave the room as quickly as possible.

"Two plainclothes officials just walk into the kitchen and arrest our Halina—that's criminal, that's against the law." She said it as if she were recapitulating an incident that had just taken place and that she couldn't yet comprehend. And that's about the way it was.

"I have to blame myself," she continued. "If we had been home, maybe it wouldn't have happened."

"I don't know," said Wondrak, who thought more realistically. "We should have watched her more carefully. With her new teeth, she could have gotten herself another man."

Halina had not been exactly delighted by the plans of her Pani. She didn't understand why she had to go to Dr. Kozuschek's on Breslauerstrasse twice a week. First, she had to wait a long time in the waiting room, then she had to sit down on a leather chair, which the doctor suddenly tipped back, so she was practically lying down, then he poked in her mouth with gleaming instruments that made an awful sound. While he scraped and filed at her last remaining teeth, this man talked and laughed incessantly, and rubbed his knee against her legs in a quite obvious manner. Halina saw and heard everything, but she didn't understand a single word, because she had to cope with her fear and her pain. And when she was finally permitted to leave this terrible house, the fear was gone. But the pain remained, sometimes for whole afternoons. She could stand it only with the help of the pain tablets that the Pani dug out of a tea canister. The beautiful and consoling tales that Frau Valeska told her, that at the end of her sufferings brand-new teeth would grow in her mouth, and that with these new teeth she would be a new person, well, she didn't and couldn't believe them, because in her lifetime she had already had to endure lots of pain without having become a new person because of it—it was only the patience acquired over twenty-six years that let her submit to the procedure.

In the end, Dr. Kozuschek had finally stuck new teeth in her mouth. Now, as he expressed it, they would stay put in the same place for the next hundred years, never decay, never break, never fall out, and never cause pain. And in fact they were new teeth that she felt in her mouth resting firmly without a wiggle when she sucked at them or pressed them with her tongue. In the evening she could simply remove them with one motion which made a gentle sucking sound, and could put them back in again the next morning.

Matka Boska, she came home and stood in front of the mirror and stared and stared at herself, opened her mouth wide, pushed her lips back with two fingers, and could hardly keep control of herself: real white, beautiful, well-formed teeth gleamed in her mouth, each more perfect than the next, as beautiful as in the movies, and much more beautiful than her old ones ever had been. Her cheeks were tight and round and flushed with excitement now, and she really didn't need the balls of wax anymore, but she didn't dare throw them away, so she simply hid them in her apron pocket.

She had real teeth now and looked like other people. Halina couldn't believe it. She reassured herself in every mirror she passed that the teeth were still in her mouth and had not been whisked away by magic.

"Now you'll get a husband," her Pani had told her, "with those teeth. With your fantastic teeth," she had said.

But before she had been afraid of every strange man and wouldn't look at them; she was more afraid now. She was even scared that Chaplain Nowak, whom she went to for confession, might be attracted to her because she had such beautiful teeth now. Basically, she couldn't cope with it.

The teeth were so beautiful that she didn't dare eat. On the second day she still hadn't taken any nourishment. Of course, she didn't know how she would get through the time to come, but she simply couldn't imagine that she would have to sit with the others and eat beets, beets of all things; they would spoil her white teeth. She opened a compact that the Pani had given her years ago but that she had never used, and laughed into the tiny, round mirror, and was pleased by her own laughter because she could see her teeth sparkling. They really were far too symmetrical and perfect to be brought into contact with such simple things as potatoes, turnips, bread, or hot cabbage soup. She would rather starve.

Valeska had not noticed this until Halina suddenly turned pale in the kitchen, stumbled, and finally fell down next to the stove on the new linoleum floor. It was an attack of weakness. Halina had to be fed like a baby. Valeska held her head on her lap, and with two fingers parted her lips and then her teeth, and poured in a spoonful of hot potato soup, potato soup with melted fat. And after each meal she showed her in a hand mirror that the teeth were still unchanged and thus would stay that way for quite some time—if she was lucky, until the day when she was lying in a coffin and really wouldn't need the teeth anymore.

Now she was like other people. She sat at the table with them and laughed like they did, and she got used to smiling, which the Pani had practiced with her in front of the mirror. With this smile she sometimes even dared look at a man, if only from a distance.

And that's what happened with the man who turned up at the garden fence one day and spoke to her in broken German. *Please, Frau, have a piece bread, hunger, hunger,* and he made the gesture that is understood everywhere, by slapping his stomach several times with his open hand. She had seen the EAST on his jacket clearly enough, because he had made no attempt to conceal it. She had stood there and looked up at him, for he towered more than a head above her. She saw his stubbly chin and the open, shabby shirt collar and the thin jacket over it, and she didn't know whether she should have sympathy for this man because he had begged for food, or whether she should send him away because he was big and, underneath some black fuzz, his cheeks were glowing feverishly. Before his gaze could fasten itself upon her, she ran away to escape her confusion. She cut two slices of bread, spread them with lard, and then, after some hesitation, put two slices of sausage on them—they couldn't even afford that for themselves anymore—and wrapped them up in a piece of newspaper, the *Wanderer* from last Tuesday, which even Lawyer Wondrak probably wouldn't miss. A few minutes later she was back at the garden fence and had just lifted her hands to give him the little package over the pickets when their eyes suddenly met.

She didn't evade his glance this time and didn't move from where she was standing, either. Although it was cold outside and her breath was white in the air, she suddenly felt sweat running down her skin beneath her smock. I have to look him in the eye, I must. She no longer knew how to put on the smile she had so often practiced with the Pani. She left her hand on the fence when the stranger put

his hand on hers, and waited. They stood that way for an eternity
and a minute, silent, astonished, and without any anxiety. Not until
they heard steps from the end of the street did this peculiar alliance
of complicity and silence shatter.

"We see again?" the man asked.

Halina hesitated. Then she said in Polish: "Come back next Saturday, at the same time, I'll be waiting here."

She turned around and went slowly back to the kitchen. He didn't
come until Sunday. She had spent the whole of Saturday in an
unfamiliar state of excitement. In the kitchen she had stayed near
the window, because she could get a good view of the street from
there. After it grew dark, she invented various pretexts for going
outside again. Once she even claimed that she had to take the garbage
pail out to the yard, the garbage seemed to be fouling up the air.

Valeska was surprised at this, for earlier wild horses couldn't get
Halina to go to the cellar after nightfall, let alone outside. Halina
stayed in the kitchen a long time, discovering more and more tasks
that she absolutely had to perform at this late hour. She refused to
be disappointed and didn't give up. On Sunday too she kept an eye
on the street.

If Valeska Piontek had been worrying about Halina as much as
she claimed, she would have noticed how often Halina went out to
the garden on this October Sunday to pick an herb, to cut a rose
that was about to lose its petals, or to tie up a creeper that she had
already tied up once. But no one in the house had noticed, they were
all so busy with themselves, especially on Sundays.

In the afternoon he actually did come. She had seen him from far
off and had walked toward him. Inside everyone was taking an
afternoon nap; no one witnessed their second meeting. With brief,
careful gestures she signaled to him to turn around. She followed
him at some distance and finally directed him to a little grove at the
end of the street. Only behind the old brickyard, where she thought
they would be alone and unobserved, did she go up to him and put
her hands on his. She gazed at him as if she had known him for a
long time already, and he accepted this pleasure in silence. And only
then did she give him the sandwiches.

She said something to him in Polish, and he understood her. He answered in Ukrainian, and she understood him. Arkady Shevchuk was his name.

Then they walked on, Halina always a little ahead, so people wouldn't notice they were together. He held a hand over the EAST tag on his jacket, but you could tell from quite a ways off by his quilted cap that he was a foreign laborer.

Later she had brought Arkady a cap belonging to the lawyer which was a little too big for him. She put a folded double sheet of newspaper inside the headband, then somehow it fit. She looked at him and laughed. It would have astonished Valeska Piontek to see Halina like this. She didn't know a Halina who could laugh and kick up her feet, dancing in the grass!

Arkady came from a little town on the Dnieper whose name she couldn't pronounce. It said Arkady in his passport, but everybody called him Kolya and that is what he wanted her to call him.

Halina was puzzled. On her identity card it said Halina, and that's what she was called: Halina.

He called her Galina.

He embraced her down by the creek. It had frozen the night before for the first time. Many of the patches of grass that lay in shadow were still quite white.

Twice they had gone to the movies. They had bought their tickets separately and had gone in separately, and had not sat down next to each other, but sometimes, when the projection lamp grew brighter, they raised their heads and looked at each other across the rows of seats. One of the films was titled *Andreas Schlüter*, and later she could only remember that a cathedral collapsed and a fat old man was crying. She had been thinking only of Kolya. The other was titled *Circus Renz*.

Once he brought her a pendant of amber that his sister had given him when he and the other men of his little town had been packed off to Germany in freight cars. Halina was flustered. No one had ever given her such a precious gift. She didn't dare wear the pendant around her neck on a piece of string—that would have attracted attention, and everyone would have asked about it, and she wouldn't have known how to explain it to them. So she hid it in the little pewter vase in which dried flowers had been gathering dust for years. No one would find out that a precious amber was lying on the bottom of the vase. Sometimes she took the flowers out and tipped the vase upside down. She felt the stone in her hand. The secret was hers alone.

She had changed since then. She had only wondered why no one in the Piontek household had noticed anything. No hints were dropped in her presence, at any rate. Only Aunt Lucie (Widera) had said to her once: "Halina, your cheeks are nice and red. According to Eichendorff, that's where love builds its nest. Tell me, who are you kissing with your new teeth?"

She had dropped a soup plate out of sheer fright. As if you kissed with your teeth! Aunt Lucie wasn't married; who knows, maybe she had never kissed a man. She felt sorry for her, Aunt Lucie. Halina forgot that she was twenty-six years old before she got her first kiss. And in spite of her excitement, she had been very much afraid that Kolya might notice she wore false teeth.

A few times she thought of telling Pani Valeska everything. She wouldn't be able to keep it all to herself forever, anyway. She had to confide in somebody, and if not the Pani, who else? In secret she had hoped that someone would notice and ask her about it—once she had even been so bold as to have Kolya come pick her up at the garden gate. But no one had noticed. Lawyer Wondrak certainly wouldn't have tolerated her going with an Eastern laborer. So Valeska was the only possibility. Irma had her own problems, and Josel still didn't know what real love was, in her opinion. She wanted to confess to Valeska, when the time came . . . But the time never came. She was arrested in the kitchen as she was busy cleaning the stove pipe. The first warm days had been the messengers of spring; they no longer needed to heat the house, and for weeks the stove had been drawing poorly. They took her away just as she was, with soot on her hands and face; she wasn't even permitted to wash or to change her clothes. The Pani was not even in the house, nor was the lawyer. Only Josel. He had stood in the doorway and had said that he wouldn't let Halina go, not until his uncle, Attorney Wondrak, was back from his trip. Then the two men from the Gestapo had simply pushed him aside, so brutally that he landed on the floor. And said nothing more.

The last time that she had seen Kolya, he had said to her: "I now learn German. Hear *pozhalusta*: Bread. Hunger. Eat. Work. Sleep. Love."

That covered about everything.

9

"THEY MUST HAVE met several times," Valeska said. "How often, they'll probably get that out of her at the Gestapo. She never said anything to me."

She was a little offended, even now, and it showed. Nevertheless she was determined to do everything for Halina that she could.

"Until after the holidays, nothing at all can be done," Willi said for the third time. "None of the offices are open, we'll have to wait until Tuesday. I can phone Judge Kanoldt again on Sunday, but since she's in a Gestapo prison, he won't know anything either."

Willi was standing in the doorway, and didn't dare sit down or go back into his room. His sister would take that as a sign of indifference and scold him. But he didn't know how much longer he could just stand around like this. He held on to the panel of the door and stretched his back against it.

From her piano stool Valeska looked across at her brother over the photograph of Gieseking. His hairnet bothered her even more now. "*Muj Bosche*, the poor thing will have to stay in prison until Tuesday . . ."

She tried to put herself in Halina's position, which made her feel so sorry for herself that she practically began to cry. She took out her handkerchief anyway: "We're celebrating a Happy Easter here, we're baking cake, the meat has been marinating since yesterday . . . and Halina is in a cold cell . . . I can't get over it."

Willi reached for the easy chair now and sat down cautiously on the arm: "You know that I'm trying everything, and I was on the telephone all afternoon yesterday."

For Valeska one thing was certain: If Halina had to spend the holidays in a prison cell, they could put up with a few discomforts here, too. She could tell that what her brother wanted was to go back to his room now to read the newspaper or start a new book. Usually she had nothing against this. But today she couldn't comprehend how a person could read three or four newspapers a day, when they all said the same thing anyway, and she couldn't imagine how anyone in this house could go about his daily affairs after Halina had been arrested yesterday on the charge of *unlawful relations with an Eastern laborer*. She was indignant about that, but more, as she later admitted to herself, because she had not known anything about the relationship.

"Well, I just can't get over it," Valeska sighed, forgetting how often she had already said that.

Perhaps Halina's secret had been too big for her to be able to tell it to anyone. And she was certainly not sure what Halina had started with this man, or what he had started with her. For ever since she had known Halina, she had been aware of her fear of men and if she had started a relationship with this Eastern laborer, whoever he may have been—well, she wished she had seen a photo of him, even if it were only a police photo—that must have caused a substantial change in her. Why hadn't she noticed anything? Certainly, Halina had been different lately, she had sensed that, but she couldn't have said in what this difference consisted.

Once she had surprised Halina coloring her cheeks so red with her rouge that she looked like a circus artiste, but maybe the heat had risen to her cheeks because she felt she had been caught. Valeska had only laughed and shown her how to smooth the rouge onto her cheeks with two fingers. Another time, when she was twisting curls with the curling iron, she had made a wave for Halina across her forehead, but that had seemed like a sin to the girl, and she had worked at her hair with water and comb until the wave disappeared.

No, beforehand she had not had the slightest suspicion, and even now she wasn't certain whether she would have forbidden Halina the company of the Eastern laborer—if she had only known about it. But she would have advised caution and would have informed her brother, and he would have known what to do. Maybe they could have prevented the worst—she was thinking of Halina's arrest and the fear she must have experienced. She refused to let herself think what would happen if Halina were found guilty, and maybe even sent to a concentration camp. You heard such terrible things about them.

Her brother had listed various possible things that could happen to Halina, and she had listened to him; she understood what he said, but she still couldn't comprehend it. In her opinion, women should marry men with a higher social status. And if for some reason they did not, like Irma, who had taken Skrobek the taxi driver, you just had to come to terms with it—regretfully. But whether it was a Pole, an Ethnic German, a Czech, or a Lithuanian—Erika Schmattloch had married a Lithuanian fur dealer, why not?—she couldn't care less. It was only a few kilometers across the border to Poland and not much farther to Moravian Ostrow in Czechoslovakia, but who could afford to travel to Breslau or to Neisse to meet a man at a dance? She imagined what it must be like when you're not allowed to marry the person you love, just because he speaks a different language or grew up a few kilometers farther east, or because he doesn't have the right religious affiliation stamped in his passport.

"We have new laws, things aren't like they used to be! You know how it is about the Jews!" Willi said to his sister, with a gentle reproach.

Yes, she had read about that, but had not given it much thought. She hadn't known very many Jews, and most of them had left the country. Frau Reich was the only one she had still seen occasionally these last few years; her daughter had taken piano lessons from Valeska for a long time. In the fall the family was supposed to have been resettled in the East, but the Volhynia Germans from the Ukraine were now coming west in their place. She hadn't heard from the Reichs since then. They could have written, after all, at least a post-card, so people would know where they wound up.

She couldn't understand at all why people made so many differentiations. She was quite the opposite. At the beginning of the war the wife of the president of the waterworks had come to her once and said indignantly that there were supposedly people in the Huld-schinsky settlement who considered Poles equal to Germans! You had to watch out, or next they'd claim that a nigger was as good as a white American—and there probably wasn't a soul in all of America who'd agree with that.

Valeska had never met a Negro, so she couldn't say anything about it. A white man simply was white and a black man was black; you could see such differences from the outside, fine. But she had lived next to Poles since her childhood, her whole life, and she knew them. Well, they were no different from her. Maybe they were a little poorer, maybe more pious, maybe they had more children. But that's all there was to it.

Willi Wondrak had finally found the *Frankfurter Zeitung* from the day before. Because of the excitement in the house, he hadn't gotten around to the newspapers yesterday. He picked it up and was about to go to his room. But his sister asked him to stay.

"It's getting warm outside," she said, "the sun is breaking through the clouds. But here in this house it keeps getting colder and lonelier. Today is Good Friday. And we could all be together. Why does Josel have to go to Beuthen today, of all days? The few days that we still have him . . ."

"The boy is taking his leave of everybody. That's a big turning point in his young life," Wondrak said soothingly.

He sat down in the wicker chair now and began to leaf through the newspaper. He scanned the headlines:

ENGLISH TERROR FROM THE AIR HEAVY FIGHTING AROUND CHAR-KOW FIGHTING AROUND LAKE ILMEN SOVIET DIVISIONS SLAIN AT KUBAN BRIDGEHEAD POLISH RED CROSS TO THE MASS MURDERS AT KATYN

Why didn't Halina trust her! Why hadn't she come to her and told her everything! Valeska knew that most people could express themselves only in a monologue, and she thought that she was one of the few people left who still knew how to listen patiently and learn from others. She didn't think this was special. She was simply curious about other people. And how often had women sat with her and told her everything, when she didn't even want to know. But it was precisely the people who were dear to her, the ones she was most interested in, who closed themselves off from her, sometimes with words, sometimes with gestures, sometimes through silence. This made her suffer. She had already absorbed a few defeats and didn't permit herself to think about them, otherwise she wouldn't have known how to go on living. The fact that for months on end her husband photographed nothing but himself, his naked body in all of its details, and even made enlargements—that was a mystery to this very day. The fact that her son asks a teacher whether he loves Dostoevski, and, because the answer doesn't satisfy him, leaps at him and bites him on the nose—that she could understand. But that he had simply run away over three years ago and jumped on a moving train headed for the West, just to get away from here, far away, for her that was still a wound that had not healed. And she couldn't comprehend, not to this very day, why County Magistrate Montag had nailed shut the windows in the garden cottage! What must be going on inside a person for him to board up the windows from the inside? She would have liked to know. Even today.

Those were people whom she spent time with, who were familiar to her; how would it be with people she hardly knew? That was something she didn't even want to think about. When the son of Justice Kochmann hanged himself in Wilhelmspark that hot, dry summer, some people said he did it out of desperation, others said he was melancholy or even unstable. She had taken that into account, and had felt sorry for old Kochmann. But she had asked no questions. With County Magistrate Montag it had been different. She did ask questions. But the answers hadn't satisfied her. And when she asked her son, at that time, he had not answered. And when she surprised her brother in bed with the boy from the Port Arthur district, she had not dared to ask questions. The sight of those two completely naked bodies entwined in ardent embrace had stunned her; she left the room in a daze. It had taken hours before she fully grasped what she had been witness to, and her feelings ranged from shame to indignation, disappointment, and lament, and she was not able to master the tumult within herself until she decided to maintain silence with her brother, too. When their glances crossed for the fraction of a second—and thinking back on it, it had seemed more like an hour—they had told each other everything; it was a truth that could not have been expressed in words anyway.

And that had led both of them, brother and sister, to a togetherness that had never before existed between them, but which they had sometimes wished for. Only the feeling of guilt can weld people together like that. And they both felt guilty. One because he had been the performer, the other because she had been the witness.

The first step she had taken was to have the boy from Port Arthur called into the Labor Service—out of sight, out of mind. Then she convinced her brother that it would be better for him to move into the garden cottage, particularly since he had had to give up all his rooms except for his study to bombing victims from the Reich. And finally she brought him to the point of declaring his willingness to marry Rosa Willimczyk the bookseller, and in church as well as in front of the judge. The banns had been posted in the church for some time, and the marriage was scheduled for May 22. If she had had her way, it would have happened much sooner, but Fräulein Willimczyk had asked for time to think it over. Which she couldn't understand because a chance like this, to marry the respected lawyer and notary Willi Wondrak, came once in a lifetime, if at all.

Valeska believed that she had her brother firmly in hand, but she remembered he had run away from a wedding once before, and at the time she had had a dress made specially for the occasion, with two hundred black beads sewn onto it. She looked at her brother sitting in the chair and reading the newspaper, and realized that she loved her brother, in her own way. Even with the dandruff and the hairnet on his head. And for an instant she even understood why he ran away.

She had always thought she knew a lot about him, even if not everything, of course, and then she noticed that she knew nothing at all about him, nothing at all about people. It had been the same way with Halina too. She asked herself why this always had to happen to her, of all people.

Wondrak turned a page. Now he read:

JUST PUNISHMENT OF TRAITORS
TO THE FIGHTING NATION

At a hearing in Munich, the People's Court of the German Reich had to deal with a number of defendants accused of participating in high treason with Hans and Sophie Scholl, who were condemned to death by the People's Court on 22 February 1943.

Alexander Schmorell, Kurt Huber, and Wilhelm Graf of Munich, during the crucial battle of our people in 1942–43 called for sabotage of our armaments in leaflets with the Scholls, and propagated defeatist sentiments. They abetted the enemies of the Reich and tried to fragment our defenses. These defendants, who excluded themselves from membership in our people's community by their very attacks on it, were sentenced to death. They have forfeited their civil rights forever.

He had to think of Pawel Musiol, with whom he had attended high school in Kattowitz. It had been during the war, and Pawel had dreamed of a Polish republic. He had sewn himself a four-cornered cap modeled after a *rogatywta*, and had worn it with a red and white cockade. Willi had met him again a few times, between the wars; Pawel was for some party or other, he had forgotten which one, and had traveled through Polish Upper Silesia as a speaker. Politically disappointed, he had then turned to popular education in the country, and for a while he was chairman of the Polish teachers' association. After a long interruption, during which Willi heard nothing else about him, his name had recently appeared on a red poster, which was pasted on walls everywhere in Kattowitz, obviously as a warning: PAWEL MUSIOL EXECUTED FOR HIGH TREASON.

Soon after the Germans invaded in 1939, Pawel had founded a secret brotherhood, *Tajna Organizacja Bojowa*, and he was arrested in 1941 in Teschen. Now the death sentence had been carried out, as a warning and deterrent because more and more young Polish Silesians were hiding, so as not to have to serve in the German Wehrmacht; there were supposed to be true sabotage groups in the Beskid Mountains already. And that was only seventy kilometers from Gleiwitz.

"You did know Pawel Musiol, didn't you?" he asked his sister. And he told her about the posters that he had seen in Kattowitz.

No, Valeska didn't remember Pawel Musiol. She thought it over and finally said: "No wonder he was a teacher. It's a mistake for us not to allow people in eastern Upper Silesia to speak Polish, and no Polish schools . . . just imagine, What if someday the Poles took over here and we weren't allowed to speak German anymore, I simply can't imagine that!"

When Valeska had been silent for a long time, Willi read aloud:

"In May there will be 125 grams of cheese as a special allotment. Instead of 125 grams of lard there will be the same amount of butter, a total of 500 grams per person, plus 200 grams of margarine and 100 grams of cooking oil. No more rice flakes on rationing.—Blackout today beginning 9:13 P.M., ending 5:42 A.M.

Tentative total for the results of the collection at the front and in the homeland on Wehrmacht Day, April 3 and 4 amounts to: 84,112,907 RM. Last year's figures: 56,980,647 RM. That is an increase of 47.6 percent. This great social accomplishment again demonstrates the close bond of the German people with its Wehrmacht . . .

"I'd like to know who can still contribute the money, when there's a street collection every Sunday," he grumbled behind his newspaper, as if to himself.

"I will have to do everything alone," Valeska said suddenly, with an optimism that surprised herself. She got up from the piano stool. But she still couldn't estimate how much work would land on her shoulders over the course of time. She didn't want to remind herself how it had been earlier, without Halina. It would be different now, in any case. The entire house was full. And she had invited a lot of people for dinner on Easter Sunday; they all had to bring two slices of meat, at the least. "Aunt Lucie will help me, I'll be able to manage," she reassured herself and, lost in thought, moved the signed photograph of Gieseking a little to the right.

Willi Wondrak read on, unmoved:

"The Polish Red Cross in Katyn. 12,000 murdered Polish officers discovered in mass graves near Smolensk. Shot in the back of the head by the GPU. Conclusive proof from documents that they were killed in 1940 as prisoners of the Red Army."

And to Valeska, without pausing: "Atrocities everywhere! We'll all help you, little sister, so it won't be too much for you, of course we will."

Willi searched his dressing gown in vain for a cigarette. "Here, take one of Josel's," Valeska said. "Be sure and give one back to him later, you know how he is."

She was glad that her brother didn't leave the room. She didn't want to be alone now.

"I see no way out for that poor bum of Halina's," Willi said, lighting the half of the cigarette that he had put in his holder. "If we're lucky, they'll put him in a camp someplace, then at least he won't be able to testify ... I think he's probably not even here anymore. They don't fool around, after all, he had that Eastern laborer tag ..." Willi said it very matter-of-factly, he had already heard of similar cases. Besides, What he was interested in was saving Halina, he couldn't worry about anyone else.

"My God, she'll be devastated, even if we do get her out of there," she said.

Willi stood up. He held the cigarette holder between his teeth and exhaled the smoke. He tied his dressing gown tighter with both hands and flicked some dandruff from his left sleeve. "Valeska, you still don't understand me." Only now did he take the holder out of his mouth. "There's the death penalty nowadays for violations like that, do you understand, the death penalty! It seems to me that you still don't grasp what happened. They can lock you up, too, if they can prove that you tolerated this relationship."

Valeska was too flustered to answer him. She went back to her piano and sat down on the round stool. She had always thought that she knew what reality was.

Weakly, she struck a key, then a chord. Then an ascending melody, which she broke off in the treble. The death of her husband—yes, there was no getting around it: That was reality. The death of County Magistrate Montag; she had seen him lying on the floor in the garden cottage between the table and the window bench. The death of Irma's husband, Heiko, who had fallen right at the beginning of the Polish campaign, and from whom Irma retained nothing but a broken watch, a necklace, a photograph, an official document, and a vague memory. That was reality. The death of Herbert Mainka, who had been a schoolmate of hers and who was beaten to death with a shovel in 1921, because he was suspected of spying for the Polish militia—the newspapers had all been full of the story at the time. She still remembered that today. That was reality. And perhaps death was the only reliable reality. Not even a

savings passbook or an Aryan certificate, not even her real estate
deeds and stock shares.

And her brother Willi's hairnet, which seemed from second to
second to be an ever-increasing threat. If he would only take off that
hairnet! She could no longer make out his face in all the smoke,
light, shadow, and gloom.

She banged the keyboard cover shut.

10

THEY WALKED ALONG in the direction of the public baths, faster now than before. As if they couldn't wait to clash with the Lutherans.

"Hannes will start it," decided Andy. "He'll throw the first stones."

He would see to it that Hannes actually did start it, and this would clear away his last doubts, too.

"You can prove yourself in our *ferajna* that way," Wonzak said. To this day he couldn't admit to himself that there would be no *ferajna* anymore. Maybe two or three guys together, if they were firmly determined, constituted a *ferajna*.

"Well, I'm with you. And I'll be the one to start, if you want me to," Hannes said. He would rather have proven himself some other way. But maybe this would win him a friend, that would make the investment worth it. He would never have done it for Wonzak alone. It was all he could do to keep up with the other two. Out of breath, he gasped: "Andy, what you were saying before, I mean about the Lutherans, that's not the way it is . . ."

"Don't you want to go along with us?" Andy asked, suspiciously.

"No, that's not it," Hannes said. "I'm coming with you, just like I said. I mean something else, something different, well, I mean . . ." He had to lengthen his stride, Ossadnik was leaving him behind again. "They're no different from you and me—if they believe. Naturally, only if they believe. They have the same Our Father, they pray to Christ on the cross like we do, they believe in the Resurrection like we do, and they—"

Andy interrupted him again: "How do you know all that?" It was not merely the old suspicion rising in him again; it also bothered him that Hannes was resisting before the friendship was sealed. "Are you going to be the first one to throw the stones, or not?" His voice cut like a knife.

"Yes, I will," Hannes said. "I'll do it if you want me to."

"I think that's two different things," Andy said. "What matters is whether you're with us, then you have to do what we tell you to,

87

and this is just the beginning. There are other things in store for you!"

Hannes Stein did not answer, but the look he gave Ossadnik conveyed his readiness better than any words could have expressed.

Behind the old Rifle Club they began to collect stones, white and gray rocks that they found in a dry creekbed next to the road. They filled their pockets, which kept getting fuller and heavier. Andy had to hold his up with his hands to keep them from tearing. When they were approaching the barracks of the children's evacuation camp at the corner of Neue-Welt and Passonstrasse—the Richtersdorf public baths and the cemetery were already in sight—they realized that all three of them had been silent for quite some time. They could feel the morning's silence almost physically. In the distance they saw a few boys between the barracks, but they didn't hear a sound. It was like in a play, when the curtain has risen and the actors as well as the spectators are waiting for the first cue. They approached the entrance, which was blocked by a lowered barrier, but to the right and left of it pathways led into the camp. Unconsciously they sensed the barrier to be an obstacle, a border that they didn't want to cross, although no one was stopping them. Off to the left grew gorse bushes, which were already losing their blossoms. They hid behind them. No, you couldn't really call it hiding, that would have been contrary to their intention. They just wanted to intensify the surprise.

"But what if they're not Lutherans?" Hannes whispered. It wouldn't have mattered if he had spoken out loud.

"Those are Lutherans," Andy Ossadnik lied. "Am I ever excited! How about you guys?"

To tell the truth, he was the most excited of the three. For the others it was an adventure, a prank, a thrill; for him it was more. For him it was the scourging.

"And not at the windows," Andy said softly, "otherwise they'll call it sabotage afterwards. Just at the roofs, a rain of stones. And then *abtrimoo*!"

They knelt down, dumped most of the stones from their pockets, and arranged them in piles. They kept a few so they'd have some ammunition for their retreat. They spoke hardly a word.

With a nod, Andy directed Hannes to start, and Hannes cast the first stone. They heard a soft thump on the roof of a barracks. Too soft to make their hearts beat faster, let alone drive the blood to their heads, which is what they were hoping for. And perhaps for something more, without knowing what this more would mean. But it would change their dreary, boring, gray morning.

And Hannes, encouraged by the glances of the others, threw another stone, and a third followed. That was the signal for the other two to hurl their stones into the camp. They had no exact target, they simply rained the stones down on the barracks. They kept on throwing and listening. Suddenly there was the crash of a windowpane.

Andy felt that that was the sound he had been waiting for the whole time. Now the heat rose to his face and made him hurl the stones even faster. He saw nothing, he only heard. He heard the babble of voices, doors slamming, steps on wood, a shout. Every sound made his face a shade brighter.

In the camp the boys tumbled out of the barracks and milled around for a while, before they realized what was happening. The first to spot the strangers behind the gorse bushes pointed at them with both hands, but silent and stymied; it took a while for the rest to recover from their surprise and take off after the attackers. They began to yell as they ran, to goad each other on; they picked up clumps of dirt or pieces of wood as they ran. One of them was brandishing a fence picket.

"*Pjerunnisch* Lutherans! Reformers!"

"Heathens! Evangelicals! Free-thinkers!"

"Protestants! Swine!"

Afterwards, Andy couldn't remember who had begun the name-calling. They threw their last stones at the boys storming toward them and began to flee. Andy ran in the direction of the rifle range. He heard the yelling of his pursuers behind him, but since all three of them had run off in different directions, the sound soon grew weaker. He looked back as he ran and saw about five or six boys chasing him, throwing stones at him from a distance; one of them hit him in the back, another on the head, he had only felt a dull thud, no pain really. Andy leaped over the creekbed, and as he turned around again, a stone hit him right in the face and knocked his glasses off. He was just barely able to catch them, and noticed that one lens was shattered. He ran and gasped, gasped, ran. His eye wasn't injured, but slivers of glass must have cut his skin. He felt no pain, just the taste of blood on his lips. He ran on, thinking about how a strange excitement had seized him at the sound of the shattering windowpane. He had felt fear then, fear of himself too—just as he was now afraid of his pursuers—along with an inexplicable yearning to be caught by them.

What would happen if he stopped right there? They would overwhelm him; even if he resisted, it wouldn't do any good, they outnumbered him. They would beat him up and leave him there. Or they would chase him back to the camp and deliver him up to the fury of the others. Or they would beat him to a pulp and hand him over to the police, because of the windowpane.

Let them beat him, torture him, humiliate him, yes, he deserved such punishment, not for throwing the stones, not for the stupid windowpane, naturally not for that, for something else, for a guilt, for his guilt, and he wasn't thinking of anything in particular, he was thinking of the guilt that everyone has before *him*, which would never cease. He thought about how they had scourged *him* and crowned *him* with thorns. How *his* hands and feet were pierced by nails.

All at once he came to a halt; he stopped so suddenly that he had to hold onto a birch tree to keep from falling. He turned around, stretched his neck forward, and looked toward them. His heart pounded so loud and fast that he couldn't have counted the beats. When *he* was being scourged, *he* didn't resist. His pursuers were surprised, they slowed their pace. The one closest to him took a few more steps, then he stopped too. They looked at each other, a dozen meters apart, as if trying to hold one another with their eyes. The other boys moved up as far as their leader and grouped themselves around him, as if up against an invisible line that must not be crossed. Their energy, which in the last few minutes had been directed solely to catching up with and capturing the stranger, the attacker, was as if evaporated now that they had reached their goal, now when they had nothing more to do than take a few steps and grab him. He couldn't escape them now. Instead they stood there as if nailed to the spot, and if he walked toward them now, they might even back off.

Andy Ossadnik didn't move. He felt a dull, pleasant weakness slowly saturating his body, making his arms weaken and dangle, placing a hard smile on his face, and leaving the taste of metal on his tongue. He wished the others would come closer, whack him, punch him, slug him, hit him, jump on him and kick him. He was entirely without will, he existed only to receive, and nothing else. He would not resist. Now he saw them advancing toward him, a large shadow moving toward him, almost in slow motion. No voices, no shouting. He waited for the first blow.

His father had never beaten him. As long as he could remember, he had never seen his father strike any of his children. He simply wasn't the type to beat his children, although he had occasion to often enough, with five boys and a girl. Not with the girl, but certainly with all five of the boys. But his father never ever hit any of his children. The only exception occurred a month ago: his father had hit him. Usually it was Tonik who hit him. Tonik hit all of his brothers. Tonik was the oldest. If any of them had done something wrong that had to be atoned for by blows, then his father just said: Tonik! Or if Tonik wasn't there: just wait until Tonik gets here. And when Tonik got there, he said: Tonik. And pointed at the boy. Tonik didn't ask questions, he knew what to do, and by his father's face, by the nod of his head or a gesture, he could tell how hard he was supposed to hit, whether he was supposed to take the stick or the strap, whether he was to hit him on the fingers or the bottom, or whether a healthy box on the ears would suffice. His father would occasionally administer a rap on the head himself. But only a rap on the head. Never blows! Tonik took care of them like any household chore. You couldn't say that it gave him pleasure, or that it was unpleasant or offensive to him either. He performed it like a necessary duty. He was the oldest, he came right after the father, and since his father didn't do it, Tonik had to. It was a duty that he performed conscientiously. When his father raised his hand to check him, Tonik would stop. Mother could wail and blubber, but to no avail. Tonik didn't even seem to notice her.

A month ago his father had hit him. He would never forget it. Something had begun there. All the blows, all of Tonik's frightening blows were forgotten. He would never forget his father punching him in the face. He was alone with him in the kitchen. For a long time he had been wishing he could be alone with his father for once. He wanted to talk with him about a few things that a boy of sixteen always wants to talk about with his father, and then, when the time comes, can't talk about, and so they talked about trivial things, and to him the most trivial seemed to be politics, which they had wound up talking about at the end, and he had asked his father whether he thought that the war was lost, and his father had looked at him for a long time without speaking. Then he had asked his father why he had joined the Party, and his father had given him more than one answer to that; and then he had told his father that in the office at the miners' association they said if the war was lost, all Party members would be locked up in ghettos, like what was happening to the Jews right now. And his father, usually so calm, had started yelling and wanted to know who had said such stuff, so he could report the man to the proper authorities. Because that amounted to "atrocity propaganda." And he would have told him the name, if his father hadn't said "atrocity propaganda," for that was the reason they had thrown Curate Mikas into the concentration camp, where they kept him for a year and a half. When he told his father that, he had stood up and punched him in the face. Without saying a word, he turned around and walked out, as if he were ashamed of his action. That evening, when they were all sitting at the table together, he noticed that his father was avoiding his eyes. And sometimes when he observed his father, and he looked at him more closely than ever before, he thought that inside of his father there must have been a different person who had hit him. Never had a blow hurt so much, never had he felt so humiliated, never had he been so wounded. It was already a month ago. Since then they had not looked each other in the eye.

Now he should protect his face. But his arms hung down so heavily, he wouldn't be able to lift them again. He waited for the blows. Maybe he had only devised the attack so as to receive these blows. But the blows didn't come. Instead, a voice, very close to his face, said: "Why did you do it?"

Slowly, Andy felt his strength flowing back, first into his legs, then into his body, finally into his head. He looked at the boy, who was standing right in front of him, but did not look into his eyes. He collected saliva in his mouth. He heard the boy's breath, short and panting, and the sound mixed in with the sound of his own breathing. He looked into the round, white face, slowly opened his lips, rolled the saliva forward and shot it off his tongue, straight into the round, white face.

Yelling and grunting, they rained blows on him; Andy was knocked to the ground and he pressed his face into the grass. The pain, issuing from all over his body and flowing together in his head, did not subside until the shouts grew fainter and more distant.

Anyone seeing the boys from the camp on their way home might have thought that the group of young people were performing some exotic gymnastics. Again and again they demonstrated to one another how they had polished off the stranger. And by the time they got back to camp they had come to the opinion, after a lively debate, that the boy couldn't have been anything but a Pole.

"Typical," one of them said. "He didn't say a word, not a single word, he didn't want to give himself away."

And another: "He was a coward, he didn't even put up a fight. That chicken Pole!"

They told the boys who had remained at camp how they had taken care of the stranger. But in the end they were blamed for not dragging him back to camp. The other two boys had gotten away.

Andy lay there. He couldn't have said for how long. The sky above him is white, a glistening white that blinds him, a white veil of clouds hanging in front of the sun, thin and worn through in some places, letting the first rays of sunshine through. Andy looks at the pink skin of his hand, sees the juicy green of a tuft of grass, studies the zigzags of a dandelion leaf. He feels pain and thirst.

He is alone beneath the sky. At least he feels that way. The sun warms him. The earth bears him up. The pain is now focusing at a few places in his body. Above his left eye, at the back of his head to the upper left, in his left shoulder, in his knees, the worst at his left temple. He wipes at it with two fingers and sees that the fingers are bloody. Since he doesn't have any handkerchief, he pulls his shirt up and presses it to his face. When he takes it away, he can see the impressions of his wounds on it. The left eyebrow is the worst, it is still bleeding freely. Andy pulls off a leaf, moistens it with spit, and sticks it to the eyebrow. Maybe that will stanch the bleeding.

He would like to be furious. But he doesn't know at whom. He cannot be angry at the boys who were chasing him, at any rate.

He turns around slowly and moves his limbs cautiously. At first his feet stumble more than walk through the grass. He's glad that they left him his shoes, at least. In time, though, all his limbs move again, he can see it in his shadow, which falls across the road at an angle to him. Walking on the road is a lot easier, too, than across the rough field. He senses his shadow as something foreign. Perhaps because he has never paid any attention to his shadow before. As if it were the shadow of somebody else. And when he comes closer to town and meets the first people on Eichendorff-Allee, he takes their amazement at him for amazement at somebody else, their shock as shock at somebody else, their calls as calls to somebody else. Now he feels quite all right. If only his eyebrow would stop bleeding. He'll go home and wash, put on a clean shirt, rub some Nivea cream on his face, and put a bandage on his eyebrow.

Not until he looked into the face of Felix Bronder coming toward him at Preussenplatz did he realize that he himself was that somebody else. The one who had thought up the stupid attack on the evacuation camp, who had run away, who got himself cornered and beaten up. He saw it all much more soberly now. The veil of clouds had torn, only now and then did little white clouds intrude in front of the sun to cast fleeting shadows.

"My God, Squintok," Bronder said, half shocked and half malicious, "you look as if you've just escaped from Devil's Island! What on earth happened?"

"Nothing much," Andy said stubbornly.

"There must have been at least three of them. It took more than one guy to work you over like that."

Bronder edged away a little—he was afraid that Squintok would slug him, in spite of his condition.

Andy could not tell him, after all, that there had been five of them. Maybe even more. He had no idea how to explain the whole story to anybody. Now he wanted to get home as fast as possible.

"Have you seen Wonzak anywhere around town, or the boy who sells stationery at Dolezich's; you know who I mean?"

Bronder didn't know whom he meant. And he hadn't seen Wonzak for days. He was in a different troop, too. "Sorry, Squintok," he said, because he didn't know what else to say. He was searching for a handkerchief and finally found one at the very bottom of his pocket, and he was glad he could at least mop the wound on Squintok's forehead for him. But when he saw how dirty the handkerchief was, he put it back in his pocket, embarrassed.

Pity was the last thing Andy needed now. He had never been a coward. He had always fought back. But today it had been different. Perhaps he had wanted to experience how it is to be defeated. To be beaten up. To be kicked when you're down. He smiled at Bronder, his face a grimace.

Bronder didn't know whether Andy was grimacing in pain, or whether that was supposed to be a smile.

"Know what's going on? They're taking down the bells from the tower of the Peter and Paul Church," Bronder said, excitedly brushing the hair out of his eyes.

Andy didn't understand what he meant. Only the nervous gestures indicated that something unusual must have happened. So he repeated mechanically: "They're taking down the bells from Peter and Paul? Why are they doing that?"

"That's the limit," Bronder said impatiently. "They're making artillery out of them. Didn't you know that? We were collecting nonferrous metals for the HY too. But that's not enough anymore. Now it's the bells' turn, everywhere!"

11

I COULD AT LEAST have asked that soldier what his name was, Josel thought, crossing the streetcar tracks. The rails had lost their infinity for him, they disappeared right beyond the next curve in the street, behind the houses. Even distances were shrinking before his eyes. He was already on Bahnhofstrasse, opening the front door to Cieplik's Conservatory. When the door shut behind him, he had already forgotten the one-armed soldier. The ticking in his head had grown clearer in the quiet that reigned in the stairwell and in the corridors. Earlier, during his long wait, Josel had imagined the house full of music, a student behind every door, each playing on a different instrument.

There was nobody around to ask, so he simply knocked on a door, and when nobody answered, he turned the handle firmly. The door was locked. He tried all the other doors. Just as he was about to go up to the next floor, he heard a soft, sonorous sound of strings. He stood still and listened; at first it was nothing but a distant tone, growing and receding, which he pursued until he could distinguish a continuous, almost dancelike melody. Josel walked on tiptoe so as not to make any noise. He put his ear to the door and listened for a while, then he opened it a crack. A boy was sitting behind a row of empty chairs, bowing the strings of a cello with a wide, out-stretched arm. Josel had never heard a cello playing alone and had to get used to the strange sound at first.

When the boy stopped playing and the last note died away in the room, he was sure that he liked the music. Just as the player lowered his bow, which he had held aloft a while pensively, their eyes met for the first time across the distance and the chairbacks. Josel's face flushed. Without quite knowing why, he left the room with quiet steps.

"If you're looking for somebody," the boy called, following him to the corridor, "nobody else is here, they're all gone for the holidays. I think I'm the only one practicing. Can I help you somehow?"

It was probably his friendly tone that gave Josel the courage to stop and speak to him. "I'm looking for Professor Lechter's piano class," Josel said, so as not to mention Ulla's name. As long as he had come this far, he might at least have a look at the room where Ulla did her practicing.

"That's one floor up, way at the back on the left. Maybe there's somebody there copying music who can help you. I didn't hear anyone up there today, and I think the professor went to Warsaw with a student. I heard something like that."

With that, he turned back to his cello, not paying any more attention to Josel.

Josel walked upstairs. The door with the nameplate PROF. LECHTER was shut. Josel stood in front of it, turned the handle, and jumped at the echo it made. The classroom was locked. He bent down, so as to at least see through the keyhole what it was like inside, but he saw only the backs of chairs, not even the piano. The entire conservatory seemed a collection of empty chairs to him.

He went back downstairs and sat down on one of the chairs in the room with the cello player. The boy, who had looked up briefly and now even smiled at him, kept on playing. Josel leaned back in his chair and stretched out his arms over the backs of two other chairs; he had had no idea how beautiful a cello playing alone would sound, almost as beautiful as a piano. He looked at the boy's hands and was amazed by the virtuosity with which the fingers of the left hand danced over the strings on the neck of the cello, and the right hand hovered in the air with the bow. Why didn't Mamuscha send me to a violin teacher, he thought, when I didn't want to play the piano? He kept staring at the boy's hands.

"Bach, Suite for Cello Solo in C minor," the boy said. "I played it through for the first time today. It's not good yet, but I'll get there. The change in register is difficult, it needs to be smoother, more inconspicuous, more confident. I'm fairly satisfied with the slow movement. Now I'll play the sarabande."

And he started in again.

"It sounds beautiful when you play," Josel said, when the boy had finished the movement. "*Fantastichnek*."

"Ach, aren't you the friend of Ulla Ossadnik?"

Josel was surprised.

"You're a Piontek, aren't you? Of course!" He looked at Josel and stuck out his hand. Josel shook it.

"Yes," Josel said, "but how do you know . . . ?"

The other boy began to laugh. "Ulla brought that word with her and it's going the rounds here now: *Fantastichnek*! She said she got it from a friend whose mother was the first to give her piano lessons, and now when one of us is really good, we say that he is *fantastich-nek*."

He couldn't pronounce the word smoothly, but it seemed to amuse him.

"Are you looking for Ulla?" the boy asked. "Is that why you came here?" He seemed to be puzzled that Josel had not come until now, when people had been talking about him for so long already.

"Yes," said Josel, embarrassed and still a little surprised. If only she had mentioned it! That would have given him some courage.

"Ulla's not here, I know that for sure," the cello player said. "They're going on tour right after Easter, the professor with his prodigy Ulla. Yes, our Ulla Ossada, as she calls herself now with her stage name," he said with a giggle.

"What did you say? What does she call herself?" asked Josel, dejected, although he had heard perfectly well.

"She's made it," mused the cello player.

"Ulla Ossada, you say?" Josel insisted. "But that must be brand-new? The first time she performed in Gleiwitz, she still played under the name . . ."

"Yes, Professor Lechter did all that. He'll be accompanying her on her tour. He never lets her out of his sight anymore . . ."

The pause that now ensued gave Josel time for speculations that he preferred to suppress. So he said quickly: "So she's gone to Glei-witz, then. I'll meet her there! I mean, before I go off to war. I've just been drafted and I wanted to say good-bye to her, that's why I'm here."

"Ulla," the cello player said slowly, sitting down next to Josel on one of the empty chairs, "didn't go to Gleiwitz. I know that," he said slowly. "She told me where she was going. I wasn't supposed to tell anybody else, but I guess it's all right to tell you, if you're friends. You see, she went to . . . Warsaw."

"Where? To Warsaw? Do you know that for sure? What is she doing in Warsaw?"

Suddenly he was terribly agitated. How often had they talked about it, dreamed about going to Warsaw together, to the Church of the Holy Cross, to Chopin's heart. But they never got to Warsaw. And now Ulla had undertaken the trip all alone, with that horrible professor.

"She wanted to visit an aunt in Warsaw," the boy said. "It was an old plan of hers. She's been talking about it as long as I've known her. But you've no idea how hard it is to get a visa to the General Gouvernement of Poland. She wanted to bring back music by Chopin for us. It turns out," he explained, "that Chopin is descended from Alsatian ancestors, so now he can be played again. A Chopin museum is going to be opened in Kraków, too. But then, he composed hardly anything for the cello . . ."

Josel knew very well that Ulla didn't have any aunt in Warsaw. In his mind he counted up the money he had in his pocket; it would take him only as far as Kattowitz. He would have to get organized, he couldn't just sit here.

He knew where he would find Ulla in Warsaw: in the Church of the Holy Cross, yes, he would find her there. "Thank you," he said to the cello player. "I'm going after her. There'll certainly be another train today from Kattowitz to Warsaw, don't you think?"

"Are you crazy?" the boy said. "How do you think you'll get to Warsaw? They won't even let you across the border, they're very strict now, on account of the partisans. It took Ulla months to get a visa. And I think they only gave it to her because the professor finally used his influence."

"She did not go to visit any aunt," Josel said after a pause, mainly to himself. "I know that she went to the Church of the Holy Cross in Warsaw. The heart of Chopin, in the nave, second pillar on the left, right where you come in. You have to touch the stone, you have to kiss the stone, if you want to become a famous pianist . . ."

His voice sounded tired and flat.

"You're crazy," the boy said. "Ulla's crazy, you're all crazy!"

With that, he went back to his cello and positioned the bow. He drew out a single note, long, with lots of vibrato, making it grow and recede.

"I'll go to Kattowitz and wait for every train that arrives from Warsaw, and I'll go through all the compartments and look for Ulla," Josel said to himself, chewing on his lip.

"Go on back to Gleiwitz! Maybe she's already home . . . it's the most sensible thing you can do . . . but then nobody around here is sensible."

The boy reached for the strings; with his left hand his fingers scurried up and down, he put his ear close to the bridge to hear the soft notes and the softest harmonics.

Josel felt the sweat collecting under his arms, wetting his shirt. "I think you're right," he said dully. "If she should come back here first, tell her I was here, Josel Piontek from Gleiwitz, who's going to war."

And after a long pause: "Don't you have to worry about getting drafted, too?"

The cello player looked up. He was busy with his cello and with the mistakes that he would surely make the next time he practiced, too. "Aren't they calling up guys born in 1925?"

Josel just nodded.

"Then I've still got a year! And I need it. I can't stop now, I have to make some more progress. I'd like to play all six solo suites through at once, you know, with mistakes naturally, but that's the only way to get a feeling for their greatness, for the architecture, well, how should I put it . . . for the mathematics of the music . . ."

"Aren't you afraid," Josel said, "of getting wounded in the war, your arm or fingers, just grazed, so that one finger gets stiff or has to be amputated . . . then it would all be over and you could never play the cello again?"

The boy, who was about to start playing again, lowered his bow. "I don't know what you're talking about," he said truthfully.

"I'm afraid I might get a head wound," Josel said. "Not a bullet directly to the head, then you'd be dead on the spot; I might just get grazed, or some shrapnel, then your brain doesn't work right for the rest of your life."

The boy looked away through the window, out into a gray sky that now showed islands of gleaming blue in two or three places.

"Well, I don't think that's exactly *fantastichnek*, what you're saying."

12

"ACH, BLESSED LORD JESUS, how you do look!" Anna stopped in the doorway, in shock. Andy had to squeeze past her. He was holding one hand over his left eye; with the other hand he pulled Bronder along after him. He would much rather have pushed him along in front of him, so that Mamotschka would be more interested in his visitor than his face. It was *absolutnik* great of Bronder to have come along at all, when he was just dying to go running back to the church square so as not to miss them taking away the bells. Andy had promised him he would hurry, he just wanted to wash his face and change his shirt, and then they would take off together.

"Hello, Frau Ossadnik," Bronder said shyly, when he had reached the hall. And to explain his clean shirt and combed hair, he said to her surprised face: "I was on my way to church, they're taking down the bells from Peter and Paul, and I met Andy on the way."

"What did you say?" asked Anna Ossadnik. "They're taking down the bells? Why are they doing that?"

She got no answer. Andy had hoped his mother would be at church already, and Kotik at home alone to let him in. But she never left the house before two o'clock on Good Friday, because at one time she had sworn a vow to spend the hour of Christ's death praying and kneeling on some hard church bench. Andy wished that his mother had not seen him in the shape he was in; anyway, he had the feeling that everything looked much worse from the outside than it really was, and actually he didn't feel all that bad.

"What have you been up to this time, my *diobiczek*, you look like Lazarus in the flesh!" When her son didn't answer, she turned to Bronder: "What happened, why doesn't he say anything? And on holy Good Friday too!"

Andy turned the faucet on and was about to put his head under it. Anna just managed to grab him and pulled him back by his hair. He must have had another injury somewhere on his head: he felt a sudden, sharp pain.

"You can't get any water on it," Anna said. "It'll just start bleeding again." She turned his head around carefully so that she could finally take a good look at his face. It was no use for Andreas to cover his eye with his hand now. "*Muj Bosche*, Andichek, did they ever work you over! Sit down here on the stool, I'll pat that with clay vinegar."

"No," yelled Andy. He didn't struggle, though; he knew there was no way to escape the treatment. Perhaps the clay vinegar might even help a little; Mamotschka used it to cure everything, from sprained ankles to bellyaches to punches in the kisser.

She came back with two bottles, a larger one with clear liquid, and a small brown ribbed-glass one. She also had a piece of white linen that she tore into several strips, one of which she moistened with the clear liquid and used to wipe Andy's face carefully. She kept on talking as she worked: "Holy Heaven, and I thought that Squintok was past the age where he got into fights with other boys, I thought now that he's in the HY, the wild living in the *ferajnas* would stop, it would be comradeship and discipline. And poor mother that I am, now I see you're acting like a bunch of hooligans. What kind of *djoboks* do I have for children? Every day one of you comes home in some new kind of trouble! It makes me shake to think what a mess you've got yourself in this time."

And she dabbed at his face and hair with the cloth. She was glad she only had two children left in the house now, if she didn't count Ulla, who seldom came home from Beuthen. Tonik, who was home on leave right now, didn't count.

The scrap of linen was black and bloody. She took another and drenched it with the clay vinegar. "You can't run around on Easter with your face bashed in! To the Easter mass with a face like this! And in your new suit!"

You could see how sorry she felt that the new suit would lose half its effect in combination with his battered face. She pressed his head backwards now and inspected her work thoroughly.

"It looks a lot different already. Only half as bad. Just the eyebrow, it needs a bandage." She sniffed at the brown ribbed bottle and dripped dark brown liquid on a fresh strip of linen.

"Tell me how it happened. It's easy to see you were in a fight. But who with, and what for?"

"Owwaah!" yelled Andy, squeezing his eyes shut. The iodine burned like fire.

"But it'll help," Anna said briskly and pressed the cloth against Andy's eyebrow again. "You tell me, Bronder, what was going on."

Imagine, her own son didn't even want to talk about it! It was clear to her, at any rate, that whoever Andy had been fighting with must look much worse. Her children were not *always* the stronger ones, but they usually were. She took that for granted. She pressed the iodine against his eyebrow for the third time. But really in anger this time, because Andreas didn't want to talk.

"I don't know, I wasn't there," said Bronder, who was curious himself now and wished he knew what Squintok had been through.

Andy slid off the stool. He let his mother stick a bandage over his eyebrow, standing up and straining impatiently. "Now put some iodine on your knees yourself," she said, pointing at his scraped and blood-encrusted legs. "But don't wash them! Not until tomorrow or the day after. And if you press the rag with the clay vinegar to your eye every once in a while, the swelling might be gone by tomorrow. And your shirt! Ach, blessed Lord Jesus!"

She acted as if she were noticing the shirt smeared with grass, dirt, and blood for the first time. "Take it off right away. How am I supposed to get it clean again with the greasy soap they give us nowadays. I'll be standing at the washboard for hours."

Her poor hands. Maybe Franzek could get an Eastern laborer for her, a woman for the laundry and the rug beating, at least. Those were jobs she hated. There were Eastern laborers everywhere now, and all the other Party members had one already, some even for every day. And as long as her Franz had joined the Party, then she should have at least a few benefits. You hardly had to pay the women any wages, and besides, you were saving them from hard labor in a factory.

Andy pulled his shirt off over his head and he could feel lots of places that hurt.

"We attacked the Lutherans," he said. He looked at his face more carefully in the mirror now, for the first time. The left eye was nastily swollen. He had the feeling that the swelling would press against the eyeball more and more. But his eye wasn't injured, thank God.

"What do you mean, Lutherans?" Anna Ossadnik said, pushing her son gently aside and washing her hands in the sink. She knew that earlier there had been many street fights between Catholic and Lutheran youth gangs. But that was a long time ago. And on Good Friday they had fought with the Jewish kids. But now there weren't any more Jewish kids.

Since she happened to be standing in front of the mirror, she quickly felt for the goiter under her scarf. It hadn't gotten any bigger, anyway.

"Nowadays, you *absolutnik* can't tell who's a Lutheran anymore, more and more people move here and more and more move away," Andy said self-importantly. And stretched his shirt like a flag. Only now did he see the dirt and grass marks on the back. "We attacked a children's evacuation camp out in Richtersdorf. The boys there all come from the coast. Everybody's Lutheran there, you can bet on it. All but a few exceptions." He was thinking of Hannes Stein.

"Who else was there?" Bronder's curiosity was killing him. It couldn't have been the *ferajna*, after all, he was a member, or rather, he had been a member when the *ferajna* still existed. Nowadays there was always something different to do: HY duty, collecting scrap, air raid practice, first aid, letters to the front (everyone in the troop had a soldier pen pal), and now there was duty at the field hospital, too. And he was even in the Don Bosco League. It had been dissolved some time ago, of course, but they met once a week at Curate Mikas's, disguised as acolytes.

"I won't tell," Andy said with a wink of his eye, to the extent this was still possible. "Not enough of them, at any rate, else I wouldn't be in the shape I'm in. We were outnumbered, that's for sure."

"And your glasses?" Anna said. Only now did she notice that she hadn't seen his glasses anywhere.

Andy dabbed iodine on his knees and grimaced. He didn't answer.

"Hey, that's not fair," Bronder said. "You can at least tell us who you took on this raid with you—at least you can tell your mother!"

But Anna was now much more interested in what had happened to Andy's glasses. "Your glasses?" she repeated.

"At the end they ran," Andy said between his teeth, handing the iodine bottle back to his mother. "Here." And he pulled the glasses out of his back pocket, or rather the frame. Also a lens that had fallen out of the frame during the fight. The other one had shattered when the stone hit him.

"Those beautiful glasses!" Anna Ossadnik said.

But the glasses had never been beautiful. She knew that. They were ugly, coarse medical insurance glasses, which were supposed to correct Andy's squinting, nothing more.

"I don't need them," Squintok said. "I don't squint anymore."

"What if Papa finds out!" Involuntarily she slipped into the role of a conspirator. "We'll keep it a secret from everyone, from Tonik, too, all right?" But Tonik had not given a thought to his family since he had been home on leave; he slept the whole day and in the evening he went out to chase girls.

"Relax, Mamotschka," Andy reassured her, "don't worry about the glasses. If I need some new ones, then we'll get some ugly ones again on the medical insurance. Come on, Bronder, let's go over to the church and take a look at the bells coming down."

With that he vanished into another room to get himself a fresh shirt, and they could hear him opening and shutting drawers. He was looking for one of Paulek's good shirts.

"What is your family having to eat today?" Anna Ossadnik inquired of Bronder.

"A buttered roll, nothing else," Bronder said. "And in the evening, barley broth. It's a fast day."

"Yes," she said loudly, "today is a fast day. But Andy, you should at least eat a slice of bread with margarine, son, you're skin and bones."

"Let Bronder bring it along," Andy called from the hall. He didn't want her to see that he had put on one of Paulek's shirts.

"Actually, I wanted to fast the whole day," he called, "but I don't think I can last until evening. But spread the margarine real thin!"

Anna was doing that anyway. She handed Bronder the slice of bread. "Be on time this evening," she called into the hall, where she heard Andy banging around. "After supper I'll read the legend of Saint—"

"No," Andi yelled, and showed himself in the shirt after all. "Not about Genoveva!" He already knew that one almost by heart. If she read that one he wouldn't even come home. "Read something else for a change!"

Anna was insulted. She had not read the legend of Saint Genoveva for a long time. She was thinking rather of the legend of the two martyrs, Audifax and Abachum, twin sons of the Persian aristocrat Marius, who were first reviled and then slain by heathen soldiers in a Roman prison.

"This evening Kotik will read something, something from the history of Silesia, all right?"

Andy didn't wait around to answer, he ran down the stairs, and Bronder followed him. They were hurrying, so as not to miss the bells coming down.

"I'll come along later," Anna called after them. And mainly to herself: "Those beautiful bells! They're desecrating sacred things. If only it turns out well in the end!"

13

"MAYBE I CAN help you carry something?" asked Karpe, who was resting his suitcase on his shoulder now. He wasn't very much younger than Silbergleit, but of a husky build.

"That's very kind of you," Silbergleit panted. "But you've got more to carry than I do. How far is it to the train station?"

"I don't know where we are anymore," Karpe said. "I've got the feeling they're leading us somewhere else. Not to the train station."

"It's just because I don't have my medicine," Silbergleit said. "I don't give out that easily, I'm tougher than I look."

"Don't you feel well, Herr Silbergleit? You're all red in the face." Karpe bent down to Silbergleit, who was walking bent over, and peered under his hat. "Come on, I'll take your briefcase for you, I'll carry it for a way, at least. I can still manage that much, who knows how much longer they'll be driving us through the streets. Ultimately, everyone is his own neighbor."

That was his way of consoling someone.

"No, no. I won't give up my briefcase. Not under any circumstances. I'll make it," Silbergleit said, looking at the ground.

A kapo, who had been running back and forth along the column and had been watching them for a while, yelled at them. With his stick, he pounded on Karpe, who staggered. Unnoticed, Silbergleit pushed ahead a little to protect Karpe with his back, so that he wouldn't stumble forward and fall.

Arthur
  I can't hear you
  Arthur it's your birthday and the jasmine is blooming
  do you smell it stop that Ilse
  you came back and left the bouquet of jasmine in front of the door I saw you I didn't leave the window even when it had gotten dark outside I didn't want the jasmine not in my room Herr Karpe took it and the smell penetrated through cracks in the door it was

everywhere in the hall in the whole house in all the rooms this heavy sweet numbing smell I couldn't escape it

you never forget it

they came one day in November I was not on the list they simply took the others from their homes they were allowed to take twenty-five kilos of baggage and two blankets and enough provisions for two days and their homes were sealed since then I have not gone outside the house

it was in 1927 when we met no you're wrong it was 1927 I have more time to think about it that's it you spoke to me in the Hotel am Zoo you came up to me after the reading and asked me what I meant by the sentence

Recently Silbergleit and Karpe had become friends. When the living space in the Jewish community house became scarcer and scarcer toward the end, they had moved into one room together. Herr Kochmann, chairman of the Jewish community, had been trying since the beginning of the war to accommodate as many Jewish families as possible in the community house. They would be more protected together. He himself had moved out of his villa on Miethe-Allee at a time when he could have kept on living there. He didn't want to be better off than the others, and above all he wanted to be close to his community.

First they took away Herr Karpe's laundry business on the Ring, then commandeered his home. He and his wife had to move into the attic, where earlier his seamstresses had lived. When his wife died, he buried her in the new Jewish cemetery on Leipzigerstrasse, and when he got back, he found his things in two suitcases on the street, and the new owner wouldn't let him back in the house, which had once belonged to him. So Karpe went to the police to register a complaint, and the police only laughed. He had to take off his shoes and socks, then they hung a sign around his neck I WILL NEVER COMPLAIN TO THE POLICE AGAIN and chased him across the Gleiwitz Ring. Herr Linz had thought nothing of it and advised Herr Karpe to move into the little Jewish ghetto on Niederwallstrasse, until the *big* Jewish ghetto was ready.

Silbergleit lived in one of the desirable rooms in the front on the street, which Frau Goldstein had sublet to him. After the Jewish star was introduced, their windows were smashed at night by stones— later even in broad daylight. Herr Kochmann was able to persuade Herr Linz to have shutters installed, and one day Herr Linz ordered that the shutters not be opened anymore and had them nailed shut.

Frau Goldstein, who was almost eighty, began to tyrannize Silbergleit. She wouldn't tolerate his playing the phonograph, accused him of wasting water, and unscrewed his fuse because he read books at night in his room and sat there scribbling, which drove up the amount of electricity used and had the Gestapo threatening to cut off the current to the whole house.

Sometimes he would lie on the sofa, putting the words of a poem in place in his mind, or planning a story, or thinking of his wife Ilse, or simply lying there thinking of nothing, and Frau Goldstein would barge in, complaining about the noise that he allegedly was making . . . She had plainly gone mad, this Frau Goldstein, who wouldn't wear the Magen David and therefore never left the house, not for over a year now. Old Herr Kochmann couldn't calm her down either; he tried to play the peacemaker everywhere in his gentle, soothing, superior manner.

Silbergleit was not surprised. He was more surprised that she had been the one who went mad, and not he. It could just as easily have been the other way around. He was only surprised that everybody didn't go crazy in this situation.

For a time he could no longer write, and that was when his heart pains started, too. So he had asked Herr Karpe, who lived upstairs in a room facing the backyard, whether he could move in with him. He had partitioned off part of the room with woolen blankets, then he could turn a lamp on in the evening and write. But that didn't happen often. His eyes had become too weak; after a while red dots would dance on the paper. That was from the work in the sewage treatment plant. The president of the waterworks was a notorious Jew hater, and he assigned them purposely to the hardest jobs, sometimes making them work for hours in the chlorine, whereas the other workers in general were relieved every three hours.

When he was no longer working at the treatment plant, he cooked the meals for Karpe and himself. And Karpe cooked on Sundays.

They didn't have much to cook, but it was enough for their needs. They got along well, Herr Silbergleit and Herr Karpe. At first Karpe had been astonished by how much his roommate wrote. Even on the Sabbath he sat at the little round, wobbly table, which he steadied with pieces of cardboard, and wrote. Most of what he wrote he tore up and later burned in the stove. When paper grew scarcer, he wrote on the margins of the newspapers. Earlier, when Karpe was running the laundry on the Ring, he had already known Herr Silbergleit was a poet. And when Silbergleit moved in with him he saw his books on the shelf; he had leafed through them, even read one or two. He especially liked the short pieces, such as the "Sabbath Description" from childhood, the legends of the "Seven-Branched Menorah," of the "Wailing Wall," of "Jerusalem," and of the "Sleep Dancer." And he long remembered the poems "Orphans" and "At the Door of the Jewish Welfare Office" and "Experience."

Once he had asked Silbergleit why he always tore up his sketches and destroyed them, when he wrote such moving things. To write so beautifully was a gift.

"It's not good enough," Silbergleit had answered. "It has to be even better. I always begin over again. What I'm working on now will outshine anything I've ever written."

Karpe was thinking that what Herr Silbergleit was writing now would probably never be printed. And when he told him that once, Silbergleit fell silent and did not speak to him for two days.

They had been counting on it daily. But when it finally did come, they were surprised. Secretly they had been hoping that the deportations would cease. There were supposed to have been secret negotiations with the Americans. There were so many rumors.

Herr Linz came with four other officials in civilian clothing to Niederwallstrasse. He had been wearing civilian clothing the time before, in November. So they knew right away what was up. He didn't even need to read them the order. They just wanted to know who was on the list this time.

They were all on the list. Except for Justice Kochmann. And two mixed marriages, the children of which were being raised Catholic. Archpriest Pattas from St. Peter and Paul had verified this in an affidavit.

This time they had only two hours to pack, and during this time the officials patrolled all the apartments. At the last transport in November, when they announced the deportations two days in advance, there were numerous suicides. The Lewin sisters, from Wilhelmstrasse; Dr. Aufrecht, the gynecologist, along with his wife— they were found in bed, their arms around each other, poisoned with Pyrimal. The whole town had talked about it. This time they probably wanted to avoid that. First of all they cut off the gas and unscrewed the fuses. Ration cards and work permits had to be handed in. They were allowed to keep only their identity cards. Their baggage was weighed. If it was heavier than twenty-five kilograms, the suitcases had to be opened and things taken out.

Herr Linz was very precise. He collected their cash, jewelry, and other valuables personally; he went from room to room, registered every piece, and handed out signed receipts. They were there and observed in what an orderly fashion everything was carried out. The valuables were placed in a manila envelope that was fastened before the eyes of the owner, who had to write his name diagonally across it. That was supposed to be like a seal.

On the front Herr Linz printed in big letters: SILBERGLEIT ARTHUR ISRAEL B 1881.

They would get everything back in Riga, Herr Linz said.

Wedding rings had to be handed over, too. Silbergleit had already buried his earlier, in the yard at Niederwallstrasse 17. If he were to come back again to the town of his childhood, he would dig it up from the black earth. Karpe, a widower, had sewn both rings into the lining of his coat. He had told Silbergleit and advised him to do the same.

"It's not the gold," Karpe said, "it's the memory that I'm carrying with me."

Silbergleit thought it better to bury his in the black earth. He had been born not far from there, on Ratiborerstrasse.

Weapons, knives, scissors, sharp objects, medications could not be taken along. He had a little bottle of *crataegutt* in his pocket, for his heart. He had been accustomed to the drops for years, he thought he could not do without them. Now above all, with all this excitement. He hoped Herr Linz would let it pass.

Then they were searched in the stairwell and the official, whom he had never seen before, discovered the bottle right away—he had not been trying to hide it anyway.

"We don't want any trouble," the man said, and poured the drops onto the tiles in front of his eyes. "So nobody will commit suicide!" He dropped the empty bottle and crushed it with his boot; the glass crunched.

Linz had been there, and to Silbergleit's request to let him keep the heart drops he had only mumbled something about regulations and continued to fuss with the watches he had confiscated. The Gestapo officer in civilian clothing ordered the others to throw away their medicines right away, each individual would be searched, and if he still found something then they would be punished. For instance, by a beating. That was quite legal.

It had been very quiet in the stairwell, and it was easy to hear tablets rustling and falling to the floor and glass clinking.

From various provincial communities, suicides by Jews have been reported. The population, except for friends with mixed marriages, takes no interest in the transport of the Jews and seems to accept it.

Silbergleit began to sweat. He felt his legs getting heavier. It was not the briefcase and not the two blankets, probably he had less to carry than most of the others. It was his heart. He had trouble getting air. His breath came short and heavy. He was dressed too warmly, too. He pushed the briefcase aside and unbuttoned his coat and jacket. He also loosened his tie. He always dressed properly. He always did at home, too; when he was sitting at his desk, writing, he usually wore a suit and vest.

Aron Szalit from the little Lithuanian town of Slabodka the dirty little Jewish boy who always stinks of cabbage soup because there is nothing else to eat at home but cabbage soup his clothes saturated with the smell of cabbage soup his skin smells of it his hair no one wants to sit next to him in the yeshiva bgcause he stinks so the dirty little Jewish boy Aron Szalit from Slabodka who goes barefoot to the nearby capital Kowno to learn to read and write

to read the Talmud and Mickiewicz Karamsin Tolstoy a little

Jewish boy runs out of the ghetto into the world he carries a clump of earth in his pants pocket and someday he will sell books in a bookstore in Berlin

The coat was worn out and shone with grease spots. The sleeves were too short and had holes in the cuffs. He had already turned the cuffs up once and hemmed them; the jacket sleeves stuck out a bit. Jews got no ration card for clothing.

The strap was cutting into his shoulder. He pushed it farther up toward his neck. Now it was the books that were getting heavy for him. Herr Linz had wondered why there were only books in the briefcase, nothing else, just books. The others had packed warm clothing, shoes, and photo albums, some memento or other. He had packed only books. They were the only things he possessed. He would never give them up.

When Herr Linz discovered the books in the briefcase during the inspection, he started to dump them out. Silbergleit threw himself over them. He would rather let them kill him than give up his books. "These are books that I wrote myself, war poems from the First World War, here, one of them is called 'Flanders'—I fought for Germany there! And this one here: 'The Maiden A Legend of Mary.' And this book, *God's Cornucopia*, you can't take that away from me . . ."

Silbergleit began to have doubts about how far he could get with the briefcase full of books. This was the first checkpoint, and how many more checkpoints would he have to pass until they arrived at their destination? And no one among them knew their destination. He believed in the ghetto in Riga because he wanted to believe in something. Books will be needed there. Not just his. He had books by Hermann Hesse along, too: *Beneath the Wheel*, personally inscribed.

The manuscript of his novel, *The Menorah*, and the *Diaries* that he had been writing in secret until the end, he had hidden all that in the cellar on Niederwallstrasse, behind the thick wall that Herr Kochmann had had built shortly before the war. As if he had anticipated all this. The ritual objects of the synagogue were hidden there too.

Someday someone would find everything. When all this was over. Then his diaries would bear witness to what the Jews here in Gleiwitz had experienced and suffered since the beginning of the war. Up to the day of deportation. But he wanted to take his printed books along with him. They were his identification, no matter where he ended up.

14

At the corner of Wilhelmstrasse and Niederwallstrasse they almost ran into each other's arms. They were both in such a hurry that they didn't notice one another until the last instant. "Oh, it's you, Herr Apitt," said Herr Thonk, coming to a halt. He didn't want Herr Apitt to think that he was hurrying so he wouldn't miss the removal of the bells from St. Peter and Paul. "Herr Apitt, of all people!"

"Is it possible, it's the cell leader," Herr Apitt said. When he was in a hurry, he walked a little bit crooked, with one shoulder forward, as if pulling the rest of him along.

He would much rather have gone on alone, for you never knew what kind of a conversation a Party comrade like Thonk would involve you in, and he had enough to do to shake off Block Warden Koslowski, who didn't just snoop around the houses watching people, but recently had stationed himself on the stairs and interrogated them about their position on political events. Widow Jawcrek had come to him, crying, and had told him that Herr Koslowski had demanded that she praise the heroic courage of the German soldiers at Stalingrad, on the spot, when her husband had already fallen in the siege at Stalingrad and she was still wearing mourning. But if he continued on alone, he might just make himself look suspicious, at least it might attract attention. Once some Party people had gained admittance to his apartment, and he hadn't been able to prevent them. They never come with a search warrant, after all, they just snoop around and threaten to make things difficult for you, and even at his age they could still give him a lot of trouble.

He turned to face Herr Thonk and acted as if he had to look him up and down first to see whether it really was Cell Leader Thonk. "Where are you off to in such a hurry, Herr Thonk?" But he himself was out of breath as he spoke.

"You know," the cell leader said, walking more slowly, "in times like these you always have something to do. Today all the people's strength is needed. It starts early in the morning and doesn't stop in the evening. And we must not tire, we all know that."

"Today is Good Friday!" old Apitt said. It might be that the Party man had just plain forgotten Good Friday. They had different holidays: the Führer's birthday, Seizure of Power Day, March on the Feldherrnhalle, Birth of the Nation Day, Solstice Celebration, and so on; he didn't know what they all were.

"Yes, yes, I've been thinking about it," Herr Thonk said. "But I have to think of our boys at the front, too, fighting every day. So we on the home front shouldn't hold back either. Many of our people's comrades still don't understand that we're in a heroic battle with half the world. And we're winning!"

"Yes, it's almost unbelievable, all the places our brave boys are fighting," Herr Apitt said mildly. "Even when they have to yield to superior power, in the East and in Africa, that's already been in the newspapers. But fortunately there are special bulletins every day about the ships that are being sunk by our U-boats. Herr Cell Leader! You're making the people accustomed to special bulletins, but what will you do one day when there are none? People are virtually addicted to the Liszt fanfares."

It gave him pleasure to show Thonk that he knew where the fanfare theme came from.

"If we all fight heroically, and if our communal spirit holds up, especially here on the home front, then there will be no reason to broadcast fewer special bulletins," Thonk said.

They stopped and waited for a streetcar going past them with a loud noise made by braking long before the curve.

So many pensioners and retirees volunteered for Home Service after our appeal, Thonk thought. But Apitt had not been among them. He considered the possibility of assigning him some required duty. He didn't know much about Herr Apitt, but he was sure that he was no particular friend of the new Reich. There was nothing you could pin on him, no, there hadn't even been enough for a warning from the Party up to now. In his speech he was quite careful, it was said, but he had never participated voluntarily in any project. And the block warden had once reported to him that Herr Apitt had dropped only five pfennigs into the can during a house-to-house collection; he didn't remember what the collection was for—imagine, a five-pfennig piece! Yet he was drawing an official's pension. And even Musiollek with his nine children gave ten pfennigs every time! Koslowski had once gained admittance to Apitt's apartment, with the help of the district leadership. He had authorized it, but had not been there himself, no, the word would have gotten around and he wouldn't get anything at all out of people after that. But Koslowski had found nothing, not even hoarded groceries, as a rumor had suggested since the beginning of the war.

There was so little to get out of him because he lived such a reclusive life. He was supposed to have been a Socialist earlier; by '37 he had already been pensioned off, and he wasn't old enough yet. He had been involved in the ethnic strife in 1920–21, on the German side, so you couldn't fault him on that. In his report Koslowski had written: "Goes regularly to the municipal library, checks out books on Buddhism and Roman history. Never books on the Teutons or German history." Admittedly that was no reason, however, for the district leadership to initiate anything against Apitt.

Only now did he notice the yellow armband with three black dots on Apitt's arm.

"Do you want me to help you across the street?" Thonk asked cautiously. He did not know in which direction Herr Apitt was headed. Surely in the direction of Peter-Paul-Platz, and then to the church. All of them were headed that way today. He was going to the right, wanting to be seen today at the district leadership meeting at the Hotel Upper Silesia.

"But why?" Herr Apitt said. "The legs are still spry. The only thing that bothers me is my teeth. But you know that. When the weather changes, I begin to feel it in my joints, too: rheumatism. You can get that from your teeth, too, as I read recently."

"I mean your eyes. I guess they keep getting worse, don't they? You already have to wear the armband of the blind."

"Ach, my eyes, yes," Herr Apitt said, almost stopping in the middle of the intersection. He had forgotten that he had sewn a blind armband on the sleeve of his coat. No one paid any attention to an old man these days. This way at least he got a seat on the streetcar, and at Gmyrek, the butcher's, he didn't have to stand in line—it was his turn right away if there was veal for a change. Which didn't happen all that often.

"You're right, my eyes are a lot weaker. Especially at night and at dusk. And when the weather changes, it affects my eyesight. You know, there are hours when I can't see anything at all."

Sometimes he didn't want to see anything, either.

Now Thonk walked along with him a little farther after all. "As long as I've known you, you've had problems with your teeth. Why don't you just have them all pulled out and dentures put in, then the pain will be over once and for all. Our military doctors have invented a new substance, a plastic, that seals dentures against your palate, nothing can happen. There're all kinds of inventions nowadays! That's a side effect of armaments technology. And after the war it will all be turned to civilian use. Life will be good."

He himself had a set of upper dentures, and would have liked to show Herr Apitt how easily you could take them out.

"For heaven's sake, I beg of you," Herr Apitt said, "just leave me my toothaches. I leave people their Sunday masses, which they probably can't live without, and you your Party meetings!"

The cell leader was listening more closely now. "What do you mean by that?" he asked warily.

"People need something to believe in," Apitt said, unmoved. And somewhat more softly, but now Herr Thonk was really listening: "Everyone needs something he can believe in. Especially in times like these . . ."

The cell leader didn't want to argue, but Herr Apitt sometimes had a way of expressing himself so ambivalently, which he didn't like much. I should feel him out in a longer talk, I might get more out of him, he thought, but it was not easy to get closer to him.

"Yes, you're right," Herr Thonk said. He even laughed now. "Do you believe in the ultimate victory?" That didn't sound at all suspicious, he just wanted his hopes confirmed by other people. And Herr Apitt, who had so much time to read books on Buddhism and Greek and Roman history, had a broader horizon. Herr Thonk didn't even get around to reading the political training magazines regularly, his work for the Party was such a strain. Even on Good Friday he still had to go the the RRW in the afternoon to paint stencils on freight cars with other Party members and some of the Hitler Youth. He suspected the district leadership of choosing Catholic Party members for this work. Half of them would call in sick again. You could only depend on the youth these days. The younger generation was simply the guarantee of the future. The Party was right about that. A few Party members had left the Church, but only because they wanted to be promoted. He himself had seen them slipping into the confessional after that. Maybe he would have left the Church too, if his wife hadn't always broken into tears as soon as he broached the subject. Yet they would save a lot of money on the church tax alone, but his wife was afraid that the pastor wouldn't bury her then. You couldn't talk to her about it. And he himself didn't know how he would look the pastor in the face if he ever met him on the street. He realized that he would never amount to much in the Party, basically. They had different people for that. And the things Kolmann had said, about how they took care of the partisans and the Jews in the Ukraine, even if they were enemies of the people, well, he really was too old for that, and too Catholic. That was something for the young ones. At the Somme he had seen enough corpses, and enough hate in the uprising of '21.

"What did you say?" He hadn't noticed that Apitt had kept on talking.

". . . I don't know whether the situation is like that, but we should be ready for anything. The whole world is against us, and if we don't win the war, everything is lost, this time we won't get back on top, they'll dictate two Versailles to us at once."

Ever since all of Upper Silesia had been German again, Herr Thonk hadn't given Versailles a thought. For him that had expunged the humiliation that Versailles had inflicted upon them. But Herr Apitt was right, the war was bigger this time and thus the defeat would be bigger. Once again the terrible atrocities as in 1918, when mobs raged through the streets . . . And he didn't even want to think about 1929.

"Yes," he said, "Germany itself is at stake. Woodrow Wilson's Fourteen Points, the enslavement of Germany." He had learned that in a Party course and had actually almost forgotten it. He was grateful to Herr Apitt for reminding him.

They were already past Peter-Paul-Platz, where there was more traffic than usual. Now they had to turn the next corner and they would be standing right in front of the main tower. He might just as well go the last few steps and have a look at it all. Besides, he suspected Archpriest Pattas of having the bells taken down on Good Friday on purpose because the entire town would be around. The leadership had sent Party members who were supposed to take note of every word he said, so he wouldn't be inciting the people. Pattas was capable of anything. Curate Mikas, at any rate, wouldn't be permitted to preach from the pulpit the next few Sundays; the Gestapo had forbidden it.

"Sacrifices are expected of all of us," Herr Thonk said. "From the churches as well. They must give up their bells now; they'll get them back after the war."

"Ach, I thought the Church was giving up its bells voluntarily," Apitt said.

"Well, these days nobody gives up anything entirely voluntarily, so let's say: *semi-voluntarily*."

Which was only another word for coercion. They knew that by then.

"I understand," old Apitt said, with a tortured laugh, because Herr Thonk was looking at his face expectantly. It was a laugh that pained him.

"I'm no enemy of the Church," Thonk said, "and believe me, I could be higher up in the Party if I had left the Church. Roman Catholic, in the Party that's a flaw, today you're supposed to be a *believer*, but I am just Catholic, and my wife is too. But the Church shouldn't meddle in our affairs, something like the Christmas message of the Pope, that's no good, he's rousing the people against us now."

"I have to go," said Apitt, who didn't want to listen to this. "I'll find my way all right, I just have to follow the people."

The cell leader stopped and took hold of Herr Apitt by his armband: "We need volunteers for a big project, you come too, this afternoon and tomorrow afternoon at the RRW, just painting with stencils, you can still do that, four hundred cars, they have to be done by Sunday. All we've got now are squirts from the HY, and young girls. We could use a few older people to supervise. Can I count on you?"

"Ach, I know," said Apitt, "you see that poster everywhere now: *Careful! The enemy is listening!* And then that man with the hat . . ."

"No," Thonk said: *"Wheels must roll for victory."*

Apitt stopped. He looked as if he would take out a handkerchief in the next instant and hold it to his cheek. He had already put on the expression for it. "Sounds amazing," he said. "But my eyes are already so bad that not even the strongest glasses help."

"We are in a total war, you know that, ever since February. The people want it, you heard that on the radio. There is a sense of community among us and a will to sacrifice, *pjerunnje,* one last great effort and victory is ours! And that I am permitted to experience it . . ." He really was happy. "You don't want to shut yourself out of this, do you?"

"No, I don't," Apitt said.

"It's all in the service of a higher ideal," Thonk said. "The thing with the church bells, too. Everything for the ultimate victory. Have a look around your apartment again, maybe you can find something made of brass or bronze, I'll send a boy to your place. Every piece of nonferrous metal is needed now. I've even unscrewed the brass doorknobs in my apartment and contributed them!"

"Ach-you'll-never-get-the-door-shut," old Apitt said. The bells, he could understand that. But the doorhandles in your apartment?

"What did you say?"

"Now just come along the last few steps and have a look at them taking down the bells." Apitt was practically pushing Herr Thonk.

"No, no," Thonk resisted, "I have to go to a Party meeting. I'll have someone come pick you up tomorrow for the painting project at the RRW."

"Completely voluntarily or semi-voluntarily?" Apitt shouted after him.

The little square in front of the main portal of St. Peter and Paul was black with people. It wasn't the massive crowd that there always was when pilgrims were returning from Annaberg, from Deutsch-Piekar, or from Albendorf, and were received by Archpriest Pattas with the bells ringing and the organ playing solemnly; it was more like on Sundays after the High Mass when the faithful streamed out of the church and stood around on the square for a while in groups and clusters, chatting, exchanging news, or making appointments. The difference was mainly that now they all kept looking up at the church tower. Some constantly kept their eye on it, even while they were talking with their neighbors, for they didn't want to miss the slightest development; others just cast a glance upward now and then, and some were conversing or reading a newspaper. Nothing unusual was to be seen except for the fire chief's car, the truck, and the rope from the block and tackle that was hanging down from the church tower. For most people that was unusual enough. The main portal and the square to the right, up to the first side nave, were blocked off by red and white rope barriers, and improvised signs pointed to the side entrances of the church.

15

It seemed to Rosa Willimczyk that everyone but her was accepting the removal of the bells as a matter of course. She was the only one who asked: "Who ordered this?" No one answered her. She went through the crowd and said loudly to people: "Who do they think they are, taking our bells away? Who sent them? And who gave them their orders?" The women looked at her, amazed, surprised, and a little unbelieving, to the extent that it was possible for a Catholic to be unbelieving on Good Friday. They didn't understand that someone like her, who was no different from them in any way, dared to ask that. The bells were being taken down in broad daylight, so there must not be anything wrong with it. Those in decision-making positions looked quite different, and they were not here among them, they were sitting behind desks in Oppeln, in Breslau, in Berlin, and even in Rome, and they didn't inquire whether it was all right with the people here. Christ was nailed to the cross, the high tribunal decided that, and ordinary soldiers carried that out; they drove nails through the hands and feet of a human being and erected the cross and the people stood around and wept, but no one asked why it had to be that way.

They made room for her and let her go forward to the barrier. When she reached the first fireman, she asked again: "Who ordered this?"

The fireman, who was exclusively interested in the problem of whether to root for Vorwärts Rasensport Gleiwitz or Beuthen 09 on Easter Monday, had her repeat the question again, it seemed so outrageous to him. He had been sent there that morning to secure the church square. The removal of the bells meant nothing to him, it was being carried out by men of the OD, who answered directly to the armaments minister and always cited some higher order or other. So an ordinary fireman like him couldn't do anything anyway. And besides, he was Lutheran. "Go over there to the men with the white armbands, they're responsible for the bells," he said.

He didn't allow her to cross the barrier, and so she had to go around. Finally one of the men with white armbands came toward her, because she was gesticulating energetically with both arms as if some disaster had occurred.

If she had not immediately claimed to be a member of the Parish Council (in reality she hadn't been reelected two years ago, but still, she had been singing in the Cecilia Club for nine years), she probably wouldn't have gotten any information. So she did learn that there was a legal order from the Reich government for the surrender of church bells, and that the bishops had called upon their churches to perform this bell sacrifice for victory. He was responsible for taking the bells to Cosel undamaged, where they were to be collected and loaded on barges. The pastor of this church (he didn't even know it by name) had wished expressly, yes, he said *wished expressly*, that their bells be taken down on Good Friday, and by three in the afternoon if possible.

Then she went to the rectory and demanded to see the Archpriest. After a while the assistant pastor, Jarosch, came out, along with a young curate, whom she didn't know, and a number of acolytes.

When Jarosch caught sight of Rosa Willimczyk, the bookseller, he said as if in one friendly word: "Praised-be-Jesus-Christ-Fräulein-Willimczyk-how-are-you-I-hope-you're-fine . . ." and extended his hand. After all, she confessed to him, and he saw her every Sunday at the High Mass, sitting in the fourth pew, almost always in the same place. But he didn't invite her to come in. As if he were concealing something in the rectory.

She repeated her request to speak with the honorable Archpriest. "On a rather important matter," she said loudly, in the hope that the Archpriest might perhaps hear her. She could tell from his face that the assistant pastor had appeared in order to get rid of her as soon as possible.

The honorable Archpriest, he allowed immediately, had retired to his private quarters to hold a dialogue with God; he had to prepare himself for the Good Friday liturgy now.

She had to respect that. She glanced quickly at her little watch, but felt ashamed to be measuring the suffering of Christ with a minute hand.

If it was an important matter, then naturally *he* was at her disposal, even though he didn't have much time. From the hallway two more acolytes came up.

Rosa Willimczyk kept it as brief as she could: Whether the surrender of the bells was taking place with the agreement of the Archpriest, and why on Good Friday, of all days? And whether the Archpriest would bless the bells before their deportation? The square was black with people, and the faithful were waiting for a word from the Church to this barbaric act, yes, she said: *barbaric act*.

The two priests took turns answering now, which didn't make it any clearer. She made out that it was taking place on the basis of an order from the commissioner for the Four-Year Plan, which had been issued a year ago.

And it now was affecting the churches in Upper Silesia, successively, the young curate added. He came from Saxony, where they had performed the bell sacrifice as early as 1941; there had been an hour of ceremony on the occasion, and the bells had rung one last time for an entire hour. The honorable Archpriest, however, had decided that they were to part from their bells in silence.

At the words "bell sacrifice," Rosa Willimczyk had given the young curate a look that made him flush.

"Yes," assistant pastor Jarosch said, "as far as the time is concerned, the Archpriest wanted it that way. Because the bells have to be silent on this day anyway. And so they will just be silent forever!"

To go ahead and make an hour of ceremony out of it was cynical, the bookseller thought. "Then I really do prefer to go through this on the saddest day of the year. This turns out to be a symbol for me: the silent Church . . ." She was speaking more and more excitedly. One more acolyte came out of the sacristy. And only now did it occur to her to answer the greeting of the assistant pastor: "In eternity, Amen," she said.

The priest thought she was taking her leave, and was grateful. Turning to go, he said: "Besides, we posted the order outside in the announcement box, anyone can read it there."

"Maybe it should be read on Sunday after mass and explained to the faithful," the young curate said eagerly. "It could be that some of the people here can't read."

The new curate must still be pretty new around here. For heaven's sake! And who knew what stories they told him about Upper Silesia back there in his Saxon seminary. Rosa Willimczyk punished him with a long, contemptuous glance. And she had never seen him in her bookstore, either. Her bookstore was a Catholic one, after all, and number one in town. "What the Church has to put up with these days," Fräulein Willimczyk said. "To let the bells be carted off without any protest!" She was disappointed. She would have liked to see Archpriest Pattas kneeling and mourning in the middle of the crowd. Jesus sweat blood on the Mount of Olives.

"Can't you protest?" she asked helplessly.

The assistant pastor sent the acolytes back inside. "Go on, I'll be right there," he said to them. And to Fräulein Willimczyk, seriously and decisively: "No, we cannot protest. In other towns, the churches sacrificed their bells with rejoicing. At least we won't go along with that. But we cannot refuse. Do I need to remind you that the most reverend Archpriest proclaimed the last Christmas message of the Pope from the pulpit, counter to the wishes of Prince Archbishop Bertram? He was probably the only pastor in all of Silesia who did that, and you must remember the protests . . . Praised be Jesus Christ, Fräulein Rosa, and let us pray to God that he stand by us, now and in our hour of need." And with that he left.

Rosa Willimczyk did not remember. For the first time she had not remained in Gleiwitz for Christmas, but had traveled to the Beskids all alone. She had heard the midnight mass in a little mountain church, just as she had read in a book by Rosegger when she was young. Yes, at the time she was still reading Rosegger—and since then had never looked inside a book by Rosegger again; at most she only sold them.

In the announcement box on the church wall outside, she discovered the order. Not a soul seemed interested in it.

**Surrender of Bronze Church Bells Order
for Implementation of the Four-Year Plan on the
Rendering
of Nonferrous Metals**

In order to establish the metal reserves required for long-term conduct of war, I decree:

1. *That the metal in bronze bells and copper building parts is to be appropriated and put at the immediate disposal of the German Armaments Reserve.*

2. *Bronze bells are to be reported and delivered. Initially copper building parts are only to be reported. The establishment of the time of their delivery remains discretionary. No disposition may be made of the objects to be reported without special directives.*

3. *Dismounting and transport of the bells will be undertaken at the cost of the Reich. The provision of substitute metal and an appropriate reimbursement for the value of the bells after the end of the war is guaranteed. The type of substitute and cost compensation for copper building parts to be dismounted will be settled on a case-by-case basis.*

4. *The Reich Minister of Economics will determine the means necessary for the implementation of the regulation. He may permit exceptions to the obligation to deliver.*

The Commissioner for the Four-Year-Plan
Göring, General Field Marshal

So that was it. She went back to the people waiting on the church square and joined them. Maybe it was even better that the people here had not read it. What good would it have done? It wouldn't change anything. At any rate, she had found out that the honorable Archpriest Pattas had wished the bells to be taken down on Good Friday, and that it wasn't a dirty trick of the Party, which she could well have imagined. That meant she knew more than anyone else on the square here.

She saw Hrabinsky, the cripple, sitting on his folding chair, sucking on his cold pipe and reading a newspaper. From time to time he stuck his pipe in his pocket, folded up the newspaper, and clapped his hands with enthusiasm. Then he would pull the pipe out again, unfold the newspaper, and engross himself anew in reading an article that he had probably already read before. Maybe she would even meet Herr Wondrak; half the town was out and about today. But the lawyer seldom went to church—his sister, though, all the more frequently. She would certainly see her here. They had invited her to dinner on Easter Sunday.

Many people came to Rosa Willimczyk's bookstore and she liked to pass the time with them. She was friendly, of course, but there was always a tinge of superiority in the friendliness, if not arrogance, which sometimes seemed unpleasant to others. As far as books were concerned, she simply knew a lot more about them, and she let it show. She had spent two years in Freiburg after her education, in the Albert Bookstore. She had often gone to Bach concerts there with a girlfriend, they had read poems by Reinhold Schneider together. It had been the high point of her life. She still read only poems by Reinhold Schneider.

Once a year she wrote a letter to her old friend in Freiburg in which she reminded herself and her friend of the Bach concerts. There was nothing like that in Gleiwitz. In general she felt rather lost in this town and rarely neglected to preface the name of Gleiwitz with "inartistic" whenever she mentioned it. For a time she had been friendly with Frau Piontek, at whose house on some evenings Chopin was played tolerably well, and sometimes a trio by Schubert, too. Such evenings generally ended in a sigh of how terrible it was to have to live in such an "inartistic" town as Gleiwitz.

Dr. Kamenz had once invited her to the *St. Matthew Passion* in Beuthen, probably because his wife had fallen ill; in any case, she had been so excited that the whole concert meant nothing to her, and at the end she managed to say only that the Freiburg Bach Chorus had been much better. He hadn't taken her to another concert after that. But maybe his wife hadn't been sick anymore after that, either. Dr. Kamenz had been drafted two years ago. He was busy cleansing the holdings of the library of the University of Kråkow. When he was on leave, he usually dropped by her bookstore, too, but he hadn't bought a single book from her, not even Jünger's *Gardens and Streets*, which she had set aside for him. He hoped he would be able to stretch out his activity in Kråkow until the war was over, for he didn't much like the idea of being ordered to the Eastern Front and earning a "frozen meat" medal.

Well, and who would like it.

She greeted a familiar face without knowing where she knew it from. Or wasn't that Widow Zoppas? My God, she almost hadn't recognized her. She had probably been out of town for a while with some young soldier from the Rhine or the Ruhr. Rosa gave her a friendly greeting but walked on past. Good heavens, all of Gleiwitz was on the streets today. Well, basically it would be better for her to marry Herr Wondrak. He was a good match, an excellent one, this attorney and notary, and they had all congratulated her after the word had gotten out. She had turned red when the subject came up, because she couldn't rid herself of the feeling that everyone knew or suspected how the wedding had been arranged; she wished she could give up her work in the bookstore now, so as not to have to see so many envious faces. She preferred it when they approached her with faces full of sympathy, she had gotten so used to that in the course of the years.

She knew that she could only be unhappy with him. Was she happy in her bookstore, where she praised books that nobody wanted to buy, and sold books for which she had no regard at all? She only wished that they had more to say to each other, Herr Wondrak and she. But they had practically nothing to say to one another. They sat side by side, if they got together at all, and in an uncertain feeling of loneliness attempted to assure their closeness by holding each other's hands, and didn't even dare to look at one another. They were silent. And she thought about how she would have to smell his sweat for the rest of her life, his sweat that smelled as sour as rye Zur. But maybe it was all right that way. Perhaps she would be unhappy if she couldn't be unhappy. Yes, there could be such a thing.

Maybe she could have married Dr. Kamenz, but he was already married. His wife was a silly goose and jealous to boot, the doctor had to admit that, but he had done nothing to alter the situation. That had been her luck with most men. After all, she was at an age where the majority of the men who were right for her were married to silly and jealous women. Maybe she hadn't tried hard enough. In any case, she had been surprised when Valeska Piontek had come to see her one day and asked her whether she would like to marry Lawyer Wondrak, who naturally would come to ask for her hand in person. She just wanted to feel her out on this visit. After all, they were at an age where such things could be planned with common sense and patience, surely that was her opinion too.

So she had finally met with Herr Wondrak in Gruban's Wine Room, where the attorney was still served wine in the fourth year of the war, and they had come to an understanding, looking past one another and remaining silent. She had been prepared to marry even if she wouldn't be happy with him. He would be just as unhappy with her, she felt as she sat there next to him, silent, occasionally swallowing a little wine.

Reading books and being unhappy, she loved that. That was her fate.

Hrabinsky, the cripple, clapped his hands loudly again, tearing her from her thoughts.

Yes, she wanted to dance the polka, once more. Since Irma Piontek's wedding in the Hotel Upper Silesia she hadn't danced. To dance the polka again, one last time. At her own wedding! Then she would adopt a stern, solemn countenance, take on a slow, solemn gait, wear black, high-necked dresses with white lace collars, become a member of the reading society, collect phonograph records, and occasionally travel to Breslau for a Bach concert. That much she could permit herself.

16

I'VE GOT TO snare one before the day is out, Tonik thought, and pushed his way into the curious crowd on the church square. He strained to see whether he could spot a familiar face anywhere. Here and there a face appeared that laughed at his, or in his direction, at any rate, and sometimes he remembered in a rather imprecise way having seen it somewhere a long time ago. But it was not the kind of face he was looking for, so he scrunched up his eyes. Sometimes he looked into a face for a long time, impudently long, until it turned away—no one could stare him down.

Earlier he had spoken to a girl because she wouldn't stop looking at him. He had doffed his cap and said boldly: "Pardon me, Fräulein, if you're cold, I can lend you my jacket." But the fräulein was not cold at all. Then he said: "Pardon me, young lady, if you feel like going to the movies tonight, I would very much like to invite you." But the young lady didn't feel like it, and shook her head. And although he felt that his mouth was already getting dry, he said: "Day after tomorrow is Easter, do you want to meet again then, after High Mass?" But she didn't want to, and shook her head for the third time. He ran his fingers through his hair, put his cap back on, and moved on. Who knows, maybe she was deaf and dumb.

He would try somebody else. Here where half the town was standing around he would surely meet someone he knew from before, or maybe strike up a new friendship. I've got to snare one, he thought. He was already five days into his leave, and hadn't found anything yet. After all, he couldn't go back to the front without at least getting laid first. Who knows, maybe this was his last leave. It didn't have to turn out as disastrously as it had last night.

Basically, what happened to the bells didn't interest him at all. He had come here because practically everyone in town had come to Peter and Paul Church that morning. He couldn't care less whether the bells hung in the tower, calling people to mass, or were melted down in some factory and turned into cannon balls or armor plate.

He wouldn't hear the bells anymore when he had to return to the front in nine days anyway. He didn't even look up at the sky. He was just a person who cared more about the ground beneath his feet.

It was better not even to think of what had happened the day before. But something kept reminding him of it. He didn't want to go through that again; he would jump into the ice-cold Klodnitz first to bring himself to his senses, for the more he thought about it, it seemed clearer and clearer, that he had lost them, at least for the time being. Maybe that was also the reason that he no longer had the courage to address a girl he didn't know.

Her face had not seemed entirely unfamiliar to him. But he really couldn't have said whom it reminded him of. After talking to her for a while, he thought she had to be one of the numerous daughters of Schachtner, the delicatessen owner, and that's who she turned out to be. Only he didn't know which one because they all looked rather similar. For a while he played the innocent, hoping to get closer to her that way. Her name was Helga—and he remembered this name least of all. But it was enough that they could talk about the same streets and squares, about the same springs and summers, about the same movies and hit tunes that made up their childhood.

In truth he was thinking of nothing but how to get on with it, to the deed itself, and the longer it took, the more painful it was. He could think of nothing else—it was like a screw in his head that bored an ever deeper warning into his brain when he was lost in the description of a summer or of some nutty adventure (such as the flood in 1937, when Antek Bielschowski drifted out into the Klodnitz on a chunk of ice and drowned). It was probably because he had never experienced the real thing, and—because he could not shake off this *pjerunnisch* fear of VD.

On the first evening she said good night to him right at the movie show, on the second he was permitted to walk her home, on the third evening they kissed down there by the Klodnitz bridge. The tempting thought of marrying a Schachtner daughter, which had slowly worked its way into his head, was certainly bold, but not entirely preposterous. The delicatessen owner had half a dozen daughters, sooner or later they would all come into their inheritance, and perhaps in his case that would be enough to open an auto repair shop after the war. Unless he could take over a branch of the delicatessen business, which Schachtner had established everywhere in the big towns of eastern Upper Silesia. When she finally allowed him a kiss down there by the Klodnitz bridge, hesitant, with her teeth clenched, he wanted more. He wanted it all. He pressed her against the wall of the bridge, it scratched the skin of her back and she began to cry. But Tonik didn't let go of her. Earlier someone had said to him that it's always that way with girls who are still virgins, they're afraid and begin to cry, then for God's sake don't stop, otherwise they'll never get over it. And only when she began pummeling him with her fists, furiously, did he let her loose, and heard her whisper, sobbing: "I can't, Tonik, it's that time of the month."

He kissed the tears from her eyes and stroked her hair. At the moment he really believed he loved her, and therefore asked her quite simply whether she would at least marry him. And she cried and laughed. And he said now she was a war bride. And she laughed and cried. And so they embraced for a while longer and kissed. Until he finally whispered into her ear: "Come on, blow me." And he repeated it, more than once, begging, howling, because he thought he couldn't stand it any longer: "Come on, Czinka, blow me!"

But she didn't move. And after a while she said, puzzled: "I don't understand."

In Paris once a prostitute had done it to him, and he had actually liked it. He didn't actually want to screw her, like the others, for fear of getting infected, and with a whore in Paris you could practically count on it. He had always wondered about his buddies; it didn't seem to make any difference to them—they climbed aboard anything they could get, and as a result wound up at the clinic.

All at once Helga Schachtner began to understand what he wanted, for she pushed him away with all her strength. Tonik was so surprised that he put up no resistance. He saw her make the sign of the cross and run away, up the stairs to Wilhelmstrasse. And he just wondered how she had found the steps so quickly in the dark. Tonik searched for his cap, which had fallen off. It was pitch black, he had to grope around on the ground. He straightened up his uniform, buttoned it, and fastened his belt. He had trouble finding the stairs.

Up above the bridge a painted-over streetlight gave off a weak blue gleam. It was quiet on the street, he couldn't see a soul. Far off he could make out a flickering light, slowly approaching. It was the streetcar, whose headlight let through only a slit of light. Tonik moved slowly toward the car stop. He could ride for two stops. He could also go on foot, it wasn't far. Since he couldn't decide, he lit a cigarette first. My God, his hands were still hot and his shirt was sticking to him under his uniform. He wouldn't snare anything else tonight; he was completely wiped out anyway. He would try again tomorrow. He would have to make it sooner or later. He blew out the smoke with a hiss. Maybe he had made a few mistakes with Helga Schachtner aside from its being her time of the month. Maybe he had been too impatient. But with the few days of leave he had, he couldn't afford to wait. In any case, he resolved to try a different tack tomorrow.

A groan went through the crowd. And Tonik looked up in the direction they were all staring. And now even he was interested.

"You're blocking my light," he heard someone yell from behind him. "Not even a uniform is a windowpane."

Herr Hrabinsky rose excitedly from his folding chair. Something was finally happening, and then somebody stands right in his way; not even a soldier in uniform had the right to do that.

"Ach, Tonik, it's you? Yes, I heard you were on . . . what's it called? . . . recuperation leave. Stop by sometime and tell me about the war . . . I hear you're always out after girls in the evening. You'll be in luck, no more men around, and the women are crazy for one . . ."

"Heil Hitler, Herr Hrabinsky," said Tonik indignantly.

17

KOTIK WAS ALREADY coming toward them. "Where have you all been for so long? We've . . . Man! Hot damn! *Ciulik!*" he interrupted himself with this volley. "Squintok, do you know how you look? What happened? Who did that to you?" He inspected his brother's face with curiosity, shock, and admiration.

"Don't ask so many questions, *hoppek*," Andy said, "questions make you hungry."

"If the answer doesn't satisfy you," Bronder put in, "then you can grill him tonight at bedtime."

He had been with Squintok so long now that he almost thought he had been there for the fracas.

"Did you get into a fight with the Lutherans?" Kotik grinned.

"How do you know that?" This morning when Andy left the apartment, he had not even been thinking about it yet.

"Well, I've heard from the grown-ups that it used to be the thing to do, in the foundry district, for instance. Only—now they don't dare anymore. There are more Lutherans all the time."

"That's it," Andy said.

"Come on," Kotik invited them, "we've got good seats, back there by the rowan trees. If it gets exciting, you can climb up in them. There's half a *ferajna*'s worth of us already." He led the two to the other side of the church square. "You're sure late enough. Two bells are already down. It's time for the third by now, it's supposed to be the biggest."

Tex Weber almost fell out of his tree when he saw Squintok. He had made himself quite comfortable in the fork of an acacia. From there he had the best view and if anything happened that the others on the ground couldn't see clearly, he had to supply the commentary. The suspense came only when the bells were being hauled down. In between a lot of time passed when nothing at all was happening. But you could throw stones—that scared old women. Talk in a

disguised voice. Pick the newspaper out of Hrabinsky's pocket. Play
soccer with a tin can. You could even gamble for pfennigs. But
naturally all that was nothing compared to a bell snapping its rope
and falling.

"Haven't you ever seen anybody with a black eye before?" Andy
ignored the questions peppering him from all sides. It wasn't all that
rare for a boy to be running around with a shiner. It would take
three days for it really to blossom: dark blue.

"I don't know if I'll stay much longer," Tex Weber said. "The
whole business is taking such an insanely long time, and I've got a
heck of a lot to do at home."

"Have you seen Wonzak or Hannes Stein? You know, the one
who's left from the children's evacuation camp?" Andy said.

"No, not so far." But that didn't prove anything, even after he'd
been in the tree for two hours. "But the square is so full that even
a U-boat Captain Prien could sneak through all the way to Scapa
Flow."

"A what?" Kotik asked.

"*Elemele dudki*," Tex Weber said, dangling his feet.

"It's good that the weather's getting better," Bronder said. "Now
the sun's coming out. Maybe it'll really be nice today."

"I'll stay for the Bell of Mary, then I'm leaving," Tex said.

"What do you mean, Bell of Mary?" Kotik asked. "I thought the
Bell of Hedwig was next. That's what everybody said."

"No, no, it's the Bell of Mary, it's almost two hundred years old.
The sound is insanely beautiful. You can tell it by the sound," Tex
Weber said.

"What kind of crap are you telling Kotik? Our *hoppek* has to learn
something, but not lies. It's the Bell of Hedwig—it is! The Bell of
Mary is hanging in the Church of Mary, just like the name, and
that's in Breslau."

"But that's insane," Tex called down from his branch. "The Church
of Mary isn't in Breslau, it's in Danzig." He was proud of knowing
that, when he was so much younger than Squintok.

"There are churches of Mary everywhere," Andy said disparag-
ingly. "And Peter and Paul churches too—even the big church in
Rome where the Pope lives is named that."

"That's insane, that's insane." Tex Weber squirmed up there in his tree.

"And there's probably a Hedwig's bell in Breslau, too, I won't deny that," Andy continued," but the Bell of Hedwig here is called that because Saint Hedwig is the patron saint of Silesia, and you should have learned that in the Don Bosco League. But you're a group leader in the HY now, in Petersdorf, when everybody knows that's a pile of crap."

"Insane," said Tex Weber. "The Pope's church in Rome is called St. Peter's, and not Peter and Paul's. And the bell here is called the Bell of Mary because the Holy Mother protected the town of Gleiwitz from the Danes with her blue mantle in the Thirty Years' War. That's how it was! You should know that too, Squintok. You learn that in your lousy school!"

"That's enough of that," Bronder put in. "All this squabbling disturbs the prayer atmosphere. You can just ask the pastor for the information, right? We'll ask the curate afterwards. *Hoppek*, are you coming?"

"It's the Bell of Hedwig, if you mean the big bell," Andy persisted. "And besides, I'm not called Squintok anymore. Because I don't squint anymore. You can call me Andy now, like the others do, or Andreas."

"Insane!"

It was enough to make you afraid that Tex would fall out of the tree from sheer enthusiasm.

To Tex Weber, everything was *insane*, and it had been for some time. They were surprised that he hadn't long since found another favorite word, because he kept changing to new ones. Heaven knows how he chose this one. Earlier he had said *murderous*. Or else *swell*. For a time he thought everything that he liked was *colossal* or else *colossalous* and *fantastichnek*, but he got that one from Josel. Tex was admired because he was always the first to start something that the others emulated.

Thus he wore the shortest pants in the whole town or at least in the neighborhood. Even his HY pants were so *insanely* short that he had been warned by his squad leader. But outside of HY meetings he turned them up an inch higher. And in winter he ran around in long pants that had bell bottoms so broad they spread out over his shoes. He even hit on the idea of sewing in a different-colored wedge. He was clever at such things and sewed them himself, even a pair of pants with the opening and buttonholes at the sides, like sailors wear. Try and beat that. He was probably the one who started the white silk scarves, too. By now you couldn't go to the movies in the evening without wearing a white silk scarf under your jacket, and all the boys looted their parents' closets. White linen would not do, it had to be silk. Occasionally Tex brought a French magazine to school, with photos of Negro bands and dancing girls with top hats and feather boas and "colossalous" breasts, and the latest fashions just as they were being worn in Paris—that was his source. His soldier father was stationed in Paris, and brought booty home with him on leave, things that you hadn't seen here for a long time, and the boys and the girls in the whole school fought over the magazines; he could practically have auctioned them off page by page.

"Hey," Tex Weber said, "something's up."

They looked up at the church tower eagerly. But you couldn't make out any change, not yet at least.

18

SHE HAD READ a while longer in the *Miracles and Deeds of the Saints*, but not with sufficient concentration after Andy had told her about the bells being taken down at St. Peter and Paul. She certainly couldn't bear to stay at home until two o'clock with just herself and her curiosity, so it was better for her to set out right away. It might be that with today's technology the bells would go pretty fast, and she might even be too late. Well, this was something she didn't want to miss. She had also found something in her book that was excellently suited for reading out loud, the legend of Audifax and Abachum, and the story of Alexius underneath the stairs, too, would not be bad in times like these. If only Andy didn't trot out some horror story from the history of Silesia again; he had gotten her mad at him that way last year.

She didn't know yet who would be there that evening. Andy and Kotik for sure, perhaps Ulla would come, too, she really hoped so; together with her and Franzek, that would make six—there hadn't been that many of them together for a long time. But she couldn't count on Tonik; this was his fifth day at home on leave and up till now she had seen him only three times, and then only briefly. Heaven knows where the boy was hanging around these days. But no one could tell him what to do, least of all his mother. What should she do, anyway—in two weeks he was going back into the field, and who knew what would happen to him there; you didn't always have to think of the worst. Poor Bruno, she thought, they didn't even know where he was buried. Well, Tonik should have fun and enjoy himself. But at least he could have told her where he had spent half the night and with whom.

Kotik was the only one of her children who had taken after her in this hunger for reading, and he was permitted to read all the books that she brought home from Kaffanke's Lending Library on Germaniaplatz. Right at the checkout counter Frau Kaffanke pointed out the books that a teenager should probably not get his hands on. She hid these in her night table at home so that Kotik wouldn't even be tempted to take a look at them. She was happy about his love of reading. From the very beginning the only condition she had set was that he keep away from the books until she had finished reading them, for she knew from childhood what difficulties it had caused with her sister, because naturally they always wanted to read the same book at the same time.

Kotik didn't read only at home, he read outside on the street, too, while the others were playing mumblety-peg or were running with hoops. He read in the yard, he read on the stairs, he read during recess, and if she didn't check up on him now and again he would probably read every evening with a flashlight under the covers—but she had never seen him reading a children's book. She had given him *Grimms' Fairy Tales*, and brought him the fairy tales by Hauff and by Andersen from the library, the Silesian sagas and the Battle of Troy for children, but he just paged through them dully. In contrast, he liked talking about grown-up books and sometimes surprised her with his judgments. For example, she had never thought about whether the solution of a murder case in the detective novels by Paul Rosenhayn, which she liked reading best, took place logically or not; that was the way it was written, and that must be how it was, and it was the Herr detective's, Joe Jenkins', business to solve the case. It had to be suspenseful, that was all. Kotik, on the other hand, asserted that it had to be suspenseful and logical too.

Recently she had been reading Westerns, above all Zane Grey. She imagined that she had developed a lively interest for America's Wild West. In reality, it was Kotik who had talked her into it, because he himself was really hot for books by Zane Grey. She much preferred Hans Dominik, whom she had discovered one day on the shelves of the library and since then her favorite subject was futuristic novels; but none of them were as good as Hans Dominik's, and she only regretted that there weren't more by him. *Atlantis* she had read twice and she liked it even the second time. *Atlantis* was his best book, of course, or maybe *The Burning of the Cheops Pyramid*—well, she wouldn't argue about that. *The Heritage of the Uranides* had really swept her away with excitement, but she couldn't read something like that twice—the suspense was gone. She consoled herself with other, poorer fantasies, and waited for the latest book by Dominik.

Anna looked out the window. Outside it was clearing up, and in the west she could already see blue sky; it would be enough if she just slipped on a jacket, she could do without her umbrella. Instead she would put on a hat—no, better the simple black wool turban, which made her look more serious and was more appropriate for the day. And a velvet shawl around her neck, which she arranged in front like a breastplate. For many years she had timed it so that on Good Friday she went to church at three o'clock, the hour of Christ's death, made her confession, prayed a litany for deceased relatives, and also the sorrowful mysteries of the rosary for those who were alive. That was part of her ever continuing dispensation.

Anna took her prayer book and rosary and set out for the parish church. She saw the people on the church square from far off. So they were still in the process of taking down the bells; otherwise the faithful would long since have been inside the church.

"What's going on here with all these people?" an old woman asked. "Is there going to be a special blessing?" She said it as if it were going to be a special ration on their grocery cards.

"Look for yourself," Anna said condescendingly, "they're taking down the bells." Nothing else needed to be said.

Widow Piontek was coming directly toward her, she wouldn't be able to avoid her. At least not for the time being. Ach, blessed Lord Jesus, what pitiful clothes Valeska Piontek had put on again today, on Good Friday. It was almost ostentatious. So at High Mass on Easter Sunday she would look all the more elegant. Most people here did that, it was the custom. She couldn't do so herself, not on Franzek's salary, even though he had been promoted to senior engineer now. With so many children, and their daughter at the conservatory, even though she had a scholarship, everything cost so much money. Not that she regretted it. Ulla was so talented. And almost famous by now, someday she would earn a lot of money. She was already very proud of her daughter. Sometimes she asked herself where Ulla had got it from. She herself was quite unmusical, she could hardly tell a piano from a violin. Listening to music on the radio was too much of an effort for her, she preferred reading biographies of famous musicians; Harsányi's *The Hungarian Rhapsody*, that was really something . . . None of the piano teacher's children was talented, at any rate. Not even Josel would amount to much, they had almost thrown him out of school. If Lawyer Wondrak had not been his uncle! With connections you could do anything these days. Biting a teacher on the nose, blessed Lord Jesus Christ, he must have a screw loose somewhere. And once she had wished this boy would become Ulla's husband someday!

She put on her friendliest smile, which looked more like a mask. She hoped that Frau Piontek wouldn't notice it.

After the two women had greeted each other gushingly and bemoaned the loss of the bells for a while, Anna said innocently: "Everything's okay again with Josel?"

"With Josel? Why shouldn't everything be okay with him? He'll be in the army now, the poor boy!" Valeska sighed.

"I only meant—didn't something happen, recently, at the high school? There was some talk," Anna said, so casually that it underscored her curiosity.

"Oh, that," Valeska Piontek said with a sigh of relief. "About the report cards? I'd already forgotten it. That just shows you how time passes."

But so much had happened! She took pains to smile. "Our Josel brought home the best report card in his class," she said triumphantly. "But apparently no one was talking about that!"

19

EVEN BEFORE JOSEL came home, Valeska Piontek had found out everything, at first only in fragments but gradually almost the whole story. Word must have spread through town like lightning, which she was actually glad about, for she knew that Josel would probably be the last reliable source of information. Lucie (Widera) —the *djobok* only knows how the news reached her in her loneliness—had come by the next streetcar from Hindenburg-Mathesdorf, because she was always there when she was needed, and she hoped so much to be needed that sometimes she showed up in places where she really wasn't. Well, Valeska heard from her about an uproar at the high school that Josel Piontek was supposed to have been involved in. Further fragments, but likewise nothing precise, from Ingeborg Schygulla, who, under the pretext of wanting to borrow some salt, had turned up at the door. On the telephone she learned from a quavering voice, which belonged to her friend Verena, that Josel was supposed to have jumped at a teacher. From another friend she learned that he had proclaimed the revolution while brandishing a book, and if Valeska would be patient for a while, she would find out what kind of book it had been—but she didn't want to be patient.

She had to take a few drops of valerian on a lump of sugar to calm her nerves.

She believed only her brother Willi, who also provided the most exact description of the incident, and who implored her above all not to run off to the high school as she was, without hat or coat.

Through a colleague whom he had dispatched to Coselerstrasse immediately after the first rumors, he had found out that Josel Piontek had not been arrested, had not even been kept after school after the report cards had been distributed, and it seemed as if the faculty was more interested in playing down the incident and not letting it turn into a political scandal.

Valeska wasn't thinking of anything like political implications, she was only thinking about what must be going on inside a person who did such a thing, in a person she had given birth to, after all, Who was her own flesh and blood. But she didn't succeed in establishing a connection between what had been recounted to her and the face that she sometimes observed in sleep in the morning, which belonged to her son.

When Josel Piontek was called on by name and climbed the stairs to the dais, where the principal handed him his report card with a handshake, he is supposed to have bowed, saying something or other that the others didn't understand, which must have satisfied the principal thoroughly, for he shook Josel's hand longer than those of the other students. Walking away, Josel is supposed to have turned back and loudly asked the principal and the faculty behind him whether he was permitted to put a question to the principal. And the principal had even been pleased and had called out "yes, of course," and then Josel asked his question, by now somewhat excited and speaking more softly, so that none of his fellow students understood him, and not all of the teachers either. Then the principal, perhaps one of the teachers, too, is supposed to have said "louder, please," and then suddenly Josel spoke so loudly that they all understood him, his fellow students below and the faculty up on the stage, even Bulla, the half-deaf mathematics teacher. Indeed, it was supposed to have sounded almost like a scream: "Do you like Dostoevski?"

And so loudly that the principal involuntarily pulled back, not just with his head but with his whole body. And then Josel is supposed to have jumped at him and pulled on his ear. According to another version Willi Wondrak claimed to have heard, he had seized the principal by the ear and had bit him on the nose. There had been quite an uproar after that, the teachers were finally able to pull Josel off him. One of them is supposed to have hit him in the face; in any case, his nose was bleeding, just like the principal's, who stood in the background patting his face with his handkerchief for quite a while, after everything had quieted down, while Bulla, the mathematics teacher, handed out the rest of the report cards. And Josel, his arms pinned by two teachers, had followed the rest of the proceedings after that quite peacefully from his corner, as if nothing unusual had happened. He had been allowed to go home with the

others, too. The principal had sworn again and again that he did
not want to press charges against a student, particularly not one with
such outstanding grades, and he considered the whole affair as a
pardonable overreaction on the part of someone who lost control
of himself before the end of the school term because of intensive
studying.

Josel was urged to explain himself and to apologize to the principal,
which he did finally do, after some hesitation, because his homeroom
teacher Skowronnek made it clear to him that the matter could have
political consequences, since the principal was a Party member. Josel
declared himself prepared to do so and added something to the
general apology that was received with perplexity but with no objection, namely, *that anyone who did not like Dostoevski was sick and
was suffering from freezing of the heart*.

Where on earth did the boy get that, Valeska thought—the part
about freezing of the heart.

Now they were waiting dinner for him. Lucie (Widera) had already
heated the plates over the gas for the third time. Irma wanted to
wait in her room until Josel came; she remembered that he had
disappeared once before, and what a commotion that had caused,
and now in her condition, she didn't want to go through it again.

Willi Wondrak was already sitting at the table, tying one knot
after the other in the fringe of the tablecloth. In secret he did fear
that the whole affair might grow into a political case, after all. This
evening he wanted to call up the district leader, just in case. Considering Josel's youth, he would probably get him off, but it wouldn't
be easy.

Valeska couldn't stand to look at her brother's fidgety hands and
the restlessness on his face any longer, and she turned her back to
him. She watered the flowers in the window nervously, although
she had already watered them in the morning.

Finally Josel walked in through the door as if nothing had happened, and put his report card on the piano as if it were some
document that concerned all the rest of them, but not him. He could
tell by their faces that they must have heard about the incident at
school, although it was unclear from whom and how much. In any
case, he wasn't going to bring up the subject.

He sat down at the table, and Mamuscha served the soup with a somewhat reproachful face, which he ignored. When Irma came and sat down, he enjoyed the silence of the others for a moment, but he sensed that they were just waiting for an explanation.

"You probably all think I'm *plemplem*," he finally said, "but I'm not."

His mother certainly wasn't, she was clear and direct in everything. And Uncle Willi wasn't either; for him every weekday passed like every other, only Sundays were different for him, but even a Sunday was like every other Sunday, at least as far as Josel could tell. Maybe Irma had been *plemplem* at one time, but ever since she had been hanging on to that Skrobek, always wanting to make babies with him, you couldn't call her that anymore. Papusch was the only one who had really been *plemplem*, but to Josel's sorrow he hadn't noticed that until it was too late and he could no longer tell him.

While Valeska sawed at the tough roast beef and her gaze shifted back and forth between the knife and Josel's eyes, she thought: Why Dotsoyevski, of all people? Her son was at an age where she could no longer prescribe what he was to read, and he paid absolutely no heed to Willi, whom he had listened to for a long time. On the other hand she was glad that Josel read so much, since he had shown no desire to play the piano. Sometimes she had read the authors and titles of the books in his room, and was surprised, because most of them meant nothing to her. Young people read quite different books nowadays than she had in her youth, and that was probably just as well. At his age she had read Eichendorff and Gustav Freytag and Wilhelm Raabe; and the book about the fat man who had been a glutton in his youth and therefore was called Stuffcake had pleased her the most. But for many years now she had not gone beyond reading *The Upper Silesian Wanderer*, the Michaelmas Calendar, and the Petrus Newsletter. But she intended to read this Dotsoyevski now, if it was true that her son had attacked the principal of the high school on his account, although she was pretty sure that this Dotsoyevski wouldn't be much to her liking.

Valeska looked at the others, who were wielding their utensils embarrassedly and too loudly, as if in some way or other they had been participants in the incident. "What was the connection," she asked, "I mean, the principal . . . I mean, what does that have to do with this Dotsoyevski?"

She scrutinized the white tablecloth intently, as if she perceived in it a secret, not yet discernible pattern.

Lucie brought in the dessert in a big bowl: pickled pumpkin, which she had refined with some Milei-W. She had beaten it with a whisk until her hand hurt, but it hadn't produced much foam.

Helping himself liberally to the pumpkin, Willi thought: Actually, that was quite a stroke on our Josel's part, quite a stroke. To jump at the principal while report cards are being handed out and bite him on the nose! Maybe someday the boy will amount to something . . . if only the principal were not in the Party! He regretted always having behaved in his own school days. Now, as an attorney, he was a kind of principal himself. He gave speeches and handed out report cards, defended and accused, publicly and privately, and hid behind what he had learned was the law—but there was another man somewhere within him who applauded inwardly anyone who broke loose. He wouldn't be surprised if someday someone came along and bit *him* on the nose.

In his school days—and this he could remember quite accurately—he had ignited the paper stored in the boiler room, and the whole west wing of the school had gone up in flames, and he was the one who had rescued valuable historical objects from the burning building, such as the old globe, for which he was later awarded a certificate. This document hung framed in his law office—his guilt had remained undiscovered to this day.

"*Fantastichnek!*" He used Josel's favorite expression and poked him with his elbow. "Why did you ask about Dostoevski, of all people —couldn't it have been some other author? When we're at war with the Russians?"

And Irma thought, while going quickly back to her room to check on her child, who had fallen asleep: Ever since Josel ran away that time, Mamuscha lets him get away with murder, he can do anything he wants to, as long as he stays at home. But she won't be able to excuse so lightly what has happened now. Sure, she'll dream up some kind of excuse for him, that's true, like back then at my wedding with Heiko—she didn't want to think about that anymore. That's just the way Mamuscha is, she lives in this world and at the same time she doesn't. To this day Irma didn't comprehend how adeptly her mother juggled this, and she didn't know whether she should be astonished or indignant about how little her mother was cognizant of this reality, at the same time warping it to her own ends. And she always stretched it farther than the others.

She, at any rate, was of the opinion that Dostoevski was not exactly the appropriate pretext for attacking a high school principal, and thus the highest authority.

When she came back from her room, she wondered, who is this principal, anyway? You see him maybe once a year, and, as far as I've heard, ever since Stalingrad he doesn't run around in his Party uniform anymore. You should have jumped Przybillok instead, he's been picking on you for years in German class!

And Lucie (Widera) thought, as her gaze strayed disapprovingly from one plate to the next: Has everyone here gone crazy? They sit there talking about whether they should tear this man's ear off or bite that one on the nose, as if it were the most ordinary thing in the world to attack an authority figure of the first rank, like the high school principal. They sit there and discuss an incredible incident as if it had not occurred right here in this town, but somewhere far away among the Hottentots. They should thank their lucky stars that Josel is allowed to be sitting here at the table with them at all, and not at the police station or in some prison cell, where they would chain him to the iron bed as a threat to society . . . She, in any case, would not have been surprised if they had turned him over to the madhouse at Tost.

She let the pumpkin dissolve slowly on her tongue and observed Josel very closely out of the corner of her eye to see whether he would reveal his madness in any of his reactions. What must be going on inside of a person like that? she wondered.

Josel was trying to piece together all that had happened. When I walked up on the stage, I wasn't thinking of anything bad; it didn't start until the principal shook my hand: some kind of an impulse that was emitted by that fleshy, hairy hand and transferred itself to me and filled me with a sudden rush of revulsion against everything, and strongest against this man. I remembered a story by Dostoevski;

that is, I didn't remember it, it was inside of me because I had been living it for days. Just like that official in his hole of a cellar, I paced back and forth in my room, and decided not to do any more studying and just wait until I get called up and sent to the front, where maybe I'll get a head wound, and if I'm not dead on the spot, then I'll be mad, a moron for my whole life, doltish, retarded. I couldn't get it out of my mind . . . people are all so busy because they're mad, doltish, retarded, and want to make themselves forget it with all their busyness. That's why I wanted to feel the debasement, no, in Dostoevski it's the *enjoyment* of debasement, at least I wanted to try it, and resolved simply to run into Uncle Willi, for instance, when he was coming home from court or from his office, so hard that he would fall down, and then be cursed by him, or Herr Apitt, or Countess Hohenlohe when Aunt Milka came pushing her along in her wheelchair, or scare one of our teachers at school in the hall— but at the last instant I always stepped aside, like the official steps aside from the old Russian general. I once ran into a total stranger on the streetcar, ran my head into his belly. But in the end he apologized to me, because he must have thought he caused the collision when the streetcar braked suddenly—yes, he was the one who begged pardon from me, and I'm only a student!

Up there on the stage, all at once the principal seemed to me to be the kind of person I had to run at, even in the awareness that I would smash my head, and if I named Dostoevski when I did it, then the other would have to understand right there why I was doing it and that I was obliged to do it, and so I yelled at him and when he moved, I jumped at him and bit him on the nose.

That's the way it was.

But what should I answer to Mamuscha, Irma, Uncle Willi, Aunt Lucie (Widera), who expect an explanation from me? No matter what I say to them, they'll never understand. No, that would only leave them more confused than ever. He could scarcely understand himself as the person he had been at that moment.

"I think I just couldn't stand these times anymore," he said to himself, but loud enough so the others could hear it. "Everybody's talking about the war, but except that we read about it in the newspapers and have to pay attention to blackouts, and more and more people are coming here from the Reich because they're being bombed there but not here, we don't even notice that there's a war on . . ."

They listened to Josel, as if struck dumb.

And Josel continued, louder: "I'm already drafted and now I'm being called up; I'm not afraid of getting in some battle in Russia, I can't change that, nobody can. But do you know what I'm afraid of"—and now he turned directly to his mother—"I'm afraid of getting a head wound and not being dead on the spot, maybe even living on, but like a moron!"

Aunt Lucie (Widera) was the first to regain her composure, and she started to clear the table. She did so as matter-of-factly as possible, and in this confusion she wanted her question understood just as matter-of-factly: "Tell me, young man, what is going on inside of you? You are sinning before God when you talk like that!"

Valeska got up from the table and began to help her.

"But really, Joselek, you can't have gotten all that from this Dotsoyevski?"

Josel took two cigarettes from his pack; he had been eighteen for three months and since then had been eligible for a tobacco ration card. He had twenty-four cigarettes for the week—twenty-three, because he offered one to Uncle Willi.

"Just imagine, Uncle Willi," he said, "something like that happening to me. That's what it is—the fear it'll happen to me hits me so hard that sometimes I have to do something crazy just to prove to myself that I'm still perfectly normal."

"I'm not quite sure," Willi Wondrak said, and divided the cigarette in two; he would smoke the other half later. "You think up some, well . . . very strange, very odd things." He spoke gently, as if to someone who was no longer of sound mind.

"I don't know," Josel said, "if I'm only thinking it up. I'm simply afraid of it. I can't do anything about it. I wake up in the morning, lie in bed like I'm paralyzed, thinking: it's almost time now . . ."

"I will pray for you," Lucie said softly. "You are not in God's grace . . . when you talk like that."

Josel shivered. "Stop it, Aunt Lucie. You've all acted like you were paralyzed for years. Maybe you don't notice it anymore . . . You, Uncle Willi"—and Josel's voice grew fanatic—"you used to drive away all the time, somewhere every weekend, just to get away from here, out of this hole, because you didn't want to put up with what was happening here, but I see what they've been making of you, they've clipped your wings, all the women in this house!"

Lucie carried some dishes into the kitchen. Irma made use of the opportunity to vanish from the room with her; she wasn't supposed to get excited for any reason, and didn't want to. Valeska began to sneeze, a nervous sneezing that wouldn't stop.

"I don't believe you're right, Josel," Willi said, still just as gentle and forbearing as before, but his hand was trembling.

"You think I don't see how you're suffering," Josel said heatedly. "You're not the man you used to be, admit it! Since you moved in here, and ever since Mamuscha has been babbling about this marriage, something must have happened. *Pjerunnje*, why don't you want to tell me what really happened?"

Valeska gathered up everything she had in the way of maternal authority (and admittedly it wasn't very much), brushed the hair from her forehead, and said in a nasal voice: "That's none of your business, my son. It concerns only my brother Willi and Fräulein Rosa Willimczyk, not even me, and everyone just has to respect that, don't they. You have to admit that your uncle Willi is long overdue in getting married, and Fräulein Willimczyk is an educated person, she's read more than all of us put together—I'll ask her whether you got all that from this Dotsoyevski . . ."

Willi Wondrak puffed on his cigarette, almost burning his lips. It embarrassed him that his sister was speaking for him; on the other hand, what else could he have said?

"I consider you old enough, Josel, to trust you with the truth, but sometimes it's not the time for the truth, or we ourselves don't know where the truth is to be found. I'm just telling you that it really is good and right that I marry Fräulein Rosa."

"I wish," Josel said between his teeth, "that you had the courage to bite a certain person on the nose, then you would be spared quite a lot."

Willi looked over at his sister.

"And as far as the war is concerned," Wondrak continued unmoved, "I too could be drafted any day, they're calling in almost everyone now ... and who knows who'll come back from there. Let's talk about it then, after the war."

Josel gestured impatiently, but he said nothing. *Afterthewar*, he had heard that all too often, for four years now; who knows who among them would even live to see it. Everything was postponed for *afterthewar*. Even the truth.

Lucie (Widera) was standing in the doorway, hiding her hands under her apron. She had heard the bad news. She swallowed hard. Somewhere, hidden in a corner of her heart, she had harbored a hope that the lawyer would marry her, simply because he could use an efficient housekeeper. Oh, she wasn't fooling herself, naturally Fräulein Willimczyk was an educated person, as a bookseller she could read as many books as she wanted to, but the attorney had enough educated people among his colleagues. What he was lacking was an efficient, inconspicuous housekeeper, and she was certainly much better suited for that. She was not jealous, no, that she was not. Perhaps a little disappointed. Jealousy, that was a sin, and she practically never sinned anymore. The older she got, the less there was for her to confess. Sometimes she invented a few venial sins, just so she would have something to say to the pastor in the confessional. She didn't want to disappoint him, after all.

Valeska went to the piano and picked up the report card, which no one had dared to touch until now. It was as if she were returning to reality with this piece of paper. Valeska read it, and her brother looked at it over her shoulder.

"We have to drink to this," she said, while she was still reading. "Josel has brought home such a good report card." She was proud of her son, but she was unable to be happy.

"Maybe there's one more bottle of champagne in the cellar," Willi Wondrak said, "then we'll have a toast!" He knew very well that there was no champagne in the cellar, because he had conducted a thorough search in vain several times.

"I'll go get the glasses," said Lucie, relieved, and went into the hall, where tableware for especially festive occasions was kept in a wall cupboard.

Valeska Piontek looked at her son, then she walked over to him and put an arm around his shoulders: "I would just like to know," she said gently now, "what it is you've learned from this Dotso-yevski?"

"Ach, Mama," Josel said, pushing her arm off. "Don't keep calling him Dotsoyevski!"

20

Hʀᴀʙɪɴsᴋʏ ᴄᴏᴜʟᴅ ᴀʟᴡᴀʏs be found where something was going on; as a cripple, he had plenty of time on his hands. Most recently he could be seen almost anywhere, sitting on a little chair, and when he got too bored, also paging through a newspaper. The government insurance had provided him with a wooden prosthesis —just recently, enormous progress was being made in orthopedics —so that he no longer had to walk with his crutch and strap on that peg leg. But walking with the prosthesis was an effort for him, and forced him to rest frequently. For this purpose he had designed a folding chair for himself, from canvas and dowels, that could be carried comfortably under the arm.

The first two bells had already been lowered and loaded on a truck; now it was the turn of the biggest bell, the Bell of Hedwig. To observe this properly, he had already had to set up his chair at various spots, because people kept blocking his view. He didn't know most of them who stood in his way, big and dark. Where did they all come from, anyway? *Pónbóczku*, it's as bad as a dedication of a new church!

Hrabinsky had painted Hʀᴀʙɪɴsᴋʏ on the back of his folding chair in big letters because in a newsreel he had once seen Veit Harlan sitting in a chair like that, directing hundreds of extras on a Prague street set with a big funnel in front of his mouth; that had impressed him. He also owned a sun visor like Harlan wore on his forehead. But today, when the clouds were scudding across the sky and only letting a sunbeam through here and there, sunglasses were enough. You had to keep your eye on the bells constantly, for when something happened, it would be fast, and he hadn't come here just to miss the disaster. After all, what if the rope snapped . . . ! That would be a big event for the town.

He could scarcely do without his folding chair anymore, it was so immensely practical. He took it to Schachtner's delicatessen and sat down in line when there were special allotments of rice flakes or beet syrup. As a cripple he didn't have to wait in line, of course, but he didn't want any special treatment, not during the war, no, and besides, he liked talking to people. He opened up his chair on the streetcar, and in church when the pews were full—and the longer the war lasted, the fuller the churches were. He had even shown up for pilgrimages with his chair, but also at Homeland Day in Gogolin and at the sports regionals of the Silesian HY, at which Gauleiter Wagner had personally shaken his hand.

He no longer needed his cane for support, but rather as a weapon. In his opinion, too much riffraff was hanging around the town— Poles, Ukrainians, Gypsies, and Negroes. No genuine German could be safe from them.

Whenever someone said that he had never seen a Negro in town, that the Jews were all gone, and that soon there would be no more Gypsies either, then Hrabinsky would reply crossly that Ukrainians, Poles, and Negroes were all the same and besides, there wouldn't be fewer thieves when there was nothing left to steal.

Hrabinsky was the kind of person who was always enthusiastic about one thing and contemptuous of another. The object might change, but the passions remained. He could get involved in a pilgrimage to the Annaberg in the same way that he worked his way along Wilhelmstrasse with a collection can for Winter Aid. With an ardent voice he sang in the Rorate masses at Advent:

> *Drop down dew, ye heavens, from above,*
> *And let the clouds rain the just;*
> *Let the earth be opened*
> *And bud forth a Saviour.*

And at the community potluck on Reichspräsidentenplatz, he linked arms with the mayor as well as with Herr Helling, the chairman of the Southwest Africa Association:

> *You Upper Silesian homeland,*
> *You country of rustling woods,*

How gaily the silvery ribbon,
The Oder, adorns the fields.

And when they had arrested a group of alleged Communists at Oberhütten, he had laid in wait for them before police headquarters on Teuchertstrasse, and had struck them in the face with his crutch and yelled: "Down with the Red Front!"

Now he took his crutch and pushed away the people who were blocking his view. He didn't want to give up his good spot to a Schönwald farmer's wife who was pushing forward in her starched and embroidered cap, her mouth wide open in curiosity and wonder.

He caught sight of Valeska Piontek, who was inspecting the whole square slowly and curiously. She's running around today like the poorest miner's widow, he thought. At Easter he himself used to let the rich Jews on his street give him something that they weren't wearing anymore because it was out of fashion. But now the Jews in family ghettos had been resettled in Poland, the last of them only yesterday. Naturally, he had been there. All the Jews were supposed to be gone now, except for old Justice Kochmann, who had been honorary citizen of the town even before 1933; you couldn't deport him so easily. He had felt sorry for them, the Jews, the way they walked bent over and woebegone through the gate from Niederwallstrasse, each with one suitcase and two blankets; they weren't permitted to take any more, he had heard. He had recognized Dr. Blumenfeld, Herr Weissenberg, and Herr Karpe from the laundry on the Ring only at the last moment, because they had looked so changed—gaunt, pale, their clothes threadbare.

Frau Piontek hadn't even had her hair done, Hrabinsky thought. After all, you can still get a wet wave without ration stamps. The business with Halina must really have affected her. Other than that, God knows, she's got no reason to grieve: a widow for four years now, and the real estate agency that she started with her brother is supposed to be flourishing, all the way into the Kattowitz region.

In his mind he lined up a few questions that he had long wanted to ask Frau Piontek, but then she moved off in another direction.

It was the wife of the locomotive engineer Ossadnik who was waving to Frau Piontek with broad gestures.

Not a soul would know who this Frau Ossadnik was if she were not the mother of that Ulla, the child prodigy! How something like that could grow up in this town! Strange . . . Recently she even appeared in a concert and charmed the people with her piano playing, and she's only eighteen years old! It was even in the newspaper. She still looked good, this Frau Ossadnik, and even though her husband was only an engineer, she was always dressed smartly, except for those awful scarves.

He didn't want to watch the two women exchange greetings, he would rather keep reading his newspaper. He was already reading the article about Katyn for the second time. What terrible things were going on in the world. He sucked on his cold pipe. He didn't have a crumb of tobacco left, and he had already swapped half of his clothing stamps for tobacco. He could do without a new shirt, but not without smoking. Maybe Frau Fleissner would advance him a small pouch of tobacco against his May ration card. Otherwise it would be a long Holy Week.

"Have you seen my daughter Helga, by any chance?" Schachtner, the delicatessen owner, asked the cripple.

"You'll find everybody here on the square," Hrabinsky said magnanimously, "you'll find your daughter here too. But listen here, have you read this?" He slapped the newspaper: "The massacre of Katyn? The Bolsheviks killed twelve thousand Polish officers, with the typical GPU shot in the neck, and buried them in mass graves near Smolensk. And the Polish Red Cross is there, Herr Gorcycki, Herr Skracynski, and Herr Lachert, so it must be true and not just propaganda. Want me to read some of it to you?" And before Herr Schachtner could object, Hrabinsky started to read: "Here it is . . .

> *"On the basis of the examination of three hundred bodies exhumed to date, it has been established that these officers were murdered by pistol shots in the back of the neck. Execution by professionally trained executioners can be deduced by the typical uniformity of the wounds.*

Third: The victims showed no signs of a struggle; the dead are still dressed in uniforms and boots, and are still wearing their decorations, and considerable amounts of Polish money were found on the murder victims.

Fourth: It must be concluded from the papers and documents found on the bodies that the murders took place approximately in the months of March and April 1940 . . ."

Hrabinsky looked up from the newspaper: "How could it be possible? What kind of people could do that, put a bullet in somebody's neck. Can you understand it? Well, that's more than a person can understand. No, a people who can do something like that must be damned!" Hrabinsky fumed.

Herr Schachtner scanned the article himself. "Terrible," he said, after reading it. "But I have to go find my Helga, she's running after Anton Ossadnik, you know what a skirt chaser he is."

21

ANDY OSSADNIK WAS in no mood to argue, not at noontime, and certainly not on Good Friday. And definitely not with this swollen eye. Besides, he was pretty sure that the oldest and largest bell in town was in the Church of All Saints, because it was the oldest church in town, and St. Peter and Paul wasn't built until around the turn of the century. All the bells here were relatively new, except for this one, which was supposed to have belonged to All Saints once; he had learned that it had been taken as booty by the Danes in the Thirty Years' War, but the wheels of their cart had broken under the weight of the bell, so they had to leave it behind. This bell was then later presented by All Saints to the Peter and Paul Church upon its dedication. Andy had heard this earlier in the Don Bosco League from Curate Mikas, and Tex Weber must know it too, but for some time he had been interested in nothing but the U-boat war; he pasted up entire fleets from cut-out books and collected every newspaper clipping about his idol, corvette captain Prien, the victor of Scapa Flow, and he attempted to create something like a marine HY platoon with ten other boys in Bann 22.

"The bell! Here it comes!" shouted Hrabinsky. Everybody looked up. If you looked closely, you could see that the rope hanging down from the tower window was now stretched taut and even vibrating with the tension. In the tower window the outer side of a bell was visible. The whispering on the church square grew softer and ebbed away. Quite slowly and with small jerks, as if being pushed by invisible hands, the bell slid farther and farther out the tower window, until it was suddenly visible in all its immensity. Even at this height it still looked huge; for Andy, who had never seen it before, it was absolutely majestic. Most of the spectators on the church square had never seen this bell before, but looking at it they could imagine that in the four bell tones of Peter and Paul, which all of them believed they could still remember clearly, *this* was the bell with the darkly admonishing, booming tone. For a few seconds it seemed as if the

bell were hovering in the air, then it was released from the tower
crane with a little jerk and was taken up by the rope of the block
and tackle. It swung very slightly, so slightly that the clapper didn't
even strike the metal, which the people had probably been expecting.
There were also some among them who hoped that the rope would
snap and the bell plunge to the ground. And a few were even praying
for it. But although the bell now truly hovered "between heaven
and earth," as it says in the hymn, minute by minute it was coming
a bit closer to the earth.

Andy remembered a ballad that his grandmother had taught him.
He wondered if he could still piece the whole thing together. "Do
any of you know the 'Ballad of the Bell Casting in Breslau'?" And
without waiting for a reply, he began:

> *"There once was a bell caster*
> *at Breslau in the town,*
> *skilled at what he thought and wrought*
> *a master well renowned.*

> *"Many bells he'd cast by then,*
> *some yellow and some white,*
> *all for the church and chapel,*
> *God's glory and delight."*

Tex didn't know this one at all. And it was no use talking to him
about it anymore either; he'd just keep saying "insane" and coming
up with the craziest words in the world.

Andy knew that Breslau had previously been known for its bell
casters; bells from there had been sent to Cologne and Munich and
Amsterdam and over half the world. You didn't learn this kind of
thing in school, either. But his grandmother in Turawa, she knew
half the *Ballad Treasury* by heart.

"So, do you know the rest?" asked Andy.

"Well, it sounds familiar," said Tex from up in the tree. "I know
the first verse too, say it again."

"The heck you do," said Andy, reciting further:

> *"And so full, so clear, so pure*
> *the master's bells do ring,*

> *for the master cast as well*
> *his love and faith within."*

Then he was stuck. "Come on," he said to Bronder, "let's go up front, maybe there's more to see up there." He didn't want to have to tell Tex Weber that he didn't know any more verses . . .

"I know another verse," Bronder said, "but I don't know where it goes.

> *"Yet of all the bells he'd cast*
> *the one which is the crown*
> *that is the bell of sinners*
> *at Breslau in the town."*

They never got all the way up to the church. But if Herr Hrabinsky wouldn't mind getting up from his folding chair for a moment, then they would be able to see what was happening. The cripple stood up willingly, first placing his newspaper on the seat. There was nothing to see except the two trucks, on which two bells were already lashed down with ropes, and the workmen handling the block and tackle and shouting orders to each other. Most important, no priest had made an appearance, not even an acolyte.

"I know some more," said Kotik.

"Some more what?" asked Andy.

"Some more of the ballad.

> *"In Magdalena's Tower*
> *his masterpiece is hung,*
> *and soon many stubborn hearts*
> *back to their God are won.*

> *"Has not the noble master*
> *his work in truth conceived!*
> *His fingers moving day and night*
> *Without a moment's leave.*

> *"And when the hour approaches*
> *when everything is done,*
> *then . . . then . . .*

"I don't remember any more."

Hrabinsky had listened in at the end. "I can't help you out either," he said, disappointed. "When I was in school, we had no time for things like that. We only learned hymns by heart, and I know a lot of those." He wanted to start in on one: " 'The Lord shall I praise . . .' "

"I learned it once myself," said a man next to them. "That's 'The Bell Casting in Breslau,' by . . . by . . . isn't it, yes, we learned it in school, a beautiful ballad."

Another man broke in. "Learned and forgotten," he said, "learned and forgotten. That's the way it is in life. 'Then he calls . . . his . . . boy . . .' Isn't that how it goes? Yes, of course:

> *"The master called his helper*
> *to come and watch the fire:*
> *'While I am gone be certain*
> *it flare not nor expire.*
>
> *" 'I wish to take a drink now*
> *for strength to shape the ore.*
> *For only a liquid meal*
> *can mime the perfect pour.' "*

And Kotik recited along with him:

> *" 'Tend the fire carefully*
> *and never touch the tap*
> *for it will mean your life if*
> *you're such a silly chap.' "*

Now other listeners joined in. Andy noticed the bookseller, Fräulein Willimczyk; that is, he heard her voice growing louder and louder, for she wanted as many people as possible to be astounded at her literary knowledge:

> *"The boy stood by the cauldron*
> *and watched the glowing beast*
> *unruly, boiling, bubbling,*
> *it wants to be released.*

"It hisses in his eardrums;
his mind is turned to sap.
Relentlessly his fingers
are drawn toward the tap."

Andy made a movement with his head and the three boys vanished from the center of the circle. He had seen his mother with the piano teacher, Frau Piontek; he didn't want to run into them. And besides, the crowd had started to bother him. So it was almost better to shoot the breeze with Tex Weber or climb a tree, where you could get an *insanely* better view of everything.

Andy held one hand in front of his swollen eye, partly to protect it and partly because it hurt. He ought to have put on an eye patch; besides, you looked pretty interesting with one of those on. It's true that a black eye looked like a defeat, while an eye patch looked like a victory. Hadn't that Lord Nelson always worn an eye patch? Anyway, it was one of those naval heroes. He would go to the Easter High Mass with an eye patch on, even if the swelling had subsided by then. The shiner would last a while yet at least. Easter with an eye patch!

Andy and Bronder stopped. They looked at the bell and at the rope and down at the block and tackle. They were straining to see something, as if they had to decide about something that had to do with the distance and the men and the rope, and certainly with the bell too.

"There's nothing to be done," Bronder said pensively after a while.

And Andy, who had no doubt thought the same thing, said, "There is *absolutnik* nothing to be done."

"I've got it," said Kotik, who the whole time had been thinking about how the rest of the ballad went. "Now I know how it goes."

"So tell us," said Andy, "and don't keep us in suspense!"

"As his fingers touched the tap
he felt it turning on.
It made him scared and anxious,
he knew not what he'd done.

"He ran out to his master
to him his guilt confessed
falling down upon his knees
da-dum-da-dum don't know this line

"And as the boy was speaking,
regretful of the harm,
rose up in sudden anger
the master's good right arm.

"The master plunged his knifepoint
into the young boy's breast,
then hurried to the cauldron,
unknowing in his quest.

"The boy would work no more now,
his body cold to touch.
O master, wicked master,
you push yourself too much."

"Jeez," said Andy, "how do you know all that? Do you know the whole ballad by heart?" He could see that he had underestimated his quiet brother. Well, naturally, he buries himself in books just like Mother! But she doesn't read anything but those idiotic fantasy novels! *"Pieron!"* he said in admiration.

From behind a black triangle that turned out to be an old granny with kerchief, shawl, and thick skirts, Wonzak suddenly appeared. "Ach, you holy sack of straw," he said as he saw Squintok from the front, "you look terrible!"

From the back, Squintok had looked much more like himself than he did from the front. But it *was* Squintok, as his voice proved to Wonzak. "They didn't catch *you* anyway!" Andy said.

Andy was glad about that. He had to assume it was true because Wonzak didn't have a scratch on his face or a speck of dirt on his shirt.

"So what happened to you?" Wonzak stuttered. Hannes Stein appeared behind him; he had to suppress his surprise at first too, and he wiped the back of his hand across his damp mouth.

"I sacrificed myself," Andy said nonchalantly.

"You should have run away with us." Hannes Stein pushed closer to him. "We ditched the Lutherans by the allotment gardens. We just know our way around in that area better, don't we?"

"I stayed to fight them so they wouldn't get all of us," said Andy.

They didn't have to believe him, he just wanted them to take a look at him—that's why he took his hand away from his eye—so they would have some idea of what they had been spared.

"They outnumbered us," he said. He shrugged his shoulders. "But I managed to keep all my teeth, that's the main thing." He laughed as he said it and drew back his lips so the whiteness gleamed. For him that was really the most important thing, because he was as proud of his smooth, blinding white teeth as his brother Tonik was of his hair.

Wonzak and Hannes were impressed. Only now did they realize what could have happened to them. Even all three of them would have been no match for that superior force.

"It was a mistake on our part," said Andy, "to show up with three *pierons* in front of that evacuee camp. If we'd had our old *ferajna*— sure, but who knows?"

Wonzak nodded enthusiastically to Andy. If it were up to him, he would revive the old *ferajna*. But he'd never get it back together without Squintok.

"You defended yourself!" said Hannes admiringly, inspecting every single wound and scrape, from his head to his knees.

But Andy didn't want to play the hero. "I did not!" he said firmly. "I just wanted to stall them. I knew that if they took out their rage on me they wouldn't follow you guys any farther."

Of course that wasn't true. But somehow it was true even so.

"I only protected my face," he said. "The thing with the eye happened earlier, when I got hit by a rock."

"And your glasses?" asked Wonzak.

Andy only made a gesture of disdain. "I don't squint anymore! Kotik—where'd Kotik go?"

"He's taking the ballad book out from the Borromäus Library, no doubt; he wants to know exactly how it goes, and then he'll read it out loud to us! I know him," said Wonzak.

22

"THEY'RE TAKING US to the freight yard," Karpe said, "back over there, I can already see it. Can you make it, Herr Silbergleit?"

"Yes, I can," he hastened to say. He could stand it for a while longer, if the pain didn't get worse. He didn't want to be beaten by the kapos.

"I'll make sure that we get in the same car," Karpe said. "Then we can be of assistance to each other. It'll be a long way to Riga; we've probably got some difficulties in store for us, I'm afraid."

Now he too had said Riga, Silbergleit thought.

Nobody knows about the hiding place in the cellar except Herr Kochmann and me and he wouldn't have told me either but he needed someone to help him with it and young Aaron Brauer knew about it too he crawled in through the hole and stayed in there a long time

there was so much to see

you must save the battery it's the last one we have

a golden menorah that sparkles and the Torah the embroidered silk cloth

a little boy named Aaron Szalit runs out of the ghetto into the world

one day I will stay in the hiding place and never come out again I'll wall up the hole behind me with bricks and you must promise me to pile up the old crates in front of it no one will find me then

by the time they come to look for me the mortar will have set I'm not going along when they send us to the ghetto in Lublin I don't know what Lublin is but I know what Gleiwitz is and so I will stay in my hiding place until another time comes

how the boy talks he's not even fourteen and how he talks

"Did you see little Aaron?"

"Who?"

"Aaron Brauer—you know."

When they reached the freight yard, the kapos suddenly began to yell and flail blindly at the Jews with their sticks. They drove them along a wire fence, and up a ramp. It was as if they wanted to spread an atmosphere of fear, so that no one would attempt to flee in the tangle of tracks and idle trains. But no one was trying to flee. They struggled up the steps to the platform with their baggage. An old woman stumbled and fell, the others trampled over her, screaming and praying, and clutching their baggage. Karpe and Silbergleit helped the old woman to her feet and dragged her to the platform, another Jew brought her torn cardboard box, stuffed with rags. The woman was not crying. She sank to the ground next to her cardboard box, her hair disheveled, her coat filthy, staring blankly into space.

A long freight train was waiting at the platform; the locomotive not visible because the front of the train disappeared around a curve. Faces were pressed against the slats of the cars and hands were sticking out. Only in the last four cars were the sliding doors open.

The SS men began to count the Jews and channel them into the cattle cars, and when these were full, they kept on jamming more and more people into them, backed up by the kapos with their sticks. In the end five people were left over, and an SS man ordered two of the forward cars to be opened to make space for them there.

Silbergleit and Karpe were standing close to each other; they wanted to be in the same car. When the sliding door was rolled open in front of them, they looked into a heap of human bodies; a stench of urine and chlorine that took their breath away hit them, and then they were shoved in by the kapos. They fell over the bodies, and while the door rolled shut with a screech, they crept on all fours looking for some free space.

then the jasmine had faded in summer I went to the cemetery on Leipziger Strasse and Herr Kotzur sometimes gave us lettuce to take along little radishes how long it's been since I've seen anything like that a green apple yes always on foot we aren't permitted to take the streetcar yes the hill by the Hindenburg Bridge is hard for me my heart I kept that from you the trouble with my heart in the front garden why did I everywhere the jasmine is blooming spreading its fragrance

at eight in the evening we have to be back in our apartments after that we cannot go outside I saw the way you were waiting with the jasmine in your arms

I couldn't hear you

don't come back again it's better that way

don't come back again

no one knows where we are going a curse rests upon us Good Friday that's what day it is I didn't know that today was Good Friday this fragrance of jasmine

There was only dim light in the freight car so that Silbergleit could make out nothing at first. He groped his way between the bodies until at some point he found a gap into which he could at least stuff his blankets. Then he sat down. Next to him someone was cursing in a language he didn't understand. He excused himself softly, but remained sitting where he was. He had lost sight of Karpe, and he was too exhausted to call to him. A child began to cry and was comforted by its mother.

An elderly voice next to him called out a few words to her. The language sounded like Dutch to Silbergleit, but he didn't dare to ask. He felt a hand touching him. The elderly voice had probably meant him.

"Pardon me," he said again, and tried to focus. From the half light emerged the figure of an elderly woman with a black hat on her head; she was sitting on the floor, leaning against a suitcase.

"Where do you come from?" the woman asked in pure, slightly nasal German.

"From Gleiwitz," Silbergleit said.

"Where's that?" the woman asked.

Silbergleit explained. He saw her more clearly now. The hat was the most striking thing about her, perhaps because she was wearing it in such surroundings. A bird's wing of starched silk was affixed to the front of it, giving her an air of elegance, if not sophistication. The black dress also contributed to this, its collar held together by a fastening of three silver rings. On her left breast was a yellow star, on which he could read the word *Jood*. She had sharp, almost masculine features, with slightly slanted, deep-set eyes. He guessed her age at sixty, but seen in normal light, she might be a few years older. She held a handkerchief to her nose and removed it only when she spoke.

She translated for the others what Silbergleit had said. Now questions flew at him from all sides: how many Jews had joined them, and were they all Polish Jews?

Silbergleit told them that they were German Jews from Silesia, who had been assembled here in the prison in Kattowitz. About two hundred, by his count.

"There are about two thousand of us," the woman said. "All of us Jews from Holland. Exactly one week ago we left the camp at Drente-Westerbork. Two thousand Jews at once, all with the yellow star. I've never seen so many Jews at once."

She leaned back and wiped her face with the handkerchief. She was thinking about how they had marched to the train station, guarded by police and dogs, in a long column, and how they had been stuffed into freight cars like cattle. It had taken a long time for her to realize what was going on. And actually she was still trying to evade the reality of it with memories and a perfume-soaked handkerchief.

"We spent the night waiting here, in . . . what's the name again?" the woman asked. "In Kattowitz? They switched the cars back and forth. It was cold."

"And you've been under way for a week already, in this train the whole time?" Silbergleit asked, alarmed. He couldn't imagine how they could manage for a week in such confines, in such stench.

"They push us onto sidetracks when troop transports pass through, that's why it's all taking so long," the woman said matter-of-factly. "So, you've never heard anything about the camp at Drente-Westerbork?"

She had thought that the whole world knew what was being done to the Jews at Drente-Westerbork.

Silbergleit had never heard of the place.

"How about Hilversum?"

He knew about Hilversum only from the dial on his radio. But that too was long ago. At the beginning of the war, their radios had been taken away.

"I come from Hilversum, you see," the Dutch woman said. They had owned a hotel in Hilversum, and they had leased the Hotel Lux in Zandvoort. When her husband died, she had given up the hotel in Zandvoort.

"Now I think it's good that my husband didn't have to live through all this. The hotel in Hilversum, you see, was the best in town, I had thirty employees! And the Germans took it away from me overnight."

"I was born in Gleiwitz, here in Silesia," Silbergleit said, "but I lived in Berlin for forty years. I have never been in Holland, unfortunately."

Oh, yes, she knew Berlin. They had been in Berlin a few times before 1933, and they had always gone to the Wintergarten. Her husband had loved vaudeville, you see, more than the theater. She herself had preferred going to Max Reinhardt productions at the Deutsche Theater. *A Midsummer Night's Dream* at the Circus Schumann she would never forget.

He had seen it, too. And the guest performance of Habimah in *The Dybbuk*!

Yes, with Hanna Rowina. She had seen it in Amsterdam. That had been right after the war.

They were almost lost in nostalgia, and in remembering a time that seemed light-years away, they hadn't noticed that the train was continuing on its way. Silbergleit carefully pushed over the old man who lay huddled in sleep on the other side, and sat down next to the Dutch woman. He stuffed his blankets behind his back. They sat there like that, listening to the clicking of the rails.

"Please excuse me, I haven't even introduced myself," Silbergleit said, and told her his name. "I'm a writer by profession, and I have all my published books here."

He pointed to his briefcase, which he had placed next to him, but he kept the strap wrapped around his elbow, so that no one could get the briefcase away from him unnoticed, not even when he was sleeping.

"I knew right away that you were something special," the woman said. "I could see it in your face, when you came in. And your genteel speech! You know, I'm so thankful to have the chance to talk to an educated person at last."

She was whispering from behind her handkerchief. "People just let themselves go. There's a pail with chlorine back there for the call of nature. But some of them are so apathetic they just lie there where they are, in their own urine and filth."

And as if she were just remembering this again, she opened her purse and sprayed a few drops on her handkerchief from a little bottle, and held it under her nose. She inhaled deeply. "I'm surprised the Germans say that Jews are dirty," she whispered past her handkerchief.

"I'm a German, too," Silbergleit said. "For a long time I didn't know that I'm a Jew. The Germans have made me into one again. And now I want to be one . . ." he said softly as if to himself.

And he added aloud: "I wish I could show you one of my books. But it's too dark."

Some light filtered in through the hatch in the side of the car, but too little to read by. The bigger boys had positioned themselves in front of it and were watching the landscape flying by. From time to time they called to the people in the car, telling them what they saw outside. There didn't seem to be anything unusual up to now, for the woman was listening, but didn't consider it necessary to translate anything for him.

She wanted to know whether he wrote novels.

"Poems!" Silbergleit said. "I like writing poems best, and little *Pastelle.*"

"Pardon me?" the Dutch woman asked with newly awakened interest, playing with the silver rings at her collar.

"That's what we call them in German," he said. "They're short, atmospheric sketches, the words washed in like watercolors. I like writing them. Yes, I've written a novel, too, but it's still unpublished."

The woman didn't understand. "In Riga," she said, "when we have more time, you must read something to me." She loved poems that rhymed.

"Why in Riga?" he asked cautiously.

"Oh, didn't you know?" the woman said, a bit puzzled. "Our transport is going to Riga. We're going to be exchanged there for American trucks. And then we go to Sweden."

She said that with a certainty capable of banishing Silbergleit's doubts. Perhaps Herr Linz really had been telling the truth. He believed it because he wanted to believe in something. And maybe also because the hero of his novel *The Menorah* had set out into the world from Slabodka near Kowno, and that was not far from Riga. It was no more than a hope, which received new impetus here in this dirty, stinking cattle car packed with Jews.

"I was the only one in the hotel who spoke fluent German," the woman said. "It was the best hotel in town, and only German officers with the best manners stayed with us. I got along well with them. But then the Gestapo came, and took the hotel away from me. It was my name," she whispered. "I'm a Morgenthaler, Rebekka Morgenthaler. That was enough for them."

She paused to emphasize what she had said. She had always been proud of her name. To this very day.

"I had to scrub floors and clean the toilets in my own hotel—in my own hotel! The humiliation of it all . . ." She groaned at the memory of it. And took off her hat and placed it carefully in her lap. She loosened the silver rings on her collar.

Silbergleit glanced past her to the hatch. A gray patch of sky could be seen, and he imagined a city on the sea where there would be room for Jews too. For a Silbergleit and for a Morgenthaler.

She had finally found a doctor who had certified her as unfit for work—in exchange for gold, naturally—and she had moved into a smaller apartment, where they left her in peace. In the spa hotel in Mondorf, where she had traveled annually with her husband for a rest cure—twenty-two years in a row, in the same hotel. Then all at once there was no room for her: Jews and dogs not admitted. Two days before the deportation she had been notified by the Dutch police, and she was able to put her affairs in order. She had even succeeded in hiding a few valuables with an Aryan neighbor, with whom she had also left a key, so that someone would keep an eye on her apartment until she came back. She was convinced that all Jews would be able to return after the war.

"Do you really think we're going to Riga, and from there to Sweden?" Silbergleit asked. He couldn't get it out of his mind.

"Yes," the woman said. "They need us to get the trucks."

Silbergleit wished he had some of her certainty.

Someone crawled over them on all fours. In a corner an old Jew with his hat on was praying, rocking his torso back and forth. Silbergleit stretched out his legs. He shoved the old man next to him over a little more; he was still sleeping with his coat pulled up over his face. In time he would make enough room so that he could call Karpe over here. By now he had gotten used to the jolting of the freight cars with no springs, and he was rather glad that they were lying so close together, otherwise they would just be tossed about.

A smell of chlorine hung in the air. Someone began to cough and didn't stop. It sounded as if he would choke. A child began to cry. The old Jew prayed more loudly.

The monotonous rhythm of the clicking rails filled them, made their sentences richer in pauses, their thinking slower, their reminiscences longer.

I do not want to believe it no not until I have read it myself this decree and then Herr Linz came and posted it in the hall we all read it and on the next day Herr Linz brings five meters of yellow material gleaming yellow material we had to pay for it

Herr Kochmann advances the money from the community treasury and Frau Goldstein sits there and cuts six-pointed stars out of the yellow material with long shears big ones for the adults and somewhat smaller ones for the children only Nathaniel doesn't need to wear one because he is not yet six years old TO BE WORN CLEARLY VISIBLE AND FIRMLY SEWN ON THE LEFT FRONT SIDE OF THE GARMENT when I go downtown with it for the first time I wear the Magen David like a medal on my chest I never knew how yellow the color yellow can shine like leprosy

I walk along Wilhelmstrasse I want them to see me to the railway station and back it's the time when the faces of the dead begin to speak and people look over at me and look past me they have never

seen a Magen David before and don't know what to make of it but
the boys learned about it in school they walk along next to me they
point at me begin to whistle behind me they throw stones at me
and one of them comes and shoves me off the sidewalk and another
takes my hat which has fallen off my head and throws it off the
bridge into the Klodnitz

and more and more people join them I turn around I start back
they follow me they hound me I watch them from the corner of my
eye as they walk along behind me whistling yelling shaking their fists
at me

JEW the boys whistle louder I walk faster they follow me faster
JEWISH PIG one of them hits me in the side I start running SCHID-
DOK they scream SCHIDDOK

and run after me I turn onto Niederwallstrasse they follow me
until I disappear into the house

I stand upstairs in my room and look down from the window and
see them standing there

23

"Is it possible? Can it be? Who's the first person I see, the moment I get back to Gleiwitz but Emilia Piontek as a nurse, with a white cap on her head! And no cigar in her mouth! How times change. What has become of our Milka, who read our future in the water, from the Ostropka and from the Klodnitz . . ."

Emilia Piontek, called Water Milka, was so busy steering Countess Hohenlohe-Langwitz in her wheelchair past the gaping spectators that she didn't notice the pushy, gesticulating woman at first.

"Yes, it's me," Milka Piontek said, and stopped the wheelchair. It was impossible to get any farther anyway. "But who are you?" The face beneath the Labor Service hat seemed somehow familiar to her; she strained to remember where she knew it from, which didn't make her expression any friendlier. But of course, that was . . . what was her name again, the woman who lived out there by the new transmitter, and had been widowed so early. That's right, her husband was killed in a methane explosion in the Concordia mine—Widow Zoppas!

"Marga Zoppas, you're Marga Zoppas from Zernik, aren't you?" she said, happy to have found the right name for the face after all.

"Yes, yes, of course," the other woman crowed, seizing Milka by the hands, although Milka didn't let go of the handles of the wheelchair. "You recognized me! Have I changed so much?"

She hoped she had changed a great deal. "Yes, I was away for a while," she added. "But you always come back to your hometown. *Jekuschnej*," she said, but it sounded a little artificial. And it sounded even more artificial when she started to sing an old children's song in Water Polish:

> *"Ein Piesz kam in die Kuchnia*
> *und stahl dem Koch ein Chlyb,*
> *da nahm der Koch Widoka*
> *und tat den Piesz zabić."*

She wanted to recall something from long ago, something that Milka didn't like to remember.

"We haven't seen each other for ages," she said.

"Yes, a lot has happened, a lot has changed," Milka said. She bent down to the countess. "Do you see the bell there!" She was astonished, for she had never seen a bell up close before.

"Let me think," Frau Zoppas said. "Right after the war started, I left Gleiwitz . . ."

"And you haven't been back since then?" Milka asked, skeptically. "You haven't been here in all that time?"

She couldn't comprehend how someone who had been born in Gleiwitz could stay away so long without being forced to. And she hadn't even noticed! She hasn't gotten any younger, at any rate, she thought, but more stylish, that's the first thing you noticed. She was wearing a sportily cut trenchcoat and a dyed Labor Service hat that she had altered somehow. The pendant with the fly in amber that dangled on her breast, however, was too gaudy for Milka's taste.

She introduced Frau Zoppas to the countess as an old friend.

In reality they had never been friends. But for a time they had seen each other rather frequently. Frau Zoppas had come to see her at the river, and made Milka show her how tobacco is processed and rolled into cigars, and in exchange Milka got Frau Zoppas to tell about new movies and sing the new hit tunes to her. Later Milka found out that Frau Zoppas was meeting a Labor Service man down on the Klodnitz; he came up from Emanuelssegen. Whether she was related to Milka's sister-in-law Valeska Piontek in any way was impossible to figure out. Milka had seen her for the first time at Valeska's at any rate, but maybe she had just been taking piano lessons. If you took lessons for long enough from "Piano Wally," she might end up proclaiming /you a relative. She had promoted this Aunt Lucie (Widera) from Mathesdorf to aunthood, for example, only so that she could use her around the house when there were festivities. And she knew how to give parties, you had to admit that.

After they had taken Halina away, poor, innocent Halina, Frau Piontek had sent for Aunt Lucie right away. She would certainly take care of everything, but how long would it last? She couldn't stay away from the miners' association longer than two weeks. Irma, nine months pregnant, Josel with his draft notice in his pocket, and the lawyer, who was supposed to be marrying Fräulein Willimczyk, the bookseller, next month . . . none of that concerned Milka anymore. No, she wouldn't even go to the wedding. After all, she wasn't related to Valeska's brother. But maybe for Rosa's sake, whom she simply felt sorry for, an unhappy woman who never could get herself a man, and now she would get married and still wouldn't get herself a man.

After the death of her brother Leo Maria, Milka had gone back to the house only one or two times to pick up a few things that he had saved from their parents and that she wanted to keep—a few letters, photos, and an old samovar that hadn't worked for ages, all worthless things, but full of memories. Anything valuable Valeska wouldn't have parted with, anyway.

It was lucky that Milka hadn't gotten involved in the lawyer's chancy real estate deals. It was better to have kept busy as the companion of Countess Hohenlohe-Langwitz, a basically kindhearted person, even though very moody at times. For the last six months she had been assigned as a nurse in the regional Women's Clinic, half of which had been converted to a field hospital for the wounded—so Milka had the good luck not to have to leave Gleiwitz for some other town. She wouldn't have been able to leave the countess alone. They had both gotten used to each other. In times like these the countess wouldn't have found a new companion, anyway.

"Yes," she said, "and this is the esteemed Countess Hohenlohe-Langwitz, whose companion I have been since then. Since you ran off with that soldier."

"How do you do," the countess said, asking to be turned a bit in her wheelchair. She would like to take a closer look at this person who had eloped with a soldier.

"Good day, Frau Countess," said Marga Zoppas, amazed. A genuine countess! She could hardly believe it. She held her hand tightly for quite a while. She didn't know whom to admire more, the countess in her wheelchair in the high-necked suit jacket with the shiny collar, a hat that looked like an upside-down flowerpot, decorated on the side by a butterfly made of glass—or Milka, who associated with a countess, even if she sometimes had to wipe her nose or her *duppa*.

"What do you mean, ran off with?" She acted rather offended. "We got married!" And this was no exaggeration. "Herbert Kotzenhauer from Osnabrück," she said. "It was love at first sight. Besides, he was an officer."

She suppressed the *noncommissioned*; that was unimportant. She would never get a real officer, anyway.

"He wanted me to move to Osnabrück and live with his mother, who had to take care of the furniture store all by herself after her son had gotten drafted. And I had no one left here. They say you should go out into the world," she defended her decision.

Finally the furniture store became a general bartering center for merchandise, where people brought things and exchanged them for others of equal value, and they pocketed a healthy commission in return, naturally in merchandise, too—there hadn't been any new furniture for a long time.

"So you're paying a visit to your old hometown," Milka declared, sizing up the "officer's wife" from head to toe. This officer couldn't exactly be stationed in France.

"Actually, I'd like to live here again, home is home." Frau Zoppas sighed.

"Yes, particularly in times like these," the countess joined in, "one should stay where one is at home. Nowadays anyone might become dependent on help." She knew what she was talking about.

"Above all, there aren't any of those terrible air raids here," Frau Zoppas said.

"Were you able to get used to the people up there at all? They're supposed to be so dour, they say; they never celebrate. That's nothing for people like us. But will your husband let you move away?" Milka inquired, sympathetically.

"Him?" she said. "He was killed."

"Ach, you poor woman! Ach, you poor thing!" The two women uttered the words as if with one voice, they had had to pronounce them so often recently.

The twofold widow considered for a moment whether she should touch her handkerchief to her eyes. But she refrained. It had been a while ago. And she hadn't gotten along with her mother-in-law at all. She was glad to be out of Osnabrück.

"It's supposed to be pretty hard to find a place to live now, I've heard, although I haven't been back in town for more than an hour yet."

"Yes," Milka said, and noticed that Marga Zoppas, or whatever her name might be now, was not even wearing black stockings in mourning. "We're packed with air-raid victims from the Reich. And many of the brass send their families here. We've become the air-raid shelter of the Reich . . ."

"First I'll go visit Valeska Piontek. Does she still keep as busy as she used to? Surely no one has the time these days to learn to play the piano."

"Don't say that! It's almost the other way around. Life has become so sad that everybody has taken up something or other to forget about it. You know, today, when everything is so scarce and rationed . . . thank God you can still play the piano without ration stamps."

She was about to laugh, but then the joke seemed too silly to her. She bent down to the countess and wedged into place the pillow that she had just fluffed up.

"Now they're lowering the third bell," the countess said, and clapped her hands. "Ach, Milka, let's watch for a few more minutes. Nothing will come of the outing to the Richtersdorf Hills today, anyway. Let's go to the Church of the Cross instead, to the Holy Grave."

A Good Friday like this at least brought some variety. Otherwise Milka went with her only to the park at Preussenplatz or to the Richtersdorf Hills, or along the same path by the Klodnitz or on Sundays to Wilhelmspark, too. On Good Friday and on Holy Saturday she went with her to the three parish churches, to see the "Grave of Christ" and to pray. The most beautiful was in the Church of the Cross, illuminated by one hundred light bulbs and with a copy of the Shroud of Turin over it.

It was an old custom to go to at least three churches on Good

Friday, to pray before the Holy Grave; in the old days, the men had taken a dram after every church.

"If we're going to get to the Church of the Holy Cross, we'd better leave now. They'll take down this bell just like the other two."

And with that, she pushed the wheelchair on.

24

Noon had to come before Traute Bombonnek could stop suffering as a handicrafts teacher and start living as a human being and artist. The distinction was clear to her. In the morning she felt herself to be a soulless creature, nervous and skinny, with an overdose of stomach acid, condemned to teaching young girls who were constantly combing their hair and smelled of sweat, who giggled stupidly and ruined delicate embroidery patterns with their clumsy hands. More dazed than filled with real curiosity, Fräulein Bombonnek walked through the classroom now and then and had the girls show her their embroidery frames, crocheting samples, and knitting patterns, and then fled back to her lectern, pained at the results. She bore these humiliations over the years only because she secretly hoped that a single real talent would prove to her that the mornings in school had not been in vain. In the meantime, she grew smaller and thinner and more and more dried up.

At home at her potter's wheel, in front of the kiln, or while modeling a terra-cotta bust, she was a completely different person; indeed, anyone observing her in the morning and in the afternoon would have thought these were two completely different people.

She had just given Steffi Kozura two hours of tutorial help, for pay in kind, naturally: a whole pound of smoked bacon—for that she would even leave the house on Good Friday. Someone greeted her in an overly friendly manner. She smiled back. Only then did she think about who it was. It was Fräulein Scendzina, to whom she had tried in vain for three years to teach cross-stitching. Now she was selling fish at the "North Sea," and was called Fräulein Schanda. For one hundred grams' worth of meat stamps you received two hundred grams of fish. She was as exacting now with the scales as she had been sloppy then with the cross-stitching.

In spite of its being Good Friday, the teacher wanted to work a little on the clay model of a worker's bust, with which she was not yet satisfied; but something was holding her on the church square.

Maybe she was waiting for a disaster, like all the other people here, without wanting to admit it to herself.

"Good day, Fräulein Bombonnek!" Rosa Willimczyk, the bookseller, pushed her way up. "How nice to see you."

And so as not to show that she had been following Fräulein Bombonnek, she first looked up at the church tower and acted as if she were uncommonly interested in what was happening up there with the bell. "Isn't it terrible?"

"Yes, it's terrible," the teacher answered indifferently. "But I guess it's necessary. We didn't want the war, they encircled us from all sides. Now we have to stick it out. Everyone has to sacrifice."

She believed what she was saying.

"Ach, you mean the bells?" Fräulein Willimczyk said defensively. "That too, yes, but even worse: they arrested Halina, the Gestapo. The servant girl of the Pionteks, you know? She had a relationship with an Eastern laborer. They say she was practically a slave of passion. Such things do exist."

"Oh, yes," Fräulein Bombonnek said. She knew something about that. "That's really terrible! When did it happen?"

"Yesterday morning. Frau Piontek wasn't even at home at the time. They say she didn't know what had been going on, poor Frau Piontek . . ."

"But surely he'll get Halina out again, her brother, the attorney?!" Fräulein Bombonnek said.

"Did you read in the paper," the bookseller said, as if wanting to change the subject, "Sobisiak fell in action, young Lieutenant Sobisiak, our first holder of the Knight's Cross from Gleiwitz."

"Yes." Fräulein Bombonnek remembered. In the show window of the Dresden Bank the *Portrait of a Holder of the Knight's Cross* had been hanging for a long time. Inge Haase-Richter had painted it. Fräulein Bombonnek thought the portrait unsuccessful. Frau Haase just could not paint portraits, she simply lacked the technique of perspective, but ever since she had been doing portraits of the big wheels in the Party, she had been a success. She had even won the town's art award. Only for her politics. Not for her art!

Only six months ago he had been on leave here and had spoken to the Hitler Youth. "A fanatic, you know, but he looked handsome in his black panzer uniform. My God," Rosa Willimczyk said, "I just mention it because you did know him, didn't you?"

"Naturally," Fräulein Bombonnek lied.

Fräulein Willimczyk had seen him only two or three times when he had come into her bookstore and browsed a little. He had bought a book only once, about minerals. That was all. She hadn't remembered him again until she saw his picture in the newspapers. She liked to claim that she knew all the famous people from Gleiwitz and the surrounding area, and indeed that was almost true. Even if most of the time she had only taken a book down from a shelf and sold it to them.

Only now did it occur to her why she had pursued Fräulein Bombonnek. "Let me congratulate you! It hasn't been in the newspaper yet, but naturally I've already heard about it: you're getting the Gleiwitz art award for this year! How nice! My best wishes!"

She shook the teacher's hand much too long as she spoke. "I'm so happy for you!"

"Thank you," Fräulein Bombonnek said matter-of-factly, and withdrew her hand. She saw no reason for excessive joy. She had been fighting for it for four years, and hadn't won it until now. Yet her ceramics were well-known far beyond the borders of Silesia. She had even received a silver medal at the big exhibition of arts and crafts in Dresden in 1941. But here in town, people still saw just the handicrafts teacher, and only a few knew that she had been contributing embroidery and pottery to traveling exhibits for more than twelve years now. And if she had not fired the bust of the Führer in terra-cotta, she probably wouldn't have received it this year, either.

"My name had been proposed for a long time," she said. "But you know how it is: The intrigues! People are so envious, especially nowadays. You know how artists are!"

The bookseller nodded.

When she thought of all she had had to do to win the prize. She had almost joined the Party, which, of course, had nothing to do with her creative work itself, but rather with making her living as a teacher—who could survive as a freelance artist anyway?—but most of all with the Church. For only as a protest against the Church had she applied for membership in the NSDAP. She was a member of the NS Teachers Association, of the NS People's Welfare, and of the NS Women's Auxiliary, the NS Culture Community, and the League of the German East. But being in the Party was a different matter, that involved philosophical and thus also religious commitments, and it was difficult for her as a faithful Catholic to make those commitments.

But in the end it was the pastor who had driven her into the hands of the Party, with his remark that she could not keep on living with Herr Prohaska in an extramarital relationship; that was fornication and sin. Especially as a teacher she had to be a model for youth. In the Party, which was always trumpeting things like "model for youth," she would at least not have to listen to anything like that. She had gone to district leader Preuss and had filled out the application form, but fortunately they hadn't accepted her yet.

Then Schabik, the town building inspector and chairman of the art commission, landed her the assignment for a terra-cotta bust of the Führer, and made it clear to her that he couldn't scrape together the majority of votes that he needed for her without this bust. So she had accepted the assignment and had thought it was better to do something for the Party *once* than to be committed, even artistically, to serving a world view for her whole life.

She was opposed to tendentious art, and she had been even before '33.

The building inspector had promised her a complete exhibition in the Gleiwitz Museum for Arts and Crafts, with a catalog, which was something special in view of the paper shortage, and a frontispiece of the terra-cotta bust was to be included in it. So she could even send the catalog to her friends in Copenhagen and Oslo. Maybe Schabik was a little overzealous, but as one of the few officials who had been a councilman before 1933, he always had to prove himself a two-hundred percenter if he wanted to keep his head above water.

She couldn't tell any of that to Fräulein Willimczyk. But according to the things she had heard about her, maybe she would understand. You had to be so careful nowadays about what you said to whom. The school administration had once called her on the carpet for allegedly using some Polish words in the classroom. She couldn't remember. Perhaps she might have uttered a Water Polish word in an exclamation of surprise or fright, that was possible. But it was a severe punishment that she had to "volunteer" to help with the harvest on two Sundays. It seemed worse to her that now there were informers even in school.

"How much money is it? I mean, is the prize worth it financially, too?" the bookseller asked, curious. "Aside from the honor, the reputation. And then you'll be in the *Gleiwitz Yearbook*, too. The new one won't be coming out, I don't think, because of the paper shortage. Well, after the war, then."

"Five hundred," Fräulein Bombonnek said, and swallowed. "Most of the money will go for materials. I would like to have a bronze cast sometime. But you can see what bronze is needed for these days!"

And she pointed to the bells on the truck.

"So I guess I will have to wait until after the war."

25

Wondrak had remained in the garden cottage and had written letters on into the afternoon. Letters that he had long been intending to write, but had put off again and again. He postdated them by two days, because he knew that the recipients would be happier with an Easter greeting than with a Good Friday letter. But his mood was appropriate to this day. And this was communicated by his sentences, although he didn't intend it. It came through the most clearly in the letter to Edgar in Königsberg, which, however, didn't strike him until he read the letter over. It wasn't in what he actually wrote—he mentioned nothing of Valeska's discovery and of his planned marriage—but in the melancholy undertones, abrupt leaps of thought, which betrayed something of his despair. He decided not to send it after all. But he couldn't bring himself to tear it up or burn it. So he would put it aside and read it in two or three days. Maybe in a different mood, it would affect him in quite a different way. This wasn't the only letter that he had written but not mailed. He kept them in a metal box in his desk. Or hid them, inconspicuously, between old bills and newspaper clippings. And forgot them.

His sister had come in and brought him the first tulips of the year from the garden. He had looked at them absentmindedly because he was busy with a letter, and even more engrossed in the *Jupiter* Symphony, which, conducted by Hans Rosbaud, was just being broadcast over the station from the Reich. Valeska didn't have the impression that she was very welcome at the moment, and since all the chairs were covered by books, folders, or various garments, she left.

With a Good Friday face, it seemed to him. For an instant he felt sorry for his sister, but only for an instant; after all, it was Halina whom they had arrested. He wanted to listen to the rest of the symphony, but not to the piece by Reger afterwards—he didn't like Reger—and then get dressed, take a walk, and pay another visit to

Dr. Kanoldt. Even if he didn't have his hopes up, it would placate Valeska. Tonight he wanted to eat earlier, for at 8:20 the third act of *Parsifal* was being broadcast under Knappertsbusch, and that was something different from Rosbaud, after all. He fervently hoped nothing would happen with Irma, so he could listen to his *Parsifal* undisturbed.

Wondrak stood up and crossed the room, which was stuffed so chaotically full of furniture, books, and plants that you might think a special system was necessary to work your way from the door to the desk, located near the window. Or vice versa. He, in any case, moved with confidence in the room, even though he shifted something around almost every day. Now he just brushed against the rocking chair, which creaked back and forth for a while, and a botanical orchid that was hanging from the ceiling, its leaves trembling in the air.

Willi Wondrak had moved into his sister's garden cottage on Strachsitzstrasse a while ago. Initially it had seemed to him that he would simply not be able to part from the things that had surrounded him for so long, and so he stuffed the furniture, books, lamps, and houseplants into the one big room of the garden cottage. Even now, when he came home from the office and opened the door, this room still seemed to him like one big labyrinth; but once he was inside it, he felt secure. He would move a table farther away, switch a comfortable chair for a regular one, assign the lamps to new places, arrange his glass balls according to the latest system he had devised—but to be surrounded by these things in such cramped space pleased him, and he sometimes asked himself how he had stood it in the big, sparsely furnished rooms in his old apartment.

So now, whenever he was in Valeska's music room, he liked to be in the corner across from the veranda, because the vitrine, table, armchair, and grandfather clock surrounded him in such a cozy way. To his own surprise, he could always find an empty spot in his room where he could put down some books or a glass ball, a free wall where he could hang one of his portrait miniatures from the eighteenth century, or a niche for the little English mahogany folding table. In recent years he had collected the little portrait medallions on his travels, and bought glass ball paperweights. He enjoyed studying these finely painted miniature portraits; the brush strokes could be seen only through a loupe. The portrait of the young Duke of Courtenay from the year 1704, which he had bought at an antiquary's in Prague, turned out to be a very special rarity, because Lens, its painter, was using ivory as a background for the first time.

And the two Millefiori from Baccarat were also true rarities among his numerous but not particularly valuable crystal balls with glass flowers, colored glass threads, or air bubbles sealed inside; he loved them simply for their clear transparency or the ever-changing light refractions. Precisely because he was not a particularly knowledgeable or impassioned collector, such occasional finds gave him pleasure. And when he went to foreign cities, he still looked for them today, although nobody wanted to sell valuables anymore.

He moved the vase with the tulips in it to a different place, directly in front of the white wall; this showed the colors off to better advantage. He poured out half the water; with less water the stems of the tulips would take on bizarre forms and hang down. He had that from Fräulein Heiduczek, who also took care that there were always fresh flowers or perhaps just a green twig on his desk at the office.

He was surprised that his sister said she had known nothing about Halina's association with that Eastern laborer. She always kept an eye on things, even if she didn't necessarily have a hand in them. She had uncovered his secret, after all, although there was nothing he had guarded more carefully from her and from everybody else as well. He had brooded over whether she had found out about it some time beforehand, or whether she might even have known for a long time, and had just been waiting for an opportunity to surprise him. He had come to the conclusion that she had suspected nothing and had come into the unlocked room by chance. Hours, indeed days had passed when they had only looked at one another silently, measured one another silently, and had accused each other silently. Basically, that had only made it worse.

At the time he had resolved to speak about it in all candor with his sister, now that she had become a witness to his secret, and perhaps he was even a little relieved that he didn't have to take refuge in the old deceptions, lies, and dissimulations anymore, at least not with his own sister. And sometimes he thought that something hidden inside him had driven him to it, so that there would be more truth between them, and he had planned everything that he would say to his sister, everything he would explain to her, everything he would confess to her. But it had never come to that. Even before he could begin, she confronted him with a proposal that stunned him. It was so monstrous that he needed time to grasp it at all. He had never thought of such a thing. She, on the other hand, when he understood her ideas, thoughts, and remarks must have been planning it for a long time.

Since it was high time he got married, it would be best for him to do it soon, and best of all to Fräulein Rosa Willimczyk, the bookseller, who was an educated person with a good reputation, not entirely without means, and who, for her part, regarded the lawyer very highly. His sister had already put out a feeler in this direction "extremely tactfully," and had received an agreement in principle from the bookseller who, by the way, neither wished nor expected what is referred to as "marital duty."

He didn't realize how serious his sister was until she brought up all the possible objections to this plan and then destroyed them convincingly with arguments that in general could have been his; so that in the end there was really nothing else for him to do but nod in assent.

Valeska had presented her plan in a calm but determined voice, as if that was the sole possibility of freeing him from his guilt—and this had only shown that she was a genuine Wondraczek. And perhaps this was the right way of doing things.

She had arranged a meeting between him and the bookseller, and so they suddenly were sitting facing one another at Gruban's Wine Room on the Ring. He had known her for years, as one knows a bookseller from whom one buys a book occasionally. He had seen her at his sister's house too, to whose circle of friends she belonged, and she had probably participated in one of her *tableaux vivants*, in Leibl's *Three Women in Church*, if he remembered correctly. That was all.

And he hadn't thought of marriage at all, ever since the time he had almost stumbled into marriage with Erna Gottschalk, and was able to escape only at the last moment, because he had realized it would destroy both her and himself. They had met in the Wittig Congregation, and their need of faith and their fear of faith had brought them so closely together that they soon fell victim to the beautiful and wild dream of discovering their souls in total unity, while their bodies grew more and more distant from each other. He had tried to make the problem clear to her in long, impassioned conversations at night, but wasn't able to convince her. Perhaps she also didn't want to leave him alone in his misery? He, in any case, wanted to part with her, and had to.

Herr Wolf, of Gruban's Wine Room, even served them a glass of Rheingau; yes, he could still produce a bottle of wine, as if by magic, for the attorney from his extensive hoarded stockpile, whereas for ordinary customers, in this fourth year of the war, only some fermented fruit wine or an indefinable house drink was dispensed.

They sat at the back of the premises in a corner, sipped awkwardly from their glasses, and listened to a group of officers at another table swapping war stories with loud laughter, which didn't exactly make the two more cheerful. He caught himself staring at her breast again and again, which (he remembered exactly, it was at the beginning of the war and the town was full of soldiers) Fräulein Rosa had mutilated with the poultry shears in the kitchen of the Hotel Upper Silesia at the wedding of his niece, Irma; it had been the talk of the town. He had forgotten the reason.

He took her hand in his and held it tight, that seemed more appropriate to the situation. "Why don't we give it a try," he said softly to her.

. . . he saw how the boy was walking along the riverbank, he had attracted his attention before, because he reeled as he walked, as if he were drunk or dazed, he left his bicycle there and followed him to the river, the boy didn't look back a single time, he ran along the river, and more than once he was afraid that the boy would fall down the embankment, and then he saw how he let himself drop into the water, not like someone jumping in to swim across, the water was too cold for that, he simply let himself slide in and drifted away, and then he jumped in after him and grabbed him right away, and the boy let him tow him to shore without resisting; he took him home to his mother in the Port Arthur neighborhood, his father had died in the war, as he told him on the way, and then his mother shrieked at him, in the midst of war, when so many people were giving their lives on the front these days, how could he do something like that, and then the boy said that he was sick and tired of it, nothing but this war, which was happening somewhere far off in Russia, and the bombs in Hamburg and Berlin, what did that have to do with him, he didn't know Russia and he didn't know Berlin, and he had never been there and would never go there either, maybe as far as Mathesdorf or Odertal or to the Annaberg, and he had a perfect right to be unhappy, to be desperate, what did that have to do with the war . . .

Wondrak went to the wardrobe and selected a proper suit. He liked wearing pressed suits, and he thought about who would press his suits for him, now that Halina was no longer there. Then he took out a shirt and looked for a dark tie to go with it. He didn't dress elegantly, but with a certain care. Perhaps he believed that it would make him a different man.

Wondrak remembered the time in boarding school when he was initiated into the sacrament of confession. When they were herded into the confessional as well as into the bathhouse every Saturday, and what pleasure it was to be washed clean in body and what a torture to be washed clean in soul, and how greedy the confessor was for details, particularly as far as *impure thoughts* were concerned, even if you hadn't done anything, but had only thought or imagined it. In the confessional he had once thrown up, from excitement, fear, or shame, and another time in sheer fear he had rattled off the entire list of sins and confessed to everything. To this day he could still see a fellow pupil who had run screaming through the dormitory and had scratched his face bloody with his fingernails. He was put into the infirmary with a nervous breakdown. Later it turned out that the confessor had refused him absolution. When the same thing happened to Wondrak more than a decade later, he had sworn to speak out publicly against auricular confessions, wherever it was possible. At the time he had joined one of the numerous Wittig Congregations that had been formed after the excommunication of the theologian and writer Joseph Wittig, and had found among the young people there the same crisis of conscience and fear of faith, and this provided him with consolation and for a while redemption.

Many ways lead to God, even one through sin, and that is perhaps the shortest. Maybe it was just this one sentence from Wittig's novella *The Redeemed* that had given him strength and faith for years to come. *How cold one is toward God, when one has not committed sin for a long time; one goes past the cross like past a historic monument. Phariseeism descends upon the soul. My Lord! Is not sin necessary in order to experience God's most divine characteristic, mercy?* It wasn't his fault that he had to take this path, so he had to resign himself to it.

He founded a committee and then left it, he published pamphlets and financed brochures, and when he finally called for a boycott of the confessional in a leaflet and at the same time criticized the *Dear Lord's Tales* of Joseph Wittig as all too naive, he was excluded from the congregation. Later he had visited the writer in his house at Neusorge, a man grown stout, with a vehemently reddened face, preaching in a hectic, somewhat eunuchlike voice, haranguing about his battle with the Church bureaucracy. To hide his disappointment, Wondrak had had him inscribe one of his books for him, *The Life of Jesus in Palestine, Silesia, and Elsewhere*. And he had left without speaking about his problems. He never read the book.

So he was left alone again with his weaknesses and temptations. He hadn't given up his fight against this sacristal church until after the seizure of power, when the Catholic Church was getting into difficulties. When he had to decide, he did decide for the Church of his childhood, after all. But he had not gone to confession anymore since then.

He put on the jacket and straightened his tie carefully. In the mirror he actually did look like people look who pursue their work conscientiously, who listen to the request concert on the radio, who pay their taxes promptly, who consider the telling of a harmless political joke a heroic act, who don't particularly esteem the Party in power, yet at the same time despise England, and who are finally decorated with a medal, which they then wear discreetly but visibly enough as a rosette in their buttonhole. He could have been satisfied with himself.

He put on a light raglan coat. Although the spring was warm outside, he was wary of the cool April winds that arose so quickly. He wondered whether he should wear the coat open or with two buttons buttoned or just fasten the belt. It was as if he were making externals so important to conceal what was on the inside.

Suddenly his courage left him. As he was, in suit and coat with the carefully groomed water wave in his hair, he threw himself onto his bed. Wasn't it better to volunteer to go to the front after all than to marry Fräulein Willimczyk?

The sunlight was reflected from the glass balls and cast strange iridescent patterns on the wall. In the crystal on the bookshelf facing him, the light focused so intensely that it stabbed him in the eyes like a sunbeam. The light made his pupils hurt, and for an instant he felt as if he were blinded. He got up, went to the window, and drew the light muslin curtain closed, which, already yellow and frayed in places, dipped the room into a white, milky light. He had forgotten to turn off the radio, now they were playing Max Reger after all. He wasn't really listening. Wondrak's gaze swept over the room, through the jungle of the furniture, the plants, and the glass balls; all at once he hated this room into which his sister had lured him as into an inescapable primeval forest. And he wished he had stayed in his old, noisy, roomy apartment. And as if to break out, he strode out of the house decisively, knocking over a chair as he did so, and making a flowerpot wobble, and he didn't discover until he was outside on the street that he had left his labyrinth. No matter what freedom he strode into, he would always remain a prisoner. That had to do with more than just this house. It had to do with his childhood, too.

Most of all, he wished he was still that boy who had draped himself with fabric from the bolts in his father's store and postured in front of the mirror and waited for his sister's applause. That was a long time ago and could not be repeated even in thought, even if he were to try to do so with songs and dreams and phrases and gestures. *Lord, I want to be good I have tried to be good I haven't succeeded we wanted to be cheerful and we were sad we wanted to speak with one another and we were silent I wanted to encounter others and found only myself I have sinned before Thee I am not worthy to be called thy child thou hast created me in thine image and called me to greatness and I have sinned thought and spoken and acted so meanly through my own guilt.* Perhaps he should remain in his room forever, amidst the omnipotence of the furniture, and the books, and the objects, and wait until he too was nothing more than a dead object.

26

FOR QUITE SOME time, Valeska Piontek and Anna Ossadnik had been on friendly terms. After all, Ulla had been Frau Piontek's best pupil for a few years, and Franz Ossadnik had come to her house on Strachwitzstrasse once a month to pay the tuition personally, and while there he had practically always found an opportunity to make himself useful by driving a nail in the wall, oiling a creaky door, or changing the washer in a dripping faucet. There had always been something to fix at the Pionteks' ever since the man of the house had become bedridden, and all the more after his death. And after these little jobs he would sit down in the music room and listen to his daughter play the piano. In these surroundings everything seemed much more beautiful and sublime, and he reported this to his family at supper, almost gushing, as the seven of them were sitting around the oilcloth-covered table in the kitchen, where there were no expensive carpets or candleholders.

Later the two women ran into each other more often, and occasionally visited one another, but if they wound up referring to each other as "my friend" or sometimes as "my good friend," it was not because they had grown any closer.

For various reasons, Valeska Piontek didn't want to seem as if she were better than Anna, and zealously tried to downplay it. So in Anna's presence she didn't talk about music or about her real estate deals, but about household problems and raising children, yet almost of its own accord the conversation turned to the Persian rug, which, rubbed down with snow, was gleaming in its old colors again, or to the sugar bowl of Meissen porcelain, which had just been broken. Problems of which the Ossadniks knew nothing and which therefore did not exactly further the friendship of the two women.

Sometimes Valeska invited Frau Ossadnik to the municipal theater, too, or to the New World Club, for a guest performance of Grete Weiser in some Berlin comedy or other, where the audience practically died laughing; but the two of them did not laugh, although for quite different reasons. In the intermission they sipped at a sticky red fruit drink, as Frau Piontek constantly made disparaging remarks about other people's clothes.

Anna felt ill at ease on such outings, and sweated in embarrassment, because, for example, she never succeeded in fishing the money out of her coin purse in time and so she was always the one being treated. Keep your money in your purse, Valeska would say, it's a crime to spend money on this awful punch anyway.

Anna much preferred vaudeville shows, she loved jugglers, magicians, and trained dogs that were dressed like people and acted like people, too. She couldn't get enough of the lady without an abdomen, who got sawed in half at the end; at any rate, Grete Weiser's performances were feeble by comparison. She went there alone or with one of the boys, while Valeska Piontek and her brother amused themselves at *Love and Intrigue* or *The Weaponsmith*.

It was important to Anna Ossadnik that social distinctions not be blurred; even if Frau Piontek was a widow now, that made no difference. She was seen more frequently with her brother, the well-known lawyer Wondrak, who, since there were no Jewish lawyers left, was perhaps the best known in town. Anna didn't know much about it, and just hoped that fate would spare her from ever being in need of an attorney.

After they had paid a few visits to each other's homes, they soon gave up on it, thank God. Frau Piontek couldn't have found it very pleasant in the Ossadniks' live-in kitchen, even though Anna had cleaned up beforehand and aired out the place for hours. After a while Frau Piontek regularly came down with a kind of nervous sneezing, which would stop immediately when she took her leave.

Anna herself did not feel exactly comfortable in the genteel music room of the Pionteks, because you had to be constantly on guard not to bump into a vase or an expensive candelabrum. Besides, she couldn't tolerate one of Frau Piontek's terrible habits, namely, drinking her coffee while standing up. With one hand she held the saucer, with the other she took sugar and milk, and while she brought the cup to her mouth with her pinky extended and drank in tiny sips, she would walk back and forth, talking about her expensive Blüthner grand piano, which she had not had for long, on which her teenaged

pupils played Czerny and Schumann and Schubert with their awk-
ward fingers, and about what bliss it was to listen to Ulla playing
on it. Beginners had to practice on the old piano anyway, where it
didn't matter how they banged, she said with a laugh, balancing the
coffee cup in one hand as she played a trill with the other.

Anna followed such performances from the table; it made her ill
just to think of standing up and how she would stumble over the
carpet or over the step to the veranda, with the coffee cup in her
hand which surely was not the same cheap Meissen that the broken
sugar bowl was supposed to have been.

Since Ulla had been at the conservatory in Beuthen, the two women
seldom visited one another. When they ran into each other in town
by chance, they assured each other that it was high time they got
together again, for an operetta in the municipal theater, for a guest
performance of Theo Lingen, or for a cup of malt coffee, but usually
nothing came of it.

For some time Anna had noticed that although Frau Piontek did
inquire after her numerous sons, mixing up their names with ad-
mirable precision, she never asked about Ulla. She virtually avoided
saying her name. Perhaps this was because Frau Piontek was better
informed about Ulla through colleagues than she herself, Ulla's own
mother, was. However, what seemed closer to the truth was her
suspicion that Frau Piontek, by refusing to talk about Ulla, wanted
to indicate that, in her opinion, Anna and Ulla Ossadnik had nothing
in common except their last name. One of them was nothing more
than the simple wife of a locomotive engineer, while the other was
a musical prodigy unlike anyone else who had ever taken piano
lessons from Valeska.

For these reasons and others, Anna had been avoiding her more
and more recently. But now there was no way out. Valeska Piontek
had already spotted her and was steering past Hrabinsky, the cripple,
heading straight for her. And she told her immediately of Halina's
arrest, which Anna Ossadnik had already heard about. Gesticulating,
Valeska declared how sorry she felt for both of them, Halina and
the Eastern laborer too, whose name she did not even know, which
showed that she had not had even an inkling of the whole affair.
But her brother would certainly get poor Halina out of prison right

after the holidays. She had already forgotten about the Eastern laborer again.

"We all have a heavy cross to bear," Anna said sympathetically, thinking about her goiter. And naturally about Bruno, who had fallen in battle.

Anna still looked good in her wool turban and the velvet shawl that was caught up across her breast by a hatpin, thought Valeska, who now asked her friend for the latest news. She only hoped it would not be as terrible as the news she had had to report.

Anna had no news. That Andy had been in a scrap with the Lutherans today, on Good Friday, and, judging by his wounds, had gotten the short end of the stick was certainly not worth telling about. That her son Tonik was home on leave everybody knew, because he was chasing all the girls and he invited them to the pastry shop with his special ration stamps. And that Ulla was going on tour to the field hospitals Frau Piontek surely knew already.

But then something did occur to her: "I heard that Archpriest Pattas has locked himself in the sacristy and is crying."

"Well, well," Frau Piontek said. A weeping archpriest in the sacristy, that was worth something. At least it was a piece of news with which she could maybe impress even her brother. But it would certainly impress Lucie, who was running about the house in her white apron proclaiming some new measures of hygiene that she believed had to be observed in the forthcoming delivery. She might even surprise Irma with it, if she could be surprised by anything at all except the impending labor.

She might soon be at that point; Valeska had to hurry. She wanted at least to pray her litanies in the church first and do the penance, since she had hurried home with Irma that morning right after confession.

"It's a damned outrage," a strange woman said, who had joined them, her eyes riveted on the tower, "for them to take our bells away. They're nothing but criminals!"

Anna only murmured. She was of the same opinion, but at least in these surroundings, the words seemed a little improper. And besides, she had never seen this woman before, who was dressed completely in black. She pulled Valeska aside a few steps, for these days you could never tell whether someone might be trying to provoke you.

There are people, she thought, who have been living in Gleiwitz for twenty years and perhaps even in the parish of Peter and Paul, and have not seen each other even a single time. Yes, supposedly there are people like that. To her, in any case, most of these faces were unfamiliar. But people had probably hurried here from all over to witness this spectacle, which didn't exactly take place every day or any old place, least of all on a Good Friday.

"Isn't that Ilse Spinczyk?" Frau Piontek asked. She didn't even have to point, because Anna spotted her right away. She walked very slowly, almost levitating above the square, the deaf-mute master glazier Berthold on her arm.

"She's having her third baby already," Valeska said, "and they still haven't been able to get married, because his genetic health certificate has taken so long. Yet both the children are perfectly normal. Everybody knows that deaf-muteness isn't hereditary in the Bertholds."

"They're totally crazy with their ancestry researching," Anna said heatedly. "It's much worse than that with the Bertholds, they're supposed to have found a Jew somewhere in the family tree. Way back when, in the eighteenth century somewhere. That's the worst disease."

Valeska Piontek, who was about to leave, turned back to Anna to confide something important to her, with a serious expression. But then she only said: "That is the end."

Anna didn't understand her. Yet she wanted to prove to Frau Piontek that, although she was only the wife of a railway engineer, that is, of a senior railway engineer, she did understand allusions. But she couldn't make head or tail of the whispered reference to "the end." Therefore she said simply: "Yes, I understand."

"Do you know," Valeska said, "they came for the bells during the last war too—and we lost the war. Look, in 1870 we kept the bells and ultimately won the war against France. All by ourselves! You need bells if you want to announce victories . . . it's not a good omen, believe me, Frau Ossadnik. There's an old Gleiwitz proverb: 'If the bells are silent, then God has turned His back on us.' "

Anna thought about that.

"People are losing their faith," she said. "When the bells go, faith goes too. Bells are more than their sound. Just as the organ is more than music . . ."

She hoped that what she was saying was right, too. She thought it was, in any case, but she looked worried anyway.

"Come on, let's pray for the bells! And for Irma! It could come at any time now. We were at silent prayers this morning, that's when it started, not the actual contractions, but with a spasm in the back. How was it with you? You've been through it often enough!"

"Yes, that's how it starts. Sometimes it goes very fast, but it could take quite a while," said Anna judiciously. "Where is Kotik, anyway?"

She saw Milka Piontek in her Red Cross cap slowly pushing the countess's wheelchair. Next to her was a woman but you could only see her black-dyed Labor Service hat.

"Ach, blessed Lord Jesus," said Anna, "the bell is stuck!"

A murmur was going through the crowd. The bell was caught on a projecting piece of masonry on the middle gable and was tipping to one side.

"Good Lord," Valeska said, "it'll tear off the whole gable."

Everyone was looking up now. But nothing happened. The bell had wedged itself fast into the masonry.

Herr Thonk would have passed by if Hrabinsky hadn't stopped him with his stick. "What are you doing here on the church square?"

"It's positively annoying," Cell Leader Thonk said. "Have you noticed anything?"

Hrabinsky was surprised. He hadn't noticed anything unusual, if you didn't count dismounting the bells on a Good Friday as unusual.

"The people are grumbling. They need to be told that the bells are destined for the final victory, but Pastor Pattas locks himself in the sacristy and cries," Thonk said angrily. "That's an insult!" And with that, he walked on.

"The bell!" someone screamed.

Hrabinsky looked up at the church tower. *Panbozcek*, he thought, here comes Precentor Zobtschik with the collection bag. "You wouldn't think it's possible but now they're collecting with the collection bag, even outside of the church!—well, is that even allowed?" he asked loudly, and made his way with his chair to the other side of the square, where there was less of a breeze. Above all, Zobtschik had already collected over there. He met Herr Apitt, who had been about to sneak away inconspicuously as Hrabinsky approached, but he didn't let him get away.

"Did you hear about Halina's arrest, Frau Piontek's servant girl? Such a hardworking person, and now that she's got her new teeth . . ."

"Yes," Apitt said, "I live right close by. I was the first to hear about it! That must be terribly difficult for Halina. For Frau Piontek, too, naturally. And now they're taking away our bells!"

"This is all for the final victory," Hrabinsky said, against his own conviction. He was a patriot, had fought at the Annaberg in 1921, on Hill 110, and had lost a leg there. But he didn't understand how you could fight at Stalingrad. He had looked at a map to see how far away it was. That couldn't possibly succeed!

"I hope you're right," Apitt said, and grimaced. "All's well that ends well." And with that he wanted to take his leave.

"One moment, Herr Apitt. I must tell you honestly, I don't believe it, that we'll ever get our bells back, I don't believe in anything anymore. They've made so many promises, but how many promises have they kept? Not a one! So—we gradually stop believing. We won't live to see it and our children won't either, they're all dying in the war, at first far away, and now they're bringing death closer and closer."

Then Apitt stopped after all. "Sometimes," he said slowly, "I think this will all turn out terribly."

Tonik Ossadnik pushed forward in his uniform.

"Well, Tonik, how is it at the front, don't you want to tell us about it?" the cripple asked.

"But Herr Hrabinsky, you know: the Enemy is Listening!"

"Not even about how you got hit? Like to know where our boys are winning."

"We're fighting. We'll talk about winning when we get that far," Tonik said dryly.

"I read that in the Atlantic they sank sixteen ships, and two destroyers and one U-boat. And this morning there was a special bulletin on the radio, another 121,000 gross registered tons sunk, that's really something, isn't it?"

It sounded impressive. But he didn't know what one gross registered ton meant, let alone a hundred thousand.

"That's fine," Tonik said, "but that doesn't help me any. And not our buddies in Africa. They have to pull back from Tunisia, there's nothing for them there, Rommel's withdrawing."

"I don't know, either," Hrabinsky said, "what business we've got on the Volga, in Africa, in Narvik, and on Crete. We won't be able to hold them all."

"Crete!" said Tonik with yearning. Yes, he'd like to have been there with the paratroopers who conquered the island from the air. Floating down from above, and then blasting away with machine guns until the enemy surrendered. And then lie on the beach in the sun, he wouldn't have minded that at all. Except for two months in France, he had always been in the East, that was his bad luck.

"Once I saw a book about Crete, with colored photographs. Herr Hrabinsky, it must be wonderful there. When do the likes of us ever get to a place like that if not during the war?"

Yes, that's true, Hrabinsky thought. During the last war he had gotten as far as Italy, to the front at Isonzo. In peacetime he hadn't got beyond Oppeln and Neisse.

"After the war, we're sure to get new bells, bigger and more beautiful," Tonik said, and looked up at the church tower.

"Now you're starting to say the same thing, too," old Apitt said indignantly. "After the war! After the war! I can't listen to it anymore. They all keep talking about *afterthewar*. Yet nobody knows what it's going to be like after the war, not even *when* that will be. Tomorrow, the day after tomorrow, in a year, in ten years, in fifty? Who knows. And if you fall in Russia? Then what does *after the war* mean for you?"

27

A WOMAN DRESSED in black fluttered across the street toward the church square. Her movements reminded Milka of a black jackdaw scurrying after a shiny piece of metal that it wanted to take back to its nest and hide. A bulging handbag swung from her arm.

"The poor thing," Milka said, looking after her.

"Wasn't that one of the Nieradczyk sisters, who were always crazy about attending every funeral?" Marga Zoppas asked. Another two weeks and she would feel as at home here as before. With every face that she recognized, her sense of belonging and self-confidence grew.

"Yes," Milka sighed, "one of them. You can hardly tell them apart. They're like twins."

"Nonsense," interjected the countess from her wheelchair, without turning around. "There are people who claim that they were not even related."

"That's not true," Milka responded. "They weren't twins, but they really were sisters. One of them is supposed to have been married once to a tailor in Bielitz, who died of consumption. Then she bought the mangle business on Germaniaplatz with the inheritance."

"Which one was that?" the countess asked.

"I don't know."

"And which one was that, who just went by?" Marga completed her question. She felt an itching on her neck. She rubbed it with the flat of her hand, because she couldn't locate the exact spot. Her neck had never itched in Osnabrück; she was barely back before it started again. It wasn't her neck, it was the air.

"The other one is no longer living, you know," Milka Piontek said. "One day one of the two sisters started acting crazy, they were never able to figure out which one. Then they stuck her in a prison, called Kukulla's Private Sanatorium, near Ratibor, at her sister's expense. She was crocheting a tablecloth there that she was going to spread out on a big table when the Lord would come to the Last Supper. And since he would be coming with all twelve of his apostles, her tablecloth got longer and longer, but it was never finished. One day she was picked up and driven away from the sanatorium in a car—the other Nieradczyk heard that from a nurse—and shortly after that the death certificate arrived, according to which she died of heart failure. But that couldn't have been true, because Fraülein Nieradczyk knew that her sister could have died of any other disease, but not of heart failure. Shortly before, she had still been collecting hay seeds, drying them, treating them with iodine, snipping them up fine, and smoking them in a pipe—it would have burst anyone else's heart, but they say it only made her more cheerful."

"What happened to the mangle business?" the countess asked.

"It's been leased, as far as I know," Milka said. "Just look at the bulging handbag! She totes everything around with her, savings passbooks, documents, money, and certainly the lease, too. They say she's invested in diamonds, if only they're not phony! Ever since her sister has been gone, she hasn't trusted anyone. And she didn't trust her all that much, either."

"She looks as if she'll be going crazy soon, herself," Frau Zoppas said, and looked after her until she disappeared among the waiting crowd.

"I can imagine," Milka Piontek said, "that she'll be crocheting on the tablecloth of her dead sister someday, until it's long enough for Christ and the twelve apostles. I can imagine that easily enough."

They were staring up at the church tower, where a man with a broad white belt around his belly was now climbing out a window and was lowered, slowly swinging back and forth; he constantly pushed off from the wall with his feet. When he got to where the bell was stuck, it was obvious by comparison how massive the bell was in size and form. The little man, or so he seemed to Andy from this perspective, had himself pulled back up and came down again on the other side of the bell. Even though you couldn't make out the face of the man at this distance, it seemed to Andy that from his body he was radiating not insecurity or fear, but rather the joy and recklessness of a trapeze artiste, like the one he had seen just recently with the Camilla Meyer troupe on Germaniaplatz. All that was lacking was for the man up there to turn a somersault to express this feeling. When he was pulled back up, the man waved to the spectators staring up at him, who had been waiting for a sign like that, for now they heaved a collective sigh of relief, and a few people even began to clap. The man up there climbed into the tower window and disappeared.

"A file," Bronder said between his teeth.

Andy knew immediately what Bronder meant. They had both been thinking of it for a while now. But the cordon had been expanded even more. It was not only dangerous, it was hopeless.

"Yes, it would be good if we had a file," Andy said in any case. "Wonzak, can't you get a file from home?"

"What do you want with a file?" Wonzak asked.

"We'll tell you that when you get back," Bronder said.

"A file, on Good Friday?!" Wonzak said. He looked mistrustfully from Bronder to Squintok, and from Squintok to Hannes. He sensed that the others had a secret from which he was excluded.

"Go on," Andy said. "We'll wait for you here. We've got a plan. You can be part of it, if you want," Andy said consolingly.

Naturally Wonzak wanted to be part of it. "All right, a coarse file," he said as if confirming an order.

"Don't you want to work in the field hospital with us as a nurse? You get basic training, that takes two weeks, and the administration has rooms and apartments, too, that they give only to the nurses."

"I was thinking more of office work," said Marga Zoppas, who couldn't stand the sight of blood.

"Office work!" Milka pronounced the words like a reproach. "Office work! Have you got children? Well then, very probably they'll take you for Home Air Defense. Or for armament. Turning shells on a lathe, breathing metal dust all day long. I don't know whether that's the right thing for you."

"What church are we going to now?" the countess asked, after they had turned onto a small side street from the church square.

"To the Church of the Cross, naturally," Milka said. And to Marga Zoppas, who was following them because she didn't know what else to do: "Well, if you can't find a place to stay at the Pionteks' on Strachwitzstrasse, I'll ask at the clinic, there are always openings.

And lots of young soldiers!" She nudged Marga in the ribs. "And they're not all of them so badly wounded. Most of them are just pretending. Who wants to be at the front, anyway? There's a lot going on at the clinic," she said.

She pushed the countess along a little faster now, because she was excited. When she even thought about what had happened recently! Every evening she told the countess about the day's work at the field hospital. But she couldn't tell her about this. Not even Marga Zoppas.

They had a soldier there, a simple, pious, peasant boy from Passau who had both arms amputated at the elbow; then he got gangrene in one of the stumps, and now another piece had to be taken off, up to the shoulder. He lay there, the stump wrapped thickly in muslin and cotton. But he was in good spirits again soon after the operation; he laughed and joked with the nurses, and entertained the whole overcrowded ward. She could hear him in the corridor when she went past the door; they weren't having such a good time in any other ward. And once when she was on the night shift, he said to her: "Nurse, please don't run away, I have to tell you something. I can't stand it anymore, you've got to help me, it's driving me crazy!" Naturally she wanted to help him, but he kept beating around the bush, so she couldn't figure out what was wrong. Until he said: "Nurse, lie down next to me." She had turned pale, and could only stammer softly. And he said: "See, now you're running away too, like the other nurses." She saw how his neck was sweating, and there was unspeakable torment on his face.

"I understand you," she said bravely. "But I'm an old woman, it would only revolt you." She wiped the sweat from his forehead with her bare hand.

Then he whispered: "Nurse, put your hand down there. Please, nurse, I can't stand it anymore, do it, I'm cracking up, it tortures me every night." He begged and begged until she put one hand on his mouth and slid the other beneath the blanket, slowly, until she reached his leg, and then higher, up to his member. The body beneath the blanket began to squirm, then came a spasm and he was still. "Heaven bless you, nurse," he whispered. That was all.

But she couldn't even tell Marga Zoppas about something like that.

"Where are your things, your clothes and your furniture?"

"Oh," Marga said, "they're all still in Osnabrück."

"You'd better send for them soon. The West is being bombed. Better store them somewhere here if you don't have enough room."

Marga couldn't tell her that she had arrived with two suitcases, which she had left at the baggage counter in the train station. That was all that was left of her marriage with Hermann Kotzenhauer, the noncommissioned officer. And a name that she had never been able to get used to.

"Yes, I'll do that," she said hastily.

"Invite your friend over for the radio play this evening," said the countess, who felt neglected. "This evening it's *The Gods Are Athirst*, based on the novel by Anatole France." It was a repeat, but that didn't matter to her. She loved radio plays and never missed a single one. And if it was a repeat, she could talk during the broadcast, and tell the others when the most suspenseful moments were coming, and explain them—she liked that best of all. That's why she liked having other listeners.

"I can hardly wait," Marga said, "to be able to sleep again without sirens howling. Not to have to go to the air-raid shelter at midnight with a suitcase full of valuables and papers, even in winter when it's freezing cold! There's nothing left of you but a bundle of nerves. Here you live like in peacetime," she said without envy.

"It's not so simple here either," Milka defended herself. "All day in the hospital, with badly wounded men all around you, all of them from the Eastern front, I'm totally *kapores* when I get home from my hospital shift. On a normal shift I have just one hour at noon to take the countess for a walk. Ozone and chlorophyll—everyone needs that, don't they, Countess?"

"I'm happy to be experiencing Easter in the homeland. Oh, if you only knew how happy I am," enthused Frau Zoppas. "To go into the forest and see the pussywillows coming out, the anemones blossoming, and the birches stretching out their fresh green leaves . . . A birch green like that, Frau Countess, such a juicy birch green like here in Silesia doesn't exist anywhere else."

They walked along the deserted Moltkestrasse.

"Earlier," Milka said after a pause, "I always used to read something to the countess in the evenings, but now I'm too beat, I simply can't manage it."

"*Pschinzo*," the widow said, laughing. She was glad that words that she thought she had lost kept coming back to her. The foreign speech of the people in the West had made her feel lonely. A few more of these old words and she would feel at home again.

Milka was not laughing. How could she let her know that they didn't use any Polish words these days, not for some time, not since the war had begun. And no Water Polish, either. And that children in school were already being urged to report on their parents.

"In the evening," she said, "we always listen to the radio now."

Frau Zoppas bent forward again: "And the water splashing at Easter, does that still exist, when the young men sprinkle the girls with water on Easter morning, which has been mixed with perfume first . . . ?" She fell silent, as if abashed by her own enthusiasm.

They kept talking as they walked side by side.

"*Schwienta Maria*," Milka cried out, as a horde of boys emerged from a little side street and raced past them; they were banging loudly with the *klekotka*. "Can they ever scare you!"

"Ach, the *klekotka*," Frau Zoppas said, remembering gratefully. "So that still exists! Like in my childhood."

"Like in the Middle Ages," Milka said. "When the plague was in the city, they went through the streets with wooden clappers then too."

28

"Ach, my goodness," said Jutta Wieczorek, holding her friend firmly by the arm. "Did you see that! If the rope snaps! There's no protection! All he has to do is start feeling sick, at that height."

She felt a little sick just thinking about it. Nevertheless, with a slight shudder, she looked up at the church tower, where the worker was dangling from his rope.

"But the rope can't snap," said Verena Schimitschek, contemptuous of so much ignorance. "It's been tested, and the men are used to it. After all, they can't set up a net down below like they do for the Three Codonas!"

"Why can't they?" Frau Wieczorek asked earnestly. "All of the Camilla Meyer troupe had ropes attached to their backs, I saw it, and those are trapeze artistes, they've been practicing since they were children." She loved circuses, and whenever she could scrape together the money, she had gone to see the Busch Circus from Breslau every time it played a guest performance at the Little Exer. Most of all she loved the aerial ballet. Since she was afraid of heights, even a mediocre trapeze act was enough to impress her. But the Camilla Meyer troupe, on the trapeze fifty meters in the air, was too exciting for her. Once she had gone to see them with her children, and got all green in the face and had to throw up.

"At least you had luck with your husband," Jutta Wieczorek said, out of the blue.

"What do you mean? Recently he's hardly ever been home," said Frau Schimitschek, "sometimes he's on the road for a week or two at a time."

They strolled across the square, past the spectators.

"But at least he does come back!" Frau Wieczorek said. One day her husband had not come back. She didn't even know where they had buried him. Fallen in the Crimea, it said on the document. She got an atlas from Klaus to see where that was. A region bigger than all of Upper Silesia, how could she find the plain birchwood cross there? That was all a dead soldier got. And besides, it was so far away, how would she ever get there? In the meantime her eldest had also become a soldier, in France now; he was relatively safe there. Occasionally he sent a package with things that you could no longer get here, in wartime. She had worn mourning for a year, and now was looking for a new husband; she couldn't raise her five children alone, and each one was a bigger *gorolik* than the next. She sighed just thinking about what the four of them got into every day. She would probably have to wait until after the war for a husband. War widows were not in demand, and men could have enough women nowadays, even without getting married.

"My Erich has been classified draft exempt, a specialist they've only got a few of. The others can't do his job! In the General Gouvernement," Frau Schimitschek continued, while waving to someone, "they came and took the bells in 1940. The Poles go around with wooden clappers now, to call people to mass. In the cities they mostly left the big churches with one bell. They're leaving us with one, too!"

For her friend the lowering of the bells was something like a high-wire act, a thrill, a drama, that frightened and fascinated her and held her spellbound with the expectation that something unforeseen, a disaster that never did materialize, was going to happen. At the end the trapeze artistes bowed and the audience clapped; that's how it always was, the artistes changed clothes and took down the tent, the next day they were already somewhere else. But here no one would take a bow, and there was no reason to applaud, either.

"One bell?" she asked.

"Yes, the smallest one."

"The little funeral bell! Oh, my goodness," said Frau Wieczorek, "that one!"

"I know that from my husband, he gets around everywhere," Verena Schimitschek tried to explain. My God, she practically had to apologize for her husband's not being in the war and at the front. But there had to be a few responsible men at home, too. Not just children and old men and Party members. She had been telling that to anyone who would listen, and not just once: that her husband had been exempted from the draft not because he was a Party member, but because he was an irreplaceable specialist. She had also done this because a few weeks ago slogans had been painted in the night on the walls of the Hotel Upper Silesia, where the regional Party leadership had their offices: AT THE FRONT WE DONT WANT THOSE CONFIRMED BY THE CHURCH BUT THOSE RECLAIMED BY THE PARTY.

The whole town had been talking about it.

"Don't say that," said Frau Wieczorek in a tone of voice as if warning against too much optimism. "They'll come and take all the men, if things keep on like this. They already have my oldest, now it's the second one's turn, a new crop every year. We should have had more girls, at least they stay at home. I still remember, when the boys were born, one right after the other, I said to my Engelbert, how nice, we'll keep them a long time, they won't get married off like the girls when they're twenty, and they're not so expensive, either, because they don't need any dowry. Now it's the other way around."

Frau Wieczorek had a way of presenting her simple philosophy so convincingly that her friends could not challenge her arguments.

"The man up there seems to have done it," Frau Schimitschek said. They had probably missed the critical moment. The bell, which must have been hoisted a little, now slid down past the wall and swayed unhindered in the air. For a moment it looked as if the man were riding on the bell.

"Oh, my goodness," was all Frau Wieczorek said.

29

"**D**o you have relatives in America?"

Silbergleit didn't remember where he was until he heard this question.

"No," he said. "I don't know anyone in America. I applied for a visa for the U.S.A. through Switzerland, the last summer before the war, but it was too late, the borders were being closed, and no more mail was coming in from abroad. Hermann Hesse was supposed to sponsor for me . . . you have heard of Hermann Hesse?"

No, she hadn't heard of him.

"You have to excuse me," she said, "but I don't like reading fashionable authors, they're so nihilistic. Books ought to be different from life, more exciting, more interesting . . . more spectacular . . . if I may say so. I like reading Huysmans. Have you read Huysmans?"

No, he didn't know Huysmans.

"I could be of use to you," the woman said.

Silbergleit edged closer. The train was moving rather fast, and the sound of the tracks was so loud that he had trouble hearing her.

"You see, anyone who has relatives in America can travel there from Sweden," the woman said. "Everyone else has to stay in the camp. What are they supposed to do with all those Jews?"

"But how do you think you're going to get from Sweden to the U.S.A.?" Silbergleit asked. "There are no longer any passenger ships. They're all being used as troop transports now. And then with the U-boat war going on . . ."

He wouldn't get to Switzerland, either, for that matter.

The woman hadn't thought of that before. She couldn't dismiss these arguments no matter how hard she tried. "In a camp until the end of the war—I won't be able to take it." She sighed and pulled up her coat, which was covering her.

Gradually Silbergleit had staked out enough space so that there was room for Karpe, too. Just to make sure, he asked the Dutch woman if she minded whether he brought over his friend from another corner of the car.

"As long as he is an educated man!" she said, hidden inside her coat and sunken in her memories.

Silbergleit called loudly for Herr Karpe, but he couldn't hear him over the noise of the tracks. So he crawled in the probable direction and found him asleep in the middle of a tangle of bodies. For a moment he pondered whether he should wake him up, but when he saw him lying there so squeezed in between the others, Silbergleit's own space seemed more comfortable. He poked him gently and Karpe opened his eyes at once, but it took a while for him to orient himself and realize who was bending over him.

He couldn't have been sleeping very deeply. Silbergleit could read in his face that a dream had taken him far away from the reality of this train car. He took hold of his hand.

"Come on over to us, Herr Karpe, we have room for you!"

He was rather proud of that, for he had acquired the space bit by bit in the last hour.

Karpe hesitated. He didn't want to give up his spot here without being sure of getting a better one. That was one of the lessons he had already learned. He decided to inspect the new spot first, and left his blankets behind as a sign that he was not yet relinquishing his territorial right to a few hand-breadths of plank.

Silbergleit introduced Karpe to the Dutch woman, whose name he had forgotten. But the name wasn't as important as the ritual of introduction, because it reminded them of a time that they wished they could return to.

Karpe said something friendly that was drowned out by the noise of a train rattling by in the other direction. But his amiable expression said it just as well. He inspected the new spot and seemed satisfied with it, for he crawled back to get his blankets.

The sun must have broken through the clouds; it was noticeably brighter in the car now. The Dutch woman took out her compact, looked into the little round mirror, and began to powder her nose. A discussion developed between the boys at the hatch and the others in the car, and the woman joined in with short, emphatic sentences.

Silbergleit listened attentively, but he understood nothing, although the words seemed familiar.

"The boys up front there at the hatch," the woman said then, "claim, after calculating from the angle of the sun and the way we are headed—or however they're figuring it out—that the train is going toward the southeast. But to get to Riga we would have to travel north or maybe even northeast, by way of Warsaw. What do you think?"

Silbergleit was stymied. He asked Herr Karpe, who had traveled a lot in the East earlier, as a salesman. But Herr Karpe had no satisfying answer either. It could be that the train was making an arc around a city or around a large factory—they would almost be going in the opposite direction, then.

The boys at the hatch were observing the sun. They turned out to be right. The train was traveling unmistakably to the south.

The Dutch woman had devised a new theory. "Could it be," she said, "that they're taking us to Romania, to the coast? From Constanţa ships go through the Bosporus to Palestine. Maybe they'll pick up the trucks on their way back? Maybe Stockholm is already too full of Jews?"

She attempted to assuage her doubts with questions.

She had presided over a charity benefit for the Keren Hajessod before the war; land in Palestine had been bought with the proceeds. She would surely find a few Jews from Amsterdam or Hilversum in Palestine . . .

She was getting excited at her own words. She even had the courage to tell the others this, and had already forgotten that they were supposed to be exchanged for American trucks in Riga.

"They're going to kill us all," screamed an old man at the back of the car. At least that's how Silbergleit and Karpe heard it.

The woman turned deathly pale. It was obvious what an effort it was for her not to betray the turmoil of her emotions.

"People's nerves are on edge," she said. "These are simple people, and they have never learned self-discipline. Yet precisely in such situations, one must preserve one's self-possession. Otherwise chaos breaks out."

And as if wanting to arm herself against it, she put her hat back on.

"It's still a long way to Romania, to Constanţa. How are we supposed to survive that?" Silbergleit said to Karpe.

"They sent the Jews to Poland to have them work in armaments factories. But we're too old for that. The Americans are intervening for us now, that's world finance. The Germans have no respect for the English, but they do for the Americans!"

"Herr Linz never mentioned anything about Palestine," Silbergleit wondered. "But it is possible." Nobody in the first transport from Gleiwitz had written, not a letter, not a card, nothing, and that was almost five months ago, too. If they were taken to Palestine by ship, that was understandable; after all, no mail comes from there.

His back was hurting him, he pushed his briefcase underneath his head to prop himself up a little. As he did so, he bumped against the old man next to him, and asked his pardon. But the old man lay there on his side and didn't move.

"Herr Linz, you always say Herr Linz, who is he, this Herr Linz?" the Dutch woman inquired.

Karpe explained, because he had known Herr Linz longer than Silbergleit had.

Linz was the Gestapo liaison officer to the Jewish community house on Niederwallstrasse, where most of the Jews had lived at the end. He brought them their ration cards and took care of their work assignments; he looked the other way if, when they were working in the fields, they brought some potatoes and cabbage home with them. But sometimes he would come to Niederwallstrasse drunk, slug someone in the face for no reason, or kick in a door with his boots. They all hated him, and yet they waited for him, because in the last days he was their only connection with the outside world.

"He smashed up my records," Silbergleit said bitterly. "He didn't want Jews to listen to Beethoven!"

"They have their regulations, too," said the elderly lady, who seemed to have regained her optimism. "In Drente-Westerbork women examined me, very ordinary prison matrons, they touched me all over, even under my dress, with their coarse, rough hands . . ."

It revolted her even to think of it.

"They took my manicure kit away from me. On account of attempted suicides. There are people who don't believe in God, and do things like that . . ."

She leaned back, exhausted. She still did believe in God, but in a rather general way. She had not celebrated Passover since her childhood. Not until they celebrated it here, in the crowded cattle car. An old Jew had taken a well-used little book out of his coat pocket and read aloud from the Passover Haggadah, and, since no wine was available, he blessed the water four times, and distributed matzo, a tiny piece for everyone. But it had tasted delicious. And the Hebrew prayers sounded so impressive! She resolved to learn a little Hebrew in Palestine, and to go to the synagogue occasionally.

They go through the house through all the apartments and break down a door they come at any time of the day or night that's what they want that we'll be afraid smash a window that we'll always be afraid of them they left me my books up to now

once Herr Linz swept them off the shelf with a single blow but they have left me the books I picked them up one after the other I read in them again in my books

Herr Linz dumped my records on the floor and stomped around on them with his boots until they were shattered Beethoven and Wagner are not meant for Jews not for Jewish ears

Aaron little Aaron came to me we listened to Beethoven together on the old phonograph with needles that were already worn out there aren't any more new needles I rescued one record the Creatures of Prometheus it's badly scratched

a miracle that it wasn't broken

we listened to it again and again

and little Aaron Szalit who will run from the ghetto someday into the world a different Aaron who sits in my room and listens to Beethoven or to what he imagines to be Beethoven from the tinny sounds on the record that's too loud Frau Goldstein says if we don't stop it she'll tell Herr Linz about the record that isn't broken we put a blanket over our heads and listen to our sole rescued record the Creatures of Prometheus come here Aaron close the window I can't stand the fragrance of jasmine.

30

"IT MAKES ME very happy to be singled out from the others by such a prize," Fräulein Bombonnek said with emphatic modesty. "So much crap gets passed off as art these days. Please excuse the expression, but that's the way it is. Anyone who paints a picture of the Führer these days or slaps together a bust of the Führer, thinks that makes him an artist and then he wants to become a member of the Art Ministry of the Reich." She, at any rate, had been a member of the Upper Silesian Artists' League since 1931, and for a time she had been the elected treasurer of the Union of German Artisans, Province of Silesia.

"The Führer," the bookseller said with conviction, "surely is not happy about the cult that is being built up around his person. Actually, he was always such a modest man."

"And that sculptor, Storek," Fräulein Bombonnek said softly to Fräulein Willimczyk, "who pockets all the public commissions for himself, well, who calls himself a sculptor, combination of chisel wielder and Arno Breker! Those never-ending laborers in relief. Cute! Insipid! Empty!" She spat out the words like curses. "And that Haase-Richter: Tinted photography with a dose of Raphael . . . What I do is only craftwork, I've always said that, I don't presume any more, but it is skilled, solid, and beautiful!"

"Do you mean the Frau Richter whose wall painting is in the new administration building of the miners' association, do you mean her?" the bookseller asked.

"Yes, that's the one," the artisan said derisively.

"Ach, just look, the bell," Fräulein Willimczyk said. She preferred to change the subject. If Fräulein Bombonnek kept on talking like that, and in public too, she would talk herself out of the next public commission. Perhaps out of even more. Her affair with Prohaska was known throughout the town. They could cause her even more trouble about that. And nothing against Haase-Richter—after all, she had done the portrait of Scholz-Klink, leader of the Women's

Auxiliary, and the portrait had been exhibited in the House of German Art, the big new museum in Munich. She had seen it in the catalog. Besides, the bookseller had liked the mural of the peasant women binding the sheaves.

"And I wanted to tell you that you're invited, *naturally*," the bookseller said. "You'll get an official invitation, too! On May 22, that's exactly four weeks from now. Family and just a few friends," she emphasized to make the invitation more precious.

"Yes, of course, I look forward to it, thank you," Fräulein Bombonnek declared. "I read the banns in church. Now it's high time for me to congratulate *you*," she said, staring fixedly past Fräulein Willimczyk.

For days the talk had been about the wedding of Lawyer Wondrak and Fräulein Willimczyk, the bookseller, and the town was puzzled about why the prominent lawyer wanted to marry the hysterical bookseller, of all people. But Fräulein Bombonnek would rather go to a wedding than to a funeral, especially in times like these. Naturally, she would have preferred to go to her own wedding. But Prohaska didn't want to get a divorce. Although he had not gotten even a single letter from his wife in four years, yes, he probably didn't even know where she lived. "A Catholic cannot get divorced," he said. And secretly waited for his wife to be killed in an air raid in the West. She had even prayed for that to happen. But she didn't want to think about it now, better to think about Rosa Willimczyk's wedding. The piano teacher knew how to organize things, and a lawyer always had connections, even in times like these, so you could count on them to pull out all the stops. And behind closed doors she could even dance the polka again, with her Prohaska.

An artisan like her had little to offer in a barter market. A farmer wouldn't give her a single potato for a decorative plate of fired clay, and she had hardly any of the beautiful embroidery left. She had bartered it all for Prohaska; he simply needed an extra piece of smoked bacon now and then, his work was so hard. Now that people were coming here from the Reich to store their valuables, in fear of air raids at home, she couldn't keep up with what the farmers were being offered anyway. The farmers used to be the poorest people around here, even poorer than a poor *grubjosch*.

"Herr Prohaska is invited too?" she asked. Without her Prohaska she wouldn't go.

"Of course," Fräulein Willimczyk confirmed. Prohaska was related to Widow Piontek somehow, so they would have to invite him anyway. Besides, everyone knew that Fräulein Bombonnek and August Prohaska were living together like man and wife.

"I know what I can give you for a wedding present," Fräulein Bombonnek said. "I'm thinking of a handsome glazed plate, with the zodiac signs of the wedding couple on it, a custom design."

"Wonderful," the bookseller enthused. She was still having trouble with the notion of being a bride, but she was slowly warming up to it. Since she saw the bridegroom so seldom, it was a little difficult.

Now the teacher wanted to know their astrological signs.

"I'm an Aquarius," she said, "child of rain, child of pain." She gave a tormented smile. "What the sign of the lawyer—my fiancé— is, I don't even know. But I'll ask him." She had not spoken with Willi often, and never at all about the zodiac. She couldn't quite imagine him talking to her about it, either. No doubt he considered it superstition. She could inquire of his sister, yes, she would do that.

"I should also tell you how splendid you look, Fräulein Willimczyk. Lately you've been really blossoming, as if everything in you is preparing for the summer," the teacher said. She wished it were the same with her. If she could finally marry Prohaska, she would give up her job as a handicrafts teacher and dedicate herself solely to pottery.

"Here comes your Herr Prohaska," the bookseller cried out, almost relieved.

Fräulein Bombonnek blushed and quickly turned around. She could see Prohaska's coarse yet gentle face pushing its way above the others, searching, half shaded by the visor of his cap. Whenever the teacher saw Prohaska outside of their apartment, it always gave her heart a twinge. She had grown used to seeing him as a piece of the furniture, because he was always at home—except for his work at the VOH. He was part of her apartment, like the old Bohemian wardrobe, the work table, the tile oven, or the dressing table.

"I have to go now," Fräulein Bombonnek said, already distracted.

"Then we'll see each other on Sunday, after the High Mass," the bookseller said confidentially. She really was looking forward to the Easter High Mass; she sang in the choir, and in the chorale "Christ Is Risen" her voice trumpeted as it did in no other song.

Prohaska had spotted Fräulein Bombonnek by now and was coming straight toward her. Yet they had agreed that they would never show themselves together in public. She gave him a hand signal, and he answered her likewise, from which she could tell that something urgent was up. So she motioned him with her head to the other side of the church—at least there they wouldn't attract so much attention as here in the middle of all these people. What could be so important that he wouldn't wait for her at home?

As she left, she said bitterly to Fräulein Willimczyk: "Nobody will get me into a church again!" She took up her purse and started off. "I'll tell you why some other time."

31

"I'VE BEEN LOOKING for you everywhere," Prohaska said. First, he took her handbag for her. Then he fished a piece of paper out of his jacket pocket. "I've been transferred," he said, as neutrally as possible, "to the Ruhr. By the Ministry of Labor, you know, it's like in the military. I have to leave tomorrow."

She didn't even want to look at the paper. She had been expecting something like this. She had been expecting something like this to happen some bitter day. Maybe Good Friday was even the right day for it.

"Where to?" was all she said.

"To Bergkamen," he said.

She remembered vaguely that he had been married there, somewhere. But that was a long time ago.

One evening, shortly after the outbreak of the war, Herr Prohaska had stood at her door and asked whether she could rent him a room; he had found a job at the VOH Wireworks and wanted to stay in Gleiwitz at least until the end of the war—not for very long then, since the Germans were already besieging the Polish capital. In the twilight he seemed a much different man than the one she remembered from the wake at the Pionteks'. She would have preferred to send him away on the spot, but his way of merely looking at her and talking more with his eyes than with words made her react differently than she intended. In any case, later she couldn't understand why she had shown him the room under the stairs so readily. He rented it without even taking a good look at it. Sometimes she thought he would have accepted the coal cellar.

She acted as if they had never met before, or only fleetingly, and certainly not after Leo Maria Piontek's funeral. At least in the beginning, she avoided encountering him at all. If she wanted something from him, she wrote him a note and stuck it into the frame of the mirror in the hall; he couldn't miss it when he came home. At first it seemed as if he were not particularly interested in seeing her or speaking with her either, for he too made use of this form of communication. But it puzzled her that he never went out in the evening, as long as he had lived there, not to go shopping, not for a walk, not even to go to the movies or for a beer. He was at home every evening; she could hear that from the sounds in the room under the stairs. Like an animal, she thought sometimes. Only late at night, when she turned out her light and got into bed, did she hear him busy in the kitchen, or in the hall. She would lie there motionless and listen. She was waiting for something, without knowing what. Sometimes she thought she was waiting for the end of the noises, that was all. Until he went back into his room under the stairs, and calm returned to the house. But that couldn't have been it, for she was as restless afterwards as she had been before—until she finally fell asleep.

Mostly he came home from work before she did, and made his supper in the kitchen. But he also prepared hers by peeling potatoes for both of them or scrubbing vegetables. He toted the briquets for the kiln into the yard; he brushed the rugs and chopped the wood. She had been surprised when he moistened the clay one day and piled it on a piece of canvas, so that she could start at her potter's wheel right away. In the beginning she had lain in wait for him, because she wanted to thank him, but whenever he came up the stairs and noticed that her light was still burning, he turned around and went back down. In time an agreement developed between them, so that they avoided one another, virtually like sleepwalkers.

When she was shopping for him, now and then she would add a slice of bread or a piece of bacon, or fifty grams more sausage than he had left her in ration stamps. Or she would leave him a bowl of potato salad in the evening, with lots of smoked bacon in it, for which she would accept no stamps at all. In return, sometimes he would put a bar of synthetic honey, which he had bought with sugar coupons, under her embroidery frame. Or a little bottle of lavender water. And she would darn his socks and sew buttons on his shirts in exchange. Things went along like this for a while, and all at once the teacher noticed how much she liked having him in the house with her. She stopped inviting guests and stopped accepting invitations from others. She sat at the wheel in her pottery workroom

until late at night, working more than ever before. Finally she ven-
tured into larger formats, too, reliefs and portrait busts.

After she had lived with Prohaska this way for a while, she thought
about whether this might be something like love. Sometimes she
would linger longer in front of the mirror and she now washed her
dry hair, which was brittle in places, in water to which she added
dried rose petals. She caught herself making curls with a curling iron.
And she didn't merely put lotion on her hands anymore; she had
concocted a skin cream of Vaseline and dried, ground lavender petals,
which she applied to her face, hands, and shoulders and rubbed into
her skin. Because of Prohaska's presence, even though she didn't see
him any more often than before, changes were taking place within
her, but she didn't want to think about them. Prohaska was her
lodger; he paid her fifteen marks for the room under the stairs.

One time she had written: *Can you go to Oderwalde with me on
Sunday, I need some especially rich clay.* And he had written: *I'll go
with you wherever you want.* So they had brought back a whole hun-
dredweight of rich, reddish clay from Oderwalde.

Later she had also written him: *Can you help me open the kiln
tomorrow evening, at eight-thirty?* And he had written: *I'll be waiting
for you at the kiln at eight o'clock.*

She had never seen him like this, with these gentle, astonished
eyes, when they opened the kiln and he carefully lifted out the individual pieces with his big hands and set them on the table. He
admitted to her that it seemed like a miracle to him that those gray,
ugly, dull plates and vases, pitchers and bowls of dead clay that she
put into the kiln now had turned into gleaming, sparkling objects
that you could pick up in your hand and stroke, and sense their
shapes. He had immediately felt the miracle of the metamorphosis,
which she had stopped feeling because it had become routine for
her.

One day later she had found a note in the frame of the mirror: *I
want to tell you that you are a great artist. I love you!!!!*

If anyone had told her that people would say that her lodger was
her lover, she probably would have laughed. She had already noticed
that there was whispering about her in school. But that didn't worry
her. And ever since it had become known that she had applied for

membership in the Party, no one dared to whisper about her behind her back.

Yet she had only done it because of the pastor.

Archpriest Pattas had come with two acolytes during the *Kollende* procession to bless the house. It was a cold day in January and she had heated only one room, to save coal; he had gone through all the rooms with her and had sprinkled them all with holy water, including Prohaska's room under the stairs.

As the pastor was leaving, he had asked her softly but admonishingly whether she didn't want to free herself from a severe sin and give up the illicit relationship with a married man. Yes, he had said "illicit."

That was no laughing matter. But she hadn't been shocked either; she had no idea what had come over her. Pattas, of all people!

She called in sick at school, and kept to her bed for three days. Prohaska came out from his room under the stairs, and brought in wood and coal, stoked the stove and prepared food for her. He acted as if he were constantly busy with something, and always kept his back turned to her. She knew that he'd been married somewhere in the Ruhr. His wife had run off with a traveling salesman, and he hadn't heard from her in years. They had spoken about it briefly once, in the beginning; after that it was not a topic for discussion. But obviously it was for the Church. She recited the Archpriest's sentence a hundred times a day, and inspected each word for its hidden meaning. They wanted to take Prohaska away from her, it was that simple. She no longer went to confession. And after a while she stopped going to mass, too. But a person has to believe in something, she thought, having been brought up that way since childhood.

She went back to her teaching, and in the evenings sat at her wheel. She worked like a woman possessed. Once Prohaska came in, sat down in the shadows in the corner of the workshop, and watched silently as she worked. After a while she asked him to turn toward her, and she adjusted the light to shine on his face. She modeled a portrait of his head that night, until the early morning, and didn't stop until she was done with it. Not a word was spoken.

She left the door to her room open at night now. She washed

loudly in the kitchen, splashing the water around, put on her night-gown as audibly as she could. She tossed and turned in her bed, and then she kept quiet, to listen for his steps on the stairs and in the hall, but he didn't come. Until she had a crying fit one night. It had come over her just like that. Her whole body began to quiver, her teeth chattered, the muscles of her face twisted, tears ran out of her eyes. He finally came to her then. In the darkness. Since then she no longer recognized herself. She was a different woman. And she was surprised when she observed the other person in her activity. That's how little she had been herself sometimes.

Now she wanted him every night, that heavy, fleshy, sweaty body. And she waited for him somewhere different every night. She didn't want to be reminded of a marriage, of the habitual repetition, of something that his wife had possibly run away from. She found ever new hiding places in her house. He pursued her everywhere.

She began to discover her own body; she began to discover herself—feelings and abilities, joys and desires that she had only read about in books. She laughed. She laughed more often than ever before in her whole life. Sometimes she would hum a song to herself, which she had never done before. She touched her body, her skin, her face, and it gave her a feeling of contentment and desire. If the Archpriest had come now and had told her that she was "living in sin," she would not have gotten pains in her chest or red patches on her face; no, she would have hauled Prohaska out of his room under the stairs and said: "Yes, I'm living in sin, and you drove me to it."

She wanted to have her Prohaska all to herself now. In her house, in the dark. And when she saw him outside with other people in broad daylight, then it still gave her a twinge in her heart.

"They want to send you to the Ruhr," the teacher said, "where the bombing is going on! I can't understand it at all. Now that all of the armament production is being shifted to Silesia . . ."

"It's an official order," Prohaska said. "I'm going to the Ruhr like a soldier to the front." He didn't have the courage to tell her the truth.

"Yes," Fräulein Bombonnek said, "now the war is coming to us. There's no way of stopping it."

They walked along together holding hands. They didn't care about how people would talk. It no longer mattered.

She stopped and looked into his eyes. Suddenly she knew everything.

"Have you heard from your wife?" she asked tonelessly.

He just said, "Yes."

His wife had actually written him, the letter had reached him a few days ago. And he had not known how to tell the teacher. His wife had cancer and didn't know how much longer she would live. So he had to go to her. They were chained to each other forever by the holy sacrament of marriage.

"Take care of yourself," the teacher said. "Now, with all the air raids. If anything happens to you, I'll kill myself."

32

"Archpriest pattas has locked himself in the sacristy and is crying," said Erna Dolezich, who had slowly chatted her way through the crowd to her friends. This news was like a greeting, which the two women received gratefully.

"Poor Pattas!" Frau Wieczorek said. "This must have hit him hard."

"Yes," Frau Schimitschek said, "those bells aren't so ordinary, like the new ones at Christ the King's or Bartholomew's. Ours were consecrated in 1901. One of them comes from All Saints' and is supposed to have been cast right after the Thirty Years' War; the Danes had already taken the bells down once and had taken them along as booty. The big one has a few pounds of gold in the alloy, that's why it has such a beautiful tone. Oh, yes, there are differences!"

Where did she know that from?

"My husband travels a lot, you know, in the occupied zones to the East, confiscating precious metals for armaments, that's how I know that." She said it almost apologetically. "It's no longer just bells, they're taking the copper from domes, towers, and roofs now, everything is being used."

"But I can't figure out why they're doing this on Good Friday, of all days. People are so excited, none of them want to go into the church, they're all waiting outside."

They only had to turn around to see that for themselves. Frau Dolezich smelled a vast conspiracy against the Catholic Church behind this. They should resist. The state had always been against the Catholic Church. Even back in Old Prussia. Her father had told her all sorts of things about the "cultural struggle." She had forgotten the details, but the term *Kulturkampf* had stuck.

"This is a *Kulturkampf*!" she said.

"This is a dirty trick, is what it is," Frau Wieczorek said.

"Yes, that is what it is," Frau Dolezich confirmed. That term was easier to grasp.

"A dirty trick on our dear Archpriest Pattas. They'd really like to transfer him to someplace in the Reich. If he hadn't been here for so long already! After all, he read the Pope's Christmas message from the pulpit on Christmas!" She emphasized it strongly, so that they would all note how bold he had been. None of them had thought there was anything special or unusual or courageous about the Pope's Christmas message at the time. They hadn't realized it until later, when they found out that Pattas was the only pastor in all of Silesia who had dared to read it from the pulpit.

"And isn't he protecting Curate Mikas, too?"

"Yes, he has to, especially now that he's just returned from a year and a half in the concentration camp—or was it two? How much things have changed; you don't realize it when you're so close to it," she said. She had visited Curate Mikas and talked with him, but he had pointedly avoided speaking about the period of his internment.

"No one ever really figured out why they locked him up," Verena Schimitschek said. She had known these women for years, but nowadays you had to be careful even with your best friend. You were surrounded by so much envy and resentment, especially if you still had a man in the house.

"But you can imagine why," said Jutta Wieczorek, who couldn't imagine at all.

"Does he still have contacts with Polish priests, our Pattas?" Frau Schimitschek asked. "There are supposed to be some who abuse their office. They smuggle propaganda material against the Germans under their cassocks. Pistols, too, I heard, and hand grenades that the Communists in the General Gouvernement use to blow up railroad tracks."

"You can't be serious!" Frau Dolezich acted astonished. She had always known you had to be careful around Frau Schimitschek. Particularly now, since her husband had not been drafted and was always traveling around in the Eastern zones.

"The curate is innocent," Jutta Wieczorek said with conviction. "I would put my hand into the fire on that. Otherwise they wouldn't have let him out again. My brother says that when someone has been in a camp, that's reason enough not to let him out unless they have to, because he's seen too much."

"What about the Wild Monk?" Verena Schimitschek said. "He's been in and out of prison and camps five times already. You hear so much! You have to be careful what you say these days. The enemy is listening. We've got Poles, Eastern laborers, Frenchmen, Belgians everywhere, they're all spies, everybody knows that."

Erna Dolezich wondered how she could step on her friend's foot unnoticed. She wished she knew how long Frau Wieczorek and Verena Schimitschek had been on such good terms. But it seemed to her to be a big trap! Her friend was too garrulous and careless, and what was worse, she thought that nothing could happen to her, as a war widow with four children at home, a fifth son at the front, and with the Mother's Cross in silver. Yet they could send the son to the front in Russia, for instance, or simply put a bombed-out family into her apartment with an informer among them.

She observed Frau Schimitschek's powdered face attentively and said: "When we are victorious, we won't even be able to ring the bells."

"Ach, yes," Frau Wieczorek enthused, "all the portals of the churches will be opened, flowers strewn in the streets, the soldiers in a rain of confetti, like at the big pilgrimage in May . . ."

She even forgot that her husband wouldn't be among the soldiers returning home. She hummed a melody to herself that she had not been able to get out of her head for days:

In parting I reach out my hands
and softly say Auf Wiedersehn

"Yes, that's what we're all waiting for," Frau Schimitschek said.

"Then I would like to travel to the Mediterranean, finally, with my husband. He was at La Spezia and couldn't stop talking about it when he was home on leave. After the war we want to carry toiletries and perfume in the store, you can't make any money on stationery alone. You don't get to the Mediterranean that way."

Frau Dolezich was already making plans for peacetime, over and over again, because peacetime was so slow in coming.

"My husband has good prospects of getting into the Ministry of Air Transport after the war. It would be nice to live in Berlin for a few years—theater and concerts and vaudeville and all the things there."

She was already looking forward to it. Earlier their name was Szymiczek; in 1939 they had changed their name to Schimitschek, and if they moved to Berlin, they would transform it to Schmidt. Schimitschek would always remind the Berliners of Poland.

A pretty tale reaches its end
And yet it was so beautiful

Frau Wieczorek sang to herself.

"Have you heard, Widow Piontek's servant girl got herself involved with a Pole—they came and took her away yesterday and locked her up. Jesus and Mary, poor Frau Piontek, she must be in a bad way."

"With an Eastern laborer," Frau Schimitschek said, who must already have heard. "That's even worse! How can such a thing happen in your own house, under the eyes of the woman of the house . . . Don't people realize where we live? We're surrounded by agents and spies . . ."

"Look, the bell!" Frau Dolezich called out. They all watched as the bell was lowered slowly onto the flatbed of the truck. A few people applauded halfheartedly.

"*Muj Bosche*, how could they lock Halina up on account of that. She's half Polish herself."

Frau Wieczorek was fighting against a melody that was stubbornly lodged in her head. A while ago it had been played on the radio every day, and she had liked the song. Then other new songs had come along and she had forgotten the melody. But on Sunday evening her children had said to her. You have to listen to the request concert with Heinz Goedecke, and suddenly this already forgotten song was played. After the song was over, Goedecke had said, and his voice alone could make you swoon: ". . . and for the fortieth birthday of Jutta Wieczorek from Gleiwitz, Upper Silesia Raudener-strasse 25, from her children in the homeland and from her eldest son Klaus guarding the homeland at the Atlantic Wall!" What a surprise that had been. When her birthday was not until a week later.

If only her Engelbert had lived to hear it. Now she would no longer be waiting at the gate to the mine on Saturdays after his shift, to grab the pay envelope out of his hand. Now she wouldn't have minded if he drank some of it up. And she couldn't get the song out of her head:

> *Your picture I carry in my heart*
> *oh how sweet it was with you*
> *and tell you as we part*
> *that I love you true.*

"When shall we three meet again, in thunder, lightning or in rain?" Erna Dolezich said jokingly.

"When this mess is all over."

"It could happen quickly, but it might take a long time." Frau Wieczorek sighed.

"How do you mean?"

"We should stand here and not let the trucks through, then they couldn't haul the bells away!"

"Eichendorff didn't write such long poems," Bronder said. "I know a lot of songs by him."

"Then we'll just have to go into the rectory and have Curate Mikas give us the *Ballad Treasury*. We've got to find out the ending!"

They had to take a detour around the barricade. That took them underneath the acacia from which Tex Weber was still dangling his legs. He had rolled up a sheet of paper and was now peering through this telescope into the world. He was no longer interested in the church tower. By now the bell had been deposited on the flatbed.

"Have you gotten any farther with your insane ballad?" Tex Weber called to them from above.

"Ossadnik, your mother is looking for you!" a voice called out. It sounded like Froschek, the teacher, or Herr Krawutschke. Neither of them was visible.

Instead Kotik popped up, a book in his hand. "I've got it, the 'Ballad of the Bell Casting in Breslau,'" he called excitedly. "It's by Wilhelm Müller."

He had placed a stone between the pages so he could find the place more quickly. "Should I read it to you?"

"Our Kotik, you see, he thinks of things like that. You're a real *pieron!*" Andy patted him on the head. "Read it to us, *hoppek.*"

While Kotik read, more and more people came up to listen:

> *"His last request was granted,*
> *a small thing, it was said:*
> *the church bell would be ringing*
> *as he to death was led.*
>
> *"The master heard the tolling,*
> *so full, so pure, so clear;*
> *it must have been from pleasure*
> *his eyes were filled with tears.*
>
> *"With confidence he lowered*
> *his neck to meet the stroke,*
> *for what in death is promised*
> *he'd not, in life, revoke.*
>
> *"That, of all the bells which he,*
> *the master'd cast, is crown—*
> *the bell of Magdalena*
> *at Breslau in the town.*
>
> *"As though he were transfigured*
> *his eyes, it seemed, then shone;*
> *much more than one bell ringing*
> *did he hear in its tone.*
>
> *"'Twas dubbed the Bell of Sinners*
> *in memory of his crime,*
> *and there has been no reason*
> *to change it in our time."*

No one had interrupted Kotik. Even when he was finished, they were silent for a while. Even Hrabinsky. He just sucked at his cold pipe.

"That's beautiful," said Fräulein Willimczyk, the bookseller, quite simply. They even believed she meant it.

And Apitt repeated the last verse, more to himself, but everyone listened, and still others whispered the last two lines as he spoke.

"And there has been no reason
to change it in our time."

Andy pushed past the others and walked away, without saying a word. Kotik looked after him; then he looked at the others, because he didn't know what he should do now. He clapped the book shut and ran after Andy; it took a while to find him in the crowd. People were already streaming into the church.

Kotik walked along a few steps next to Andy, who was looking stoically at the ground, and asked him cautiously: "Did I do something wrong, Squintok?"

"No, no," Andy said, and wrapped his arm around his brother's neck. "I was just thinking of something that I haven't been able to get out of my head all day. Sometimes I forget about it, but then it comes back. You know, I keep thinking about how could anyone pound nails through the hands of a living person. I don't understand it . . . well, I just can't understand it . . ."

"Get out of the way! Move it!"

"Ladies, be reasonable!"

"Did you see that? Archpriest Pattas!"

"He blessed the bells from up in the tower."

"Let me through, damn it all . . ."

"Good Lord, someone is cursing. On Holy Good Friday. *Pjerunnje!*"

The motors of the trucks roared. A few thin whistles could be heard, along with a few isolated voices.

"If all the women stand in place, like a wall, then they can't get through with their bells," Herr Apitt said.

"Get out of the way, beat it, or else we'll clear the square!" one of the men with an armband yelled. The threat would have to suffice, for he didn't really have enough men to clear the square. As if to demonstrate, the motor roared.

"Can't you go get the pastor to send these hysterical females away?" yelled the truck driver.

"I'm going into the church," Rosa Willimczyk said. "Everything's over now, anyway." Somehow she was disappointed, like most of the people here. She didn't want to admit that basically she had been waiting for a catastrophe. Everything was breaking up so routinely now.

"Take your chair and go," Apitt said to Hrabinsky, the cripple. "If a panic breaks out now and they stampede, you only have to fall with that wooden leg, and they'll trample you to death. But let me climb up on your chair first for a minute; I want to see what's going on up there." Hrabinsky put a newspaper on the seat first, then Apitt was allowed to stand on it. The chair wobbled so dangerously that Apitt had to steady himself with one hand on Hrabinsky's head. He saw the first truck driving slowly forward and the crowd retreating just as slowly.

"They're falling back," Apitt said. "But at least they put up some resistance."

"When the Jews were taken away from their community house on Niederwallstrasse," Hrabinsky said, "the women just gawked, none of them were angry."

"I will never forget that they stole our bells from us on Good Friday, 1943," a woman screamed loudly. She screamed from the middle of the crowd, so it wasn't possible to identify her.

"I think I'd better go now," Valeska said. "I've been on my feet long enough. Something might be happening with Irma. Maybe she's already in labor."

But first she wanted to do the penance in church that the pastor had assigned her that morning. My Lord, what a day this has been, she thought, I haven't even gotten around to washing myself clean of sin.

"I have to do my vows," Anna said. "I'd just like to know what Kotik and Andy are up to. They were going to be here, too." She no longer had any hope of Tonik's coming.

Now the hollow sound of the wooden clappers could be heard

from everywhere. A few women began the Good Friday song, and
then the people outside on the square joined in:

> *"O head of blood and wounds*
> *By mockery covered and pain"*

The trucks drove past blowing their horns loud and long, as if trying
to drown out the singing of the crowd. Then they turned onto Peter-
Paul-Platz and drove away in the direction of the train station. The
crowd, now no longer so tightly packed, kept on singing and pushed
slowly toward the main portal of the church, which was wide open.
The cordon had been removed in the meantime.

They continued to sing loudly:

> *"Oh, Lord, what you have suffered*
> *Is all my burden.*
> *I am to blame for*
> *That which you have borne."*

33

Tᴏɴɪᴋ ᴘᴜsʜᴇᴅ ʜɪs way through the crowd. Wasn't that Hedel Zock, the one with the dark hair rolled at the back of her neck? That could only be Hedel Zock. He reached for her arm and held it firmly.

"Tonik, it's you," she said, startled, and stared at his face and his epaulets. "You're on leave?"

For a second Tonik thought that she was really happy to see him. Many women actually were happy when they saw a soldier in uniform, for soldiers were already a rarity. And besides, he had danced with her once out there in the New World, at a railwaymen's ball.

Tonik began with his invitation to the Café Schnapka, but she refused immediately, without even hearing him out. As if she had heard that one from him before. *Pjerunnje!* He resolved to think up something different for a change.

"Not on Good Friday," she said. "Cake is a sin today."

Yet there was so seldom cake anymore that she would have eaten it on any fast day—just not in public. Since a woman was listening to them, Hedel attempted to talk Tonik into going into the church with her, today, on Good Friday, to pray the sorrowful mysteries of the rosary.

Tonik would not go into the church at all. But by the time they had reached the gate, he had to have a date for that evening. And he hoped this white lie would not miss its effect on her: "I'm sorry I can't, I've been ordered to appear at command headquarters."

After all, that was a higher authority than God. At least in times like these.

The woman in the white turban turned up next to them again. Hedel, in any case, had to go into the church. But before that she was all too glad to have the promise wheedled out of her to meet Tonik in front of the Capitol Cinema at eight that evening. Tonik was so happy that he simply reached for her hand and squeezed it and didn't want to let it go again. She let him do it, and even smiled at him. His boldness was making him dizzy. At any rate, he curled his index finger twice in the palm of her hand until she pulled away and vanished into the church. A buddy from his company had advised him to do that, as an unmistakable signal; and only now did he flush at the thought that he might have gone too far with Hedel Zock. On the other hand, if she knew this kind of sign language, she would know what he wanted from her, and that was fine with him, and if she didn't come to the Capitol Cinema that evening, well, that would be an answer too. He had only two weeks' leave, so it was good for relationships to be clear.

He had imagined his leave differently, anyway. The first three days he had just slept, and then Mamotschka had told him all sorts of unnecessary things about the children and about her novels, sometimes mixing up the two topics, finally coaxing his travel ration stamps from him, at least most of them—he kept only a few bread stamps, so that he could invite someone to a pastry shop.

All of his friends were in the war, and Norbert Pawlik had already fallen in Africa. So he just went to the movies by himself, or to some bar, but it was difficult to strike up conversations with strangers. He sensed a certain hostility on the part of the others, who stared at him and drank down the flat wartime beer in silence; they seemed to regard him with reproach because he was running around Gleiwitz in his uniform, while their husbands or sons were fighting at some front or perhaps had already fallen.

All at once he discovered that he had nothing to do with his time. In the military, every hour had been filled, and if they ever really had nothing to do while on duty, some s.o.b. of an officer would think up something *pjerunnisch* for them to do so they wouldn't have time to think. Now, all of a sudden, he was completely his own man, and he didn't know how to get along without orders, which had been structuring his days, indeed, his life for a long time now. If he got his way with Hedel Zock that evening, then he would know what to do on the ninth day, and maybe on the tenth day too. On the eleventh day he would look around for somebody new. Who knew whether he would ever be coming back to his homeland again.

He should have married Hanna Baron! Now she was in Cologne, with the Homeland Flak. That was too far away for him—and besides, he had no desire to travel there, where they constantly had air raids. To be married in wartime did have lots of advantages. Very simply, you had someone who was waiting for you. Horst Müller, with whom he had been in the field hospital in Litzmannstadt, told him, as they were riding back to Germany on the same train, that on his leave he would do nothing but shut himself and his wife into their apartment and screw for the whole two weeks. Do nothing but eat, drink, and screw, until he had to climb back on the train to the Eastern Front. He envied Horst Müller.

From inside the church he heard singing. Tonik imagined Mamotschka sitting in a pew up near the front, praying her rosary, the sorrowful mysteries, for her perpetual indulgences. And somewhere in a different pew sat Hedel Zock.

I've got to zero in on someone before the day is out, Tonik thought. A gang of teenagers ran past him; he recognized his brother Squintok among them, but without his glasses, and with a bandage on his face. What a sight he was!

No, he would not go into the church. He hadn't been in a church since he was eighteen. There had been lots of quarreling at the time, and for that reason he had stayed away from home for six months. He had spent that time living at the Kolping House—in the Kolping House, of all places. Mamotschka had forced him to go to church every Sunday for long enough, to scrape his knees on the hard benches, and, what was worse, to go to confession to tell the pastor his most secret thoughts in some narrow, dark, stuffy wooden box that they called a confessional. Things you didn't talk about with anyone, not even with your best friend, let alone with your mother, and now he was supposed to confess: that he thought and did unchaste things, to himself and to others. The curate in the dark confessional questioned him extensively, and wanted to know more—what did he think about while doing it, and what did he feel? And he didn't know what to answer, because he simply thought of everything and anything in the process, whatever occurred to him, least of all girls, which is what the curate always wanted him to say. Anyway, he hadn't been to confession since then, and soon after that he stopped going to church, too. Whenever the family was getting ready to go to church, he had demonstratively picked up some installment of a Rolf Torring novel, which he intended to read at just that time, and Mamotschka would always break into tears. In the military he had met guys for the first time who had never gone to an auricular confession in their whole life, and they were not just Lutherans, who, as he already knew, rejected confession. But he was disappointed that they treated his refusal simply as a normal occurrence, and not as a heroic deed or at least an act of rebellion—the claim he made for himself.

The gang of teenagers encircled Tonik, Squintok at their head, making signs to the other boys.

"Is that really you, Squintok? They really took care of you! Where're your specs?"

Andy took his frames out of his pocket. With a grin, he poked a finger through one rim. It was the Lutherans, he said proudly. He held the frame of his glasses up in the air like a trophy.

"Still the guerrilla warfare between Catholics and the Lutherans? That's a joke. I thought you'd all be in the Homeland Flak by now, learning how to operate a light 3.7, a heavy 12.8, and the quadruple antiaircraft, and practicing marksmanship. Enough of this kid stuff! You'll be soldiers in only two or three years, and you'll be at the front. Don't you have to go to church?"

The boys claimed unanimously that they had been in church that morning, before the men came to take down the bells, and had kissed the stigmata of the crucified Savior on the steps of the altar.

Tonik wanted to get away from the church square. He suggested to the boys that they visit the artillery barracks near the town woods. Two days ago he had been drinking with a soldier in town who was in charge of the horses at the barracks. He could meet him behind the stables. In weather like this it was very possible that he would be outside with the horses. He was going to go visit this buddy of his. Whoever felt like it could join him.

The boys wanted to so much that they broke into a roar, and because they all wanted to go along, Tonik had to choose. He chose Squintok, Wonzak, and Bronder, and finally the boy with the freckles and platinum blond hair, too, whom Andy spoke up for. Kotik was sent into the church, where he belonged, next to Mamotschka in her pew. She was probably looking for him all over, anyway.

But Kotik wanted to go see the horses with them so badly. Andy had to put his foot down and finally push his little brother into the church through the side entrance. Well, at that age you belonged in church next to your mother!

On Germaniaplatz they climbed onto the No. 4 streetcar, for it did seem too far to walk to the town woods—and they paid only half fare: schoolchildren and soldiers. MORGENROTH was on the front of the streetcar and Tonik wished he could travel as far as Morgenroth. Before the war, Poremba had been the last stop.

"What are the old *ferajnas* doing, Andy?"

"There aren't any anymore. Since the beginning of the war, there haven't been any. Two or three times a year we still get together, more or less by accident, and then we can't think up anything to do."

"Tell him the story about the old house next to the brickyard," Wonzak whispered, "you know!"

That was quite a while ago. But what of it, at least it was an excuse to reminisce.

Wonzak looked admiringly at Tonik. He wished he had a brother in the army too, with a uniform as handsome as Tonik's. Above all he admired the cap—no soft folding cap, but one with a real visor —well, that's where soldiering really began for him.

"There's *absolutnik* not much to say. There was just this old house by the brickyard, way over almost in Sosnitza, you know where I mean. We watched it a long time, nobody went in, nobody came out, nobody was living there. Somebody must have been in the house before us and looted it: the drawers were wide open and there wasn't any silverware or valuables left. And we couldn't figure out who used to live there, either. We just went on in, the remnants of our *ferajna*. We ate up all the supplies—there were lots of canned goods left in the cellar; then we slit open the mattresses and dumped the feathers on each other, tore up the books and smashed the crockery, and finally broke the furniture to bits . . ."

Andy fell silent, because all at once he felt that what they had done was ridiculous.

"What else, what else?" Wonzak urged him on. And when Andy still hesitated, he continued himself: "Then one day we set fire to the house. Well, it burned like tinder—the flames leaped up to the sky, and you could see them all the way from Sosnitza and Ellguth-Zabrze. Wasn't that a great demonstration, Squintok?"

"I already told you that I'm not Squintok anymore!" Andy said angrily.

"Did they catch you?" Tonik asked.

"Of course they did," Andy said. "*Absolutnik* nothing stays a secret. The police came and took us down to the station one by one and questioned us. We talked our way out of it; there hadn't been anyone in the house for weeks . . ."

"The house belonged to two Jewish sisters, you see, they lived there in the summer," Wonzak joined in, "and one day they came to get them in their apartment in town, and then they—"

"Shut your trap," Andy said sharply.

The one they called Hannes asked: "What is it like in the war, when shells are bursting all around, and you're advancing against the enemy behind the tanks, aren't you afraid then?" In the movies he had seen soldiers marching across a snow-covered landscape in a hail of shellfire. It wasn't easy to forget pictures like that.

"Do you wear white capes in winter, too, like the soldiers in the newsreels?" He had liked that. In the snow they simply could not be spotted by the enemy.

"At the front it's not like it is in the movies, I can guarantee you that," Tonik said. "I've never seen a white cape like that out there. But enough frozen arms and legs. What's it like at the front, well . . . you don't think, you get your orders and you move on out with the others, after all, you're never alone. And then you just fight . . . Where'd you get that?" He pointed at a scar on Hannes's temple.

His brother went after him with a knife when he was little, Hannes explained.

"Weren't you afraid?"

"No, I wasn't afraid," Hannes Stein said, "it happened so fast. Only afterwards it really made me sick, when I realized that he could have hit me in the eye."

"I think it's the same way with us," Tonik said. He was lying by a river waiting for the Russians to attack, and a piece of shrapnel had hit him in the left shoulder. He hadn't felt any fear, not even pain, it had just bled terribly, and it wasn't until later that he was afraid because his arm might be paralyzed. But everything had turned out all right.

"I only get really afraid," Tonik said, "when I have to go down into the cellar and don't have any matches." He laughed, but the boys believed he was serious.

First Valeska had to get used to the dim light. They were crowding into the church now as they did for the High Mass on Easter. She looked for a seat not far from the altar, then she heard the *klekotka*. She slipped into the nearest pew, kneeled down, and made the sign of the cross. She saw a cluster of acolytes proceed down the middle aisle, Precentor Zobtschik with the cross in front, which was enveloped in purple velvet, followed by two acolytes with the censer, after them a group clapping the *klekotka*. Archpriest Pattas alone followed the acolytes, then assistant Pastor Jarosch with Curate Mikas, and after them two other curates whom Valeska did not know. Pastor Pattas held his hands clasped, as if in prayer. He was wearing a plain black gown and nothing on his head. The group stopped at the steps of the main altar. The wooden clappers stopped their hollow, rhythmic monotony. It was very quiet in the church. Many people were craning their necks to see what was happening up front. Never before had all the priests proceeded through the church with the Archpriest at their head on Good Friday.

"O thou Lamb of God, that takest away the sins of the world, have mercy on us," Valeska whispered, and struck her breast. "O thou Lamb of God, that takest away the sins of the world, have mercy on us. O thou Lamb of God that takest away my sins with thy death on the Cross, have mercy on me."

They all rose from their seats. As long as Valeska could remember, the church had never been so full on Good Friday. She saw the Archpriest raising his hand in blessing. Then he turned around and virtually threw himself on the steps of the altar—a few women leaped from their pews, thinking the priest had collapsed—and kissed the stigmata of Christ. And it was a long time before he rose again. He waved away the other priests, who were trying to help him stand up.

"Thou who sweated blood on the Mount of Olives," Valeska prayed.

The Archpriest went into the sacristy between the two curates, who were supporting him. Not even the sacristy bell was ringing. The others waited, kneeling on the steps of the altar, until the Archpriest had dressed for the Good Friday liturgy. The wooden clappers were silent.

Valeska looked for her rosary.

"Thou who wore the crown of thorns. Thou who wast scourged. Thou who took the Cross upon thyself. Thou who fell beneath the weight of the Cross. Thou who had nails driven through hands and feet."

She looked around. In the diffuse light she could recognize only Frau Wieczorek. Valeska was finished with her penance. She was just about to include Halina in her prayer and beg for her protection, when the woman next to her leaned over and whispered: "Pastor Pattas had the bells recorded, and he will have the records played Sunday morning at the Resurrection Mass, through loudspeakers. Pass it on." Valeska did so, and watched the whispering pass from pew to pew, throughout the church.

Suddenly she heard the clatter of wooden clogs, at first almost like a brighter *klekotka* sound. Valeska glanced around, and saw a group of women walking along the middle aisle to the altar. They were wearing white kerchiefs and gray padded jackets. They had to be Eastern laborers, you could recognize them immediately, even if the EAST on the patch was not evident in the dim light. They stopped close in front of the altar and kneeled down on the stone floor. The faithful in the pews craned their necks. Some of them even stood up, to see the women better. Valeska was sitting not far from them. She watched them making the sign of the cross and striking their breast with one hand, just as she did.

And then Valeska noticed that they did something different when they made the sign of the cross. What was so different? Yes, they did not cross themselves from the left to the right, but from the right to the left. Valeska observed them closely, and imitated them. The fingers to the forehead, IN THE NAME, then to the center of the breast, OF THE FATHER, then to the right, OF THE SON, then to the left, AND OF THE HOLY GHOST, then back to the center again, AMEN.

The women left the church again close together, the way they had come in. Their wooden clogs clattered like a hollow, threatening, uncanny drum. Valeska remembered hearing someplace that the Eastern Church had split sometime in the Middle Ages, and that the Orthodox Russians had been making the sign of the cross from the right to the left ever since.

Maybe it was good to know how the Russians made the sign of the cross. It might come in handy some day.

34

THEY GOT OUT at Bergwerkstrasse and continued on foot along Lindenstrasse and past the Forest School, to the rear stables of the barracks at the town woods. On the sandy terrain young gunners with horses were practicing moving the heavy 10.5- and 15-centimeter howitzers, positioning and aiming them fast as lightning. Commands snapped through the quiet of the afternoon, and occasionally the neighing of the horses could be heard.

Back by the stables, Fritz came toward them. He had met Tonik in town two days earlier. He was wearing a uniform without insignia, which Wonzak noticed immediately but didn't dare to comment on, because their conversation initially was about Squintok's face; Andy wanted to leave again, because he was not in the mood to dispense information "about my pretty puss" to every soldier who came along. This Fritz was supervising a group of Eastern laborers, who were busy leading the horses outside and tying them up to iron rings that were set into the outer walls. Then they began to groom horses in the sun. You could observe everything in detail from up above, on the slope, the animals and their attendants. With quick, broad movements, the grooms stroked the backs of the horses with metal brushes, and in reversing their stroke, the brush passed over a metal comb that collected the dirt. They took turns with the work. A few of them were standing around, leaning against the wall, holding pieces of cardboard with tinfoil pasted on it next to their heads to reflect the sun's rays on their faces.

Andy went over to them to take a closer look. He had never seen anything like that.

"They're inventive, all right," Fritz commented. "But they're lazy." He clapped his hands and drove them back to work with loud yells. There were fewer and fewer clouds in the sky, and here at the foot of the wind-protected slope it was much warmer. Fritz took off his uniform jacket. Red-striped suspenders crossed over his undershirt, which was open wide at the neck showing a patch of black, curly hair. Fritz knew more than the names and ages of the horses; he knew their special characteristics, too, even their quirks, as he called them. "This dark brown stallion," he said, pointing to a heavy, peaceful animal, through whose coat the skin was already showing in many places, "was a draft horse at the Scobel Brewery until a short time ago. He's full of quirks; without blinders you can't even lead him out. He must be fourteen or fifteen, that's about the average. Our young horses are all at the front. The ones here usually wind up in the glue factory. Many of them you can't even train with on this sandy terrain. If they ever fall, they don't get up again."

Well, when you watched the poor troopers over there being put through their paces, Andy Ossadnik said, you almost wanted to forget about becoming a soldier. He had been looking over toward the training area the whole time.

The horse handler just laughed.

"As a soldier," Wonzak said, "at least you get to meet women easier."

Tonik bit the tip off a blade of grass and spit it out. That was his answer. He took off his cap and placed it carefully on the grass, and unbuttoned his uniform jacket.

Bronder never saw girls anywhere except at church. But there they were kept separate by the middle aisle. The women sat in the pews to the left, the men to the right. You could only get close to them when you were leaving. If you were sly enough about it, you could even touch their fingertips, if you dipped your hand in the holy water just when they did. At school they were separated by a wire fence, and often enough they had their recess at different times. For a long time Sundays and going to church had been associated with girls for him, and girls with going to church, and because they never got any closer, he dreamed about them, and hoped to become a soldier someday, but only so he could finally get close to them.

"When I think," Fritz said, "about how I banged that old broad in Port Arthur!" He snapped his suspenders and laughed, remembering. "Do you know Port Arthur?"

Naturally Tonik knew Port Arthur, but nobody knew why it had such an odd name. That was the settlement out in Zernik, where earlier the jobless had lived, half Gypsies or Polacks, all of them families with ten or twelve children; it was supposed to be worse than "Cameroon" and was infamous, above all, because of knife fights. It must be a lot different, now, though; the place was called Gröling now.

"Yes, sure," he said, "but I've never been there."

"Well, the women there are really hot," Fritz, the horse handler, said. "You get anything you want for a loaf of army bread. The men are off at war. You just have to be careful! While you're busy with some broad in the bedroom, her kids are emptying the pockets of your uniform in the kitchen. They'll swipe anything they think they can use, and you can't imagine what stuff they find a use for. They're like magpies."

With his eyes Tonik followed a red ant that was stumbling across the little hairs on his hand. If he didn't get anywhere with Hedel Zock that evening, maybe he could try Port Arthur for a change.

"They took everything a buddy of mine had," the horse handler continued, "after he had been making it with two of them all night, and chased him away literally in his underwear. And then when he marched in the next day with a real commando to get his uniform back at least, they had already dyed it and altered it."

From the rage in his voice it was easy to guess that he himself had been the buddy. The boys were listening attentively. They were thinking less about what a soldier would do without his uniform than about what he would be doing with two women at once.

Fritz took a packet of cigarette papers from his pocket, took out a paper, which he placed on the palm of his left hand, and plucked some tobacco from another pocket. No one could see how much tobacco he still had left.

"I've been here for over a year already," he said: "G.F.H.," and he explained it to the boys: "Garrison-Fit, Homeland," and pointed to his chest. "Bad pump. They need a few men at the home front, too, right?" He licked the cigarette paper and rolled the cigarette between his fingers.

Wonzak lit a match eagerly.

"*I* would be afraid," Tonik said, thinking of the Port Arthur story, "on account of VD." And waited while Fritz took the first few drags. Then he took the cigarette carefully with two fingers.

"If you're in one place for any length of time, you look for something steadier, of course," Fritz said. "And you guys"—he turned to the boys—"you probably think you can just go down to the Klodnitz, behind the theater, where the whores hang out, and soldiers and kids get it for half price . . ."

But the boys just stuck their hands in their pockets and said nothing. They were waiting for the cigarette, which Tonik now passed around the circle.

"You have to be careful," Tonik said, "on account of VD." He took the blade of grass out of his mouth and threw it away, revolted. There was nothing he was more afraid of than VD.

Andy, who had lain down on his stomach, took a long drag on the cigarette, and then passed it on. "Yes, but what can you do about it?"

"A rubber," the horse handler said dryly. "Pull a rubber over it. You can get yourself in trouble in spite of it, naturally. Some broads don't like it. Besides, it can bust. No quality anymore."

"There are people who are totally rotting away because of VD," Tonik said. "Like Heine, for instance."

"Who?" Hannes asked.

"A poet," Andy said tersely. That was all he knew on the subject. "Poets often used to die of syphilis, which afterwards they claimed was consumption, otherwise they couldn't have shown it on stage, like in the opera *La Traviata*."

It was obvious that you needed to know things like that nowadays. He knew this from Paulek, who had learned it at the reform school in Schakanau. You learned more there than you did in school. He hoped that nobody would ask him what syphilis was or *La Traviata*. It had taken him long enough to get the pronunciation right. The first was a venereal disease and the other an opera, of that much he was sure.

"After all, you can't make the broads show you their yellow certificate in advance," the horse handler said.

Tonik could tell that he wouldn't get along with him in the long run. Once he had seen an exhibit with a *woman of glass*, that had been the main attraction at the Museum of Hygiene in Dresden. If you pressed a button, then all the sores and ulcers that you could get from the various venereal diseases lit up on her; it had really made him sick. There was a sign hanging above the woman: ENLIGHTENMENT IS NECESSARY, and since then he had felt a sort of mission to enlighten everyone else, too. He had done so in his company, in Poland, in France, in Russia, but the soldiers had usually laughed at him, even when they long since had been getting quick-silver treatments. But the boys here, still half children, they didn't have the faintest notion, and maybe they could be spared this blight.

"Of course that won't work," Tonik said disdainfully, without looking at anybody directly. "You can't expect them to show you a guarantee first, you have to take your own precautions. I said precautions—that's as much as you can do. The women" (and he stressed the word, to mark the difference between himself and Fritz, this horse handler) "often don't even know that they have VD, that's the worst part.

"There are," he lectured, "three kinds of venereal disease: the clap, also called gonnor . . . gonor-ear, syphilis, also called syph, and the soft chancre."

Fritz even forgot about the Eastern laborers, who were finished grooming the horses and were shining the sunlight on each other's faces with the tinfoil mirrors.

"You can tell the clap, because you get a yellow, pus-y discharge in three to five days. When you piss, it really burns, and it's off to the infirmary. That's fairly easy to tell . . ."

"Well, how do you spell that?" Andy said, who was trying to keep up. "Can you give it to me letter by letter, gonnor . . . or whatever it was?" He wished he had a pencil and a piece of paper, this was important enough to write down.

Tonik was not too sure himself, so he ignored the question and talked on, after a brief glance at Andy: "Syphilis is more complicated. If you've gotten infected with it, a so-called primary symptom forms in two to three weeks, a sore spot that turns into a boil about the size of a lentil. This boil is hard, like a coin, it has kind of a greasy shine, and that's why it's called a 'hard chancre.' "

"It sounds like you've already had it three times." Wonzak admired his precise description.

"Be quiet," Tonik said. "In eight to ten weeks, you then get a rash on your skin, most of all on your belly, your chest, and on your back; round patches the size of a penny, which knot up and cover your whole body. Now treatment is really urgent. Otherwise you'll begin to rot."

The pause he made was heavy with significance.

"If it's the soft chancre," Tonik continued, "you get a boil on your tool in one to five days—well, at least you'll notice it right away."

The boys were breathing heavily. Even the horse handler was not saying anything. Hannes Stein was already regretting having come along.

"But I've got a few basic rules and if you follow them, you can protect yourself and don't have to be afraid of having sexual inter-course," Tonik said patronizingly. "Well, the first one: Always wash your *ciulok* right afterwards, with soap, of course. And pee first thing, that's a good thing to do, it rinses everything out. And check your *ciulok* later too, of course, for instance in the morning, when you wash. Then always look at your chest in the mirror, to make sure there's no rash. And be careful: Before screwing, check out the lady, her sexual equipment, whether there are any sores or boils down there."

One of the boys snorted. Maybe his imagination was too lively.

"What do you mean by a rash?" Wonzak interjected. "I can't run to the doctor every time I get a pimple on my shoulder. We've all got pimples."

He laughed as if it were a joke.

But the others didn't laugh. Andy would have liked to pull Won-zak's shirt off and conduct an inspection with his oldest brother of the pimple status of Wonzak's shoulders. He had pimples all over, particularly on his face.

"Just as I said, like patches at first, pustules, then they turn into little boils." He paused.

"Now your prescriptions, we want to know them!" Andy said.

"Yes, I've got my rules for how you can protect yourself before-hand; I've tried most of them out myself. The whole thing has to be extremely inconspicuous, of course, that's obvious. Well, here's the simplest way: If you're a heavy smoker, and your index and middle finger are very brown with nicotine, like Fritz's there, then just hold your fingers lightly in place on the female sexual equipment, one or two minutes, that'll be enough. If the lady is sick, then it'll itch and she won't be able to stand it. If you don't have enough nicotine"—he was looking at his own fingers—"just clamp match heads between your fingers and hold them in place—you need five or six match heads. Sulphur," he said, "has the same effect."

The boys stared at Tonik in astonishment. The cigarette went around once more; it was so short now that they had to hold it with their fingernails.

The horse handler, who was listening attentively, remembered something else: "They can't stand copper or brass, either," he said. "It can be a golden wedding ring, too. Just stick your finger in inconspicuously and leave it there. In an hour it'll turn green—that means she's got it."

He twisted at his wedding ring.

Inconspicuously! Well, that was too much even for Tonik.

"How am I supposed to get my finger in there?" Hannes asked in a hoarse voice.

"And a whole hour," Andy said, "isn't that kind of long?"

Bronder said nothing out of sheer excitement. Maybe they would send him away for being too young. So he kept quiet and listened.

"Some of them like the finger, the French women, for instance," Tonik said, worldly-wise. After all, he had been a soldier in France. But an hour really was too long.

Fritz stuck to his guns. "I didn't think that one up," he defended himself. "It takes that long. It's simply a . . . chemical reaction. It takes an hour to change color."

"Can't you put in a copper coin instead, like a pfennig?" Tonik asked. He didn't wear a ring, but he always had change in his pocket.

"That should work, too," the horse handler decided generously.

None of the boys had anything more to say now. They were busy in their thoughts trying to declare their love to a girl and at the same time insert a copper coin in her slot. Each of them was discovering various difficulties with it.

"They can't stand alcohol, either. I mean, down there," Tonik said. "Naturally it's not enough to dip a finger in a schnapps glass ahead of time, and then stick it in. You have to take a whole mouthful and blow the schnapps into her. Well, if she's got the clap, she'll leap up, because she won't be able to stand it."

Hannes began to gag.

"Some girls are supposed to like it with schnapps," Wonzak said boldly. "Because it makes them hot."

"Don't you have to be careful too, I mean, so you don't get a kid?" Andy asked hoarsely.

None of them had thought about that.

"Use a rubber," the horse handler said again. "But there's no quality these days. At least, you can't depend on them."

"Or," Tonik added, "when you're almost there, just pull out your *ciulik*." But that sounded even less convincing.

"Well, if that's the way it is," Wonzak said pensively, "either the clap or a kid, I wonder why we want women so bad?"

"That's pure nonsense," the horse handler said irately. "Normally you just have fun, and nothing happens."

"Normally," Tonik said slowly and skeptically. As if he had not believed in anything normal for a long time now. "There's no guarantee unless you have a girl who has never done it with anyone else."

"I could tell you a hundred stories. You're not safe then, either," the horse handler said. "And you know, this is a funny region around here, I tell you. The people have sort of a religious quirk. Some broad asked me beforehand if I always go to church. Well, what does that have to do with a good lay?"

The horse handler glanced at the Eastern laborers, who were leaning against the wall between the horses, and still catching the sun with their homemade mirrors. The sky was shining brightly now. Fritz clapped his hands and jumped up. "If you don't keep your eye on these steppe rats every minute, they'll quit working on you."

He ran down the embankment toward the horses, yelling.

"You do have to be careful," Tonik said. "But that doesn't mean it's so much trouble that you shouldn't do it at all."

"You have to be careful about everything," Hannes Stein said, his voice strained.

"Right you are," Tonik said. He was thinking of Hedel Zock, and about their date at the Capitol Cinema.

Pjerunnje! Things had better work out tonight.

35

WHEN VALESKA TURNED onto Strachwitzstrasse on her way back from the Good Friday service and her house came into view, she quickened her pace. She was seized by a restlessness that made her heart beat faster. She imagined that she would enter the house and sounds would come from the kitchen and Halina would be standing before her with a stove pipe in her hand, her face slightly sooty, and say, *Stove draw bad in last few days*—and things would be as they always had been. She was hoping for this so much that she almost went right past Irma's room.

Irma was pacing back and forth barefoot, and her mother's entrance did not disturb her. She had gone for a walk in the garden with Lucie for a while. Now Lucie had gone to the kitchen to do the dishes, and she kept on pacing back and forth here. The pains in her back were bearable, and labor had not yet started; it might even be a few days before it did. She no longer remembered how it had been the last time, and from one hour to the next her overheated imagination invented a different story of how it would happen this time.

"It was exciting on the church square," Valeska said. "One bell had gotten caught in the masonry. Then they had to let a man down from the tower . . . is it really Lucie working in the kitchen?" She listened to the sounds and then shook her head at her own question. How could she even think that!

"Yes, of course," Irma said, puzzled. "She took Helga into the kitchen with her."

"Wouldn't it be better for the child to sleep somewhere else tonight? We could set up her bed in my room," Valeska asked carefully.

"No, no, it's better for her to stay here with me, she's used to it that way," Irma said, pacing. "And who knows when it will happen. I want everything to go on normally, everything as usual. But you've probably already told everybody in sight. Tina had her son bring over a bouquet of narcissus. I don't know whether she should have . . ."

"And the liturgy"—Valeska changed the subject—"you know, the most beautiful part for me is when Pastor Pattas says the *ecce lignum crucis*, and first unveils the left half of the cross, the second time the right half, and at the third *ecce lignum crucis*, the entire veil falls . . ."

She had really been impressed. And then when the acolytes went striding through the church, clapping the *klekotka*, and took the velvet veils down from all the other crosses, tears had actually come to her eyes.

"Uncle Willi told me about the bells," Irma said. "I don't believe in anything like that, but it is uncanny all right: they pick a Good Friday to take down the bells, a Good Friday when the weather changes so suddenly, a Good Friday on which, maybe, I'll have my baby . . ."

Valeska saw things more practically. "That must be it—the change in the weather is bothering you."

She told her about meeting Widow Zoppas, who had come back to Gleiwitz.

She interrupted herself hastily, because she couldn't tell Irma at that moment that Widow Zoppas had become a widow for the *second* time.

"She wanted to stay here with us for a few days," Valeska said, "but we don't have room. So Milka is going to take her in for the time being; they can take turns caring for the countess. The countess doesn't look good. You can already see her bones shining through her skin. I have the feeling she won't last much longer."

Valeska took two drops of her new migraine remedy and rubbed it into her temples. "I just wonder if Milka will inherit anything!"

The air in Irma's room was muggy, stale, and suffocating. But Valeska didn't dare to suggest that she open the window. She lifted her arms and sniffed at her armpits without embarrassment.

"I need to go get changed now, I practically stink," she said. But before that she made sure that it was really Lucie who was busy in the kitchen. And little Helga was sleeping in her small bed in spite of the noise.

"Did you remember that the president of the waterworks said he would be here at five o'clock?" asked Lucie, who was noisily scraping out a pot.

Jekuschnej, she really had forgotten that. Then it was high time to change. She had been running around all day in this old and much too tight housedress. It wasn't at all convenient for the president of the waterworks to come to the house on Good Friday, of all days, with Irma in her condition; Valeska could be called in to her at any moment. But on the telephone he wouldn't take no for an answer, because he had to go on a trip the next day. What he had to communicate to her was of the utmost importance. But he announced all of his visits as "important," although sometimes she couldn't even figure out whether he wanted to visit Willi, who was his lawyer, or her. Recently he had come more frequently and without any particular reason, to drink a bottle of wine with them or to play a few hands of rummy, or to borrow some newspapers from Willi. Sometimes he brought half a pound of butter or a pound of bacon that he'd gotten under the table somewhere. And because of that, they had occasionally invited him to dinner on a Sunday or a holiday. His wife had died of consumption two years ago. The climate here hadn't agreed with her; she'd looked skinnier and skinnier and more angelic, until one day she had given up breathing. To the surprise of everyone, he had her buried in the Lutheran part of the Linden cemetery, and not somewhere in Mecklenburg, where they came from.

What did he want today, on Good Friday? She hoped it wasn't about the strange affair that her brother had hinted at: that the president had the intention of marrying again. Naturally she had discussed such a "contingency" with her brother, without mentioning anyone specifically.

She asked her brother to receive the president of the waterworks, who not only was always punctual, but also liked to exaggerate it. She wanted to change her clothes first.

Valeska stood in front of her wardrobe, wondering what to put on for this occasion, when she saw the rectangular figure of the president coming up the garden path. *Jekuschnej*, he was much too early. She wished she could have rested on the sofa for a quarter of an hour. Just to lie down with her eyes shut and think of nothing at all; she needed that sometimes to get through the day. After all, she wasn't as young as she used to be, and the day might be a long one. She decided on the dress that buttoned all the way up the front, with the high collar; it wasn't modern, but it did lend her a certain sternness, and she could use that in the next half hour. While she dressed, she looked at herself in the mirror and discovered a new wrinkle engraving itself on her forehead. Recently she had had to admit certain signs of aging: gray strands of hair, wrinkles, and her skin was becoming drier and drier, even though she rubbed her face every day with whey. She tried to massage the wrinkle away with two fingers, but she wasn't much impressed with the results. She had lots of worries these days; the main one was that Josel had been drafted, and nothing had been able to prevent it. And now, since Halina's arrest, there would soon be more gray hairs.

She heard voices from the garden. Willi seemed to want to show the visitor the flowers, but except for crocuses, narcissuses, primroses, cowslips, and the pansies that Halina had planted in the fall, there was not yet much to be seen. But the daisies, scattered through the grass like yellow and white splinters!

The president was wearing a black suit, which she had never seen before except at the community potluck on Reichspräsidenten-Platz and at the funeral of his wife. As ever, he was of an intimidating blockiness as he pushed toward her now. He didn't look at her as he came up, because he was struggling with the paper to free the flowers, and if Lucie had not come to his aid, he would have knocked the heads off more than two roses with his thick fingers. So eight of them reached a vase, at any rate—red roses, at this time of year! Such splendor was only for the big wheels at their Party celebrations.

Then they stepped into the music room. Herr Müller was breathing heavily; indeed, he was snorting. The change in the weather must have been bothering him too, and when he wasn't sticking two

fingers between his shirt collar and his neck, he was rubbing his
hands dry on a crumpled handkerchief. Valeska had thought him
quite different, and he probably was, particularly if you compared
him to other officials. His massive body, almost rectangular but not
clumsy, his lumbering grace, his deep, rasping voice, his sentences,
which he larded with nouns. His peculiarity had once seemed even
greater, when his whispering wife had been around him; she was so
delicate and angelic by contrast.

They sat at a proper distance around the oval English table upon
which Lucie had already decoratively placed the vase with the red
roses. Willi took a silver cigarette case from his pocket and passed
it around; even the president helped himself to a cigarette, mostly
out of nervousness. Then he awkwardly offered them a light and
fiddled with the ashtray. Valeska arranged the roses again. Wondrak
reported their plans to redo the garden this spring; the bed of lavender was to be dug up, strawberries and tomatoes would be planted
in its place. And Valeska described the removal of the bells in imprecise and thus constantly changing terms. So they talked and sweated
until Lucie came in with the peppermint tea. The president of the
waterworks had several times already betrayed his intention to change
the subject to something far more important to him, but since he
tipped them off each time with a grotesque grimace, Willi or Valeska
was always able to head him off with a new conversational ploy. The
good man was sweating buckets.

After they had tortured him long enough, Willi Wondrak finally
leaned back and said, "As the president indicated to me beforehand
in the garden, he would like to discuss something very important
with you alone, dear sister."

But Willi didn't look like he was going to get up and leave.

Valeska didn't even wait for the explanation that Herr Müller was
obviously about to begin. She said in a kindly tone but firmly: "My
brother Willi has my full confidence. There is nothing that cannot
be discussed in his presence."

The president groaned and inserted his fingers between neck
and collar again. You could tell by his face that he was shaping
an excuse or an introduction or an explanation, and then gave it

up after repeated inhalations, finally to blurt out the single sentence that really mattered to him: "Frau Valeska, will you be my wife?"

Half an hour later Valeska was in her daughter's room. Irma was sitting on the edge of her bed with her legs apart. She was propping herself on the bed with her hands. Lucie was sitting next to her, rubbing her back through her bathrobe. Little Helga was sitting in her playpen, playing with a crudely carved wooden horse.

"So that's the way the president expressed himself," Valeska said, "and Willi and I looked at each other and didn't say anything for a while. And he thought we didn't understand him, so he repeated himself, sweating so much that he turned red. In a way I felt sorry for him."

And then she told Irma and Lucie, who giggled and forgot to massage Irma's back, how things had gone after that.

"The poor man!" was all Irma said. "Couldn't you have let him know in advance somehow, to spare him from this embarrassing situation?"

"Willi thought of that," Valeska said, "but how? After all, I never gave him so much as a thimbleful of hope. We could hardly ask him whether he had any ulterior motives with his frequent visits and gifts."

"How can anybody squeeze an old man into a black suit and have him show up on Good Friday afternoon? I think that's what's embarrassing," Irma said.

"But he called it urgent! Do you think I wanted to listen to him, after all that's been going on? And besides, it didn't seem to embarrass him much. He just took off his tie afterwards, loosened his collar, made himself comfortable in his chair, and now he's chatting with Willi and Herr Schimmel in the music room."

"Why was he in such a hurry, then?" Lucie asked innocently.

"Because he was ordered to the General Gouvernement as a war economics minister. He'll be in charge of all the water problems for the whole Warta-Vistula region," Valeska explained, somewhat self-importantly.

"He's exactly what they call a *good match*," Lucie commented thoughtfully.

"Tell me, Mamuscha, who talked you out of it?"

"Out of what?"

"Out of the president. I don't think he's exciting enough to make you fall over, but I have the feeling that Uncle Willi would talk you out of any other man, too. You don't have to stay a widow forever, you know. Neither Josel nor I would have anything against your getting married again . . ."

"After three and half years, Irma, what are you saying! I can't forget Leo Maria as fast as all that; I'll be mourning him a few more years. Besides, the president is Lutheran."

"But Mama, that's silly. Still mourning after three and a half years! Papusch would never have wanted you to. And in reality you've given away or hidden everything that reminded you of him . . ."

"Yes, because otherwise life would be even harder for me." Valeska put an appropriate expression on her face.

"That's all just a lot of words! You're not trying to claim that you ever had any consideration for Papa and us, are you? Your brother talked you out of it because he wants you to be just as lonely and unhappy as he is, that's why!"

Valeska felt the blood rising to her head. "Lucie, couldn't you go to the kitchen and straighten things up?!"

When the conversation took a turn like this, it would be better if Lucie weren't there. Valeska waited until she left the room.

"The president is a good match in any case," sighed Lucie as she left. "Even if he is Lutheran."

"So, it's your opinion that my brother doesn't want me to marry again, and you also think that I do whatever he wants?!" Valeska said this coldly and caustically as she opened the window. "How did you get that idea?"

"As a matter of fact, I do," Irma said defiantly. "He doesn't just want to stop it, he'll use any means to prevent it."

"And what is the meaning of this"—she searched for the proper word and only out of consideration for Irma's condition did she choose a milder one— "this impudence?"

"Because you can see that with your own eyes. Because he wants you to be as unhappy in your own way as he is in his. He couldn't stand it!" Irma said.

Valeska sat down on the bed next to Irma. She had to force herself to keep calm: "I don't know what kinds of notions you've been getting in your head about your mother. But you're wrong if you think that I'm unhappy. I feel lonely sometimes, I admit that, ever since Papusch has been gone, and you and Josel are always busy with your own affairs."

"I don't know where you find the time to be lonely, you're always so busy! You're imagining things, Mother. Your brother wants you to be unhappy just like you want him to be; you're both just as bad—you are genuine Wondraczeks! You're marrying him off to this unloved woman, this Rosa Willimczyk, so he will suffer for the rest of his life and so his love will be kept just for you . . ."

Irma stood up and walked back and forth a few steps.

"For you, love was never anything but possession," she continued, "and the more you can possess a person, the more you love him, that's the truth. You fought with Papusch and tried to take everything from him that was his own, and when you'd accomplished that, and he went and hid in his bed and gave in to his asthma, then you were good to him—no, I won't deny it, then you did love him and suffocated him with your love . . ."

Valeska's face turned pale. She looked down at her hands lying in her lap. "You have no right to talk like that," she gasped.

"Josel and I have both removed ourselves from your possession, not from your love, no, Mamuscha! Only because the two are the same thing for you, you think we don't want your love . . . When you realized that I wasn't turning out the way you wanted me to, then your relationship with me became one long series of humiliations, which you covered up with your 'goody-goody' attitude . . ."

"Please don't get excited, Irma," Valeska said. She was the one who was getting excited, but she didn't want to let it show. "In your condition that's not good!"

Irma sat down again. "My condition! It's no different from what Father did when he claimed he was paralyzed . . . You know quite well that he never was . . . It was his protest against you, just as I'm protesting against you with my big belly! I'll have Skrobek make one baby after the other in me, just so I'll grow stronger than you, because that's something you can't destroy for me . . ."

Valeska sensed that it was no longer enough to defend herself only with silence.

"My God, child," she said, "what are you saying? How desperate you must be to talk like that . . . I gave my children love wherever I could, and I sought out your love . . . I work like a slave for you, lower myself by giving piano lessons to snot-nosed boys and the silly geese who add a junior high school education, new linens, silverware, and a passable rendition of a waltz by Johann Strauss to their dowry; I sit up half the night figuring how to make some sort of a profit from the real estate agency; and I do all that for the two of you, so that things will be better for you someday . . ."

Irma stood up and held onto the table. She felt the first contractions, but she didn't let it show. Her hand just clutched at the edge of the table and turned white.

"You haven't understood a thing, Mama, and you never will, either, because you've boxed yourself in with self-delusions like mirrors . . . You let Papusch die in the belief that Josel was at your brother's, yet he was on the road somewhere, fleeing from you. Yes, from you, maybe from all of us . . . You wouldn't give me Skrobek when I loved him, so I threw myself at Heiko, only because I finally wanted to do something you couldn't decide for me. And when Heiko was killed, I took Skrobek, but when I finally could marry him, I didn't love him anymore . . . because I can't love at all anymore, that must be it, because you've destroyed everything inside me . . ."

Irma stopped when she saw her mother's face, on which her words were mirrored; only now was she conscious of what she had said. It had sprung from her with a vehemence that frightened her, too —perhaps because it had remained hidden within her so long.

Valeska forgot her daughter's condition, she forgot the holy day, she forgot the entire world. "I thought you were an adult. You're married, you have a child, and you're waiting for the next one, but in reality you're still the nasty, mean, conceited little girl that you were in your childhood, that always made the others responsible for the broken toys. And now you talk yourself into believing that your mother is to blame for everything, because you can't bear your own guilt any longer . . . But you'll have to bear it and come to terms with it. I have taken your guilt upon myself long enough. Do you think I could have let Papusch die with the terrible truth that I myself didn't know where Josel was? Could I have let him live with the terrible truth that he didn't earn enough with all his photographing even to pay for his materials, let alone to support his family and pay off the house? I let you humiliate me to spare you a hundred humiliations at the hands of others, and that's fine with me, too, I'm just horrified that you're in the process of ruining not just yourself but Skrobek as well. What makes you think I didn't see how you broke open the cupboard where he was keeping his poetry books hidden from you, and that you couldn't rest until you found out that he copied his poems from anthologies, you monster, you . . ."

The women stood facing each other. These were not the indifferent glances they exchanged with one another for days at a time in this house. These were looks of hatred. And of recognition. And yet deep down in Valeska's soul there was a spark of hope. They stared at each other until they were breathing calmly again. Both of them had been caught up by a guilt from which they might never break free. And each discovered herself in the other woman, slowly and with ever greater certainty, and they knew that they belonged together from then on. Warily the mother placed her hand on her daughter's shoulder, and the daughter no longer resisted.

Essentially I am like her, that is what frightens me so, and I'm already beginning to behave like her, and how much worse would it be if everything descended on me that came down on Mamuscha . . . God protect me from having to go through anything like that. If she hadn't been so strong, everything would have been ruined, she kept us together until today, and whether we love her or hate her, it amounts to the same thing, we will never break away from her. I wanted to get away, yes, I resisted, wanted to tear out whatever could hold me here, and yet I suspected that I would never get free of it. Not see the chimneys and slag heaps anymore, not breathe in the soot and the stench anymore, not hear the clattering of the shaft elevators or the unholy shrieking of the mine sirens anymore, no more of the black rivers and the clear streams, no more of the black, dense,

*endless forests, and the fear and the yearning to disappear in them like
Iron Hans or Sleeping Beauty, to be woken up again a hundred years
later . . . I wanted to forget all of that and rip it out of me, and that's
why I did it with crazy Kaprzik, because there was no one who could have
been uglier, more repulsive and revolting, who could make the deed more
vile and draw more hate upon me. I wanted them to drive me out, cast
me out, vomit me out, so that I could never come back. I wanted to be
dead, everything in me was going to die out, all of the yearning that had
still remained within me, and after it happened with this* idiot, *it took
a while before I realized that you must die not just one death but many
small ones to be dead for good, and I was still far from that, maybe I only
wanted to kill a desire inside me that was so big and so horrible that there
was no other way I could get rid of it, and when I saw the* idiot *I avoided
him, and one day they came and took him away to a sanatorium, and
not long after that, they say, he died of heart failure, the strong, dull,
crazy Kaprzik, and I heard that with a certain satisfaction . . . O Fallada,
as you were hanging . . . Nothing can take me from this wild, dark land
anymore, and now I have decided to penetrate into it even stronger and
deeper, and perhaps that began with Heiko, whom I wanted to pull into
this land which he couldn't figure out, perhaps he sensed that he didn't
belong here and for that reason didn't come back. And so I took Skrobek,
who speaks his words so slowly that they sometimes turn into poems and
who is ashamed to write down his own words because they are heavy and
cursed like this earth, and at the same time so beautiful and gentle and
a single melody, like this land. And how I must have frightened him so
that he would exchange them, his words, for the artificial ones in anthologies. Now I want roots in this land, with this Skrobek, and I will
not stop bearing children as long as I can, because my passion my love my
anger my outrage my hate my worship my tears my embraces my screams
my breath are not enough for this dark land for this black earth because
to endure it takes more life more passion more love more anger more hate
more tears more worshiping more screams more embraces and more breath
and I know that I am dead but with every new death I will bear new
life for this thrice-cursed thrice-blessed land*

"You must lie down," Valeska said gently after a while. "Do you
have pains?"

It seemed to Irma as if she had been far away. She felt her mother's hand on her shoulder. She wanted to push it away, but then she held on tight.

"It's all right," she said softly. "Please, send for the midwife, I think my time has come." With one hand she was still holding firmly to the edge of the table.

"My God, child, you got so excited! Whatever have I done! My God, how could I have let things go so far . . . ?"

"It's all right, Mother," Irma said. "It's fine like this . . . It's just fine, Mother."

36

A T THIS HOUR Kotik set out into the world. Yet he was only going home to Teuchertstrasse from the Peter and Paul Church. With a long detour through the foundry district, of course, and across Hindenburg Bridge. He didn't want to go home right after the Good Friday liturgy, especially as he had stayed for an entire hour next to his mother in the hard church pew. She was so glad that at least one of her sons was a churchgoer that she had given him free rein. But he was supposed to be home in time for their fasting soup and for the reading from *Miracles and Deeds of the Saints*.

When Kotik didn't have friends around for games or adventures, he liked to go to the big Hindenburg Bridge over the switchyards. Hundreds of gleaming rails ran under the bridge, and something was always happening. Express trains roared through, freight trains clanked along comfortably and endlessly in both directions. The loaded coal cars were now sprinkled with white lime for identification; but that didn't keep any more of the coal from being swiped, it was just easier to tell now. Best of all was when the switch engines drove through underneath, steaming, sometimes spraying a rain of fire, too, and then coming out the other side on a completely different track.

When the tracks began to glimmer red, he noticed that the sun was setting and evening was coming, and he remembered that he wanted to read aloud out of the book from Curate Mikas after supper today, so that his mother would not start in with Saint Genoveva again. He trudged on, and when he spotted his face in a store window, blackened by the steam of the engines, he wiped away the soot with his shirt sleeve and some spit. After all, he couldn't go all the way through town that way. He wondered whether Tonik would come to supper that evening, and if not, whether Mamotschka would begin to wail or would simply be silent. Tonik could at least be at home on the evening of Good Friday.

Since Tonik had been here on leave, Kotik hadn't seen him at home a single evening; he never got back until late at night, and then usually drunk. And what made Kotik the maddest was that everybody went Shhh! and walked around on tiptoes, as if someone were on his deathbed. Once Tonik had even brought a girl home with him; at any rate, Kotik had heard a squealing, giggling voice, with Tonik's placating rumble mixed in. Mamotschka had gotten up and had gotten the girl's voice out of the house and Tonik into bed—and even then there had been no scandal. Everything was different if you were a soldier. They wouldn't let Andy get away with that, although he was already in the Homeland Flak and would soon be called into the Labor Service, too. Not to mention Kotik himself.

You shouldn't put up with just anything, he thought, and he strengthened his resolve to read aloud from Curate Mikas's book tonight. That'll really open their eyes, or rather ears; surely his mother had never found anything like that to read in her books.

Kotik had not known anything about the great typhus epidemic in Upper Silesia before, and if the boys in the Don Bosco League hadn't gone to the film *Robert Koch* with Curate Mikas, he wouldn't have known about it to this day. The curate had explained to them in the subsequent class that the film's depiction of Rudolf Virchow was not only one-sided, it was false and even distorted; in reality he had been a progressive doctor who had combated not only diseases but also their cause, poverty itself. As a young staff doctor he had traveled across the Upper Silesian countryside and had written a report for the Prussian government that caused a stir. Parts of it had been reprinted a few years ago in the *Gleiwitz Yearbook*, and he would read to them from it now.

And what Curate Mikas read to them started out to be rather boring at first, because it was a little long-winded and stiff, but when he came to the conditions that had dominated life in this province back then, and when the names of towns were given where Kotik himself had been or which were located close by, such as Rybnik, Pless, Sohrau, Ratibor, Nikolai, Bilchengrund, and Gleiwitz, and when he realized it was not all that long ago, not even a hundred years, then he didn't want to believe it. He looked at the pictures in the book, the monks of the Brothers of Mercy in their cowls, throwing the corpses on carts, the half-starved children—and it really hit him when the statistics were given: more than fifty thousand people had died of typhus in this last great epidemic in Germany, which had broken out in what was probably the poorest of the Prussian provinces, Upper Silesia, after two crop failures and a great famine. He had tried to imagine it, fifty thousand people: that was half of this town that he lived in, so every other person he met on the street—dead. One side of every street devastated, and the other side in fear. He wanted to know more about how something like that could have happened, and why nobody had come to help the people until it was too late. They had studied the Thirty Years' War in history at school, but this must have been much worse.

It was already some time ago that Curate Mikas had read that to them, but Kotik couldn't get it out of his mind. He had memorized the title of the book and had gotten Klaus Koziollek to check it out of the municipal library for him, for they wouldn't give it to him, they just pointed him to the children's section, it had already happened a few times. By now he had finished reading the whole book, and even if there was much that he didn't understand he had still found the most important passages. For example, what Virchow wrote about the priests in Upper Silesia, and what the curate naturally could not read, otherwise he would get into trouble with his pastor.

Mamotschka would be amazed at the supper table when he started to read. He had hidden the book well, under the woodpile in the cellar. Paulek, of course, was no longer there—he would have discovered this hiding place with the somnambulant certainty of a water dowser. In any case, he didn't want it to fall into the hands of his mother.

Kotik thought about Paulek selling the best specimens in his butterfly collection! And he hadn't even told him how much he got for them. After Paulek had gotten back from Schakanau, there had been some new trouble with him almost every week. The worst was when the still where he made schnapps out in the allotment gardens was broken up. He had swiped Mama's sugar ration stamps (she of course never would have admitted it), and with the sugar and half-ripe fruit that he swiped from the allotment gardens, he had distilled schnapps. So that no one could smell it, he had set fire to rags and lumps of tar in front of the arbor, until the neighbors complained, because the stench was becoming unbearable. But he didn't care, it was fine if it stank like rags, just not like *schnapsik*. But the police came one day anyway, because old Frau Kulka wouldn't leave them in peace, and his primitive still was demolished. If Mamotschka had not taken the responsibility for it, they would have sent Paulek right back to Schakanau.

First Kotik got the keys to the cellar and brought his secret upstairs. He hid it behind his back at first, and then stuck it under his rear when he sat down at the kitchen table. When Mamotschka caught sight of him, he had to get up and wash his hands and face, he couldn't come to the table like that. So he pushed the chair under the table to conceal the book and sat down again right away, without taking the time to dry his hands. Papa was home from work; you could hear him splashing behind the oilcloth curtain in the shower he had built himself.

"How often do I have to tell the story," Andy said crossly. "As if guys never got into fights . . ." He was pressing a little cloth with clay vinegar to his eyebrow, with the result that the bandage was slowly loosening.

Their mother handed out the plates. "At your age," she said, "to come home with your face like that! It's usually the Ossadniks who do that to the others," she said, to reassure her Franzek. He didn't investigate further, being satisfied with this meager information.

He sat down at the table with a serious expression, but then stood up again to open the window. "It's turning summery outside," he said.

There was bread soup with garlic and browned onions, as always on Good Friday. Usually Anna would apologize for serving something so simple. Today Good Friday apologized for her. She was thankful for that, and smiled at all of them.

Kotik sat on his book, thinking of nothing else.

"Squintok doesn't want to be called Squintok anymore," Anna said. "He says he doesn't squint anymore."

Andy took the cloth from his forehead and shot it into the coal box in front of the stove. For him that was no longer an issue.

"Oh, of course," Franz said. Andy really didn't squint anymore, as far as you could tell with that eye so swollen up.

The two boys told their father about the removal of the bells from the church. Each told it from his own viewpoint. And sometimes they agreed, too. Kotik did most of the talking. Perhaps he wanted to divert his mother from her intended reading with his report.

Franz looked at his spoon, in which half a clove of garlic was floating, and said: "Ulla could at least have come for supper. Even if we're only having something simple. Today everybody's having something simple. After all, it's a fast day."

"I told you," Anna said, "she just came for a few summer clothes; she had to leave right away. She's coming on Easter and she'll stay the whole day."

"She hasn't been home for three months, even longer, not since Christmas," Franz said, making an effort not to let too much disappointment creep into his voice.

"We must get used to having a famous daughter," Anna said.

Ever since their daughter had performed in public and been applauded by the audience, someone had told her, and it was not just Frau Piontek the piano teacher, that she had a *famous daughter* now. That had impressed her. She repeated it at every opportunity. It was as if she had to say it out loud again and again, so that it would remain a reality. Actually she couldn't really picture it, except that Ulla would travel more now and come home even less. At least that's what Ulla had said.

"Maybe Ulla is ashamed of her family. I mean, it could be, because we're simple people," Franz said. "But she must know that we've done everything for her that we could."

Andy and Kotik did not look up from their plates. Ever since their sister had been going to the conservatory, she had been a different person to them. Basically, she had always been a stranger. You could never play with her, Andy thought, never pull her hair, never trip her, or dig for potatoes with her; she always had to be careful of her hands, and when they built their tree houses, went on wild hunts through the forest, or celebrated at the campfire, she was sitting at her piano, plunking away.

Andy remembered that Ulla had once said that maybe they had taken home the wrong baby when she was born. She said it as a joke, but maybe she meant more by it than I thought. Maybe it was even true. She had so little in common with them. And what was worse—they had so little in common with her.

"She'll certainly be coming to say good-bye, before her tour," Andy said encouragingly.

"I'm glad that we don't have to listen to that eternal *Szopenczyk* anymore," Anna said abruptly, and in a tone of voice that betrayed how she must have suffered over all the years.

"Did Mamotschka tell you that people protested when they drove away with the bells?" Kotik turned directly to his father, who didn't even look up. "A few women were standing next to me; they said they really wanted to lie down in front of the trucks, then they couldn't take the bells away." His father was shocked at this. He thought of what might happen if women would ever lie down on the rails in front of his locomotive.

"So, is that what they said," he said thoughtfully.

"The trucks wouldn't drive over the women, would they?" Andy said.

"No," his father said, with conviction, "they wouldn't do that. But the police would arrest them."

"Just as a matter of curiosity," Andy said, looking past his father, "what if other women lay down in their place . . . After all, they can't arrest half the town."

"No, they can't," his father said. "But sooner or later the women would give up, and they would come for the bells in secret, maybe in winter. Who would stay outside all night in winter?"

"They come take the bells on Good Friday, on Good Friday, of all days! It's not so bad that they removed the bells from the church, I guess that's the law, you can't fight that, but that they did it on Good Friday. Naturally, some high Party officials thought that up," Anna said. "If they win the war, they'll treat Catholics like they're treating the Jews. They don't like us, you can tell that!"

"Anna!" Franz admonished her gently. He had already talked to her about this a few times, and he was of a different opinion.

"Then it won't help you or us either that you're in the Party, it'll be just like with the Jews, and then the ones who are baptized Catholic, it'll be their turn then. Herr Breslauer, for example . . ."

"Anna, not in front of the children," Franzek said, more sharply now.

"Oh well, you're right," Anna said, and reached across the table for her husband's hand. She was already regretting what she had said. And she hoped that it would never happen.

"Tonik didn't come either," Andy said. It was a rather inept attempt to change the subject.

Kotik had better luck.

"The Archpriest is supposed to have recorded the bells on wax, he'll have them played on Easter for the High Mass, through loudspeakers. It's supposed to be a surprise."

"Really? Where did you find that out?" Anna asked in disbelief.

"They were talking about it on the square. I heard it, too," Andy said, rather surprised that his mother didn't know about it.

"Well, is that technically even possible?" Anna asked.

"Today anything is possible, of course!"

"That's a joke!" Anna began to laugh, a sharp, brittle laugh. "Ach, blessed Lord Jesus, they take our bells away and then ring them through loudspeakers! Someday they will close the churches and broadcast masses over the radio. How practical! Then they won't need churches anymore or priests either, then one bishop will be enough for the whole Reich."

Her voice grew bitter.

By the time they had finished their fasting supper, they had talked, argued, and fallen silent about lots of subjects, subjects that were important to them and subjects that were not important to them. And at the moment that it occurred to their mother to read aloud from the book *Miracles and Deeds of the Saints* Kotik had already pulled out his book from underneath him.

"Please, let me read something today, Mamotschka, only today! You promised me." And he didn't even wait for her to answer. "Papa, this will interest you too, it's a description of our homeland a hundred years ago."

"Well, go ahead," Andy encouraged his brother.

Kotik found the page right away, and he began to read.

"Written by a doctor, by Rudolf Virchow in 1848, after the great typhus epidemic in Upper Silesia . . ." he began and glanced at his mother, who had remained sitting out of sheer curiosity.

"Well, it says:

"Almost seven hundred years have passed since Silesia was separated from Poland; the greatest part of the country has been completely Germanized by German colonization and through the power of German culture. But for Upper Silesia, seven hundred years have not sufficed to remove the Polish national stamp from the inhabitants, which their ethnic brothers in Pomerania and Prussia have lost so completely. Of course, these years have sufficed to destroy the consciousness of their nationality, to corrupt their language, and to break their spirit, so that the rest of the people have labeled them with the contemptuous name of Water Polacks, but their entire appearance, which is described to me as quite similar to that of the Polish population on the Lower Vistula, still clearly shows their ancestry.

"Nowhere does one see the characteristic facial features of the Russians, which one immediately hears designated as truly Slavic, and which so strongly remind one that these representatives of Asianism are the neighbors of the Mongols. One finds beautiful faces everywhere, fair skin, blue eyes, blond hair, prematurely altered by care and filth, but frequently present in rare loveliness in the children. Their way of life also recalls the true Poles. Their garb, their dwellings, their social relationships, and finally, their uncleanliness and indolence are found nowhere so similarly as among the lower classes of the Polish people. And especially with regard to the latter two characteristics, it would be hard to imagine their being outdone . . .

"In general, the Upper Silesian does not wash at all, but leaves it up to the solicitude of heaven to free his body of the crusts of dirt accumulated by means of an occasional vigorous downpour. Vermin of all kinds, lice in particular, are virtually permanent guests on his body. Just as great as this uncleanliness is the laziness of the people, their disinclination to mental and physical effort, a wholly sovereign inclination toward idleness, which, in connection with a wholly canine submissiveness, creates such a repulsive impression on any free man accustomed to work that he tends to feel nausea rather than sympathy."

Kotik skipped a few pages. "Yes, and it goes on here:

"The Polish language, which the Upper Silesian employs exclusively, has certainly not been one of the minor causes of his sunken state. German schoolmasters with the most limited knowledge possible were sent to the country of Poland, and it was left up to the teacher and his pupils to teach each other their native tongues. The result of this was usually that the teacher finally learned Polish, but not that the pupils learned German. So that instead of the German language being disseminated, the Polish language kept the upper hand, and in the middle of the country, one finds countless families with German names and German physiognomies, who do not understand a word of German."

Now Franz Ossadnik did interrupt in a soft voice: "There's so many difficult words in that. And what does that have to do with the epidemic? Where did you get that book, Kotik? Are you reading that in school?"

"Certainly not!" Andy answered for Kotik. "That's just the introduction, the part about the terrible typhus comes later."

"But that shows you how far we've come under the Prussians. There are no longer any famines and plagues anymore! And not even a hundred years, and no one here speaks Polish anymore, that's progress," Franz said.

"The misery back then was possible only because of the *Polish economy*! Things are different now, aren't they?" crowed Anna. "Let me see it, what kind of book is that?" She had never seen it in her lending library.

But Kotik didn't hand over the book.

"Keep reading," Andy said, fearing that Kotik wouldn't get to the section on the Church. Perhaps it would be better for him to take the book himself now, they would believe him more too. "Give it here," he said, "I'll read it.

> "Hardly any book except the prayer book was accessible to the people, and thus it came about that more than half a million people exist here who lack any consciousness of the inner development of their people, any trace of the history of their culture, because, terribly enough, they possess no development, no culture.

> "A second barrier has been the Catholic hierarchy. Nowhere else, except in Ireland and in Spain at one time, has the Catholic clergy achieved such absolute enslavement of the people as here; the cleric is the unrestricted master of this people, which is at his beck and call like a pack of serfs. The story of its conversion from hard liquor affords an even more shining example of this spiritual bondage than Pater Matthew among the Irish. The Upper Silesians were devoted to the consumption of hard liquor in the most extreme way. On the evenings when the people were returning from the markets in towns, the roads were literally strewn with drunks, men and women; the baby at its mother's breast was already being fed with schnapps. In one year, Pater Stephan Brzozowski succeeded in converting all these drunkards at a single stroke. Of course, all means were employed, legal and illegal, clerical and secular; church penalties and corporal punishment were employed with impunity, but the conversion finally succeeded, the vow was taken by all and was kept. How great the trust in the clergy was, this epidemic also demonstrated in full measure. Many credible men have assured me that the people awaited death with a certain confidence, a death that would liberate them from

such a miserable life and would assure them a compensation in heavenly joys. If someone fell ill, he didn't seek
out the doctor, but the pastor . . ."

"That's a polemic," Anna said, and stood up. She didn't intend to
listen to that, you could read things like that nowadays in the papers
everywhere.

"Free thinkers! They're against religion! No, Andreas, stop reading. Our church has it hard enough as it is today. In other times,
all right, but not in a time of crisis! They take the bells from church,
act hostile, arrest the priests, and now the Church is going to be
made responsible for the *misery*, too? What's the author's name? That
belongs on the Index! A book like that doesn't belong in my house."

Anna's voice grew louder and louder. She felt a sharp pain in her
neck and automatically touched it. She felt the thick place as big as
a plum now. It had never seemed that big before. She fled into the
bedroom.

"What have you done now," Franz Ossadnik said disapprovingly.

"But Mamotschka!" Kotik almost began to cry. "That's not the
way it's meant, it was written a hundred years ago . . ." He looked
at his brother Andy helplessly.

"The book only proves how far we've come today," Franz said.
"Give it here!" He took the book, leafed through it. "So, you got
it from the municipal library. And you read things like this?"

There was recognition in his voice.

"I'll hold on to this a while, Kotichek. I want to have a look at
it. We'll talk about it tomorrow, then." He brushed his hand over
the boy's hair.

From the bedroom they heard Anna's voice: "Ach, blessed Lord
Jesus, what a Good Friday this is! April 23, 1943, I'll never forget
this date as long as I live!"

37

The train was traveling more slowly and came to a halt on the open track in a birch forest. The boys at the hatch reported that the SS men were patrolling around the cars. They were hoping for the noon meal, for to judge by the position of the sun, it had to be one o'clock already, and they were hungry.

After a short interval, the train traveled on, now at a steady, slow pace. All at once the boys began to babble: "Barbed-wire fences," they yelled, "watchtowers, barracks!" They they reported men in striped suits, who were digging ditches. And after they had traveled on a little farther, they described the camp gates to the others, which they were just passing.

The Dutch woman translated for the two Germans in the car.

The boys were shoving one another away from the hatch, they were talking loudly, all at the same time, so that finally nothing could be understood. From outside they heard march music, which blared more and more loudly from the loudspeakers, the farther the train went into the camp. Then the train halted, and the silence in the car was uncanny. They all remained in their places, listening to the sounds outside for what would happen now. An uneasiness seized them, which was evident in their soft and hurried breathing. The woman hid her fearful eyes behind her handkerchief.

The music broke off. And it was as if the voice from the loudspeaker would free them from something: "*Achtung! Achtung!* Welcome to Birkenau! Welcome to Birkenau: Leave the cars calmly and with discipline, take all of your baggage with you and wait for further instructions on the platform."

Then the march music blared on. This time Silbergleit translated for the Dutch in the car, but most of them had understood already. The Jews began to pack up their suitcases. Silbergleit helped the Dutch woman. Then he tied up his blankets and hung the briefcase over his shoulder.

They had not been under way from Kattowitz for more than three hours; they had not traveled fast and they had stopped a few times on the way, thus they could not have come far. If they were supposed to get out now with their baggage, it meant that they would be spending at least some time in this camp.

They heard the doors of the cars up front being shoved open from outside. The loudspeaker voice ordered them to leave their baggage at the front of the platform after they got out; for delousing, the women were supposed to line up to the right, the men to the left.

Silbergleit shook his neighbor, who had been sleeping the whole time, and obviously had not heard the march music or the announcements. The man still did not move. He shook him harder now; suspicious, Silbergleit slowly turned him over toward him. He was looking into glassy eyes, the mouth open wide, the chin hanging low. Silbergleit rolled the stiff body back.

The woman was sitting on her suitcase; she had put on her coat and pulled her hat down over her forehead, as if she didn't want to see what was going on around her. The sound of sliding doors being opened came closer and closer, from car to car. And in between the march music. In the car, couples embraced. Someone had translated for them that women and men were being sent to delousing separately.

Now their door too was thrown open. The light, the sun, the air, they were so unaccustomed to it all. They wavered for the first few steps, staggered, and helped each other along. The woman saw that the old man was still lying on the floor and did not move.

"Well, wake him up!" she cried, apprehensively.

Silbergleit took the woman by the arm and pushed her out of the car. He felt her begin to tremble. She said nothing. She understood now that she would never reach Riga or a Black Sea port, would never arrive in Stockholm or Palestine. And she would never return to Hilversum, either. She left her suitcase where it was and walked slowly over to the women.

The kapos were swarming around too, prodding the Jews to hurry and making sure that the baggage remained up at the front of the platform. A boy with a shaven head wanted to take away Silbergleit's briefcase, but he resisted, holding his hands in front of it to protect it. He would rather let them beat him to death than give up the briefcase with his books in it. Karpe hurried to Silbergleit's aid, and there was a commotion on the platform, during which his glasses slipped off.

Two SS men came up, and the bald-headed boy finally let the old Jew alone. Silbergleit stood there, gasping for air. He was unable to answer the SS man who was roaring at him. It felt as if someone were slicing into his heart.

Stammering, he finally explained that he had nothing in the briefcase but books that he had written himself. And up to then they had let him keep them at every checkpoint, and he wouldn't let the boy steal them from him now.

The SS man had a kapo search the briefcase, and when he really found nothing in it but books, he allowed the old Jew to keep it. Karpe had picked up Silbergleit's glasses from the ground in the meantime. The left lens was shattered.

Uninterrupted, the march music blared on. It had not stopped the whole time.

Silbergleit hung onto Karpe; his vision was flickering. He had rescued his books once again. But now he knew that he would not put up a fight the next time. The books no longer belonged to him. He no longer belonged to himself.

They were standing in rows of ten on the platform, waiting, the women to the left, the men to the right, separated from each other by only a narrow gap. Sometimes a woman and a man stepped toward each other and embraced. Then they returned to their rows.

Up front at the head of the line a group of SS men were gathered; a doctor in a white smock was there too. They had the Jews step forward one by one and made the choice, some to the right, to the bathhouses, others to the left, to the work camp.

"The young, strong ones," said Karpe to Silbergleit, noticing what was going on, "they're sending to the work camp, and they're sending us older people to the residence camp on the other side."

They were toward the end of the column, along with the other Gleiwitz Jews.

"Have you seen little Aaron Brauer?" Silbergleit fiddled at his glasses and squeezed one eye shut. He could not get used to looking through only one lens.

The kapos were clearing out the cars; they dragged a corpse out of nearly every one. And numerous pieces of luggage, which could not have belonged to the dead alone. Many of the Jews had left their suitcases behind; they no longer believed they would have any use for them.

The corpses were thrown on one cart, the luggage on another.

Silbergleit remembered having traveled to Agnetendorf one day. He had sent his books there in advance, he had written letters, but had never received an answer. Just like the time before the war, when he had written to Montagnola. But there was no border between him and Wiesenstein. So he traveled there. By train to Hirschberg and then to Hermsdorf, then by mail coach through the Valley of the Snow Pits, past the Kynast, past the Great Storm Helmet, and he remembered the ballad by Ruckert, which he knew by heart. The house looked more massive than he had expected from the photos he had seen, a fortress. Here one could forget what was happening in the world.

He was not permitted to enter. He wrote something on his calling card and handed it over. Herr von Wiesenstein was indisposed and was not receiving visitors. With this name on the card . . . This house, it had long been his hope, but now no longer. It was already dark, and there was no way to leave Agnetendorf. He took a room at the Upper Silesian Inn, for one mark ten per night, cheaper out of season. The innkeeper took the money, but did not enter his name in the register, this name . . .

They shuffled forward on the platform. The sky was almost cloudless now, and the sun warmed them. It was almost three o'clock and they had not yet been given anything to eat. Immediately after delousing, they were told, they would be assigned to their barracks and given provisions, they had to be patient until then. Silbergleit shared his slices of bread, already dried, with the Dutch Jews. He wanted to give some to the woman, but she refused, claiming not to be hungry. He knew what her name was again; her black suitcase stood at the front of the platform, the white painted letters clearly legible: REBEKKA MORGENTHALER HILVERSUM.

She called over to him from the group of women: "Would you like to give me a book? We'll probably be in separate women's and men's camps. Then I can read in your book and remember you."

She felt warm and took off her coat. She kept her hat on.

Silbergleit hesitated a moment. Because he was surprised by her request, and because something like emotion overcame him. He had never heard her talk like that before.

He nodded and searched in his briefcase. Then he walked the two paces over to the women and placed a slim volume of poems into her hand.

"There you are, Frau Morgenthaler," he said, holding on to her hand for a few seconds longer. It made him forget the pain he still had from the blows of the kapo.

She glanced at the book. "*The Eternal Day,*" she read. "Thank you, Herr Silbergleit." And she lowered her head. Perhaps she did not want him to see her face at that instant.

They all moved up a few more steps. Silbergleit moved back into the row of men. He observed her from there. She opened the book and read in it, behind the back of the next woman, and after she had read the first poem, she looked over at him. She smiled.

Suddenly the woman was standing next to him, her coat over her arm, the book in her hand.

"Listen, Herr Silbergleit," she said. "We're not going to Riga, or to Palestine. Actually, I suspected it all along, but now I know it. A work camp! I'm too old for that, I won't survive it."

And she whispered: "Take this coat. Please, take it, I don't need it anymore. There are diamonds sewn into the hem."

And as he stood there, not moving, she simply put the coat over his shoulder. Then she went back to the column of women. Silbergleit did not want the coat. *Man lives for a short time and is full of restlessness opens like a flower and wilts flees like a shadow and does not remain should his days be numbered then the number of his moons is with thee and thou hast set a limit that he cannot exceed for a tree has hope even when it is hewn down.* He stood there, feeling the coat heavy on his shoulder.

He would take the coat and give it to someone younger. Someone who could make use of it. He thought of Aaron, young Aaron Brauer, who had known about the hiding place in the cellar on Niederwallstrasse . . .

Silbergleit didn't dare to think further than that. He looked around.

He didn't see any of the Brauers. They had probably already passed through the selection point.

Now it was their turn. It went very quickly. No one asked their names. The man in the white smock said only: "To the right! To the right!"

First Karpe had to step forward. Then it was his turn. And behind him, Dr. Blumenfeld. And then Salo Weissenberg. "To the right! To the right!"

The kapos circled around them, channeling them in groups to the bathhouses, which were located a few hundred meters from the platform, behind the train tracks. They walked between birches that were sprouting their first green, under an indifferent April sky that did not darken, and a few of the Jews who had already spent a week in the dark, stuffy cattle cars stretched their faces to the warming sunlight.

The men had arrived at the first bathhouse and had to wait until a kapo opened the door for them.

In the dressing room of the bathhouse they had to undress for the shower; the kapos ordered them to fold their underwear and clothes and put them in a pile, so that they would find them again on their way out. Silbergleit took his briefcase from his shoulder and put it on the wooden bench, next to his shoes, and on top of them the Dutch woman's coat. He took off his socks and saw that his feet were swollen; while he was walking he had not even noticed it.

Karpe stood in front of him, already half naked; Silbergleit saw his thin, bony legs and wondered how they could carry such a strong man. No one spoke. Only the sounds that the men made undressing could be heard. It was cold between the thick concrete walls. A faintly bitter smell was in the air.

Two attendants in dirty white smocks came in. The naked Jews had to sit down on the cold stone bench, and the attendants began to shave the men's heads with small, glittering clippers, one man after the other. A kapo swept the hair into a pile. The attendant said to Weissenberg, who had reacted with a jerk: "Don't put up a fight, it's only on account of the lice . . ." And he showed the yellow stumps of his teeth in a grin. Silbergleit shoved his shirt under his seat, he put his hands to his shoulders, but that did not make him shiver any less. The attendant came over and shaved away the wreath of hair at the back of his head with three or four swift strokes. Silbergleit looked down at the concrete floor. His whole life long he had not known what a frightening sight naked old men with their heads shaven could be.

A kapo opened the heavy iron door to the shower room and the men entered willingly. In spite of that, the kapo all at once told them to hurry up. As Silbergleit went through the door, the kapo took his glasses away. Silbergleit let him. He was no longer resisting. He entered the shower room, in which the bitter smell was more intense than in the dressing room. There were no windows here. Six pipes jutted from the ceiling. How were they all supposed to shower under them? Someone asked for soap. But no soap was available.

When the jasmine was fragrant I always thought of you I saw you the last time when you were standing down there in front of the house with the bouquet of jasmine in your arms the smell of the jasmine penetrated all the corridors through all the doors through all the cracks into the hiding place in the cellar on Niederwallstrasse where we hid the Torah scrolls

after writing each sacred word the writer must take a bath where is little Aaron now it is the jasmine that smells that reminds me of you . . . Ma nishtana ha-lejla ha-se

More and more men pushed their way into the narrow shower room from outside, although they were already jammed together in here. Silbergleit heard Salo Weissenberg's gentle and calming voice, which was suddenly drowned out by screaming in the dressing room. He could not see what was happening there, because he was pinned in between the naked bodies of the others. Weissenberg's voice grew louder *for a tree has hope even when it is hewn down it can sprout again and its shoots will be forthcoming but if a man dies he is gone if a man perishes—where is he? As water runs out of the lake and as a stream trickles away and dries up thus is a man when he lies down he will not rise again he will not awaken as long as the sky remains nor be awakened from his sleep*

Silbergleit heard the gasping of the man who was being shoved into the shower room by two kapos. Silbergleit craned his neck, he could see only the man's head, blood-smeared, tilted slightly to the left—and now he saw the heavy iron door closing behind him.

In the dressing room, the kapos began to gather up the bundles left behind. They stuffed the things into sacks that they dragged along behind them. Under one bundle a kapo came upon a briefcase and rummaged around in it greedily, and when he found only books, he tore them apart. He bent over as he did, so that he could not be observed by the SS man, and looked for a hiding place for gold, jewelry, or diamonds; he couldn't imagine why else anyone would drag books all this way. But he found nothing, and stuffed it all into his sack. At the end an attendant came over and collected the hair in a bucket.

Outside they threw the sacks on carts and pushed them to the warehouse, where they sorted shoes, underwear, coats, glasses, hair into different piles. In half an hour they had to be back in front of the bathhouse with their carts again. This time at the door on the other side.

38

THERE ARE SAND crabs and water spiders that move sideways but still progress forward. Valeska was always reminded of that when she saw old Apitt walking along: one shoulder forward, hips canted slightly, which probably resulted from his holding a handkerchief to his cheek for years on account of toothache, his head shoved far forward on his long neck—and actually he didn't walk, he sailed along. You got this impression because his feet moved like a weasel's, but his upper body remained relatively still. Thus he sailed into Valeska Piontek's house, right into the music room, which, because air-raid victims were being quartered in the house, had by now become parlor, living room, reception room, and—with Valeska's bed behind the folding screen—bedroom as well. Apitt was holding a bouquet of white narcissus in his hand. "For Irma," he said into the silence. He waited for someone to come and relieve him of the flowers. Anyone. But Halina wasn't there. And so he stood in the doorway shifting the bouquet from one hand to the other. There was an oppressive silence in the room, and he didn't know what to make of it. Until then he hadn't thought that silence could be so oppressive.

Valeska Piontek was sitting on the piano stool withdrawn into herself, cracking her knuckles softly, as if there were nothing in the world more important at that moment. Her brother Willi was standing at the window; he was holding a book in his hand and was pensively examining the pattern on the drapes. Lucie (Widera) was absentmindedly scratching the skin of her left forearm with her fingernails; the spot had reddened by now. She was thinking with growing discomfort about what she could offer the visitors to eat, if they were not considerate enough to leave in case the birth turned into a long-drawn-out affair. Herr Schimmel had already nodded off a few times in his white wicker chair because it had been so quiet in the room. He gave a start at every sound, and ascertained with quiet satisfaction that nothing had changed. He had been on a walk through the forest with his wife all day, and this spring air makes you nice and tired, he thought. His wife's gaze wandered through the room; she hoped that the event for which they were all waiting would happen soon, then they would congratulate each other, and perhaps drink a toast, and then she and her husband could go upstairs. It was a shame that the father wasn't there. As far back as she could remember, the father had always been present at such occasions. But there had been no war then, either.

The president of the waterworks was settled in his rectangle. Only his head occasionally moved back and forth, as if it were merely perched atop the blocky body. He had stayed even though there was nothing more for him to do there. He had gotten his answer. Since nothing ever changed in his face, no one could say how this answer might have affected him, not even Wondrak, who knew him better than the others did. Maybe it was just more comfortable for him to keep on sitting there, talking, than to be alone at home, listening to the radio. He loved classical music, as long as it wasn't too heavy. On Good Friday only pieces like *Parsifal* or the *St. Matthew Passion* were on the radio. He loved Haydn and Schubert and Carl Maria von Weber. But they were never played on Good Friday.

Lucie finally took pity on Herr Apitt and relieved him of the flowers. "Irma will like them so much," she said in an indifferent voice.

"Everything has been going all right . . . up to now?" Apitt asked, because their faces all seemed so serious.

"I'm glad that you came," Valeska said from behind the piano. "Stay here with us for a while. We're waiting here, just killing time. That's all we can do."

"Any chance of a hand of rummy?" the president of the waterworks asked. His face showed that he was not exactly excited at the prospect.

A card game—the Devil's game, Aunt Lucie thought. And on Good Friday, too!

Wondrak walked the few steps from the window to the grand

piano and back. "I never paid any attention to the ringing of those bells," he said, "but now I'll miss them." He tried to remember what the melody of the bells had been like, and what in the future he would be missing.

"I always knew when it was twelve, I didn't have to look at the clock at all when they rang at noon," Valeska Piontek said. "You got so used to it."

"They left us *one* bell," Apitt said. "It will keep on ringing at noon."

"Then I'll plug my ears," Valeska responded. "One single bell reminds me of the funeral bell. Bells are like an organ. You have to hear them playing in harmony."

Wondrak walked over to the grand piano and back.

"If we only knew that it was worth it," Valeska continued. "I mean, what the relationship is between the loss of the bells and the gain in war matériel. After all, they can't build tanks out of them . . ."

"Oh, more important things. They make more important things than tanks out of them," the president said, and moved his head back and forth. "I have to keep quiet about it, but they're being used for the secret weapon now under development; it will be the deciding factor in the war.

"I've been hearing about this secret weapon for two years but it hasn't amounted to more than a rumor," Apitt said.

"It's more a secret than a weapon," Lucie said.

"When this . . . superweapon is to be activated is up to the judgment of our Führer," the rectangle said, annoyed. "You have to have faith."

"And in the meantime our child has to go to war," Valeska said.

The door opened and the midwife stepped in. She said impassively: "I need two sheets."

Valeska rushed to the cupboard and took out a pile of sheets and towels. "Is everything all right?" she asked once again.

"Everything's fine," the midwife said almost indifferently, and took the linen. "You must be patient." Lucie jumped up and opened the door for her, but the midwife did not give her the chance to peek inside Irma's room.

"Did you see anything?" Valeska whispered when she came back.

"No, not a thing," she said. "Only that Irma is sitting up in bed . . ."

Valeska heaved a sigh, as if she were relieved.

Frau Schimmel spoke up wisely from her wicker chair. "Then it could start soon. But it might take a while too."

"I heard her groan," Herr Schimmel said. He sat with his chair directly against the wall to the next room, and actually believed what he had said. But Irma's room was two rooms farther away. Nevertheless, they all listened carefully.

"From pain life arises," said Herr Apitt, a little solemnly. "That's just the way it is. Pain is the brother of the soul." He rose from the sofa.

As he was saying this, it seemed somewhat too loud to them, but perhaps only because they were all concentrating on the silence.

"Therefore we should all listen to what pain has to say to us." Apitt went over to the grand piano and gazed at each of them in turn. From here he had a better view of everything.

"As you all know, or at any rate most of you, I have been working on a system of pain for a long time, and I can inform you that recently I have been making great progress.

"I have spent the last few years cataloging pain—it went more quickly than I had expected. For precisely in these last few years, we have had no lack of examples and objects of pain, as you all know. For me, it was the task of my life. But now I need only about two years more, then my system will be perfect. Then I will publish it, and there will be a new language, universally comprehensible: the language of pain. I am fairly certain that the human race will make itself understood better in this language than in any other language used before. One does not have to learn any vocabulary for this language of pain, no declensions or conjugations, no new syntax; one can understand this language immediately, as long as one is prepared to suffer. And the longer the war lasts, the more people will learn this language."

"You mean that the language of pain will be the language of the future," Wondrak said seriously, pulling back the curtain.

Apitt paid no attention to the interruption. He had arrived at his favorite topic, and he didn't like being interrupted.

"To understand the language of pain, one need only listen within oneself," Apitt continued. "Studying is not necessary, for we learn this language in childhood, with our painful experiencing of the world. It begins the instant the umbilical cord is severed, for the first cry of life is a cry born of pain. I can't go as far as Augustine, who writes in the *City of God*: 'For it is characteristic of the soul, not the body, to feel pain.' Yet physical pain is only one dimension, in my opinion. The other and far more important dimension is pain of the soul. For as the body speaks to us with the former, so does the soul speak to us with the latter. And there my system begins. I have undertaken nothing less than to outline the grammar of pain and thereby the language of the soul. Initially I proceeded to catalog spiritual pain, for we do know through historical reports which diseases have attacked the human body in recent centuries, for instance, cholera, typhus, tuberculosis, syphilis, cancer—but we don't know very much about what spiritual pains humanity has suffered, aside from a few accounts, as in the works of Theresa of Avila. In the future, the pains of the soul will be registered in the same way, and future generations will then be able to learn what we suffered with our souls. For such pains, and I give only a few examples here, are far more severe: the absence of a loved one, the yearning for a loved one, the quest for God, the suffering of God, of the world, of oneself, loneliness and the fear of nothingness, the search for the meaning of life, despair, bewilderment, insanity, emptiness—all that is expressed in my grammar.

"Everyone can speak with his soul in this language, and now, finally, man will have an expression not only for the injury of the body by a knife, but also when his *soul* is wounded by a knife. And he will comprehend himself and his soul and God. It is the simplest, the clearest, and the most direct language in the world. Thus in the future, pain will replace words."

Apitt's speech had turned into a sermon. He felt like a missionary.

At least confronting these heathens here. And in his new religion of pain, all those present were unbaptized.

"But that sounds extremely mystificacious," Herr Schimmel said admiringly; he had woken up during Herr Apitt's explication. And he whispered about it with his wife.

"I didn't understand a thing," Lucie said after a while. "But it was beautifully said, wasn't it?"

"For my taste, that verges on defeatism," the president of the waterworks said. And sweated.

Valeska thought it over. For her, music was the language of the soul. But she had to admit that it was more an indeterminate feeling inside her. Pain was more distinct there.

"Do you still suffer from your toothache?" she asked Herr Apitt.

"Yes, naturally," Herr Apitt said almost joyfully. "That was the very beginning of my system."

She had known Herr Apitt for four or five years—nobody can have a toothache for that long, not even with the rottenest teeth, she thought. Apitt was not suffering from his teeth. He was suffering from the times. That was it.

"I can't quite figure out your system," Wondrak said. "I don't want to sound disrespectful, but may I ask you one question? Is it supposed to be a kind of Esperanto for pain?"

Apitt gazed at him with contempt. "You mustn't make it so easy for yourself, Lawyer Wondrak," he admonished. "The new language of pain is as simple as the language of the Bible, except that it no longer works with imprecise images and descriptions. A mathematical formula is an accumulation of ciphers and letters with plus or minus signs to the uninitiated; but for whoever understands it, it is a cosmos. My grammar of pain is cosmos and truth at the same time. The language of pain is a language that is lived, experienced, and suffered. One cannot learn it like the alphabet in school. One learns it through suffering."

Valeska resisted: "It grieves my heart, Herr Apitt, when I think of how my daughter is suffering now. But your toothache leaves me completely cold. That's how it is in reality, Herr Apitt."

Apitt felt himself misunderstood, like every missionary. But it didn't matter. Smiling, he said: "You will understand the pain of someone else only when you no longer resist your own pain, but accept it, Frau Valeska. Pains are signals from the soul. When we possess pain, I say expressly possess it, because it is a precious property, then we are close to the soul and to the mysteries. Pains are no scourge, but a grace of God."

Now he took out a handkerchief and held it to his cheek, sucking at the rotten tooth in his upper jaw until he tasted blood. Apitt's expression was strangely hard, as far as Valeska could make out. It really did look as if next to his physical pain he was imploring yet another pain that would provide him access to his soul.

Herr Schimmel went up to Herr Apitt. "Ach, would you please come have dinner with us on Sunday," he said. "You must tell us more about this new language, we find it very interesting. We're having *Ziegenlamm*, my wife got it from a farmer in trade for a golden necklace. And you don't have to bring us any meat stamps."

It's too weird for me, Wondrak thought, but he said nothing. But there seemed to be something or other in Apitt's lecture that was true. Whenever a *painful* yearning overcame him for something that he didn't want to admit to himself, he began to talk to himself, or he sought out someone with whom he could talk about it, but then he talked about something entirely different with that other person. He displayed one pain in order to hide another, deeper one.

And Valeska thought: Yes, maybe it is like that. I pray in pain to God. The greater the pain of the soul, the closer I am to God. She opened the piano lid and began to play a melody softly, with one hand.

"There is always somebody in this country who is discovering God or the soul," the president of the waterworks said, shaking his head incredulously. He decided to leave after all. He had once talked with someone in this house who claimed to be able to tell the future from the river.

Lucie didn't understand what Apitt meant, no matter how hard she exerted her brain. But she intuited some of it. She said: "There must be something true about it. The Archpriest cried when they took down the bells from the tower, and that's a pain that comes from the soul."

"How will it be," Valeska asked, "when all the bells have vanished from all the churches?"

"There's an old Gleiwitz proverb," mused Apitt: " 'A time without bells is a time without faith.' "

There were moments when old Apitt could look very old. But now he looked quite young.

39

"**I** THINK I HEARD the doorbell." With this comment in his deep bass voice, the president of the waterworks, who had now decided to stay, brought the others back to earth. They had not heard the bell. All of them were so preoccupied with what Herr Apitt had just been expounding that they wouldn't have noticed the wicked fairy Carabossa herself if she had been trying to get in. Valeska cast an anxious glance across the roses at her brother. Ever since Halina had been arrested, the slightest divergence from the ordinary aroused her suspicion. Who could be coming to their house at this time of day? No one had informed them of a visit, at any rate.

"That must be Aunt Lucie-in-parentheses-Lanolin," said Aunt Lucie (Widera) mockingly. "It wouldn't surprise me! She has found out that we're expecting an addition to the family and invites herself over for the Easter holidays . . ."

"Shhh!" said Valeska. If there really was someone standing outside the door, he would ring again. But since it was quiet, she took up Lucie's train of thought and said: "I wouldn't put it past her! How often have I told her to send us a card when she wants to come for a visit . . . There's no room for her."

"It was probably nothing," Wondrak said casually. And acted as if he harbored a special interest for the plan of the new Oder-Vistula Canal, which the president was outlining with some passion and copious nouns. Water was his profession. And he was happy that someone was interested. In this way they quickly put Herr Apitt's painful topic behind them. But Wondrak waited only until the others were listening too, then he stood up inconspicuously and left the room, as if he were just going to have a look outside after all. Everything seemed calm behind Irma's door. He went to the front door, mostly to reassure himself, for he didn't think for a moment that anyone could be standing out there, waiting. So Wondrak was a little shocked when he opened the door and saw a boy standing outside. He had never seen his face before, but it looked like the face of someone who wouldn't ring the doorbell a second time. Not like the faces of the Hitler Youth who would ring the bell asking for old newspapers or rags, or collecting for the NSV or the Winter Aid; if you didn't open up right away, they didn't hesitate to ring again harder and rattle their collection cans. This boy's face, however, looked sad, tired, and passive.

"Did you ring the bell?" Wondrak asked, still surprised.

The boy only nodded. He wiped the tangled hair from his forehead and said softly, with a heavy Polish accent: "I please speak Pan Dr. Wondraczek."

"Yes, that's who I am," Wondrak said reluctantly, suspicious now. He looked at the boy more closely. He was dressed plainly and neatly, in black shorts and black knee socks and a heavy jacket, which was too warm for this muggy afternoon. He guessed his age to be four-teen or fifteen, perhaps even younger; the tired, sad face made him look older. Out of his pocket the boy took a gray piece of paper, which was folded up and somewhat crumpled. He tried to smooth it out before handing it over, and Wondrak saw that it was a sealed envelope, with his name and address on it. It was his old name, which he hadn't used since 1939. And while he nervously opened the letter, he asked the boy: "Where do you come from?"

"From Katowice," the boy said. He used the Polish form of the name. The letter contained only five lines. Wondrak scanned them at a glance. He folded the envelope up again and hastily pocketed it. "Come to my place for now," he said to the boy. He spoke softly, as if the letter had advised him to be cautious. "I live in the garden cottage, but please, be quiet, someone in this house is ill."

He went ahead, leading the boy by the hand, which felt soft and hot. He pushed him into the hall of the garden cottage and listened outside to find out whether anyone had heard them. The boy stood in the door to Wondrak's room, because he didn't know where to look first, or where he was allowed to step in his coarse shoes. It was as if the accumulation of furniture, plants, and objects—which the fading light and the slightly distorted perspective displayed to him as a sort of nestling maze—was blocking his entrance. Willi pulled up an armchair for him, but he had to take the boy by the hand and push him down onto the cushion, otherwise he wouldn't have budged. Even then he remained sitting forward on the edge of the seat, half overwhelmed by the clutter, half ready to leap. His skinny, bluish-white knees stuck out. Wondrak had him tell his story. In Polish, because he could understand him better that way.

The boy had not been talking long, stammering and with pauses, when Wondrak left the garden cottage and went over to the music room for a moment. All at once he had become aware that his absence must be attracting attention, and he wanted to prevent his sister from coming to look for him and catching him here with the strange boy.

Valeska had indeed grown nervous, but because of Irma. Willi beckoned to her to come out to the hall, because what he had to tell her concerned her alone. He explained to her in a whisper what had happened.

"You can't hide anything in this house, the very walls have ears, here you even stumble over a pin," Valeska said, turning her head toward Irma's door.

"I'm not trying to hide anything," Wondrak said. "We have a visitor from Kattowitz, a son of the Bielskis. Do you remember them?"

Valeska didn't want to remember. She didn't want any Poles in the house, even a child. And the father under arrest! Two days ago she would still have said that there must be something to it if they arrest somebody, but after what had happened to Halina, she thought differently. But since then her fear had grown, too.

"And now he's in the garden cottage? Have you been abandoned by Jesus Christ and all the saints?" She ran into the garden, throwing caution to the winds.

But moments later it was she who was preparing some soup from Maggi bouillon cubes, whisking in a whole egg. She just hoped that Lucie wouldn't choose this moment to come in from the music room and ask questions.

"And why did they arrest his father, didn't he say?" Valeska asked.

Wondrak shrugged his shoulders. "He was never politically active, as far as I know. At least not before. He wasn't able to work as an attorney anymore, although he had applied for Ethnic Group III. And, until the end he was a legal aide in the Harrassowitz Chancellery."

"You'll put us all in danger. They're coming for us one after the other, I can see it." She cut a slice of bread from the loaf and put the slice next to the soup plate.

"But Valeska, he's only a child. He could have run away from home. At the age of fourteen we all ran away from home once or twice. Nobody will suspect him because of that."

"No, he's got to leave today! I'll give him something to eat now . . . the poor boy, on the road for two days and nothing to eat . . ." But she suppressed her sympathy again immediately: "I will be endangering my children if he stays here. Give him some money, tell him to take the train to Kattowitz, and if there's no train this late, let him get as far as he can by streetcar."

"Valeska! He's an innocent child, only fourteen. Just think about it, today is Good Friday!"

Valeska dropped the spoon. She bent down, because she didn't want her brother to see her face.

Then they both went to the garden cottage. Willi took care that they didn't run into anyone.

The boy had taken off his warm wool jacket in the meantime. Beneath it he was wearing a shirt that was obviously too big for him, for he had rolled the sleeves up three times. When Valeska led him over to the little round marble table, where she had set down the soup plate, he showed her a face that looked as if he had just cast a glance into Paradise. They both watched him in silence as he ate and wiped off the sweat with his shirt. His face changed markedly. It expressed tension, energy, alertness, and now Wondrak did recognize a similarity to the Bielskis.

"I'm not saying that he has to leave tonight," Valeska said. "But he can't stay in the house. It's too dangerous." And they considered where they might be able to put him up for the night. But while they were reciting the names of relatives and acquaintances, they realized that no one would help them.

"I've thought it over," Willi said. "I could take him to Ziegenhals tomorrow and put him into a school in the country. Lots of children of Volhynia Germans are being placed there, he wouldn't attract attention. And I'll talk to Dr. Henrici from the Bar Association in Kattowitz."

"But where should he sleep tonight?" objected Valeska, who was thinking of Halina. "And tomorrow morning, when you leave with him? Nothing stays a secret around here. For all we know, the Schimmels have been quartered with us as spies, you aren't safe in your own home these days . . ."

She acted as if the boy were no longer in the room, since she didn't know how else to speak with her brother about the matter. After all, they couldn't go outside and negotiate by the front door.

"He could sleep here in an armchair, or in Josel's room."

"My God, you're a lawyer!" After this outburst she lowered her voice again. Did she even have to remind him of Halina? "I don't know what kind of legal tricks you've got up your sleeve, but remember that I don't want it to go that far."

They were whispering to each other. They couldn't have known that, as long as the boy could remember, he had learned the truth only from whispers, never from loud speech. So now he too paid particular attention to what they were saying.

"I can sleep in the shed," he said from his armchair, into which he had now sunk back.

Wondrak moved three glass balls into a certain pattern on the shelf. He liked the arrangement better that way. "That's out of the question," he said, and wound his way to the window. "You can sleep here on the rug, or in my sister's house. It'll be all right for one night."

"Not in the music room, at any rate! If Irma doesn't have that baby pretty soon, they'll all be sitting in there, waiting. No one will go to bed before then. What kind of a shed does he mean?" Valeska asked her brother.

"Do you mean the tool shed out back in the garden?" And when the boy nodded, he said: "How did you know about it?"

"Because I was in it earlier," the boy said calmly. He had been counting on their sending him away immediately. But now they had given him some soup and a piece of bread to go with it. The doctor and his wife had even listened to him. That was more than he had expected.

"After I got the new address, I came here, but because the name on the door was Piontek, I didn't know whether it was the right place, so I reconnoitered the area first and took a look at the shed in the garden. And I thought that if I didn't find anyone, I'd spend the night there and continue the search tomorrow morning," he said in Polish.

Valeska understood only a part of it. "I think that's the best thing to do," she said hastily. "As soon as it's dark, Willi, you take him to the shed. I couldn't sleep a wink if he stayed in the house. Give him a few old sacks from the cellar, we could have been storing them there. And it's not so cold anymore, thank God."

"I'll give him one of my blankets," Wondrak said. He didn't want to let his sister see that he thought it was wrong to make the exhausted boy spend the night in the cold tool shed. "It could be some visiting relative, after all; that would not attract attention."

"After the trouble with Halina, I'm too afraid," Valeska said. She looked past the boy, and her glance fastened on a crystal goblet that she hadn't seen before. "Is that new?" she asked. She took the goblet from the vitrine, and as it was not bright enough in the room, she turned on one of the numerous lamps. She examined it more closely in the light, inspected the cut, and made the reflections sparkle. And she wanted to show her brother that the boy wasn't as important as they had been imagining for the last few minutes.

"Yes," Wondrak said. "I got it from Dobschinsky; even in these times he still has his sources. There are probably some people who have to sell things like that."

He stepped over to his sister. "Silesian Glassworks, in the Riesengebirge, about 1740, with ribboned vinework in the cuts. At the time there were only a handful of glass cutters who could do that . . . Isn't it a splendid piece? It's hard to find something like this outside of a museum."

He took the goblet from his sister's hand and happily admired the rich ornamentation. The way that he was holding it and examining it in the light could have exemplified their differing attitudes toward possessions—at least to such superfluous things as goblets, crystals, glass balls, and miniatures. To his sister these were merely dead objects that were far too expensive.

They had almost forgotten the boy. He would have liked nothing better. He was doing just fine there in the armchair, his legs pulled up, surrounded by expensive furniture and other marvelous things.

With a vigorous motion the lawyer placed the lead-crystal goblet back in the vitrine. He went to a chest of drawers, opened a drawer, and rummaged around in it. Then he took out a sweater and threw it to the boy.

"Here, put it on, it'll keep you warm. You can keep it, too." He did not like the sight of the skinny, gray knees.

The boy emerged from the depths of the chair and accepted the sweater gratefully, although he had no real idea of what to do with it; it was much too big for him. But he so rarely received a gift that he was happy about any present.

"What's your name? Grzegorz? From now on we'll call you Gregor."

40

TONIK WAS ALREADY standing in front of the Capitol Cinema, and the show didn't start for half an hour. What a bother it had been to get rid of those guys. *Dupka!* Bronder was the final one, and he showed no signs of wanting to leave. Bronder was the last thing he needed on a date with Hedel Zock. Tonik stopped where he was and explained the situation in all frankness. Bronder was only fifteen, but in these parts, twelve-year-olds were already in the know. "That's why I have to be alone with Hedel," he completed his largely invented story. "Got it?"

Bronder had nodded to him, with a long face, but had continued to follow him like a shadow. After all that talking, it finally turned out that Bronder simply didn't know where to sleep that night. He didn't want to go home. His grandfather had spent half of last night searching for his schnapps, and when he didn't find it, he accused Bronder of having sold it on the sly, and threatened that if Bronder came home that night without the schnapps he would *ukręcić teb.*

Tonik didn't know much Polish, but he knew that meant *wring his neck.*

For a time Bronder had belonged to the Teuchertstrasse *ferajna*, because earlier he had lived quite close by, on Ziegeleistrasse. His father had been killed in Russia in 1941 and his mother had followed another husband to the Warta region a few months later. She had left her child behind with his grandparents in Ratibor, a suburb. Bronder didn't find any new friends there, so he came back into town once or twice a week to see the boys in his old *ferajna*. His grandfather lived on tiny welfare checks as 100 percent disabled. A mine engine had cut off both his legs, but the management had refused to pay any compensation or Miners Association pension. On the contrary, they had claimed that the injury was self-inflicted because he had been drunk and had even demanded compensation for the damaged locomotive. He had taken it to court until he had spent not only his last pfennig but his children's as well, and to top it off, he lost his last appeal. He had never been a drinker, but that's when he began to drink, and now he had become a lush. Since he couldn't afford any schnapps, he raised nothing but sugar beets in his allotment garden for which he ran a still in some hiding place—Bronder thought it was in an old refugee barracks at the edge of Richtersdorf. He remained drunk for almost half the year, from harvest time until spring, as long as the sugar beets lasted.

It took quite an effort for Tonik to get this out of Bronder.

"When he's smashed," Bronder said, "he doesn't know what he's doing. As long as Grandma was there, she sort of . . . well, tamed him, but now that she's dead, there's no stopping him. I'm only afraid that I'll kill him," Bronder said seriously and quite calmly.

This was giving Tonik the creeps. Bronder looked so gentle and peaceable as he said it.

"I'll do it," Bronder continued just as calmly, "if he claims one more time that I'm not Joseph Bronder's son, brakeman for the German Railway, fallen 1941 in Russia, but instead—as he always says—the bastard of a Polish hired man who came across the border every spring and who my mother was running after."

"Listen to me," Tonik said. "Go home to my mother, you know where Squintok lives, don't you? and tell her I want you to sleep in my room for this one night. I probably won't come home tonight anyway, and if I do it'll be pretty late . . . Then I'll sleep on the floor—it doesn't matter, it's a lot worse at the front. And tomorrow I'll go see your grandfather with you and have a talk with him, all right?"

Bronder would probably have accepted any suggestion, as long as he didn't have to go home to his grandfather. He especially liked this suggestion; he'd be able to talk with Squintok, or with Kotik. As he was about to set out, the Wild Monk suddenly appeared next to them. Neither of them had seen him come up because they were both so engrossed in Bronder's story. The Wild Monk had been back in town only the last few days. The word had gotten around quickly—even Tonik had heard about it. No one knew why they had interned him this time; he didn't know either. Since he claimed the Franciscan monastery in the foundry district as his permanent residence, which did not want to have anything to do with him, however, and he actually stayed in a shack in the Laband Woods, they could lock him up again anytime on some pretext. The Wild Monk, so it seemed, had reconciled himself to this, at least to judge by the look on his face; in the camp or in prison at least he came into contact with people who liked to listen to him, which was seldom the case "outside." And he had so much to preach to them from the Gospels.

The monk greeted both of them with great cordiality. He smelled of walnut oil, which had obviously gone rancid on his skin. His old cowl was tattered in many places, particularly where it dragged on the ground—you noticed it right away. The dirt was probably all that was holding it together.

Tonik took out a pack of cigarettes and offered the Wild Monk one. The cigarette did a disappearing act into his cowl, so quickly that Tonik and Bronder couldn't follow it.

"I quit smoking a long time ago," the Wild Monk said. "But there are people who will only listen to my sermons if I offer them a smoke, so I swap a cigarette with them for a sermon."

"No sermon for me today," Tonik said, and lit his cigarette. After so long a time, he wouldn't have been able to say whether the monk's sermons really had been good; wild they were, at any rate. They couldn't be compared to the sermons delivered from the pulpit of St. Peter and Paul's to ease you into sleep. The Wild Monk was a preacher who involved himself in what he said to his listeners—with his face, with his voice, with his motions, indeed with his whole body. And some of this was communicated to his listeners. Tonik remembered how they had once asked him to preach to them about Hell, because it would break out of him like a storm and, howling, lamenting, wailing, screaming, and whimpering, he would act out the torments of Hell, at least some of the milder varieties; and the youngest listeners actually cried and their teeth chattered, while the others clapped their hands in delight. The monk had aged by now, you could see it in his face. His movements had slowed, his voice was accompanied by a soft whistling.

When the monk found out that Bronder didn't want to go home, the reasons didn't interest him much. He offered him a place to sleep in his shack in the Laband Woods for one night. But he would have

to put up with a blindfold, like in blindman's buff, going through
the forest, at least part way, so he wouldn't be able to show anyone
the place afterward. Not that he believed that Bronder might betray
him, like Judas did Jesus Christ, but there were ways and means to
compel him to such a betrayal—he had some experience with that.
Tonik left the decision up to Bronder, who didn't hesitate for
long—naturally he was looking forward to a bigger and more exciting adventure at the Wild Monk's than at the Ossadniks'.

"Let's go, young man," he said, and gave Bronder a shove, "and
I'll tell you about St. John's true and no longer so terrible prophecy,
which tells about the end of the world. And I say to you that we
are not far from it, for the signs are multiplying, and soon fire and
storm will ravage the landscape, the animals will die, men will flee
across snow-covered fields, frozen rivers, through dead cities, and
the devil who seduced them will be cast into the pool of fire and
brimstone where the Beast and the false prophet were too, and will
be tortured . . . Come on, young man, come . . . then will be day
and night, the innocent and the guilty from eternity to eternity, and
there will be a howling and a gnashing of teeth . . ."

Tonik edged away. It wasn't hard to see why they kept locking
up the monk. If he teaches Bronder how to preach, then by Saint
Anthony of Padua, Tonik thought, he'll make another Savonarola
out of him. When he looked back once more, he saw the two of
them at the end of the street. The monk was talking at Bronder; he
stopped now and then, and then they walked on some more. It
would be dark by the time they reached the woods, and he wouldn't
have to put any blindfold on Bronder. He probably didn't even have
one.

41

ANNA HAD LET down her hair—it hung like a tapestry over her shoulders. She was standing in her slip in front of the bedroom mirror, brushing her hair. Franz was sitting on the bed in his undershirt. He sniffed at his fingers, because the soap gave off an unpleasant smell. He watched his wife standing in front of the mirror, her body, which was clearly underlined beneath the slip, her bare shoulders, her hair, the movements of her arms. For him, it was a satisfaction to look at her, merely to look at her; everything about her pleased him, still pleased him, and they had known each other for more than twenty-five years. If he had permitted himself such precious words, he would have to say: I still love you, Anna. But that was not the language in which simple people conversed in this country. He said: "My God, Anna, I think you're still so pretty . . ."

"Ach, how you talk," Anna said seriously and rolled her hair into a bun. "I'm an old woman, I'm over forty. Here . . . look, all these gray hairs." She liked to exaggerate, so that others would contradict her.

"You've got six children," Franz countered eagerly, "and you're still beautiful. And I'm getting more and more rickety." He said that without resentment.

Anna rubbed some eau de cologne on her hands and face. She liked it when it smelled nice in the bedroom. And she patted some on that place on her neck, too—no, it didn't hurt, but it seemed enlarged to her.

"You know that without you I'm nothing, Franzek," she said, and sniffed at her fingertips.

"Give me a squirt, too, the new soap really stinks."

"Being a little rickety is good for a man nowadays, otherwise they would have drafted you long ago." It was typical of her always to look at the sunny side of things.

"My hair, look, it won't even have the chance to turn gray." Franz brushed his hand over his scalp, on the middle of which only a little fuzz remained. "What's going to become of it all?"

Anna sat down next to Franz on the edge of the bed. "What's the matter?" she asked. "Did what Kotik read out loud get you that upset? I got upset too, and a lot more! But I've already put it out of my mind. Before we go to sleep I'll read the legend of the holy martyrs Audifax and Abachum out loud . . ."

"No, no." Franz rejected the idea. "What Kotik was reading there, the description of Upper Silesia by that Rudolf Virchow, that interested me a lot more, I'll read that over Easter, when I have more time. I guess it's true the way it's written. In the Reich they've always forgotten about us. My grandfather said the Kaiser knows nothing about Upper Silesia, except that in the forests of Prince Pless there are still aurochs to be hunted. And my father worked in a coal mine in Scharley that belonged to a Herr Arnhold in Berlin. He came driving up once a year in a four-in-hand, visited his coal mines and coking plants, not even knowing how many he owned, and gave Kaiser Wilhelm a park with a villa in Rome for his court artists, full of ateliers; that's where those fancy artists travel now and paint Italian landscapes, and they've never even seen a worker from one of the Arnhold coal mines."

Anna put a hand on Franzek's knee. "Hush," she said, "now you're getting excited! Let's not talk about it. We're living in a different time. You've gotten so nervous, Franzek, I don't like it."

Yes, she had felt it, even though she was so preoccupied with her novels. And with Squintok, naturally, who didn't want to be Squintok anymore.

Franz stretched his back. "What do you mean, how have I become different? Do I look any different?"

"I can feel it."

She really had been feeling it, for some time already. "The bees," she said. "You know, I've noticed that you don't spend time with your bees anymore, like you used to. Two swarms have already flown out this year, and you didn't go capture them. That's never happened before."

Franz Ossadnik looked at his wife in amazement. He hadn't known that she cared so much about his beekeeping. She had gone out to the bees with him only two or three times a summer at most, but always remained at a respectful distance, preferring to gather berries and herbs and heather in the woods. Or she would sit down in the grass and read her books. She claimed that she had sweet blood and attracted mosquitoes and bees. She was terribly afraid of insect bites in general. Once when he had moved the bees to Makoschau and she had carried the honey extractor for him, she had limped around the house for days afterwards and had treated her feet, neck, and shoulders with clay vinegar. But he couldn't see a sting anywhere, and was convinced that it was all in her imagination. In any case, she had avoided his beehives ever since.

"With that swarm, you know, that was something different . . ." Franz was about to begin.

"But that's not so important," Anna said. She brushed the bedspread with her hand. "The material is all gray," she said regretfully. "Even though I scrub my hands raw doing the laundry. There's no more good soft soap for loosening the dirt, that's the trouble.

"Something or other is bothering you, whether it's here or with the bees. You have been different lately." She was simply curious now, nothing more.

"Anna, I've been wanting to talk to you about it for weeks, but it's not that easy. I don't know if I can even say it to you." His voice was calm, soft, and at the same time so clear that his wife was worried.

"Say it to me?" Anna didn't understand her Franzek. He hardly read the newspaper, and once a week, when he had his day off, he would page through a magazine—the *Beekeeper's Bulletin* or the *Arbeitsfront-Kurier*. But she read novels, at least four every week, and her husband didn't have the faintest idea what she got out of them. From this Dominik she even learned what the future would look like. She just couldn't imagine that there might be anything that he couldn't tell her.

"But Franzek! You know that you've never been able to keep a secret from me."

Yet she couldn't remember Franz ever having had a secret from her. For her Franz was a book, one that she had already read a few times and that no longer contained any surprises. It was different with the children. From beneath the pillow Anna took out the bed jacket she had knitted herself.

"It's like this, Anna," Franz said, taking her hand firmly in his. "It's not a matter of keeping secrets from you. I've gotten into an awful fix and I need some advice, serious advice, about how to get out of it. And I don't know whether you can be of any help to me. I don't want to get you involved. Can anyone hear us?"

"No." Anna shook her head. "Kotik is asleep and Andy's in his room. And Tonik isn't home yet."

"I've been wanting to talk to Lawyer Wondrak about it."

"With Dr. Wondrak? Why with him? But first tell me what it's all about. The suspense is killing me."

She stuffed the bed jacket back under the pillow and acted as if she were searching for something.

"You musn't talk to anyone about it, please, promise me."

"Yes, of course." Anna was growing quite impatient and was about to take her hand away from his.

Franz did not look her in the face as he said, "I enlisted in the army."

"Are you crazy?" Anna said quickly, as if she had been suspecting this. Now she gripped his hand. She spoke bitingly, so that she would believe it too: "But they wouldn't take you, you're much too old and too rickety for the Greater German Wehrmacht!" She paused. "Excuse me," she said, "but it's a good thing that you're too old for the war. We have two sons in the war now, and another has already been killed. That ought to be enough for Adolf! Franzek, you can't be serious . . ."

She couldn't believe that he would want to leave her.

"Calm down, Annuschka, and listen to me. That's just the trouble: I can't talk to you about things like this. You get so excited."

"Why shouldn't I get excited, when you spring something like this on me? Give me one reason why you did it! Or tell me it isn't true!"

"Anna, it's something I just can't live with. And I had been thinking whether I ought to confess it to Pastor Pattas."

"Ach, blessed Lord Jesus!" Anna shivered. She had never seen her Franzek like this. First the lawyer, now the pastor. She was filled with sympathy; it was the only feeling for her husband she was capable of right now.

The pause lasted longer than she had intended. Twice, Franz tried to speak, but didn't know how to begin. Yet he had imagined this situation a few times already, and up on the tender he had practiced some of the sentences out loud; he would have to talk about it with Anna sometime.

"The trains, Anna, that I've been driving for some time, those are freight trains full of people. From all of Germany, from France, from Holland, I usually take over here at the switchyards or in Heydebreck, where the train lines come together . . . I drive them to Birkenau, that's a big concentration camp. They're all Jews . . . They've been traveling for days. When we get to the camp and they open the doors—you see, they're all cattle cars, and they just stuff the people inside—so when they open up the cars, a few corpses always fall out. I have to wait there at the platform until the cars are cleaned, and then I drive the empty cars back. Anna, it's terrible to watch it all."

"Jews . . . you say? How do you know they're Jews?"

"They're all still wearing the Jewish star on their coats. And yesterday I asked the engineer who I took over the transport from, he drove them all the way from Drente-Westerbork. With Jews from Holland and Belgium."

"There aren't that many Jews. They've all emigrated."

"It's been going on like this for six months. And Anna, I think that it's a great sin, what they're doing. And I . . . and I've always read that the Jews are being resettled in the East. But when you see how they arrive with nothing, with a suitcase and two blankets, that's all they have . . . Surely they used to have the things we do, a place to live, furniture, clothes, a radio . . . Somehow I feel I'm partly guilty for them being there . . ." His voice made it plain that he had been thinking about it a lot. The pauses between his sentences were growing longer and longer.

"They're sending the Jews into the armament factories. I read about it," Anna said. "Since the air raids in the West started, Upper Silesia has become the arms producer of Germany. Everywhere around here." She said that because she had read it in the papers.

"I heard there are supposed to be several camps at Birkenau," Franz said slowly. "There's plenty of room. They're dying like flies there. Every day some of them are burned. You smell it sometimes."

"But if *you* don't do it, someone else will drive the trains, Franz, think of that. You just happen to be an engineer. Otherwise you'd be sent to the front."

"I shouldn't have joined the Party. For these transports they only use Party members."

"When did you send the letter?" she asked.

"What letter?" Franz began to knead the corner of a pillow.

"Well, that you were volunteering. I don't know why you didn't wait until we talked it over. You usually talk about everything with me."

She had always made the decisions. How could he possibly write this letter without her approval? It offended her that he had not asked her first. As she thought about it, she even started to get angry.

"Today," Franz said. "When I changed clothes at the depot, then I sat down and wrote the letter, and mailed it off right away. Because I knew that if I talked to you about it first, then I would never mail it. And maybe I wouldn't even want to write it anymore. But believe me, for some time now I've been thinking about writing that letter, ever since they rejected my transfer. I don't know how much longer I can keep on doing this."

He punched at the wadded-up pillow, lay down on his back, and stared helplessly at the ceiling. "You see, something happened, Anna, and I thought: now you have to do it. If you don't do it now you'll never do it, maybe you'll even get used to it. You have to do it now and talk to Anna about it this evening—but not until afterward. You've got to understand me, Anna."

And when Anna remained silent, he talked on, still staring at the ceiling, which slowly began to sway. "Yesterday a car was switched onto my train in Kattowitz; that happens often, it's nothing unusual, sometimes I drive sixty cars to the Birkenau camp. When they opened the doors, I saw that there were Jews from Gleiwitz in the car. I recognized Herr Karpe, from the linen store on the Ring where we sometimes traded, and then Frau Grünpeter and her husband, who had the grocery store . . . And then I saw Herr Blumenfeld from the

health board; I didn't recognize him right away, you know we haven't
seen him now for a few years, and I asked him if he was really Herr
Blumenfeld of the health board, and it really was. And he said that
they were removed from Gleiwitz yesterday and had spent the night
in the Gestapo prison in Kattowitz where they had been assembled,
and now they were supposed to be going to a family camp."

Franz had the feeling that the ceiling was going to fall on him.
He sat up and switched on the other night lamp too. "Do you have
any schnapps, Mamotschka? I feel lousy, a schnapps would do me
good."

Anna began to undo her braid again. "I do have some, but today
is Good Friday, Franz!"

"Listen, Herr Blumenfeld asked me to go see Justice Kochmann
on Niederwallstrasse and tell him where they were being taken."

Anna began to brush her hair again. The movements of her arms
were as forceful as if she were fighting with someone invisible.

"No, you're not going to do that," she said, gasping. "I'll get you
a schnapps, now; all right." With that she went into the hall, took
the key to the pantry, and got a bottle from a hiding place that only
she knew about. She didn't bother with a glass. Only Franzek drank
out of this bottle, anyway. She just needed to watch out that he
didn't keep it too long.

When she got back, Franz was sitting in the chair. He had turned
on the ceiling light. More light would calm him down. Better yet,
the ceiling would stop moving back and forth the way it had in the
semi-darkness. Anna's face was even paler in this light than before.

"On no account are you going to see the Jews," Anna said. "The
whole town would hear about it. My God! The others might hear
about it."

It was something that really concerned only the two of them.

Franz took a swallow of schnapps, and although it was only a
small swallow he could feel the schnapps spreading its heat inside
him. He breathed deeply, as if he would have to do without air for
a while.

"I won't go," he said. "No, I won't," he assured himself once
again. But at that moment he didn't know whether he would keep
his word. Deep down inside something told him that it might be

his duty to inform old Justice Kochmann. "I wonder," he said slowly, "if I shouldn't just tell him in an anonymous letter."

"No, keep out of it. Stop thinking about the Jews." Anna was whispering now, because it was better not to talk about Jews out loud. "I thought all the Jews were gone. I haven't seen any for a long time. They say they're all being resettled in Poland."

Now she took a swallow from the bottle herself. It occurred to her that she hadn't thought about the Jews she knew for a long time. Dr. Bermann of the health board, for whom she had been a domestic before her marriage, had moved to Berlin and had died there at his son's. The Lustigs had emigrated to Chile, and Hanna . . . my God, now she didn't even remember the last name of the girl who had taken a course in plain needlework with her—to Palestine, and the Leschziners were supposed to have grown rich in Brazil. They themselves had thought once of emigrating to Australia, when Franzek had been without a job for so long. But for her it would have been difficult, for she would never be able to learn a foreign language, and that was only the beginning. It was different with the Jews, it was easier for them to adapt. Most of them had come from Poland or Russia, after all, and had adapted to life here, and they learned languages much more easily, too.

"Anyway, your letter was a mistake. You should have applied for a transfer to someplace else."

"I did, I tried that, I reported in sick, but they kept on assigning me. I'm a Party member, that's the trouble."

It sounded like a reproach, which Anna took personally. "But we just wanted Ulla to be able to study and get a scholarship. Frau Piontek wanted only the best for her, you know that. And after all, Ulla has made something of herself."

She went over to her husband and put her hands on his shoulders. "We must talk to Lawyer Wondrak, you're right. Maybe he'll know a way out. I mean, about the letter. So it can be declared invalid, somehow."

She acted as if she were thinking it over. She was already a lot calmer now. A lawyer would be able to think of something, that's what he was paid for. Her Franz was worth the expense. The husbands of most of the women in the neighborhood were at the front.

She had been lucky, up to now. Her husband had become senior engineer in the meantime, and he was at home. And only slowly did it begin to dawn on her that there might be some connection between the fact that her husband hadn't been drafted and didn't have to fight at the front, and that as a railroad engineer he drove the transports to the camp.

Franz was silent. He pushed Anna aside, lightly, and took another swallow from the bottle. He couldn't taste the schnapps, but the heat in his throat felt good. "It'll happen pretty soon anyway," he said. "They're drafting everybody who's halfway healthy. You've heard all about it, now it's total war. Someday the women will have to drive the trains."

Actually, he didn't care. He had to worry about his train being blown up on every trip, as it was, even though they had been riding with an empty car out in front for some time now. In Russia it happened every day somewhere; now the partisans were on the move in Poland too.

"Yes, but you have to resist," Anna said. "You have to try, at least. I'll go see Dr. Wondrak tomorrow, he'll be able to do something. You're indispensable!"

She took the bottle and put it on the nightstand. I've always been the decision maker in this house anyway, her face said.

"Then I'll have to keep on driving the transports. And keep on seeing that misery. Dear Lord, forgive me!" He went to the light switch and turned out the ceiling light. He still thought it would be right to go to the pastor, maybe confession would relieve him. He embraced his wife.

"Don't look, Franzek," she said. "Misery is everywhere these days. They arrested Frau Piontek's Halina because she was keeping company with an Eastern laborer, the poor creature. You can't do anything about it. We have to see that we make it, Franzek, that's all that matters. We have to survive. Especially now that we're finally doing a little better! We get more on our grocery coupons than we used to be able to afford with six children, let's be honest about it. A pair of new shoes for the children every year! They used to have to go barefoot the whole summer. And Paulek brought me the Persian lamb coat from France and now that beautiful material, and for Ulla, you were amazed yourself, the evening dress with all those sequins on it. Now we can even rent a room to the Dittberners, who can't stand it anymore in Berlin with the air-raid sirens, for twelve marks a month. We haven't had a single enemy plane come over here, Franz!"

She put all her hope into this exclamation, so that he wouldn't destroy what they had acquired.

Franz was silent. Maybe I shouldn't have talked to her about it at all. You shouldn't talk to women about things like that, he thought.

"Basically, we've never been better off, Franz. I hope my goiter will get better, too. It's a little more swollen now, but that's because I got so excited just now . . . It's not that noticeable, is it . . . ?" She reassured herself with the thought.

"And the war," she said, "will come to an end some day. You know, old Hrabinsky always says: 'Enjoy the war, peace will be terrible!' "

She slipped into her bed jacket and carefully folded down the collar. The sleeves were a little too short because the wool had shrunk in the wash. She turned out the lamp on the nightstand.

"Don't think about it anymore, you're just doing your duty. And tomorrow morning I'll go see Herr Wondrak," she said firmly.

"You know, the bees," Franz said pensively, staring into the dark. "You didn't understand about the bees. Bees only swarm in the summer. I let the swarm fly out! If I'm not here, who'll take care of them?"

She did not answer.

After a while he could feel that Anna was crying.

Suddenly they heard two or three dull blows and a muffled cry, followed by soft whimpering. All this came from close by, indeed it seemed as if it had taken place inside their own apartment. Franz reached across Anna for the switch on the night lamp and missed it in his haste and excitement. A terrible suspicion rose within him. In the hall he met Kotik, who was leaning against the doorjamb, confused and only half awake.

"It was Squintok who screamed," Kotik whispered.

Franz went the few steps and tore open the door to Squintok's room. He saw his son kneeling on the floor in his nightshirt, his left hand on the wooden stool, the fingers clawing upward. Blood was collecting in his palm and trickling down on the sides, and a long nail jutted up from the middle. Andy's face was distorted in pain, and his lips were pressed together tightly.

Anna had come in unnoticed behind Franz and clutched at her husband's shoulders. "*Muj Bosche*, the poor boy," was all she said.

42

THE DAY HAD begun gray and overcast. Toward noon the clouds had torn open and a wind from the southeast, from the Beskids, chased the clouds, played with them, piled them on top of each other and finally drove them off to the north. In the afternoon the sky was swept clear and it triumphed in a single gleaming blue. The sun embraced the land. It was as if someone had held a match to the air, it virtually exploded, and a wave of warmth surged through the streets of the town. The people grew restless in their houses, without knowing quite why; some of them went out in the street and concealed their confusion, others talked over the back fence with neighbors about the times or about God, many went walking at the edge of town, breathing in the smell of the earth, and some waited until it grew dark and the first fireflies began to blink, then they would embrace down by the Klodnitz. And then wait again. Until spindle, shuttle, and needle began to dance.

Josel had been drifting around town, where it was quieter now with fewer people around; he had gone through Wilhelmspark, past the Hotel Upper Silesia and the municipal theater, along the Klodnitz to Lohmeyer- and Loschstrasse, under the chestnuts, which were stretching out their first leaves like green tongues. In May they formed a single green canopy here in which the blossoms gleamed like sparklers. There was a restlessness in him that he had been feeling ever since that morning and that he was trying to forget in his senseless search for Ulla, but he had only become more conscious of it because of the lonely cello player at Cieplik's Conservatory. He had been to the Ossadniks' twice. The first time the only one at home was Tonik, who was just getting out of bed although it was already afternoon, and he knew nothing, and the second time Frau Ossadnik, who was counting on Ulla visiting them on Easter. He had told her neither about his trip to Beuthen nor what the young cellist had confided to him about Ulla's trip to Warsaw. Maybe it wasn't even true and he would just upset her mother. He talked himself into believing that perhaps it had only been a pretext on Ulla's part for taking a trip somewhere else, to Breslau or to Berlin. She had told him that she wanted to take a master's class from Puchelt or from Gieseking, when she was far enough along—but she had not told him when she would be "far enough along."

Maybe now she was far enough along. He hoped that she hadn't gone to Warsaw without him. He had left a note with her mother for Ulla please to call him as soon as she got home, and the reason he wrote down made it urgent enough: I'M GOING TO WAR! Maybe she had gone back to the music school in Beuthen first. Then she would already know. There was nothing more he could do. He could throw stones into the Klodnitz. Which he finally did. He could not have said why it was precisely now that he collected some stones, as he had done when he was a kid, and dropped them from the little bridge. They had often done that back then, in the evening when darkness was falling and the Klodnitz was one big black mirror, and they had listened to the sounds that falling stones make, and each sound was different depending on the size of the stone, if you listened right. He had sometimes imagined what the sound would be like if a person fell off the bridge like a stone. In flood times people had always drowned in the Klodnitz.

The Klodnitz flowed so slowly here that you might think it was a standing body of water. Its surface glittered metallically, which came from the numerous ore-washing plants that discharged into the river. Josel noticed a smell of metal now that the water was warming up. On the way back he passed the Church of the Cross, where he bought some young birch twigs from an old woman. He would give them to his sister Irma. Young birch twigs bring good luck. Then he went home.

When Josel opened the door to the music room, he saw her. He stopped. He just stood there and left the door open behind him. He had already been warm for some time; now the heat shot to his face. Ulla Ossadnik was sitting in his mother's music room! That was the last thing he had expected.

"At least close the door," his mother said dryly.

He had been on the go all day in search of Ulla, and now that he had found her, he almost couldn't believe it. Since he still didn't know what to say to her, he simply walked up to her and placed the birch twigs in her arms.

"Ulla, it's you." He said it as if the entire day had been nothing but the preparation for this one moment, for this meeting.

"Ulla has come to say good-bye," his mother put in. "After Easter she's going on a concert tour, our artist!"

Valeska looked at Ulla admiringly from the side. She still could not grasp that the little Ulla who had come to her one day for piano lessons, whose hand she had guided over the keys, was now appearing in concert halls, and that her name was in the newspapers.

Ulla held the twigs in her arms. "Klaus told me that you were in Beuthen this morning; that's the cello player, you know, the one you talked to at the conservatory." She looked around for a vase for the young birch twigs, because it gave her the chance to make what she wanted to say sound more nonchalant.

"You have to go in the army? And right after Easter? Well, it's the parting of the ways, I guess. You'll be in the army. And I'll be on tour . . ."

There was a slight difference, after all. But she didn't notice it until she had said it.

"Yes, I've been drafted," Josel said.

What else did Ulla need to know? That's really all he had to say to her. He went into the kitchen and brought back a vase, and Ulla deftly placed the birch twigs into it.

"Yes, the poor boy," Valeska said, "he's actually still too young for the military, isn't he? They could at least have waited until graduation."

Josel didn't bother to answer that. He watched Ulla arranging the twigs in the vase, somehow cleverly producing the model of a miniature tree. It amazed him.

He wanted so much to be alone with Ulla, that's what he had gone to Beuthen for, to talk with her undisturbed. Here she would be totally commandeered by his mother. And while she peppered Ulla with questions, he was at least able to deduce that Ulla had to take the streetcar back to Beuthen that evening. That would be his last chance to be alone with her. He would walk her to the streetcar stop, maybe even ride a ways with her.

Josel listened to what the two women were talking about. How often he had heard that before! But they said it as if it were the first time they were talking about such things. He wished he knew if Ulla had really been to Warsaw, at the Church of the Holy Cross, but he didn't want to ask her in front of his mother. That was their secret, and he would keep the secret and carry it around with him to the end of the world. He couldn't believe that Ulla had gone there by herself, or even with her teacher, that Professor Lechter. It was something that belonged only to them, and he remembered how often they had talked about it and imagined what it would be like, and how they had actually tried to go once and had been sent back at the border. Later it was no longer so important to him to have been there in reality, because he had been there with Ulla so often in his thoughts.

He just wanted their secret to be preserved. When you entered the central nave, the second column on the left, that's where it must be, the secret that united them: the heart of Chopin. They walk through the empty space in the church, and their steps echo, and they kneel down on the stone floor and place a bouquet of anemones there, or a white lily. "He loved lilies," Ulla says, and she places a lily at the foot of the column. And they return from the church he has never seen, return from the city he has never visited, return from their childhood, which is moving further and further from them— and he returns to a dream that he wanted to return to again and again.

Aunt Lucie came in and whispered something to Valeska. Lucie seemed to have expected her reaction. For when Valeska started to leap up, she pressed her gently back down onto her chair. "Keep calm, there's no reason at all to get excited." And to all of them she said, "Please stay away from Frau Skrobek's room now, until . . . it's over."

She had already left the room.

Willi Wondrak came in on tiptoe, sat down by the window, and began to read. After a while he looked at the clock and turned back a few pages because he had lost the thread. Then he looked at the clock again. Frau Schimmel came downstairs alone and sat down silently in a white wicker chair. Her gaze wandered, and she took the opportunity to examine the objects and furniture in the room more closely, which she had been wanting to do for days, but Frau Piontek had always headed her off in the hall. She hoped they would be able to use her now. She had enough time. She had always had the time, but ever since their cozy two-room apartment in Berlin had been burned out in an air raid, she had even more time.

Josel and Ulla had glanced at each other a few times from a distance. Then Josel stood up and walked past Ulla to the veranda. "Do you want to come see what's already in blossom in our garden?" he said, as casually as possible. He opened the door. The warmth billowed in and made the people in the room breathe more deeply. Ulla got up and went out into the garden with Josel. They walked past the garden cottage, past the tool shed almost to the end of the garden; they didn't see the crocuses blooming, or the primroses, tulips, and daffodils, or the shining forsythia. They smelled the gorse. And they smelled the blue hyacinths.

"Ulla," Josel said softly but determinedly. As if he had caught her in a snare with this form of address.

Ulla felt uneasy. She stopped in front of a hedge of forsythia, which burned with its thousand yellow blossoms as if with a thousand tiny lights. "How warm it's become, all at once . . . as if spring has suddenly exploded . . . You can really feel it on your skin . . ." She stretched out her arms.

And Josel, who actually wanted to say something else, said that summer had already been lying in wait for a while, beneath the earth, and the sun hardly comes out before summer breaks out and can't be held back . . . Then he turned toward her and said in a different voice: "We haven't seen each other for a long time."

"At the concert," Ulla said, and broke off a blossoming twig. "That's not so long ago."

"It was a beautiful concert, yes, it was," Josel said. "I think I was trembling more down there in the audience than you were up on stage . . . I was so proud of you. And so excited that I only remember half the concert, if that much . . . At the end I was dripping wet with sweat, as if I had been playing and not you . . . I wanted to tell you that right after the concert, but you weren't listening to me . . ."

"You know, there were so many people standing around me, all talking to me at once . . . I wasn't even there—I mean, for a few hours afterward, I was dazed. I was there but I was somewhere else at the same time; that started with the first few bars of the B-minor sonata, only my fingers were playing . . . I wasn't myself again until I was alone in my own room, and that's when I noticed how exhausted I was. If Professor Lechter hadn't come to my room, I don't know what I might have done . . . I played the concert all over again in my thoughts, and I don't think it was really good until then . . . Can you understand that?" she said.

Josel walked silently beside her. He had wanted to interject something once or twice but his throat felt as if it were tied in knots. "Well, if that's the way it is . . ." he stammered and couldn't look at her. "I don't know how to begin, but I have to tell you something important . . ."

"Well, I was actually only satisfied with the A-flat major Polonaise. Did you notice what I did with the secondary theme there . . . ?" Ulla hummed a melody and struck the keys in the air with her right hand. She was already thinking of her next concert in Kattowitz, and the one after that in Oppeln. And what she would play differently then.

Josel didn't remember details. He had simply thought the concert was wonderful, and staring raptly at Ulla, he had heard only a single, uninterrupted melody. If she had asked him what was happening on her face during the scherzo of the B-minor sonata, he could have described it to her.

But Josel began again: "I have to tell you something important, Ulla! This may be the last time we meet, so it would be good, if you . . . I mean, you ought to know that . . . well, I don't know how to say it . . . It would be good if I knew whether you'll be waiting for me. Until I come back from the war . . ." He was walking backwards in front of her now, so he could say it to her face: "I would like you to wait for me . . . even if you're famous . . ."

He stopped. He had said it all wrong, but still it was right that he had said it.

"You're crazy!" was all she said. But she felt immediately that her reaction was wrong. Yet what he was demanding of her was such a surprise that it confounded her at first. And as she looked at him standing before her with his arms dangling like a condemned man waiting for his execution, she felt that she couldn't cope with the situation. She didn't know how to respond. She looked at the forsythia twig and crushed a blossom between her fingers, then a second one.

"Pardon me, Joselek," she began slowly, "you startled me with your question. Let's be frank. We're not children anymore, who dream of something that will dissolve in the next minute, or the next hour. We were childhood friends, that's a lot, but it's no more than that. We'll see each other again, someday. You're going to war, I'm going on tour. Maybe we'll wait for each other, but the way you wait for a friend. And so we'll see each other again, sometime, as the friends we were in our childhood. We're grownups now. We're different people now, Josel."

She spoke slowly, because she wanted to weigh every word as she spoke. She didn't want to hurt him. But she had to tell him the truth.

Josel had listened to her attentively. Essentially she had told him what he had already figured out for himself; she had just used different words. He had wanted the truth from her no matter how bitter and sobering the consequences would be for him; but while he had always pictured this in his thoughts, she had appeared closer to him and more intimate in these thoughts, and in the end he had invented an intimacy that no longer had much to do with reality or with Ulla.

He walked on and sat down on a bench. If only she had at least left him his belief.

"We've become different people, Ulla, that's true. But we haven't become strangers," he said. "I don't demand anything of you. I used to think we'd get married someday, but that was long ago. Those really were dreams, childish dreams . . . We loved each other in our own way, as children, and it's a different situation now, I know. But I need someone I can believe in; when I go to the war, I need to know what I'm fighting for, I need to have the feeling that someone is waiting for me."

"But you have your mother, you have your sister and the others, too."

"To know that *you* are waiting for me would give me the courage to endure, to survive . . . would give the whole thing some meaning."

Ulla sat down on the bench next to Josel. She hesitated to say anything, because she felt that anything she might say now would be wrong; but she had to say something to him. She felt sorry for Josel. He had always been so unpredictable in his feelings.

"We'll all be waiting for you to come back from the war . . . healthy . . ." she said softly, trying to put as much conviction as she could muster into the words. It was not much.

Josel felt it. But he didn't need pity.

"You were in Warsaw, to visit the heart of Chopin!" he said bitterly.

Essentially that was what had ruined everything between them.

Ulla searched Josel's face, as if she could read more in it than just what he had said. "How do you know that?"

"The cello player told me. He told me because he thought we were close friends. You probably didn't want anyone to find out about it . . . ?"

"Did you mention it to anybody?" Ulla asked warily.

"Nobody, not a word."

"Not even to your mother?"

"She's the last person I'd mention it to," Josel said coldly.

"Yes, I was in Warsaw. I suddenly got the visa I applied for over a year ago. I had stopped believing that I would ever get it. So I went there for one day."

"To the heart of Chopin?"

"I bought some sheet music," Ulla said evasively.

"You were in the Church of the Holy Cross and you touched the pillar that the heart is walled up in!" For Josel it was a certainty.

Ulla did not answer. She gazed at the evening sky, which slowly was beginning to turn color, from bright yellow all the way to dark purple.

"It was our secret, Ulla! You betrayed it! You were there with the professor."

Ulla jumped up from the bench. She didn't want him to see her face flushing an angry red. "That was childhood nonsense," she burst out. "I used to believe in it the way you believe in a pretty legend, that's all. I've given my first concert and it was a success. That should prove what nonsense the legend about Chopin's heart is! And I don't have to answer to you either . . ." She was angry now and wanted to leave. In a way she was afraid of him too. He was so unpredictable sometimes. And hadn't he bitten a teacher on the nose at school only recently? Somebody had told her about it. She had not wanted to believe it, but maybe there had been some truth in it, after all.

Josel grabbed for her hand and held it tightly. Now he was standing next to her. "Because you're waiting for your professor, that's what it is. That's why you can't wait for *me*."

"Let go, you're hurting me," Ulla said. But it was not anger, it was almost pity in her voice. The forsythia twig, from which she had plucked almost all the blossoms, fell to the ground.

Josel didn't let Ulla go; he drew her down to the bench and said to her breathlessly: "I can imagine how you'll parade across half the globe with your professor, and at the end of the performances you'll drop a curtsy, because you're supposed to be packaged as a child prodigy to the amazed public, that's why he's in such a hurry with the tour, your professor. I watched him gaping at you, devouring you with those frog eyes of his . . . I thought to myself, this is wrong for Ulla Ossadnik, this fatso, this sweaty blob, these toad eyes . . . He just wants to be alone with her on this tour!"

He had begun loudly, now he was only whimpering. And Ulla, who had at first been unable to free herself, now could feel that he had let go of her. Josel fell back on the bench, he drew his knees up against his body and hid his face.

Ulla was so upset that she had to gasp for air. She smoothed her dress and brushed the hair from her forehead. She wished the gesture could have shaken off everything that had just happened. She wanted to leave; she would go through the garden to the street without saying good-bye to the others, just to get away from here. But the sight of Josel in the pose of a child wanting to hide from himself blunted her decision. She stood there looking down at him. And to her own surprise, she put her hand on Josel's head. She could feel how he was trembling.

She wouldn't have thought it possible for her feelings to change so quickly. She sat down next to him and looked over at the house; the light of the setting sun was reflected in its windows once again. From the outside the house looked dark and deserted. Yet she knew that inside everyone was waiting for a new life.

"You, *tuleja*," she said, forcing herself to smile. "You're jealous of the professor . . ." Her voice came gentle and soft in the twilight. "I'm grateful to the professor, so grateful that I don't even know whether maybe it's more than just gratefulness. Yes, I learned a lot from your mother, she was more than just a piano teacher to me, she discovered my talent, and she knew when the time came that she could teach me nothing more. But *he* was the one who made an artist of me . . . I had never thought of performing in a public concert someday, all by myself, as a soloist, in front of hundreds of listeners . . . Maybe I dreamed of it, like in the dream of Chopin's heart, but I didn't believe in the reality of it, and then in Beuthen, where I was totally lost at the beginning, he took charge of my education, and he brought me to where I am today, and that's just the beginning. He says I have the stuff to become another Landowska!"

"You're laughing at me," Josel said. "Maybe you're right. You're thinking of your career and your future, and I'm thinking that I have to be a soldier, and might come back a cripple or a madman. Maybe that's ridiculous. I'm probably just a ridiculous person. But I've still got enough control over my senses that I'm not telling you what I've been wanting to tell you the whole time, namely that I love you, and that I would rather die than not be able to love you—but no, I won't say it, instead I'll just say wait for me, please, wait for me! At least promise me that—or I'll kill myself!"

"Josel, you're just talking nonsense. Who knows where you read that! I used to love your words, words that you got out of books somewhere, and they were so new to me and so beautiful. But now I don't need your words anymore, now I need music. There is good music and bad music, but there is no ridiculous music. There are good people and bad people, but there are no ridiculous people."

"I'll hang myself. Enough people used to kill themselves for that reason . . ." Josel said slowly. "But this isn't the time for suicide. Why bother to kill yourself when there are so many people out there lying in wait to kill you."

"Don't think of things like that," Ulla said. "Think about coming to my concerts, after the war, when I'm playing somewhere nearby. You must promise me that . . . Josel."

"After the war, after the war, I can't listen to that anymore: everybody talks about that, every other sentence begins that way. *After the war!* Everyone hopes for true life then, if not paradise, but I'm living now, I have to go to war now and nobody knows what *afterthewar* will be like, and which of us will even live to see it . . ."

Josel knew that never again would it be the way it had once been. As of this Good Friday there would be a deep crevasse between the past and the future that could not be bridged again in an entire lifetime.

"Maybe it's good that there's a war. Everything will be different afterwards."

"The war is coming closer," Ulla said. "In Warsaw a revolt has broken out in the Jewish ghetto."

"In Warsaw?" Josel asked incredulously. "And you've just come from Warsaw?"

"Yes," she said. "I heard the shots and explosions."

"So how did you get out of there?"

"The revolt is only in the Jewish quarter, it's fenced in and separated from the Poles. The Jews have been living there in isolation for years. This morning, as we were riding away, smoke hung over the quarter."

"And the Poles?"

"They're glad that it doesn't have anything to do with them this time. Life goes on normally for them, they go to church and go strolling by the Vistula."

"I didn't read anything in the paper," Josel said.

"No, there's nothing about it in the newspapers."

Ulla got up from the bench. "Let's go in the house." She picked up the forsythia twig she had dropped. And although it looked pitiful and frayed, it seemed especially precious to her now.

Nothing was stirring inside the house. "It's still quiet," she said thoughtfully.

"They haven't even turned on a light," Josel said. "If the baby had arrived, we would have heard it by now."

"I have to go back to Beuthen now, otherwise I'll be late. It might take your sister a lot longer," Ulla said.

They walked through the dark garden toward the house. Josel took Ulla's hand. He wanted to hold fast to something he no longer could hold onto. "Can you feel the summer?" Ulla asked.

But Josel couldn't feel anything anymore.

43

Tonik had arrived at the Capitol Cinema half an hour early. So first he took a look at the display cases, but he couldn't make out most of the photos in the weak light of the painted-over light bulb. *I Accuse* was the special feature for Good Friday: UNDER 14 NOT ADMITTED. Well, he couldn't stand Hatheyer. Maybe he could talk Hedel Zock into going to the CT Theater, if she came on time, or to the Schauburg; there would certainly be something better there. He loved movies with Zara Leander or ones with Marika Rökk and with Hilda Krahl. It was not always the starring roles that attracted him to a film; it was more the supporting roles with which he suffered or triumphed. Paul Kemp, for example, or Rudolf Platte, or Fritz Kampers, those were the ones he remembered. Not the heroic types, rather the shy ones, dogged by bad luck, little men, but smarter and craftier than the big shots, and in the end they were the ones who were victorious. Those were his heroes.

In the meantime he could ask the man at the ticket window what was playing at the other theaters, but there was no man at the window; after he knocked on the pane, a young woman came out from someplace. You could hear voices from the loudspeaker at least, and the whirring of the projectors, and when he asked her his question, the young woman indignantly refused to answer him. So he would see *I Accuse* with Hedel Zock if she showed up at all; he still wasn't sure of that. Anyway, he wasn't taking her to a theater to watch a movie.

Then the first moviegoers came in. They were all about fourteen to sixteen years old. They strolled in, bought tickets, combed their hair in any reflecting windowpane, and they smelled of birch water. The girls wore their hair in a bun, some of them wore a turban, too, improvised from a shawl. A few boys encircled him, edged in closer, whispering, sizing him up pretty openly, as if they had never seen a soldier in uniform. When he was just a noncom. With a lieutenant or a captain he would have understood that.

The boys wore their hair long, down to the collar. That was probably because most of them had already been in the Labor Service. When he was their age, he had worn his hair matchstick length, which was also regulation in the army. And all the boys were wearing white silk scarves around their necks. They hung out over the collars of their jackets a little foppishly; he had seen this before a few times, but it hadn't caught his attention as it did now. Tonik stood up, combed his hair too, and walked outside past the boys. It was unpleasant the way they were staring at him, and he didn't feel like getting into a conversation with them. The boys were disappointed; they looked after him as he disappeared out the door, and reproached each other for not bumming a cigarette from him right away.

Tonik waited outside now, and each time someone stepped out of the dark into the diffuse light of the Capitol's blue-painted neon sign, he felt something almost like an electric shock: this must be Hedel! But then it wasn't after all.

Since more and more people were arriving, Tonik bought two tickets just to be sure they wouldn't wind up without any seats. He bought seats way at the back where they could hide, for forty pfennigs. That was pretty expensive. Particularly if Hedel Zock didn't show up.

It smelled of birch water. The entire lobby was a cloud of birch water. In front of the mirror and the windows boys were standing, slowly and silently combing their hair, which they had rubbed with birch sap on Good Friday. You had to tap into a young birch tree a few days before Easter, a short cut into the bark, not too deep, and hang a vessel below it; by the next morning the vessel was filled with fresh birch sap. You had to rub that into your hair; it would protect you from baldness and increase your virility.

And the girls had to wash in water from the river or the pond on Good Friday, then they would always remain beautiful.

Not much had changed. Only the white scarves were new to him. Now one of the boys did come up to him and tried to bum a cigarette. He surely would have gotten one, too, if Hedel Zock had not slipped in through the door at that moment. Tonik left the boy standing there and walked up to Hedel with the tickets in his hand.

Hedel Zock was dressed plainly; only her hair attracted attention:

she had twisted it into little curls all over her head. She was just afraid that they wouldn't last long, because she had curled them herself that afternoon and let them dry under a hairnet. It would have been better if she had been able to wear the curlers overnight, but her mother would never have permitted that in Holy Week. She already had had a scene with her mother for combing her hair in front of the mirror. On Good Friday you didn't look in the mirror, especially not as long as she had! Hedel had decided to go dressed as she was, for if her mother had found out that she had a movie date with Anton Ossadnik, she wouldn't have let her out of the house; she would have locked the door and hidden the key. It wouldn't have been the first time. Once her mother couldn't remember the next morning where she had hidden the key the night before, and had had to send for the locksmith so Hedel could get to work on time, at Rebenstorf's Department Store, where she was a sales trainee.

On the way here, Hedel had planned how she would act toward Anton Ossadnik—well, rather coolly. She would wait until he spoke first and would let him do the talking, for nowhere else does a person betray his true self more than in the way he talks (her friend Helga Zimnik had said that); that's what she would stick to, at least in this case. She had even planned a few sentences that she wouldn't forget even in a moment of great confusion: "Take your hand away! Pardon, but please don't do that!"

Which only proved that she hoped he would do that.

Men only think of one thing, she thought, and immediately seemed two years older to herself. She wished she were that old.

If only she didn't have to watch this sad movie. It might even spoil the mood for both of them. Hedel had read in the paper that *I Accuse* was being shown today, on Good Friday, "by popular demand." Sweet Jesus, she would much rather have gone to something like *The White Dream*. She had seen that film seven times, yes, and she wouldn't be bored the eighth time. *I'm Mizzi of the Prater, the sweetheart of all men, they all come back again* . . . She had been delighted. But naturally they couldn't show a movie like that on Good Friday. She loved Viennese films, and sometimes she tried out the dialect, which she was not very good at.

Sweet Jesus, was she excited when she finally caught sight of Tonik.

It had gotten rather late, and Anton came right over to her in his handsome uniform, with the tickets in hand. In her embarrassment she apologized, repeating the same words. Surely she had unattractive red spots on her cheeks—she always got them when she was nervous, and she sure was now, especially since she thought that she had been spotted by Fräulein Konopka, who could hardly screw her head back on; and of course she would talk about it all over the department store, having seen Hedel at the movies with a soldier on Good Friday. At least he was a noncommissioned officer, with two decorations. You did see the Iron Cross II everywhere, of course. But she was going to ask Anton what the other medal meant.

Without saying much, Tonik put his arm around her hips, so that she would get used to it right away, and she was much too nervous really to notice it. "Ach, excuse me," she repeated, "for coming so late. I had to think up a story at home, otherwise my mother wouldn't have even let me out. You can't imagine it, but the older generation is still pretty old-fashioned these days . . ."

She was quite proud of how she had expressed herself.

Tonik didn't want to imagine it. He was more interested in getting two seats in the last row, but they had already been taken by the fourteen-year-olds and their girl friends. He just managed to get seats off to the side. Tonik would have liked to see how the war looked in a newsreel at home from a comfortable seat in the movies, but unfortunately the main feature began right away. And maybe he would see soldiers in snow-white coats sometime, on the Eastern Front, like the ones Bronder talked about. And so he shouted into the dark for the newsreel.

Next to him, Hedel almost died of embarrassment, but then she was able to whisper to him that the Capitol shared the newsreel with the CT, so that it was shown at the beginning in one theater and at the end in the other. This satisfied Tonik.

During the whole show, Hedel had to push Tonik's hand away with patience and perseverance, at least a couple of dozen times. She couldn't make use of the phrases that she had planned beforehand. She didn't dare to talk into the silence, and she was devastated by what was happening on the screen. When Paul Hartman finally agreed to give Hatheyer the poison, she began to blubber, and she was not the only one, to judge by the sounds all around her. A favorable development for Tonik, for now she let him keep his hand on her knee, because she needed her own hands to dry her eyes.

When the movie was over, most of the audience used the short intermission before the newsreel to leave. The shuffling of feet went on and on, even when the German eagle flashed onto the screen and the emphatic voice of the narrator began. Now Tonik tugged Hedel outside too.

After that sad film he would probably need twice as much time to get her in the right mood. He was worried whether there would even be enough time this evening. *Pjerunnje*, he thought, maybe I should make a pass at a widow for a change, it wouldn't necessarily have to be one from Port Arthur; at least she wouldn't have to be home by ten thirty. And maybe we could even do it in a bed.

With Hedel it would have to be in a park or down by the Klodnitz. Lucky that the weather had turned warm, you could go for a walk along the river. There was no performance at the theater tonight, so no one would be coming out of the theater to disturb them. At any rate, she didn't resist when he put his arm around her hips. She said nothing. She was still thinking of Heidemarie Hatheyer and how she had pleaded for the poison in her wheelchair. Tonik, on the other hand, was talking as if his life depended on it. He talked about the time when they were building tree houses in the town woods, about the time when they were exploding bottles and cans with unquenched carbide, about the time when they looted a department store in France after taking a town—the name of which he had forgotten, unfortunately—and he had wound up in the women's clothing department, of all things, and had come out with an armload of dresses and furs, and then that night, which his company spent in an evacuated school, they had swilled cognac and champagne, and finally had draped themselves in the furs and begun to dance, in the classrooms, in the corridor, and on the school benches . . . and how they had sung: *Good night Mother, good night, I'm thinking of you, all right* . . .

Now even Hedel was laughing. She put up no resistance when they took the path away from the main street and he led her carefully and smoothly down the few steps to the Klodnitz. Ach, sweet Jesus, she liked him well enough, this Anton Ossadnik, his arm wasn't at all offensive, far from it, she felt as if he were raising her up, she had never crossed the street as light-footedly as this. And down by the river he began to kiss her. She let him, in part because she didn't know how to resist. She liked him well enough, this Antonek, it was just going a little too fast for her, they hadn't known each other that long, and hadn't had time to get to know each other better, after all. But they would have a few days now, and next year, on his next leave, a few days more, and then . . .

He hugged her tight and pressed his body to hers, he stroked her neck with his fingers and thrust his tongue between her teeth. She couldn't get her breath; if only because of that, she had to work free of him. She pushed against him with all her strength and gurgled a few sounds that were unintelligible.

But he held her tight and stammered out something that she didn't understand until he repeated it. "Can it be that I love you, Hedel? Yes, that's how it is, Hedel. I love you, Hedel." Tonik wasn't losing any time, his hand was fumbling for her breasts, then down along her body. "When we do it now, it'll be the first time for you, won't it?"

Ahh, Sweet Jesus. Hedel was almost crying. "Yes, yes, yes," she whispered, her lips close to his ear. "Anton, my Tonik, I belong to you. But not today! We can't. Because . . . because—it's Good Friday!"

"*Pjerunnje*," was all Tonik said. "*Pjerunnje!*"

44

AFTER MIDNIGHT, when the guests had left, it was quieter in the Piontek house. Valeska had made up the sofa in the music room as a bed for Josel, because he didn't want to go to his room any more than the others; they had entrenched themselves in their chairs to wait for the baby's arrival. Valeska had been to Irma's room again and had learned from the midwife what she had heard repeatedly during the last three hours, namely, "It's all going perfectly normally, and it won't be much longer." But it was Saturday by now, so it would turn out to be a child of fortune—if you believed in that. Valeska did. She took the news back to the music room, where everyone glanced up expectantly and then sank back, because they had been expecting and hoping for something else. Soft, vapid music came from the radio. Willi had turned it on because the silence was making him uncomfortable, and nobody had minded. Not even Lucie (Widera), who had withdrawn into the corner between the wall clock and the vitrine for a little nap in her wicker chair, in the hope that the wall clock would wake her every half hour when it chimed. For she mustn't miss the birth.

In the room only the lamp on the English table spread a soft, even light, but it still seemed too bright to Valeska, at least for the mood they all were in. She stood up and looked for a silk cloth in the vitrine, and finally found one that seemed just right. She placed it carefully over the lampshade, pulled it taut on all sides, and tested it to see whether the heat of the bulb would be too strong. Then she sat back down at the table. She did this all slowly, as if to render the slowly elapsing time visible through her gestures and movements. The dim, diffuse light frayed objects and made them unreal, and it set the people facing each other in their chairs at a greater remove from one another than they really were. The silence enveloped them. It was not that they were silent because someone in the same house was about to bear a child, in a room a few steps away. Quite simply, they had said everything to one another. It had not been much, but it had been enough.

After a while Willi Wondrak stood up and changed to a different station and different music. The events had cheated him of his *Parsifal*, Act Three. At this hour the same dribbling music was everywhere, the same in every way as what had preceded it. So he sat down again. No one was listening, anyway. Not until a voice interrupted the music: *Achtung! Achtung! An important announcement: Enemy aircraft have crossed the border at Lübeck and are approaching the Hannover-Braunschweig air corridor. The civilian population is requested to heed the sirens and proceed to air-raid shelters without panic when the alarm sounds.* After that the soft, lilting monotony of the music continued as before.

Only after a while did Josel say: "That means the alarm will sound in Berlin in fifteen minutes." He knew that from Herr Schimmel, who had told him again and again how they went to the air-raid bunker on Savignyplatz after the alarm, and how they heard the flak and the bombs exploding in spite of the thick walls. And how they went back home after two or three hours with two suitcases and a briefcase. Sometimes they saw a house burning along the way too. And finally it had been their house that was burning.

"Poor Gerda," Valeska said. "The raids are about twice a week now. They can't even sleep in peace anymore. If it doesn't stop, she wants to come here this summer with both children. I just don't know where I would put them up."

"Some day the bombs will be here too . . . The whole armament industry has been moved to Upper Silesia, that'll draw them like flies," Wondrak grumbled to himself.

"They don't even let up on Good Friday," Valeska sighed, remembering that the Polish boy had to disappear from the tool shed at daybreak.

No one contradicted her. They sat there in silence. And waited. The silence in the next room continued too.

Valeska rose from her chair and went to the veranda door. "I need a breath of fresh air." She pushed the blackout curtain aside and slipped out into the garden. The curtain had caught, and made a broad strip of light in the night, but it was so weak that it wouldn't be seen very far away. She felt the warm air and the humming silence of the night like a tremor on her face. So many sounds and voices had pelted her today that she yearned for silence, for the smell of the garden in this spring night, for the numbing of the gorse and the gentle tumult of the almond tree, whose first blossoms were opening in this warmth. The sky seemed to her like a black cloth in which she herself had stitched a thousand stars. A window opened in the house and low voices fell outside into the darkness.

Valeska wanted to listen to her own voice, which came from the very depths of her soul. As she walked through the garden, only the rustling of her footsteps to be heard, she felt that the loneliness within her had grown. It had begun with that September day when Josel had vanished and Herr Montag had shot himself in the garden cottage. And when Leo Maria had died. The loneliness within her had grown ever since, and had continued and increased through pain and disappointments, a loneliness that stretched to the sky. How much longer would she be able to bear it?

Valeska made a wide arc around the tool shed and arrived at the end of the garden, at the place where she had once planted the wild lavender, to counter the stench of the nearby coking plant. And it had worked then, too. It was a scent that had attracted the women of the neighborhood in the evenings. The fragrance of the wild lavender had never been more intoxicating than in that summer. After that it had deteriorated from year to year more and more beneath the soot, and now in the spring only a few plants still sprouted fresh green from the gray bushes. Now Willi wanted to have the bed dug up and to plant tomatoes there.

Valeska kneeled down, because she had caught her shoe in a creeper. She remained in that position, feeling the cool, dry, hard earth under her knees.

There was no way to evade it anymore. The war had attacked them like a cancer. The war ate at them. Perhaps it didn't yet show from the outside. There were no air raids, no bombs, no burning houses. But the obituaries in the newspapers were more frequent than before. A requiem mass for the dead was read daily. And her Josel, still half a child, had to go to war. Irma fought against death, bearing child after child. Halina was sitting in the Gestapo prison on Teuchertstrasse and was being interrogated, maybe even beaten. Her brother would marry Fräulein Willimczyk, the bookseller, and never be released from his great and secret yearning as long as he lived. Milka would let time and life itself slip away, spending it with the dying at the field hospital and with the increasingly moody and sclerotic countess. And the Polish boy in the shed meant a new danger.

Valeska remembered how it had all begun. She remembered the last day of August 1939, when they were sitting around the radio, hearing about the deployment of the army across the nearby border. It was the last time that they had all been together, and it seemed to her as if her whole life was summarized in that picture, in that scene; the photo that she had taken of Irma on her wedding day was only a coarse counterfeit compared to the photo that she had preserved in her head.

She would never forget that summer. It had been a hot dry summer, the mullein foamed yellow in the fields, the poppy had not been so wild and red for a long time, the thistles scattered their burrs in the children's hair, the rivers dried up to trickles and stank, the fish turned up their white bellies and began to rot, blue wisps of flame danced the whole night long on the slag heaps, the wild lavender spread its fragrance in the garden, and the moon blossomed in the sky like a huge glowing red flower . . . She remembered all that and knew that she would never forget that summer, for to forget it would mean to forget all the summers of her life. Never again would there be such a summer. At the time she had not believed it, but today she had to admit it: every day since then had been a slow departure, from time, from the world, from life.

She tore off a few leaves of lavender, crushed them between her fingers, and sniffed at them; they smelled faint and musty, the scent of lavender was weak. She plucked some more leaves, crushed them between her hands, and pressed her palms to her face. She breathed in the scent greedily, with her eyes shut, as if addicted to it, to the smell of the lavender, to the smell of the past.

She stayed there like that and waited. When no knight battled a dragon in the sky, she stood up and went back to the house, in a wide arc around the tool shed. Nothing had changed in the music room. Only the music on the radio was different. Valeska walked slowly through the room to the linen cabinet behind the folding screen. She opened the cabinet and poked around in the sheets and pillow cases until she found a small, gray package. She opened it and took it to the table. In her hand shone a black, tear-shaped stone the size of a fist.

"Here, Josel," she said. "Take this stone. Papusch gave it to me for you that night, before he died. A black stone from this black earth. Take it with you, to the war."

Horst Bienek was born in Gleiwitz, Upper Silesia, in 1930. He began his literary career as a journalist in Berlin, where he studied with Bertolt Brecht at the Berliner Ensemble. He was arrested on a political charge in 1951 in East Berlin and sentenced to twenty-five years' forced labor; he spent four years in the Vorkuta prison camp in the northern Urals before being freed by an amnesty. Since 1956 he has lived in West Germany and continued his career as a poet, essayist, and novelist as well as an accomplished film maker. He is the recipient of numerous literary prizes, among them three of Germany's most coveted: the Hermann Kesten Prize, 1975; the Wilhelm Raabe Prize, 1980; and the Nelly Sachs Award, 1981.

Ralph R. Read (1939–1985) was an associate professor of Germanic languages at the University of Texas at Austin and a prolific translator specializing in contemporary German fiction.